I0680921

# CALL ME HOOP

## THE FIRST SEASON OF FUCKING SCUMBAGS BURN IN HELL


DREW STEPEK

LUCY LEITNER

LUCAS MILLIRON

JOHN SHUPECK, JR.

LEWIS KELLY

PETER CAFFREY

DANI BROWN

RYAN HARDING

**Dedicated to the Big Men. Upstairs and downstairs.**

ISBN: 978-1-940250-52-6

Cover Illustration by Anastasia Panina
Cover Layout by Drew Stepek
Interior Layout by Drew Stepek

Edited by S.C. Mendes and Lucy Leitner

*Call Me Hoop*, Sonny Hooper, and the *Fucking Scumbags Burn* in Hell created by Drew Stepek

Printed in the United States of America

First Edition

Visit us on the web at:
godless.com
bloodgutsandstory.com

# FOREWORD

When Drew Stepek founder of Godless asked me to write the foreword for *Call Me Hoop*, a series I'd been fan-girling over since day one, I was more than a little surprised. Generally, a powerhouse author with a sizable backlist of award-winning titles is selected to endorse and promise the book you're about to read is a 'good one.' But despite having average-sized feet—and being handed giant shoes to fill—I was not about to pass on the chance to mingle with the amazing authors who fill these pages.

Hopefully, you'll bear with me while I completely fuck this up in my clown shoes.

*hold for applause*

For horror fans who haven't heard about the website (and now app) called Godless, listen up. This distribution platform is a game-changer for indie authors and small presses by hosting today's best and brightest talents from all subgenres of horror.

After launching Godless, Drew had an idea for a series called *Fucking Scumbags Burn in Hell*. Originally, he was going to tackle it alone, but being a big fan of collaboration and group efforts to better the genre we all love, Drew decided to reach out to other writers and offer them a chance to create a scumbag within the universe.

He wrote the first three stories and released them to readers before handing the reins over to the seven chosen authors. After reading the first story, *A Little Bit Country*, I thought of all the possibilities that could make this series a hit. I even considered throwing my hat in the ring and penning my own scumbag tale. But I didn't, and I actually don't regret that decision at all. This series is absolutely phenomenal as a reader. By not being privy to all the behind-the-scenes secrets, I was able to uncover a lot of the intricate details that weave all the stories together on my own, making the series more fun and exciting to read. Each one of the authors added a new voice and this anthology is the better for it. And these are their stories.

*insert Law and Order *bong bong**

DREW STEPEK, author of *The Knuckler* series, opens the gate with the first three stories to show everyone how to scumbag, before handing over the reins for everyone to play.

LUCY LEITNER, author of *Outrage Level 10*, got the A-line haircut and barreled through with a little Karen action. She rampages through her turn like no one is watching.

LUCAS MILLIRON, author of *Cocksucker*—king of opening lines so offensive you consider closing the book before you dare turn the page—makes you want to shut your eyes and never use them again if it means having to visit the eye doctor.

JOHN SHUPECK JR., author of *Lilibeth*, the writer with a knack for unnerving his readers when they realize he might really be a serial killer, brings his original style and voice and introduces a new level of grit to the series.

LEWIS KELLY, author of *Hunger*, is the youngest of the bunch, but his fresh eyes make one hell of a statement with his entry into the saga.

PETER CAFFREY, author of *The God of Wanking*, the man we all assume has a screw loose, reassures us that we are most definitely correct. The glorious scumbag he contributes is a real dickhead.

DANI BROWN, author of *Ghetto Super Skank*, the Queen of Filth herself, shows us all how she got the name, with the ripest of scumbags. You're gonna want to hold your nose for this one, you can smell Amy through the pages.

RYAN HARDING, author of *Genital Grinder*, takes a *Criminal Minds* approach to his story and profiles our last scumbag in the series. Giving us the baddest bad, the boss-level evil we'd been waiting for. Don't worry though, our pal Hoop has his name.

The entire series flows cohesively, and the authors really stretch their legs and get into their characters. I promise you; this is a good one!

*Rayne Havok*
*"The Drizzle"*
Author of Killstreme

# A LITTLE BIT COUNTRY

DREW STEPEK

"There he is!"

The shout came from across the room as I walked into the office, wiping dirt and sweat off my head with my arm. The office was as white as a Smoky Mountain Christmas with one desk and two chairs. A fat man in glasses with a pencil behind his ear stood up and started clapping his flabby old hands.

I stopped dead in my tracks. It was the first voice I had heard since… I can't even remember. Seemed like I had been walking around forever.

"Well?" the fat man badgered me. He was sweating worse than me, and his fat face was all red. He had long hair pulled back in a ponytail like a girl and one of them funny beards. I think people called 'em Van Dykes. "Are you going to close the fucking door and come in? Were you born in a barn?"

I looked back outside the office, still gripping the door handle. There was nothing but black behind me. The caverns were gone. I sniffed loudly and cracked my neck.

"Jesus Christ, son! We have a lot to get to."

I jiggled the handle a bit and then closed it. "Where am I?"

"Come on over here and take a seat." He pointed at one of the chairs in front of his desk. "We have a lot to get through before I can send you out."

"Send me out where?" I shuffled my dirty, bare feet toward him. "Am I goin' somewhere?"

He pointed at the chair again. "You've been brought up to the big leagues, son. Didn't anyone brief you?" He lifted the phone and pushed a flashing button. "Phillips! What the fuck is going on?" He waited a second, then rolled them bulgy eyes of his. "Didn't anyone educate number—" He shuffled through stacks of papers on his desk and pulled out a folder. He opened it, dragging his finger down the page. "Number two, two, five, dash, six, one, six, two, three, two, two, eight, five, nine, seven, two, three, five, one, niner? I got him in my office now looking at me like he doesn't know where he is." He covered the phone with his hand. "Fucking processing. Heads are gonna roll, that's for sure." He pointed to the chair again. "Why don't you take a seat while I get your paperwork all situated."

"I'm just fine standin' right here."

He waved me away like a bumble bee and took his hand off the phone. "What do you mean he hasn't been processed yet? Did he at least get his orientation?" He covered up the mouthpiece again and asked, "Did you have your orientation yet?"

"I don't remember getting no orientation," I said.

He slapped himself on the forehead. "Okay, Phillips. He *don't* know. Ask Thompson what I should do." He pulled the phone from his ear and pointed to it. "Hold music. It's the worst."

He rocked back in that chair of his and put his arms behind his fat head. His armpits were drenched like he just got sprayed with a garden hose. He pulled that phone back to his ear and listened. He let out a big gust of wind and pulled out that pencil from behind his ear. He started writing stuff on the folder.

"Okay," he said. "Okay. Wait. What?" He snapped the pencil in half. "What do you mean I have to do it? I'm his handler. He should already be prepped and ready to go. Goddammit, Phillips! He's supposed to go out today." He started beating that phone against his head. Not hard like. I think he was making a point. "Do you really expect me to believe that the processing department is short staffed? We're in fucking Hell. There are zillions of people down here." He waited a second, listening to Phillips. "Oh, don't worry, The IT will hear about this." He put his hand over the phone and looked at me. "Can you believe this guy?" Then, he pulled his hand away. "Fuck me? Fuck you, Phillips." He slammed that phone back onto its base. He put his hands over his sweaty, lady haircut and started laughing like a mental patient.

"Excuse me, mister?" I tried to get his attention. "What in the heck am I doin' here?"

He peeked out behind them hands and took a deep breath. Then, he opened up that folder. "Come on over here and take a seat." He pointed at one of the chairs.

I limped on over and pulled the chair out from his desk, but I didn't sit down. "I haven't sat in a long time, mister."

He put on thick glasses and went back to the folder. "It's not like sitting is something you have to learn how to do." He looked up at me. "Just jokes, son." Then, he looked back down at the folder. "Yep! Looks like you've been walking for a *loooong* time." He took them glasses off. "How long do you think you've been down here?

I brushed off the seat. I had been walking for so long that the chair looked as comfortable as a hayloft. "I don't know. Can't seem to remember anything 'cept walking. Seems like forever."

He smiled. "You don't need to tell me. I've been there. Thing is that there is no time in Hell. It's just… here."

I bent to sit and fell right on my ass.

"BAM!" He shot out of his seat, laughing. "That never gets old."

"You tryin' to hoodwink me, mister?" I looked behind me to see who pulled the chair away. No one was there. The chair wasn't even there no more.

He started laughing and pounding his fists on the desk. "So classic. *So* classic."

I rubbed my legs and butt. They sure did hurt. "Where did that chair go? Why in the hell would y'all do that to me?"

He stopped laughing for a second and looked behind him. He looked back at me like he didn't know whether to check his watch or scratch his ass. "Y'all? "I'm the only one here." He took his seat and went back to that folder. "Oh. Here we go. He thumped on that folder with his finger. "You're from the American South. Duh."

I got back to my feet and brushed off the backs of my legs. "I guess so. Don't 'member much."

He snapped his fingers and that chair appeared behind me like some kind a magic trick. "No one remembers much about being up there." He pointed at the white ceiling. "Take your seat, please, son."

I stepped toward him. "Mister. I got a mind to—"

"Just sit down. I got my laugh for the day."

I grabbed the chair by its arms and lowered myself onto the seat. It didn't get swallered up into thin air this time.

He threw the folder back on the desk. "Well, you don't have a name on here other than number two, two, five, dash, six, one, six, two, three, two, two, eight, five, nine, seven, two, three, five, one, nine."

I was listenin' to him best I could, but I was thinking more about how good it felt good to sit down. Seemed like I really had been walking around in them hot, stinking caverns forever. "You're the first person I spoke to since I been here."

He looked at me like I was a squirrel in a rat trap and pointed a new pencil at me. "I'm gonna call you Country."

"Why you wanna call me that?" I started licking at my dry hands with my tongue.

He scrunched up his face, watching me. "Well, not exactly a southern gentleman, but you are a lil' bit country. Besides, I don't want to have to read off that long number every time I talk to you."

"I think I want to go back to them caverns now, mister," I said.

He put his elbows down on the desk and looked at me straight. "No, I don't think you do."

My hands were covered in callouses like I got chicken pox from a baseball mitt. I tried to lick at them, best I could. "And why is that?"

"Jesus!" He pushed the lotion bottle from the corner of his desk to me. "Licking your hands is only going to make them worse."

I squirt a lil' bit of lotion into my hand, then smelled it. "This ain't hot sauce or nothin', is it?"

"Hot sauce? Hilarious." He grabbed the bottle and delt a lil' bit onto his hands and then lathered them up. “That is a good idea, though. I need to remember that one.” He stood. “You want something to drink, Country?”

“Better not be no hot sauce,” I warned him.

He walked over to a water cooler in the corner that wasn’t there a second before. “What is your obsession with hot sauce?” He poured water into a cup and brought it back to me.

I grabbed the cup and sucked it down. I couldn’t even remember the last time that I had water. I handed it back to him. “Can I have me some more?”

He chuckled. “You bet, Country.” He walked back to the water cooler and refilled the cup. “You know. You’re real lucky. In all my time of working as a handler down here, I’ve never seen anyone make it to agent status so quickly. The IT must have seen something special in you.”

“The IT?”

“Yeah. *The* IT. Trust me.” He mosied back to me with a second cup of water. “I’m just a lowly handler and I had to suck The IT’s dick and eat The IT’s pussy for what seemed like forever.”

“You ain’t making no sense.” I took the cup and licked at the rim like a bullfrog catchin’ a fly before drinking it down. It was the best darn water I ever did have.

“The IT is what people up there call the Devil.” He giggled. “Satan? Lord of the Underworld? Mephistopheles?”

“Let me get this straight, mister. The Devil is some kind a lady?”

“Didn’t you just hear me say that it had a dick, Country? Keep up. You ever heard of a lady with a dick?”

I crunched up the paper cup over my mouth, trying my damnedest to squeeze every darn drop of water out of it. “You also said that The IT had a vagina.”

“The IT has both,” he said. “I don’t know what the fuck I was sucking and eating. You don’t ask The IT questions. The bottom line is that I did my time and I got this job. Now, as of today, I work with you. We’re a team.”

“Well, I never heard nothin’ like that about dicks an’ vaginas an’ all. I also never met this IT thing.” I unfolded the cup and put it down on his desk. “What are we gonna be doin’? Shovelin’ pig shit or somethin’?

He sat down behind his desk and started snickering. “No, Country. We won’t be shoveling pig shit.” He opened a desk drawer, took a bunch a books and folders out, and dropped them in front a me. “As of today, you are an agent. You will be sent out into the field to manipulate the forces of Heaven. Your purpose—our purpose—is to breakdown the followers of God one at a time.”

“Do what now?” I picked up one of them books and flipped through the pages.

He smirked and put out his hand to shake. “Name’s Sonny Hooper. You can call me Hoop. I will be your coach and your handler.”

I looked up from that book, licked my hand then shook his.

“You do know how to read, don’t you?”

"I assume you slept well last night." Mr. Hooper handed me a big bottle a water.

I pulled some crust off the inside of my nose and sucked down the water. It refilled by itself. "Well, I'll be." I figured it was some kind a magic or something. "It sure was nice to sleep in a bed, but that fan wasn't workin' real well."

"You're in Hell, Country!" He dug them flabby hands of his into a bag a potato chips. "Do you know how hard it is to get fans down here at all?"

He waved me up and I followed him to a new door that appeared behind his desk, over by that water cooler. As I moved across the room, I thought about that struggling fan from my new room and something jarred loose. I got a memory! "I remember something… one summer. All the hardware stores in town were outta fans. I was so hot and the fan I was using didn't blow much at all. Might as well have been tryin' to blow out a barn fire with a straw."

"That must have been like Hell. It said in your file that you're from Tupelo, Mississippi. The home of The King."

Like he just turned on a lightbulb in a closet, I remembered something else—the king. I remembered Elvis. I remembered I liked music.

He put out his hand, letting me walk through the door first.

I peeked inside the new room. It was all white with some kind a computer doohickey and some other type of trough that looked to be hooked up to the computer doohickey. "There ain't no tricks in here is there? Like that disappearin' chair?"

He put up his arms and the flab jiggled in his short-sleeved shirt. It was like a chain reaction. His body shook all the way down to the cuffs of his brown slacks. "We don't have time for tricks, Country."

I walked into that room.

He pointed to the computer doohickey. "That is the machine that will take you back to the earth realm."

I scuffled over to the trough and bent down to smell it. It wasn't a trough like the tin ones I used to fill on my daddy's farm. At least I didn't think so. "I'm gettin' out?" I licked at my hands again. "I get to leave?"

He put his hand over his face. "Oh, God, no. You just get to go on a… hmmm… vacation." He walked over to that computer doohickey and pushed a couple of buttons on a typewriter that lit up like a Lite Brite toy. "Did you read any of the books or assignments I gave you yesterday?"

I walked over to him and looked at the TV screen on top of that computer doohickey. "It was too dark to read." I touched the window screen.

He swatted my hand away like it was a fly on a hot dog. "Don't touch that, Country. Are you telling me that you don't know how this works?"

I was getting a little tired of his tone. "I said it was dark."

"I thought you could read."

"I can read," I yelled at him. "I think."

"Look. It's not that hard. I've sent several agents into the field without understanding the ins and outs of the equipment." He handed me a device that looked like a big June bug. "Put this over your ear."

"My ear?" I turned the critter over and hundreds and thousands of legs scurried around. I didn't much like that bug. "It's not gonna bite me, is it?"

"Bite you? No! It's an earpiece so I can communicate with you." I'll wear one too. He pointed at a microphone coming outta that Lite Brite typewriter in front of the computer doohickey. "I talk into that and you hear me in your ear. I will be watching you from this." He pointed at the screen. "That way I can monitor what you're doing. We can't have you breaking any of the treaty agreements with the guys upstairs."

I put the bug on the edge of my ear. It clamped over the top and the bottom. I felt all thousands of them legs prick into my skin. "You mean God?"

"God. Jesus. Angels and shit. The other team. Let me make this simple." He pointed to that white trough. "You will be in there." Then, he walked over to that computer doohickey. "I will be watching you from here. You will be doing what I say and playing for our team. It's like football."

"I like football, I think." I scratched at my ear. That June bug was locked on there pretty tight. It was making me wanna sneeze for some reason. "What position am I playin'?"

"It's not literally football. You will be taking over the body of a little girl who is presumed possessed. The device in your ear will control your crossing between the realms." He tapped on the June bug thing.

I looked at that window glass TV on top a that computer doohickey. It was seeing everything that I was seeing. I waved my hand in front of my face. "Huh?"

"This machine." He gestured his hand around the room. "It's connected to Hell's core. It allows us to communicate with the earth realm through little girls."

I didn't much understand what he was saying so I just acted like I did and nodded my head. "Why lil' girls?"

"They are the easiest to occupy. For some reason, everyone thinks that when a little girl is sad or starting her period that she's possessed. So, we breach their conscious when they are easily inhabitable. I could tell you a million stories of all the times that the other team has tried to shut down our operation because we figured that out. That's why there is a treaty in place. We can scare the hell out of anyone we want, but we can't kill anyone from their team. It's become a game of influence. We used to be able to take down whoever we wanted. But, The IT has kind of a weird relationship with the other team. Remember that. Our job is to outwit them and show the rest of the earth realm the persuasion of The IT."

I looked at Mr. Hooper and then at the TV screen. "Remember what?"

"Jesus, Country!" He put one of his hands on the microphone and pushed a couple of buttons on the Lite Brite typewriter. "Phillips!" He turned around to look at me and said, "Just a second." He turned back to that computer doohickey. I saw the back of his head in that glass window TV. "This guy isn't ready." He put his hand over the June bug in his ear. "I know that we're short staffed, asshole. I think we should send him back to the caverns. He doesn't even want to do this."

I walked over and tapped him on the shoulder. "Mr. Hooper."

"Hoop! Call me Hoop!" He shushed me like we was in a church. "Not you, Phillips. I know you know my name. He's talking to me."

The June bug in my ear started to itch more. "Hooper, I don't wanna go back to them caverns anymore. What do I gotta do?"

He put up his finger again. "Wait, Phillips. It looks like he doesn't want to go back to the caverns."

I shook my head no and talked into my June bug. "I don't wanna go back to them caverns, Mr. Phillips."

"You heard it from him. Can we send him up to show you that he's ready? Yes. Okay. Of course, I'll get him to sign the paperwork." Mr. Hooper stuck up his thumb. "I think we're in business." He walked over to the trough and flipped some doodad. "Oh, fuck you, Phillips." He smirked and winked at me. "You have a better chance of going back to the caverns than my boy Country." He waited a second. "Oh, yeah. You wanna make a wager? You're on." He paused. "Toolshed? Are you fucking kidding me? She's in a fucking toolshed? This hick will be a rockstar in a toolshed. If Country fucks this up, I'll do a thousand years in the caverns. If he does things right, you go back to the caverns. Later, dipshit." He put his hand over his June bug like he was hanging up a telephone.

"Do I gotta go back?" I took another drink from my water. Sure did taste good and even with a busted fan that bedroom of mine last night was better than walking forever.

Mr. Hooper grabbed a stack of papers that was sitting next to the computer doohickey. He handed them to me. "You have to sign this. Now."

I looked at the pages but couldn't read nothin'. "What does it say?"

"That's right, you can't read." He grabbed the papers back.

"I can read. I think."

He pointed to the first page. "This says that you are enlisted in service to the underworld and that you pledge yourself to The IT." He went to the next page. "This says that you will abide by the rules of the treaty. Blah, blah, blah. Remember… Don't kill any priests, parents, good Christian people. We *don't* kill. Our mission is to influence." He flipped through more pages. "This is the treaty." He continued through what seemed like a couple hundred pages, finally stopping at the final page. "This says that you are choosing not to walk the caverns anymore. And finally, this says that you won't try to escape once you're in the earth realm."

"Escape?"

"Yeah, man. If you rip this off—" He rubbed on the June bug in my ear. "When you're in the earth realm, you're trapped there."

I took a sip of water. "So, I'd be free?"

"No. You're not going there as yourself. Only your soul… your brain is going there. You will be trapped in the body of your host. Sure, you'll feel all the same pain that your host feels and you'll be able to smell the air and taste the food and all that good shit, but you won't be there. Imagine being in a jail where you can't talk to anyone you see."

"That sure does sound better than them caverns."

"Of course it does." He flicked his fat finger against that page. "Once you sign this, you'll never see the caverns again. I promise. You will be able to drink all the water you want. You'll have a bed and a room every night. If you help me win this bet, shit, I'll get you a working fan and some lights in your room." He handed me back them papers and a pen. "Please help me out, Country. In case you didn't hear, I just made a bet with that pederast Phillips. Man, do I hate that guy. He's been trying to steal my job for years."

I took the pen and studied them papers. "So, my brain won't be here anymore?"

He turned back to the computer doohickey. "No, your little brain won't be in Hell anymore."

"I don't much like the way you're talkin' to me again, Mr. Hooper."

"Fine," he said, punching away on that Lite Brite typewriter. "Big brain. You have a huge fucking brain."

I started to sign them papers and then stopped. "Wait, what's my name?"

He didn't turn around. "Just sign the contract 'Country.' If you can't spell that, just put an X. I'll send it over to Phillips immediately and he'll process 'two, two, five, dash, six, one, six, two, three, two, two, eight, five, nine, seven, two, three, five, one, nine.'"

I scratched an X on that last page.

Mr. Hooper snatched the papers back from me and fed them into his computer doohickey. "This should do the trick. Thing is that you need to follow the rules when you're up there because we're sending you out as an unprocessed agent. We are taking a chance on you because I believe in you."

He waited a minute.

I took a gulp a water.

"Did you get the contract, Phillips?" He snapped his fingers at me and pointed toward the giant trough. Then, he whispered at me, "Get in."

I walked over to the trough. It opened like a garage door and I looked inside. There was all types of lights, gadgets, and wires inside, but there was also a comfortable looking lawn chair in the middle. I put my hands against the chair's fabric. It sure was soft.

"Oh, fuck off, Phillips," Mr. Hooper screamed like an alley cat. "Be sure and tell the old gang down in the caverns I fucking hate them." He tapped on his June bug again and then hit the Lite Brite typewriter a few more times.

I dragged my legs over the side of the trough and laid back in the chair. "Is this right?"

"Perfect, Country." He walked up behind me and put this thingy that looked like a green bean strainer over my head. "It's going to be a bit disorientating when you slip back to the earth realm, but it will get easier the more times you do it." He flipped a switch on the side of that green bean strainer. "Are you my boy?"

"I ain't nobody's boy," I told him.

He laughed and his fat rolls smacked at my nose. "I know that. You're a badass. You're a soldier. You're a hero!" He slapped my arm. "Tell me the rules now."

I stretched out my neck. That chair sure was comfortable. I felt like a pig in shit. Sure was better than walking around them caverns. "Number one. Don't tear this off or my brain will be inside a lil' girl forever." I tapped on the June bug.

"Perfect. What else?"

"Don't kill no priests or nothin' like that."

"Don't kill *anyone*, Country. Remember the treaty. You have to remember the treaty. If you fuck this up, The IT will get in trouble with God and then I will be sucking dick and eating pussy for a long time."

"Don't kill nobody," I said.

A red light started swirling around on top a that window glass TV and a bunch of gravy started filling up inside the trough.

Mr. Hooper counted down on his fingers. "Three. Two. One. Good luck, Country. Let's send Phillips back to the caverns where he belongs. Goddamn Yankee. I think he lived in New York when he was on Earth."

"I don't think I ever been to New York. But I don't think I'd like it."

The top of the trough locked tight like a cigarette holder and the gravy completely filled it up. It didn't smother me though and it didn't taste like no gravy I ever had before.

I opened my eyes and went to spit out that gravy taste, but my mouth had gone dry. The vacation ride made my big old brain feel drunker than Cooter Brown. Whoever the hell that was.

I looked around to see where I was. I was in a toolshed, lying in a corner behind a lawn mower. I scratched at it to see if it was real and got my hand all tangled up in some spider webs. Yep, it was real, alright.

I put my other hand up my dress. There weren't no man parts down there. Oh, shit! I was inside a little girl.

The door across that shed opened and I think I heard a bird chirping. A mouse scurried into another corner.

"Violet? Are you in here?" a man hollered into the shed. "It's me, yer paw and Deacons Breshears and Prine."

I sat and peeked over the side of the mower. The barn doors into the shed were about half-way opened.

I heard a voice in that June bug on my ear. *Country, can you hear me?*

I looked out and saw the deacons enter the shed.

*Country, it's Hoop. Can you hear me?*

I pressed on the June bug like Mr. Hooper. "I hear you," I said. At least, I think I said. My voice sounded like a lil' girl. "This is weird."

*Don't worry. The machine on your ear is cloaked when you're on the earth realm. You successfully crossed the planes. What do you see?*

The deacons stepped further into the shed. "Violet, it's your Pa. We're here to help you."

I pressed on the June bug again and whispered like a cotton tailed rabbit. "I'm in a shed. Some men is comin' in here. I think they want to help me. What should I do?"

Mr. Hooper laughed.

*Flip the switch on the side of the receiver on your ear. I need to see what's happening. I need to handle the situation. Remember. No fuck ups or I'm in the caverns for a long ass time.*

I turned on that switch like Mr. Hooper told me. I felt a breeze come from outside through a hole in the shed. It smelled nice like the magnolias were blooming on a Spring day. It smelled better than the burnt pig shit in the caverns. The smell reminded me of home. I was home.

*Good work. I can see the door and the men. Keep looking in that direction. I need to know what we are dealing with. Remember. No killing.*

I did as Mr. Hooper told me. I could now see a third shadow behind the deacons. I grabbed the seat of the mower.

*Oh shit.*

"What, Mr. Hooper? What do you see?" I asked him.

*Open your eyes. Code red, Country. They have bats and a shotgun.*

He was right. As soon as them deacons and that pa got to the middle of the shed, one of them clicked on a light bulb with a string and I could see them better. Two was holding bats and the man who wasn't in a church outfit had a shotgun. I think he was Pa.

"Why do they have bats and guns, Mr. Hooper?" I asked him. I was getting chilly from the hole in the shed.

*Jesus, Country. They know that you're inside the little girl. Fucking Phillips blew our cover. We should abort.*

"Abort?"

*You should come back. They've already won. Looks like it's back to the caverns for me. Dammit!*

"I ain't goin' back to no caverns!"

"Violet?" one of the men asked. "We're here to help you. Come on out of that corner."

*Abort, Country! You hear me? Run away!*

I stood up and brushed dust off the spring dress I had on, then tapped the June bug. "I ain't going back to them caverns."

"Violet, baby. It's Pa."

A deacon shuffled toward me. He was an older gent with spotty a face. I thought it was strange because he was wearing a pretty fancy church outfit. The type a man of God would wear on Easter Sunday.

"What caverns, honey?" he asked.

I looked next to me and grabbed a digging spade. "Y'all better not come back here. I'll fuckin' kill you, motherfuckers. I'll rip off them dicks a yours and eat 'em up like possum pie."

They all froze and gasped.

*Country, Goddamit! Stand down!*

"Fuck you, Mr. Hooper. I'm gonna win this football game. You ain't gotta worry about suckin' no more dick or eatin' no more vagina."

I jumped on top of the lawn mower seat and pulled the spade back behind my right ear. The girl's hair fell in front of my face. "Get outta here, you fuckin' Yankees! Go back ta Heaven."

Two of them choked up further on their bats. "Daniel, go back in the house. You don't need to see this."

The Pa stood there, crying like a woman. His shotgun fell to the dirt floor.

One of the deacons stepped forward. "Violet, put down that spade."

The June bug blared static in my ear, and I couldn't really hear nothing Mr. Hooper was saying to me. I turned off the switch.

"I'm a gonna kill you fuckers." I jumped at the deacon in front and shoved the spade right through his dick. He bent and curled forward, begging me to stop.

I pulled, then pushed that thing in and out of his gullet like I was churning butter. A lot of his insides dumped onto the ground. He fell on his knees like he was praying. But he wasn't praying. He was trying to pick up his gizzards and put it all back inside of him. I started stomping through all them guts like I was jumping through sprinklers in the mud. I picked up a long string of them insides and wrapped it around his neck like I was putting Christmas lights on a tree.

He coughed and screamed and it smelled kinda like he mighta shit in his drawers. His face turned red then blue and he fell forward. I looked at the other two men and they was just staring at the big old mess on the floor. It was like they was watching a dog getting hashed by a mongoose. With friends like them folk, who needed enemies.

They watched me lift up that spade and dig it clean through him from the other side. It took a second, but when his body settled, and stopped flipping and flopping, I dug my little girl hands into his temples and pulled his head off.

That broke the second deacon's stare. He screamed and came at me swinging the bat, barely missing my head. Stupid Yankee.

I hopped onto the corpse so I would be tall enough to reach the second deacon. Before he could swing the bat again, I shoved my little girl fingers into his eyes. "You don't fuck with my team!"

I ripped around in his sockets and scratched his face, tearing all the skin off. His tears and blood tickled my fingers and made me smile.

Pa folded like a card table, cowering and squealing like a baby hog. All he could say was, "No, Violet. Please stop."

That second deacon didn't really have much of a face no more, but he came at me again. "Lord give me power!"

I jumped off the headless deacon and ran back to the mower. I climbed onto a work bench and snatched two hammers.

"Satan! Leave this innocent child." He growled, then charged at me.

I growled back and jumped over his bat swing like a bullfrog. I figured I had some type of superhero power when I ripped that guy's head off, and now I was convinced. I threw myself at him and grabbed hold of his neck, dragging him down to the dirt floor.

"Please, God. Give me power to fight the evils of—"

His words were silenced by the smash of the hammer. I laughed as his small, dirty teeth jumped around like popcorn on a hot stove.

I stood and danced around his sprawled body, while he tried to grab that bat a his again. I finished my one person do-si-do and drove the claw side of the hammer into the guy's throat. I pulled away a hunk of flesh from under his Adam's apple and continued to hack away at his throat. His choking sounded like he was gurling with baking soda.

I smacked the hammer into his chin, and it unhinged from his skull with a *pop*. I set the hammers down and took his slick jaw in my tiny girl hands. With a smile, I tore his jaw clean off his head.

Pa was still crying. If he knew what was good for him, he should forget about the few seconds he had left to live and just enjoy the show.

I paused to admire the sloppy mess the deacon had become and my eyes damn near bugged out. He was still alive. I was more surprised than a baby raccoon playing with a Jack in the Box to see his hands feel around the ground for his missing parts.

The deacon brought his jaw and a fistful of teeth to his face, trying his darndest to speak. His tongue was just flopped out like a dick on sex night, so I grabbed it, stepped on what was left of his throat, and yanked the tongue out by its root. I tossed it at Pa's feet, reminding him that he was next.

More static came through the June bug.

*Country! Goddamit! Abort! Do not engage. Turn your camera back on!*

"I ain't goin' back to them caverns, Mr. Hooper." That second Yankee Deacon was still alive, sputtering like a truck running outta gas. I positioned myself over him and used my new girl parts to piss all over his chest. "Fuck you, Deacon. There ain't no God to help you now. You go an' tell THAT to Mr. Phillips! I never did like no cheaters."

After that, he stopped moving, so instead of going on about the Devil and whatnot, I picked up the hammers and looked at Pa.

*Country, what they fuck is going on up there? I can't lock your location. I need to bring you back, now. You don't want to be trapped up there.*

I sniffed around like a coon hound to let Pa know that I was huntin'. He was curled up in the corner with that shotgun across his lap.

"Why are you crying, Pa?" I asked him and wiped some of the brains off my face. All sorts of goo and muck dripped down the front of my dress. The head of that first deacon was between us. I picked it up by the hair and rolled it like a bowling ball over to Pa.

"Please, Violet," he whimpered and tried to hide behind them hands of his. "Please, Lord. Please, Lord. Save my Violet."

More static came through that June bug, but I couldn't hear no Mr. Hooper.

I stubbed my toe into one of them circular saw tables on my way to go play with Pa and a blade fell near that little girl foot of mine.

Pa put his hands together like he was a praying. "Please, God. Please, God. Please dispel this demon from my sweet Violet."

I bent over and picked up the saw blade. One of the edges cut into my finger. I licked my little girl blood and spit it at Pa. He was still crying. It made me laugh.

*Country, turn your camera on!*

Before I knew it, I was standing over Pa. He stopped praying and looked up at me. "Violet. It's Pa. Please come back to me."

I raised the saw blade, then got a pretty twisted idea in my head. I buried the blade into the web between the little girl's devil finger and ring finger. Mr. Hooper was right. I could feel everything, and it was worse than getting a hand stuck in a woodchipper. I pressed it down as far as it would go, cracking and breaking bones in that little girl's hand. Then, when I finally buried it all the way down to the wrist, I bent her and started shitting on Pa's coveralls.

Pa stopped crying and I grabbed his hand. "Tell that Yankee Phillips, that the South will rise again!"

I pulled Pa's arm out with my regular hand, and as he started shrieking, I used my new saw hand to chop that arm of his clean off. I kept shitting while I stood on top of him. He laid down, taking in his own dirty defeat.

I took his severed arm and beat his face in with it. That wasn't killing him, so I took to the saw hand again, using it to pull him apart like a dog with a ragdoll. Arms. Then, legs. Then dick. Then balls. He was choking on vomit and blood and whatever ever else, so I helped him out and shoved his fingers from that dead arm into his mouth.

Still laughing and shitting, I started cutting holes in his face. After I got tired of that, I totally sawed his head right down the center. Both sides peeled away and fell onto them coward shoulders of his. There was blood everywhere in the shed like someone had shot a BB gun into the side of a swimming pool. I dug into his brain and ate away. Tasted every bit as good as squirrel. I think.

More static came through on the June bug.

*I've got you. You're coming back, Country, you stupid fucking redneck.*

I opened my real eyes and the white trough started draining water like a bathtub.

The lid popped open with a hiss.

Mr. Hooper ran over and smacked the side of the trough. "What in the fuck did you do?"

I shook the fog of transportation outta my head and grabbed on to the side of that trough. "Maybe I'm a lil' bit more rock n roll than you was thinkin'."

Hooper threw them hands of his up and down. "What the fuck does that mean?"

I pulled my body up from the lawn chair and threw a leg over the side of the trough. "Well, you said that I was a little bit country, an' I said I was a little bit rock n roll."

"Is that a joke? Is that a fucking joke?" He glared at me. "How do you even fucking remember that?"

"I dunno," I told him. "I was just playin' the sport like you tol' me to."

He stomped over to the Lite Brite typewriter and punched a few keys. "Jesus, Country. I told you not to kill anyone. What in the fuck was that? Are you so fucking stupid that you took the sports reference literally?" He tapped on the June bug. He waited a bit. He pushed some more buttons. Then he looked back at me. "You killed two of God's servants. An innocent man. The girl is dead for sure. You shoved a fucking saw blade straight through her hand, down to her wrist. It's too late to send in a clean-up crew. That tool shed is swarming with angels."

"They was tryin' to get me."

He threw a big stack of papers across the room at me. "You know what this means, right? I have to go back down to the caverns. Looks like it's thousands of years of sucking The IT's dick and pussy again. Fuck!"

"I din't mean to get you in no trouble."

His face went white like he just saw General Lee's ghost. He lifted that fat old finger of his and put it to his lips, telling me to shut up. Tapping the June bug, he said, "Hello, Phillips."

I felt hot and grabbed the water bottle. It was full again. I hadn't been up there for very long, but I already missed that cool breeze. I tickled the June bug in my ear on the belly. The arms moved in and out like a water pump at a well. Maybe that June bug didn't have to stay on my ear, after all.

Mr. Hooper laid back in that seat of his like it was a rocking chair on a porch. His belly stuck out and popped one of them buttons on his shirt. He didn't seem to notice. "Yes, Phillips. I'm quite aware of what happened."

He let out a big gasp and listened to his June bug. I drank more water.

"Yes, Phillips, I get it. Well, it was your job to process him. I'm just supposed to handle him."

I flipped the switch on the side of my June bug and looked at Mr. Hooper and then at the glass TV on top a that desk of his. It was a TV camera, I reckoned.

"Of course, I know that. I'm the one who took the bet," Hooper said. "I knew he wasn't ready, you scumbag. You took advantage of me. Phillips? Phillips? Phillips?" Then I saw him tickle the belly on that June bug in his ear and flip the switch up and down three times. The bug's legs came off from around his ear and he threw it across the room.

I was right.

It did come off.

I walked over to where he threw it. When I bent down to get it for him, he started screaming.

"You fucking idiot. Don't bother with that. I won't need that where I'm going."

When I touched his June bug, it crawled away so I didn't bother with it no more. "Where are you goin'? Don't we have more games to play?"

"Unfortunately for me, I'm going back to the caverns for Lord only knows how long." He started crying. "Phillips is going to be your new handler."

"Mr. Hooper, I din't mean no harm. I was just doin' what felt right."

He walked over to me and put his hand on my shoulder. "I get it, Country. You didn't know. It was my mistake. I should never have explained the job to you the way I did. More so, I should never have sent you on a mission without any training."

Then, outta nowhere, a bunch of red lights started flashing all around the room. They weren't there before, I don't think.

"What the hell now?" Hooper yelled as he wiped tears off his fat face. He started running after the June bug but it was too fast for him. "Help me, Country. I need to get this."

I ran over by him and chased the June bug across that floor, up and down the walls until we finally cornered it by the trough.

"Don't break it, Country. I need it."

I put my hands down and cupped them together. That June bug, with all his hundreds a legs crawled right into my fingers like a cradle. I slowly got up and held out my hands. I suppose it was the least I could do for poor old Mr. Hooper.

He plucked that lil' fella up by a few of its legs and put it over his ear. "Phillips? What now?" He paused. "Code Red five, five, niner? Not possible." He walked back to that Lite Brite typewriter and pushed a few buttons. Some images flashed on that window glass TV. "No way, Phillips." He turned a dial on the side of the desk. "I understand that we're short staffed. He just killed four people. There is no way I'm going to send him up again."

He closed his eyes. "I'll ask him."

I took a drink from the water bottle. "What does all these lights mean, Mr. Hooper?"

"We have a situation, Country. A big situation. A Code Red five, five, niner, to be exact."

"I don't know what all that means."

"It means that God and his team—I mean associates—are about to take down one of our most precious hosts. They are apparently angry about what happened earlier."

"You mean with me?"

"Yes, Country. With you."

"Well?" I asked him. "What can we do?"

"Phillips wants to send you back into this host to fight off God's associates. I told him I'd ask you."

I thought of tickling that June bug on my ear. This was my chance. If Mr. Hooper was going back to the caverns, then so was I. I sure didn't have a whole lotta interest in sucking no IT's dick. "I'll do it. I swear I won't kill nobody this time."

He let out a giant gasp of air. "Maybe we don't have to go back to the caverns after all. Get in the pod and prepare for transfer."

He meant that trough. I did as I was told.

He tapped on his June bug. "Phillips. We'll do it. You have to promise me, though, that if we succeed in protecting the asset that you will stand up for me."

Mr. Hooper snapped his finger at the trough, then tapped away at that Lite Brite typewriter. "Get in," he told me.

"Thank you, Phillips," he said. "I know we haven't fixed this situation yet, but, thank you." He tapped on his June bug and walked over next to me. "They are going to let us do it, Country. Sweet, Jesus."

"Sweet Jesus," I said.

He bent down about the same time that lawn chair started dropping into the trough. The gravy started coming up around me again. "What are the rules, Country? Please listen to me this time."

"No killin' no one."

"And?"

"And don't take this off or turn her camera off."

He put up his hand like he was saluting me. "Thank you for serving the IT, solider."

I saluted him back. Figured it was the right thing to do.

The cigarette case lid started to fold over me and the gravy filled up the trough. There was no way that I was going back to them caverns ever again.

I opened my eyes.

I was in bed. I reached between my legs and like before, there was no man parts, but there sure was blood.

I looked at my wet fingers. They were lil' girl fingers again. I reached over the side of the bed and wiped them off on some brown shag carpeting.

A song I recognized was coming from a record player in the room.

"A Little Bit Country, A Little Bit Rock N Roll." I always liked that song. I think that it was my favorite song.

A dirty old fan was barely blowing air at me from a nightstand. It was just like that hot summer when the hardware store sold out of fans. It was hot, but it wasn't as hot as Hell.

I heard crickets a chirpin' outside the window.

I tapped on the June bug. "Mr. Hooper, can you hear me."

*Yes. Now turn on the camera.*

I got up from the bed and looked out the window. I saw a nice farm outside and a rusty old swing set. The swing set looked familiar. I took a sip from a glass a water next to the fan. Outside, two hound dogs chased after a squirrel. All them years in the cavern made me forget how much I loved being alive.

I wanted to be alive again.

"I don' think that I'm gonna turn on that camera, Mr. Hooper," I whispered.

*What are you talking about, Country? Turn on the camera. We have to protect the assets. We had a deal!*

I started rubbing on the June bug just like Mr. Hooper had before. "No, we din't have no deal. You had a deal with Mr. Phillips an' that IT."

*Goddamn you, Country! You can't do this to me. You signed a contract.*

"That's where you're wrong. I never signed nothin' an' nothin' has been proceed. You said it yourself." I clicked the switch on the June bug up and down three times and it started coming loose from my ear. "I wanna be alive again, Mr. Hooper. I don't ever wanna go back to them caverns."

*Don't do this, Country! You can't do this to me!*

The June Bug jumped off my ear and onto the floor, and I didn't hear nothing in my ear no more. I was a free man. Free to be back on the earth, listening to my favorite song and feeling the breeze from a hot summer night.

I got out of the bed and started stomping away at the June bug with my bare foot to the beat of that song by Donnie and Marie that I remembered loving so much. The bug clicked and fizzed and sparked. Finally, it was all outta juice.

I walked across my new room and picked up a rag doll. I took it back to bed with me. It wasn't as good as feeling a woman next to me in bed, but it was better than Hell. It was better than them caverns and it was better than taking orders from fat, old Mr. Hooper.

Just before I started to fall asleep in my new body, in my great new life, the door to the bedroom creaked open and a bit of light shined in from the hall. A man came into the room and made his way over to my bed.

He sat down.

I knew that face.

It was… me.

*Recognize yourself, Deacon Futch?*

I started blinking and huffing. I tried talking back to Mr. Hooper's voice in my head but no words were coming out that girl's mouth. *How can you talk to me*? I asked him in my mind.

*Oh, come on, Johnny. Do you really think that Hell is in the business of giving people promotions and sending them to earth for vacation? Ha!*

"I don' understand, sir. Please bring me back now!" I kept yelling but nothing was coming out.

Deacon Johnny Futch, me, started running his wet hands through my little girl hair. Then he started rubbing up inside my bloody girl parts.

*There is no back. There are no agents. There are no handlers. There is no Phillips. Our job is to punish people for their sins. It is Hell, after all.*

Then, it all came back to me as quick as momma bird bringing food back to her nest.

My life as Deacon Johnny Futch had not pleased God.

I had my way with the girls of my flock. I raped them. I Beat them. I told them that I could rid their bodies of the Devil's evil. The girl I was inside of… well, I killed her. Her Ma and Pa told me that she had the devil in her on a counta she was bleeding outta her body and carrying on.

I buried her under that swing set outside.

*I can't really say it was a pleasure getting to know you*, Hoo

And then, just as my head went quiet again, the other me pushed my little girl head into the pillow on the bed. The girl tried to scream. I tried to scream. Nobody heard nothing. A belt unbuckled for the first time in what would be a zillion more. Forever. I felt everything as my own penis went inside that girl and those wet, bloody hands wrapped around that little girl throat.

*Welcome to your eternity, Deacon Futch.*

# The Skid Row SLUGGER

Drew Stepek

"Hey, JC. The body's over here by this dumpster."

I ignored my partner and ashed my smoke next to a pile of human shit. My target wasn't the feces. It was a disfigured city rat wiggling across the pavement, trying to avoid the turd. Like a dying turtle without arms, it struggled toward a sewer drain a few feet away, leaving a trail of blood in its wake. The foul excrement and my ashes were the only obstacles preventing it from freedom.

"Let me help you." I stepped on his tail with the tip of my boot, pinning it next to the shit. It lifted its head and bared its teeth. The little fucker was too weak to squeak, much less scurry away. It must have gotten into a fight with a raccoon or an opossum and lost. Lost miserably.

"JC!" My partner Hernan tapped on his watch. "I'm waiting."

After giving Hernan the finger, I dug my foot deeper into the rat's tail. It shook in agony. I pulled back my other foot and booted the nasty fucker in the side. The half-dead rodent let out an anemic cry as the tail detached from its ass and remained under my shoe. The mutilated body tumbled toward the sewer grate on the side of the curb. The carcass teetered on the edge for a few seconds. Then, it somehow mustered up enough courage and energy to roll fully into the sewer.

"Two points," I muttered.

I looked over at Hernan, hoping he saw my conquest over the dirty, street trash. He just shrugged his shoulders and waved me toward the alley. He was more interested in getting out of the rain than watching me kick the excrement of Skid Row into the gutter where it belonged.

A morning drizzle escalated into a sprinkle. It was a rare rainy day in LA. Sure, water was falling from the sky, but I never really considered a day without sunshine a "storm." The upside of a rainy day in LA was that the precipitation wiped the smog out of the air. The downside was that it made the smell of feces and piss saturate the alleys and streets.

With or without less than perfect weather, Los Angeles was a biohazard. The vermin that treated the streets as its toilet continually contaminated it every second that they continued to breathe. I wasn't fooled. I knew that these nameless drifters chose to live off the grid. They chose the street. They remained out of the grip of the law.

I pulled the hood of my city-issued rain gear over my head and walked toward my partner. Before I could make it ten steps, however, I felt a hand on my shoulder.

"Hey, man. Can you bum a smoke?"

I unsnapped my holster and spun around. "Don't fucking touch me, scumbag!"

The grime-coated hand and its brown fingernails belonged to one of the thousands of shitbags that made The Row their home. He was a scrawny, heavily intoxicated black dude with his hair shooting off in every direction like a witch doctor. I was surprised that he didn't have a bone in his nose and a shrunken head around his neck. As if he didn't already look like he just escaped from an institution, he had jailhouse ink all over heavily weathered cheeks. That was a thug look that screamed, "I'm a fucking criminal."

He shot his arms in the air, and the piercings all over his face shook and clanked together. "Yo, dude. Chill the fuck out."

His breath reeked of vodka. That smell, though, was overpowered by the stench of urine wafting from his body. To stay dry, he wore several black garbage bags that covered his torso. They were wrapped with tape around his wrists and pelvis.

He smelled like a garbage can. He looked like a garbage bag. To me, he was a walking and talking pile of trash.

I spat my cigarette at him. It twirled around until the lit end grazed his cheek. It didn't cause any real harm, though, and he was on his knees as soon as he saw the smoke hit the pavement. A discarded butt wasn't useful to him if it got wet. Since the LA drainage system was fucked up, an inch of rain in the air was an inch of rain on the ground.

He grabbed my old smoke, but I mashed his hand into a puddle. He cried out.

"You must really need a cigarette." I quieted my voice. "Huh, Buckwheat?"

I repositioned my boot to ensure that my heel's sharp edges dug into the back of his hand. Then, I reached down and burrowed my fingers through his disgusting hair. I turned his head to face my partner. "Hernandez. Is this what you call securing a fucking crime scene? What the fuck?"

I refastened my holster and twisted my foot on top of his knuckles. He tried to get up to a squat so he could get his hand out from under my sole. I released his hair and pushed him back to the ground. "Stay down, Wheat."

"Williams. Jackson. Get the fuck over here and take this junkie shithead down to the station for questioning."

The rotten deadbeat started squirming like a worm on hot pavement. "Come on, dude," he whimpered. "I just asked you for a smoke."

I let up on his hand. "Wrong. You're inside an active crime scene with two dead bodies, shithead. Now, you're a suspect."

When I carelessly looked over where the other officers were, he picked up a large rock from the ground by his legs. He jumped to his feet and slapped me across the temple with it—the blow connected with my head so fiercely that my neck cracked. My opposite ear buried itself in my shoulder.

His disgusting, rotten teeth and corroded tongue came millimeters from my nose. "I ain't the Slugger, bitch!"

My brain bounced around in my head, and I felt a razor-sharp sting on the left side of my face. My vision blurred as I felt blood trickle out of my partially muted, then ringing, ear.

Wobbly, I flicked out my collapsible baton and started pummeling his face with no intention of stopping. He fell backward and raised his forearms to block my bombardment. As my vision cleared, I continued to bang away on his arms, managing to connect with his face again. I loved the sensation I felt in my forearm when my club broke the skin and chipped into the bone.

"I didn't say you were The Slugger, Buckwheat." I pulled back the club and snatched him up by his garbage bag clothes. "But now you've resisted arrest and assaulted a police officer."

He spat in my face, and a tooth hit me between the eyes. I think I managed to knock out four of what teeth were left in his mouth. After a few more direct hits to the bridge of his nose, he finally cried out in defeat.

He pulled the garbage bags over his black and crimson face and started balling. "Stop, please." Blood gushed out of the top of the bag and into his hair. After a ten-second tantrum, he pulled the bags back down and began sorting through the blood, trying to recover some teeth. I don't know why he bothered. It wasn't like I was going to help him put them back in his gums. Besides, I was doing him a favor. All the drugs this walking disease used over the years made his teeth completely useless, dead, and disgusting.

The two officers who were tasked with controlling the parimeter finally ran up to us. They picked the bum up and zip-tied his hands behind his back. Williams put on some latex gloves to prevent her from contacting AIDS—which this asshole definitely had—and put some gauze into his mouth.

She surveyed my work as she shined a Maglite into the man's face, asking him to follow her finger with his eyes. "Conners? What the fuck? You gave him a concussion."

"He smashed a fucking rock against my face," I said. "I should be asking you 'what the fuck?' How is it that this homeboy can get into a taped off murder scene and attack me? It was your job to secure the perimeter."

She turned the light back on me and asked me to follow her finger. I swatted her hand, knocking the flashlight to the ground. I pointed to the perp with my club. "This mess." I tacked the end of the stick between his eyes as they closed. Tears squirted out onto his bloody mess of a face. "This is on you."

I stared her down. Then, her partner. Then, the trash bag man who refused to reopen his eyes. "Learn how to be a fucking police officer."

The two bungling cops and the crack addict turned around and walked toward the black and white. *Shockingly*, they hadn't used their squad car to block the parimeter as instructed. Young cops never understood that we lived in a world of us versus them. There isn't any time for niceties, kumbaya, and hugs. These subhumans want what you have, and they'll take it from you if you aren't always on alert. Foolishly, I let my guard down and got cracked in the head with a rock. Lesson learned.

I fired up another cigarette as I retracted my club and twirled it around, right back into my belt. I rubbed at the left side of my face.

Hernandez watched my performance and rolled his eyes. "You okay, JC?"

"Yeah. Thanks for the back-up, partner." I sucked on my new smoke. "Those two dumbfuck rooks almost got me killed."

Hernan looked at my battle scar. "Damn. He got you good. You better get that looked at when we get back to the station."

"I'll be fine," I said. "I'm sure you'd feel a lot worse right now if that punk made me the next victim."

"Sure, JC. I don't think that twerp is the Slugger."

"You never know, Hernan." Using my fingers like a gun, I shot around the street and down the alley. "Any of these pieces of shit could be the Slugger."

Hernan cleared his throat. "Whatever you say, Jessie James." He held two coffees and lifted one toward me. "I suppose we can never be too careful, can we?"

I blew on my finger as if it were smoking like a real gun. "Not on The Row, brother." I lit my second cigarette and took the coffee. "Don't worry, we'll get this scum."

Hernan crouched down and pulled a blanket off the victim. I flicked my second cigarette into the dumpster and took a sip of the lukewarm coffee.

He looked in the direction that I threw my smoke and then back at me. "Really?"

I shrugged my shoulders. "What?"

He pointed at the dumpster. "Don't we get called down here enough for dumpster fires that *aren't* caused by us?"

"Hey, genius." I leaned my head back and let the rain drizzle onto my face. "It's raining."

I considered calling him a "retard" however, during our first week as partners, another detective told me his daughter had Down syndrome. I can't remember if I called him that or not during that week, but I had been careful not to use that word around him since.

One time, he had to leave the precinct early for an emergency with Benny, his daughter. He left me with a pile of paperwork. Me—and a couple of the other guys—yelled "retard" as soon as he left the station. It felt good to get it out of our system. I don't think he heard us. I'm sure if he did, he would have told the Chief. And, since nothing ever came out of it, no harm, no foul.

"Lucky number seven?" Hernan ignored my jab and pointed at what looked like a number in the oozing mess at the center of the victim's skull. "Is he numbering them now?"

"This is the eighth victim." I took another sip of my lukewarm coffee, hunched over the corpse, and put on new gloves. "Just a coincidence."

"No." He traced the number on the face with a pencil. "That's a seven."

"That doesn't make sense. This is the Slugger's eighth victim."

He counted backward using his fingers. "I think it's—"

"It's eight." I insisted. "I should know. Officer Diez was the first. Jesus! And I'm the one who just got a fucking rock pounded against my head." Jenny Diez was my partner before Hernan. "In case you forgot, she was beaten to death by a shithead with a baseball bat nearby. The murderer has never been caught, and the bat was never recovered. It was the Slugger. Too big of a coincidence not to be."

He bowed his head and put his hand on my knee. "Sorry about Diez, brother."

I grabbed the pencil from him without acknowledging his sympathy. I stuck the point of it into some brains that were vomiting out of the front of the forehead. I pulled it toward my eye as it drooped like a rope bridge over a deep trench.

A pain drilled from the left side of my head, through my brain, and into my right. Both my ears rang, and it felt like my skull could burst at any second. I tried to shake it off and lighten the mood, so I didn't alarm Hernan. "I guess this guy wasn't the brains of the operation," I joked.

He let out a short, forced laugh.

I used my glove to untangle the brains from the pencil.

Hernan coughed into his hand and then shook his bile off into the lid of his empty coffee. "Maybe this isn't the slugger?"

I used the pencil again to illustrate. "You see this indentation here, around the top of the wound?"

He nodded his head while he covered his mouth and nose with a bandana. He inched in closer to the victim's face. "I guess I can't miss it."

"Look closer," I said. "See the abrasions and swelling that curve and fade out the closer you get to the cheekbones?"

"Ummmm." He closed his eyes and shook his head. Then, he reopened them. "Sure."

"Now, look at this." I scribbled inside the rounded outline of bruising below the nose, around the middle of the mouth. "You see the shape that makes there?"

Hernan shuffled over behind the head and straightened his back to get a bird's eye view. "Fuck me. That's a bat."

I dragged the pencil to the nose. The tip was concave, almost ironed-on to the face. Dried blood and cartilage forced their way out of the raised nostrils and into the mouth. "I assume this was the nose. It's almost as if the Slugger used it as a target or a button."

I drew a circle in the air around the eyes. One of them was crimson red and popped. The other dangled off the side of the cheek, still attached. "The eyes literally jumped out of the sockets. The left one…" I lightly pricked it with the pencil lead. "Rolled back into the barrage and burst under the bat. While the right one…"

I dug under the adhering blood vessels and the optic nerve. “It bounced out of the way.”

“What does all that mean?”

“It means the victim took the majority of the bat beating on the ground.”

He rubbed his palm over his own face. “It looks like he tried to sneeze with his eyes open, and that lit up some M80s in his mouth.”

“What is it with you Mexicans and fireworks?”

He let out a colossal breath. “What is it with you and stereotypes?”

Ignoring him and still unsteady from Buckwheat’s assault, I got to my feet. I side-stepped behind Hernan and positioned myself over him and the corpse. I scuffed my shoes and lifted my arms together over my head as if I was holding a bat. Then, I forcibly brought them down like I was pounding it on the face.

“BAM! BAM! BAM! BAM! BAM!” I yelled.

Hernan flinched behind his arm and almost lost his balance.

“Fuck, JC!” He grabbed onto the left side of his chest. “You trying to kill me?”

I helped him up by his coat lapel. “Take a look.” I used my finger to sketch an outline of the top of the bat.

“Well, I’ll be damned.” He took my coffee, continued to study what was left of the victim’s face. He waited for about 30 seconds, then asked, “So, wait. He was attacked while he was sleeping?”

“No.” I dropped back down to my knees and gently unsealed the back of the head that was adhered to the cement by a massive amount of dried blood, more brain matter, and skull pieces. “The killer first made contact with the head while he was standing… from behind. This rear wound is different. The impact point is on the crown as if he was running away from the killer.”

Hernan nodded his head in agreement. “It’s amazing how much *you* can tell about a murder after only looking at it for a few minutes. It’s almost like you were here.”

“Every murder is a story.” I smirked. “To catch this maniac, we have to know his story and his patterns. After eight victims, I can look at the evidence and think like him.”

The creaking wheel of a rusty shopping cart coming toward us drew our attention. A recognizably Boston accent rang out from the end of the alley, “That’s pretty much how it happened, officers.”

Hernan drew his firearm and aimed it through the rain into the darkness.

Not taking my eyes off the end of the alley, I drew my gun as well and bumped Hernan with my shoulder. “Seriously! You didn’t clear your side of the fucking crime scene? You really are a genius!”

“I did. I fucking swear. There wasn’t anyone here.” Hernan used his hand to shield his eyes from the rain. He surveyed the alley for a fire escape or a door.

A fat figure pushing a shopping cart filled with a collection of the most useless garbage in the history of waste walked toward us. Once he emerged from the shadows, he raised his hands above his head. He had long, wet hair pulled back in a ponytail, thick glasses, and a goatee covered in beads of wet dirt.

"Get on the ground, motherfucker!" The yell intensified the pounding pain in my head, causing my shooting hand to shake.

"We have a witness," Hernan gasped. "Oh, my God. We have a witness."

*Shit!* I thought.

"Or, we have the Skid Slugger," I quickly suggested.

"Can I please have some water?" The fat man's accent was competing with the broken fluorescent light fixture in the interrogation room; I hadn't decided yet, which aggravated my migraine more.

Hernan sat across from the bum. "Excuse me?"

The fat man pushed the empty paper cup across the table. "Water. Please. It's hot in this room."

Standing behind Hernan, I rubbed my temples. The pain caused by the attack earlier clouded my thoughts. Stupid rookies, stupid Hernan, they were the reason hardworking white cops like me would be extinct one day. They'd get us all killed with their fuckups.

I paced behind Hernan, trying to refocus my thoughts. I had much bigger problems than my skin color right now. I didn't plan on saying a word until I had a better idea as to what this scumbag may or may not have seen last night.

"Here's an idea," Hernan said. "How about you tell us your name since you don't have any ID."

The fat man crossed his arms and rested them on top of his belly. "I do have an ID, but I left it back at my cart. Since you made me leave it in that alley, I'm sure everything will be gone when I get back."

"I'm sure it's filled with valuable treasures," I said, unable to keep my mouth shut. These people pissed me off so much.

"Excuse me, detective," the suspect returned. "My entire life is in that cart."

"You should have revealed yourself to us when we first arrived. You gotta understand where we're coming from; you were hiding."

Our suspect picked at his teeth. "I wasn't hiding. I was looking for my 'friend' Phillips."

"Who the hell is Phillips?"

"Just an old friend who I seem to have misplaced."

"Great." I let out a deep breath. "You hear that, Hernan? He misplaced his *wittle* imaginary *fwiend*."

Hernan laughed but never took his eyes off our suspect.

The perp stared right back at him. "Water, please. I'm burning up."

He was right. The room was growing increasingly uncomfortable.

That's Los Angeles. The second the temperature goes lower than 60, or it rains, everyone boards up their windows and cranks up the heat. I would have gone outside the door to turn down the thermostat, but I didn't want Hernan alone with that scumbag. It was time I acted. I pulled up a chair next to my partner and rolled up the short sleeves on my shirt. For a forty-eight-year-old detective, I was pretty fit. That frequently worked as an intimidation technique.

"Please," he begged, tapping the cup on the table. His heavy breathing fogged up his bifocals. He took them off and wiped them with the end of his tight-fitting, stained white shirt. He put them back on and stared at my biceps. "You're pretty fit for a cop. Aren't you, buddy?"

I flexed my arms gently from left to right. "Name?"

"My name is Sonny Hooper." He extended his hand to shake. It was also coated in dirt and so fat it looked like it was inflated by a tire pump.

I glared at his hand in disgust.

"Sonny." Hernan wrote it down as he mouthed the name aloud.

I put my hand over his to stop him from writing. I didn't take my eyes off of the bloated toad man, though. He returned my stare and smiled. His hand remained in the air, waiting.

"Don't write that shit down, Hernan."

"Why not?"

"Because it's a bullshit name. Sonny Hooper was Burt Reynolds's character in the movie *Hooper*."

"Hey, fuckwad, what's your real name?" I asked.

"Nobody calls me Sonny Hooper, though. Call me, Hoop." He continued to stare at me as he dragged his disgusting tongue across his cold sore-riddled lips.

This fucker wanted to dance. Well, that was just fine. But it wasn't gonna be a Ménage à trois. "Hernan. Please go get Mr. Hooper a cup of water."

"You sure?"

"Yeah. I got this."

He not-so-subtly pointed at the camera above the door, making sure I keep my cool.

"I got it," I said again and shot him a wink.

He got up and left the room.

As soon as the door closed the door, Hooper started yapping again. "You better be smart, Detective Conners."

A ringing instantly blared into my left ear. It was so loud that it made my entire body feel powerless. I squinted my left eye and curled my lip to try and push the pain out of my face. For a split second, I was unable to speak. It felt like I was having a stroke.

"Detective Jimmy Conners. You go by JC because the kids used to make fun of you for being named after a tennis player… a sport which they deemed gay."

I made a fist with my left hand, hoping to help break the pressure escalating inside my head.

"They also made fun of you for being a little, little, small boy. They called you Jimmy-Jimmy-Rat-Boy because you were so small and had beady little eyes and buck teeth."

I scoffed, but sweat collected below my nose. I wiped it off with my wrist. "If that were true, how would you even know that? We've never met, Hooper."

"I know many things about you. I guess you could say that I've studied your work on The Row."

*That was it. He saw me. This motherfucker saw me and was being coy.* It was surprisingly clever for a loser piece of shit. I looked out of the corner of my eye, reminding myself that the camera was also recording everything we said.

"Let's cut to the chase, Mr. Hooper. What did *you* see last night?"

"I can't be sure." He put his finger over his mouth and entered deep thought. "I saw a white male in a black sweatshirt pulled tightly around his face, which was also blacked out with makeup or coal. First, he snuck up on my friend Charlie. Poor Charlie just minding his own business, counting out the aluminum cans and stomping them to fit into his bags."

The wasp nest in my skull buzzed louder. Every time the fluorescent light in the room cracked or Hooper intentionally left the letter "R" out of words, the dizzier I got, and the more claustrophobic the room became.

"Shouldn't you be writing this down? I'm sure your partner will be interested in this story."

I looked at my watch. Less than a minute had passed. It already felt like an eternity. I stood and leaned over the table toward him. I must have done it all too abruptly because I fell right back down into the chair. A haze danced in front of my eyes as they fell shut.

Trying to rebound, I jolted my eyes open and regained composure. Hooper hadn't moved an inch. Thankfully, I didn't think I passed out, but I was sinking fast in other ways.

"You seem delirious, Jimmy. Have you been burning the midnight oil? Too many late-night visits to your beat, maybe?"

I avoided his intimidation and turned Hernan's tablet toward me. I picked up the stylus, re-flexing my arms and pushing out my chest. "You haven't told me anything that doesn't smell like bullshit. Just keep on talking. The more you talk, the closer I get to your confession of being the Slugger. So, please. Be my guest, loudmouth."

"Oh. Okay. I haven't gotten to the good parts yet." Hooper sat back in his chair a little and put both his arms behind his head. His armpits were sweating so profusely that his shirt was permanently discolored.

"So, Charlie was counting and stomping his cans when the man—" he looked me up and down "—with your build, snuck up behind him."

*Fuck*, I thought, grinding my teeth.

"Fuck, indeed."

"What?"

"Just agreeing with you." Hooper gave a foul smile. His teeth were moldy. Old food that evolved into plaque was compressed into every crevice and lined his gums.

"I didn't say anything."

"You didn't? I could have sworn you just said 'fuck'."

He continued staring at me.

I blinked a few times and swallowed, hoping that Hernan would return with the water.

"Where is your accent from, Hooper?" I asked, trying to take control back. "Boston?"

"It's Hoop. And, no. I'm from Rhode Island."

"Is that even a real state?" I joked.

He let out a quick laugh. "Not really."

"So why come to Los Angeles. I'm sure there are a few alleys you could piss and shit in around Providence. I hear it's a real dump."

He let out a heartier laugh, and his arms fell to his sides. He wasn't on defense anymore. I was taking back the room.

The buzzing of the fluorescent light continued. The brightness managed to intensify after each time it flicked off.

"Just a second," I said, heading for the light switch.

I flicked it on and off a few times until the buzzing stopped. I took the opportunity to look into the precinct through the small window in the door. It was completely empty. I pressed my face against the glass, but there wasn't a sound or movement between the empty rows of desks.

"There's no one out there, Jimmy."

I snapped my fingers and pointed at him. "Refer to me as Detective Conners, you fat fuck."

"And, here I was thinking we were making jokes. Becoming pals."

"The time for jokes is over, Hooper." I tried to angle my face to see more of the room. Nothing. I shook the doorknob, even though I knew it was locked from the outside. I would have pounded on it, but then that slob would be back in control.

"Why don't you sit and listen to the rest of my story." He unfurled his fingers and waved me back to the chair.

I looked up at the camera. The red recording light was off. I smirked. Maybe Hernan wasn't such a dummy after all. I took my seat, thankful Hernan read into my wink.

Hooper blew his nose into his sleeve. As he pulled away, the snot drooped down like the brain attached to the end of Hernan's pencil at the crime scene. "Who came up with the name, Skid Row Slugger anyway?" He tugged the snot string free from his face.

"Why does it matter? Don't you think it paints an accurate picture of the crimes *you've* committed?"

He grinned, exposing the complete decay of his mouth.

I needed to break from his stare and the animosity behind his incessant smiling. I grabbed the case file beside Hernan's tablet.

"Why don't you tell me more about your victims." I pulled out the first picture. "We called this one 'The Doll.'"

He looked at the photo and slowly closed his eyes. I was shaking him.

"You wanna know why we called her The Doll?"

He turned his head to the side.

"We called her that because the Slugger took one massive swing at her head, broke her neck, and almost knocked her head off. When she was found, her head was dangling to the side of her body. The neck was decimated to Jell-O."

I pulled another picture from the file and studied my work for a minute. Pride flushed through my body as I threw the photo in front of him.

"You recognize this one, you sick fuck?"

He closed his eyes.

"Open your Goddamn eyes." I tapped and the photo with my finger. "We called him 'The Crater' because The Slugger beat his chest in so forcefully that he destroyed all his ribs and bored a massive hole through his torso. Then, he scooped out everything inside and threw it in a dumpster."

The fat bastard swallowed deeply and turned his head to the other side.

"Number three. This is a picture of 'Tomahawk.' This is some of your best work. He crushed the victim's neck with the sole of his boot and then completely wrecked the top of the head. So much so that her skull was pounded entirely into dust."

Hooper whimpered. "Please. No more."

I had him on the ropes. He hadn't seen shit. I should have known he wasn't smart. Same as the rest of the Skid Row scum.

"Number four. 'Bullseye.'"

"Stop, please, Officer Conners."

"Look at him, you fat fuck!" I screamed. "Bullseye. The Slugger tenderized his face. Then, he used the bat to drill a hole through the center of the face with it."

Tears built up on the sides of his eyes. At that point, I had almost convinced myself that he was the Slugger.

"Five. 'Thanksgiving.'"

"No more."

He bowed his head, so I slid the picture into his line of sight.

"You want to know why we called him that?" I slammed my first down next to the photo, shaking the table. I hadn't realized how worked up I was getting. From the collar down to my pelvis, the entire front of my shirt was soaked with sweat.

"Thanksgiving. The Slugger pulverized his backbone and neck," I whispered. "Then, he folded the victim in half and tied it's arms and legs together."

"Stop, detective!"

"Why? Don't like seeing your own work, Hooper? Aren't you proud of yourself?"

He buried his chins into his shirt and covered his mouth. He was starting to realize that playing Mister Smart-ass was a mistake. I don't play that shit. Ever.

"This is my personal favorite. 'The Egg.'

"No more." He lifted his head out of his shirt and tried to look menacing by arching one of his eyebrows, showing only one angry eye. His flabby face was bright red and wet from crying. "For the love of God," he squealed. "Use their real names."

I rushed behind him and tugged on his ponytail, bringing his head upright. My fingers touched the filthy rolls under the hair and squirmed. I held the picture directly in front of his face.

I bent down to his ear. "That's the thing, Hooper. We can't ID any of the Slugger's victims. Like you, there are as worthless as the trash on the streets. The only names they have are the ones *I* give them."

I looked up at the camera. The record light was still off.

"Number six. The Egg. I think this one speaks for itself. The Slugger smashed the skull open on the side, and the brain and blood dissolved because he filled the skull with lye. Everything inside oozed out of his head."

Hooper's body shook, and his herpes lips quivered. It was time to close. I tightened my grip on his greasy ponytail and slammed him face-first onto the table. His glasses broke under the weight of his pumpkin-shaped head.

I breathed in a rush, smelling his fear. This mental son-of-bitch was about to confess to something he didn't even do. Damn, I was good!

I mushed his face into the table. I heard the lenses on the glasses *crack* and *pop*. I bent down to his ear. "I don't have any pictures of your final kill, but I'm sure you remember him from last night.

I released his head from the table, but he just remained there, groaning and crying.

"I got you motherfucker. Confess, Hooper. You're the Slugger." I walked back toward the door to see if anyone had returned who could finger me for violating all of Hooper's rights. No one. Very strange. The Chief must have called an emergency meeting. I guessed that Hernan got pulled in a while getting the water. He had been gone for what felt like an eternity. Lucky for me.

"The Doll wasn't the first victim, though. Was she, Jimmy?"

A dreadful feeling rushed up my back. It was as if a thousand spiders crawled out of my asshole to go to war with the wasps in my head.

I slowly turned from the door. "What the fuck did you just say?"

"I said, 'The Doll wasn't the first victim.' Was she… *Jimmy*?" Hooper sat upright, confident. There was no sign that he had been a quivering mess of tears. His face was pasty, not red, and his glasses were no longer broken.

"Wha… what are you talking about?"

"Jenny Diez was the first victim, wasn't she? She was your partner. You were obsessed with her. Weren't you?" He pounded both his fists on the table.

"H... h… how could you know that?" I tried to straighten my back and reflex my arms, but my body wasn't responding to my brain.

"But she didn't love you back, did she? As a matter of fact, she was going to file rape charges against you." Hooper picked up all the victim photos. "You couldn't have that. Could you, little fucking Jimmy-Jimmy-Rat-Boy. No, you couldn't have that at all. That's why you paid a couple of meth addicts from the Inland to beat her and dump her body in The Row. Didn't you? Didn't you!"

I looked at the camera. The recording light was still off.

"You're the Slugger, Jimmy," he howled. "You randomly murdered my friends to create the illusion of the Skid Row Slugger. That way, Diez's death would never be traced back to you. But you liked this killing gig a bit too much. Just couldn't stop after you got a taste of murder."

I rushed across the room and snatched up my chair. Hooper retreated to the farthest corner of the back wall. This time, he began laughing maniacally. The sound of his disgusting accent reverberated from all the walls in the small room.

I raised the chair over my head like my faithful aluminum baseball bat. But, before I could unleash on Hooper, Hernan rushed into the room.

"What in the fuck are you doing, JC!" He grabbed the chair out of my fists. He tried to subdue me, but I was too powerful for him.

"He's the Slugger!" I screamed as loud as I could. "This piece of shit is the Slugger!"

Hooper smiled at me and blew me a kiss. Then, he mouthed 'bye, bye' as he waved.

Hearing the raucous in the room, three black and whites entered and pulled me out. They must have knocked me unconscious while tackling me because everything went black.

I sat at my desk with an ice pack on my head. I spent the better part of my time since I awoke trying to think of ways out of being fingered as the Slugger.

Hernan had continued talking to Hooper in the interrogation room while I was knocked out, and he was still in there. *Fuck!* that was the only thing going in and out of my head. *Fuck. Fuck. Fuck!*

As far as everyone else knew, I hadn't laid a finger on Hooper yet, and there was no video of the conversation. The real question was how to handle my defense if Hooper—

The door to the interrogation room opened, and both Hernan and Hooper walked out. Hernan clapped him on the shoulder and shook his hand.

Hooper turned to me and grinned. His sinister eyes turned black, and his nostrils flared. He mouthed something to me, but I couldn't make it out. I tried to duck out of sight, but I knew he saw me.

*Fuck.*

*Fuck. Fuck. Fuck-fuck.*

After one last quiet exchange between them, Hooper left the precinct.

Without wasting a second, Hernan turned to our office and marched toward me. He shook his head in anger and disappointment.

*Fuck.*

When he reached the office, he nearly tore our door off its hinges. Rather than pulling his gun on me or screaming, though, he waited for the door to fully closed.

Then, after waiting for a beat, he asked, "Did you call that black guy 'Buckwheat' this morning before you beat the shit out of him?"

"Huh?" I couldn't believe that's what Hooper squealed on me with. I was the fucking Slugger, and he knew it. "Uh, no. I didn't call him anything. He attacked me with a rock."

"You stupid fucking racist. Hooper said that someone on The Row shot you with a cellphone, and in the video, you can distinctly hear you call that guy 'Buckwheat.'"

"Did you see the video?"

"Not yet. Hooper is going to track down the phone. He said he'll bring it to me tomorrow."

"I never said anything like that, I swear. That son of a bitch came up behind me, inside a crime scene. I thought he was trying to grab my gun. So, I used force, and then he assaulted me."

Hernan started pacing around my desk. "You better fucking hope that's all that happened, JC. You know people are coming down hard on the LAPD right now."

"Hernan. You know me."

"Yeah. I sure do. That's why I think it happened." He stopped pacing at his desk and took a deep breath. Then, he darted his finger toward the interrogation room. "What the fuck was that?"

"More importantly, where were you, Hernan?

"What do you mean? I went to get Hooper water."

"For a fucking half hour?"

He cocked his head as if I was speaking a foreign language. "Half hour? I was gone for less than 30 seconds. Hooper said you passed out moments after I left the room. Then, you came to and started swinging your chair at him."

"That's not true. You were gone. Everyone was gone." I pressed the ice pack closer to the bump on my head. "You went and turned the camera off. There was no one in the precinct. I looked out the window."

"JC. I walked to get water, then I walked back. No one turned off the camera. Good thing, too. You never got the opportunity to lay a finger on Hooper's head, and he isn't going to press charges for your outburst."

"You were fucking gone, Hernan. Everyone in the office was gone. I was in there alone with that animal for a half-hour."

He walked over to me, lifted the ice pack off my head, and examined the bump. "I don't know what you're all about right now. I told you to get your head looked at. You could have a concussion or brain aneurysm from that blow this morning."

Had I imagined the whole conversation? I pressed the ice pack even harder onto my wound.

"You better pray you didn't call that guy 'Buckwheat.'" He looked at his watch. "Shit. I gotta jam. Mary needs me to take care of Benny tonight because she has an all-nighter at the hospital."

"I didn't call him anything," I repeated.

"I guess we'll find out tomorrow, won't we?"

"You've got my back, don't you partner?"

"I gotta do what's best for my family. I'll decide after I see the video. And, JC…"

"Yeah?"

"Get your head checked before you leave tonight. You're going to have to be on your best game tomorrow."

In a fog, I waved him out.

Had I imagined everything that happened in that room? Was I feeling the walls closing in and have a psychotic break? None of what Hernan told me made any sense. Everything that happened felt so fucking real.

I messaged my temple. Other than the bump, and the continued throbbing, nothing felt out of whack. As if I could decide whether or not there was any damage to my brain by touching it.

By the time I packed up my things and called it a day, I still didn't know what was real.

However, I did know what needed to be done.

Hernan lived in Boyle Heights, which was a Mexican neighborhood between downtown and East LA. It wasn't the worst neighborhood in LA, but it wasn't the best, either.

I parked about two and a half blocks away from his house, on a dark part of the street. I made sure that there were no liquor stores or banks anywhere near where I parked. Nothing that could have surveillance cameras. This job had to be clean. Besides, Hernan and his wife Mary were respected members of the community. He was the cop that spent his free time talking to kids about gang life because he banged when he was a teen. She was a graveyard shift nurse at a hospital downtown that spent every free minute she had chasing around her handicapped daughter. They were pillars of the community. I suppose that would have meant a lot more if the city wasn't a pile of shit filled with drug addicts and criminals.

In their defense, Mexicans are a hardworking group for the most part, so there was never a ton of activity after midnight in his neighborhood. That said, even though the area was dead, it seemed like kids were always lighting off fireworks at all hours of the night and morning.

Thankfully, there was nothing to celebrate on that night. If one of our teams had won a championship, most of the minority population would be downtown near the Staples Center, destroying everything. I loved it when that happened. It gave me a free pass to beat the shit out of crowds of people. It always made me feel like I was using a sledgehammer to destroy an anthill.

On those nights, my job to protect and serve wasn't called into question. They were flagrantly breaking the law. I was the law.

I used the rearview to help me blacken out my face. I pulled the hood of my sweatshirt over my hair and used the drawstrings to pull it tight. If I did run into anyone on my way to Hernan's house, they most likely wouldn't find me suspicious. A brown person with a hoodie and a baseball bat was a pretty typical "look."

Strangely enough, if I was just some white guy walking around the streets of Boyle Heights with a baseball bat, that would have raised suspicion. The only whites who hung out in that area were there to buy drugs, guns, or hookers. So, a white guy with a bat was most likely there to cause trouble.

As I put on my gloves, I grabbed the old aluminum bat off of the backseat of my car. As I got out, I put my justice stick into a cover that strapped it to my back. I also tucked an old gun that I snatched off of a crime scene years ago into the front of my pants. I turned on the car alarm and then headed to my partner's house.

Hernan usually tried to get his four-year-old daughter Benny to sleep before nine. That was never an easy task. On top of her Down Syndrome, she suffered from night terrors and always seemed sick for one reason or another. She was also spooked by fireworks and would be impossible to talk down if she got shaken by explosions. Come to think of it, Hernan should have been raising her in any other city in the world. I supposed he wasn't such an outstanding family man and community member, after all.

After putting the kid to sleep, he usually kicked back a few *cervezas*, then zonked out while watching *SportsCenter*. He didn't get to do that a lot. Benny was a handful and she got restless when Mary worked the nightshift at the hospital. The fact was that she didn't have the same connection to her father as she did to her mother. Afterall, Hernan worked a lot.

I ensured that the bat bag was secured to my back as I leaped over the chain-link fence that led down the Hernandez driveway. The shaky barrier rattled a little but nothing loud enough to wake anyone up. Their driveway was littered with Benny's toys. A pink bike there, a hopping ball there, a box filled with Barbies over there.

When I reached the backdoor, I breathed a sigh of relief at the empty Tecate can sitting on the second of the three short steps. As I expected, there were ashes around the rim and a finished cigarette crushed in the center of the ring. Hernan was so predictable. I assumed he'd have one more smoke break before turning off ESPN and heading to bed.

I reached out and turned the knob. Unlocked, bingo!

I knew I didn't have to worry about any alarm system or cameras back there, either. Hernan was the security system and always had his firearm close by. I knew his schedule, though, and would easily catch him off guard.

My intention was to be in and out.

To prevent it from creaking, I pressed my left hand against the door and pushed it open. The kitchen was dark, but it was partly illuminated by the TV from the living room.

I crept across the kitchen tile as I pulled the bat free from my back. I spun it around by the grip, which was a tradition before I used it. As I crossed through to the dining room, the TV's brightness intensified, and the familiar sound of the *SportsCenter* theme song pulled me toward the actual final victim of the Skid Row Slugger.

As the family room came into view, I saw Hernan's favorite Dodgers' hat over the couch, turned backward on his head. I rolled the cold aluminum bat on my latex glove and then bounced it off my palm nine times, fixating on the LA emblem. That would be my target. The brightness of his giant screen TV blurred out everything else in his room, besides that hat. I licked my fingers and wet my contacts at the tear ducts. I took two long strides to the couch like I was about to stomp on home plate after driving a grand slam.

I stood firm and kicked the top of the bat off the tip of my shoe. I pulled it up, over my head, and then behind my back. Knowing that Hernan was tough as nails, I wanted to deliver the death blow with one strike. I didn't want my partner to suffer.

With my eyes closed, I took three deep breaths and said the Lord's Prayer.

When I reached Amen, I flexed my arms and transferred every bit of energy from my entire body into the bat. I focused on the Dodgers logo and hoisted the bat up and over my head.

*CRUNCH*!

The bat buried itself in Hernan's skull. The dodgers hat yanked from his head as I pulled back the bat to deliver an assurance blow. I took a sideways batter's stance, wanting to see if I could knock his head clean off.

In the LED rays from the TV, two small hands emerged from the visibility of the couch's back. They twitched for a few seconds, and then the body collapsed to its side.

I poked my head over the couch. It wasn't Hernan.

It was little Benny. She was sitting on top of a pile of pillows, where she'd been watching *SportsCenter* with her father. Blood gushed from the massive notch on her head. I peeled the Dodger hat off of my bat and laid it over her face.

Desperate to help her, I reached out for her hand. It was lifeless and limp. I tried to toss it up in the air, hoping it would animate. It didn't.

"B? What was that noise?"

Taking my eyes and hands off the little girl, I looked to the hall that led to the bedrooms. Hernan was standing in the doorway. My grip became weak, and the bat slipped out, hitting the wood floor. It bounced around for a bit until it rolled under the couch.

Hernan patted his hip to hopefully draw his firearm. He swallowed intensely as he came up empty. I looked over at the coffee table in front of the couch. There the gun sat in the middle of three Tecate cans.

"JC? Is that—"

Before he could get another word out, he lunged toward me. I ripped out the stolen gun from the front of my pants. Without thinking twice, I unloaded the clip into Hernan's face, neck, and chest.

Confused and delirious, he tried to shuffle his way to the couch to caress his loving daughter Benny. After two stumbles, though, my partner for the better part of a year, Frank Luis Hernandez, crumbled to the ground.

I pulled his phone out of his jeans and used his thumb to unlock it. Then, using the bloody thumb again, I texted my own phone—that I smartly left back at my apartment.

I typed in all caps: "HOOPER. IT WAS HOOPER."

Taking a second to get all my ducks in line, I staged his hand and phone on his chest as if he were texting me the last clue before he died.

Shockingly, I got out of Boyle Heights, no problem. For the most part, gunfire goes unreported in most Mexican neighborhoods because no one can tell the difference between shots fired and fireworks exploding.

I didn't want to resort to shooting Hernan in the face. He deserved better than that. The horror he must have felt when he realized that he had unintentionally doomed Benny. Thankfully, for him, *his* guilt only lasted a few seconds.

When I planned everything out earlier that night, I had no interest in even waking Benny up, much less bashing her head in. Unfortunately, what happened… happened. There was no way to go back in time and fix Hernan's mistake.

I never had any interest in being a parent, especially to a special needs kid. I will never understand the connection between a father and a daughter. I could forgive him for his judgment, but I knew I would never forget.

After carefully sliding into the driver's seat of my car, I dropped the bat and the gun onto a large bat bag that I left open in the back. I was careful not to drip any of Benny's DNA on the path back to my escape. The thing was that not much blood from her head made it onto the bat at all. I suspected that had something to do with the Dodger hat acting as padding.

As soon as I knew I was a safe distance from his neighborhood, I flipped on my headlights. I wiped the black off of my face. Then, I took a deep breath.

Unlike my trip to Boyle Heights, there was nothing suspicious about a cop following up a lead in Skid Row… especially considering that I was the lead detective on the most significant and most horrifying multiple murder case in the history of Downtown Los Angeles.

I had a pretty good idea where Hooper would be, and I knew that the bat and gun would make lovely additions to his shopping cart filled with trash. I counted my blessings that we left the cart in that alley, virtually unchecked.

Sure, that was terrible policing. And, whether it was going to be frowned upon or not, I would surely receive accommodations for bringing down the Slugger. People would study the brutality of this case for decades. They would also always hold me up as the hero. As sad as it might have been, and as much as I genuinely regret my part in killing Benny, her murder would end up making the story of the Slugger that much more sensational.

After picking up my phone at my duplex and thoroughly washing myself off, I returned to my car. The first thing I did was try to respond to Hernan's text and call his phone. It was the way for me to establish contact from the cell tower by my house. I left a message the third time that I called and said that I was worried about him and that I would investigate the Skid Row, where we met Hooper for the first time.

Like most people in LA, I parked on the street. That night, I parked far down the road, before and after I went to Hernan's house. Since I snuck in and out through the back of my house, up and over my garage, and into an alley, I wasn't concerned about being caught on camera. If I became a suspect in Benny and Hernan's murder, my meticulous preparation would make it nearly impossible time tracking my movement.

My mission was not only to plant the bat and the gun onto the under shelf of Hooper's precious cart; I also needed to get my hands on the phone that recorded the video. That was *if* it even existed. Me calling that dirty shit Buckwheat when he clearly assaulted me would be inconsequential once LA got wind of my heroism. But, if it existed and Hooper had it, I wanted it.

With the bat bag over my shoulder, I slipped into the alley where I first met Hooper. I looked at my watch; I managed to get to the scene at roughly 2:15. I sent the text from Hernan's phone around 12:07. So, even though it might look like I spent a long time getting from point A to point B, I could always make the argument that I was asleep. Beyond that, I could also say it took me a while to find and then kill Hooper.

The alley was much longer and thinner than I remembered it being the previous morning. That was still no excuse for Hernan to not correctly clear the scene. That was the first of several mistakes and shitty police work that ultimately led to his death.

The smell of the alley had gotten more repulsive smelling in the fourteen or so hours since I was last there. The air was still thick and moist from the rain. People in LA always called it "marine layer." I just called it fog. It certainly made any investigation downtown much more difficult. Side streets and alleys acted as pockets for the mist and stench of the streets. In other words, the moisture latched onto the smell, and then they swirled around in an alley together for several hours. In a place like Skid Row, where subhumans shit right outside the tent or box they lived in, the smell was always toxic after a rainstorm. I decided to inhale the toxicity through my nose because I didn't want to open my mouth and taste the street.

Pulling a mask over my mouth, I slid against the brick and boarded-wall and started looking for the Hooper and the cart. The cover wasn't effectively doing its job. The sting of the stench was so powerful that it felt like it was burning the paper off my face. I used my right forearm to cover the lower half of my face as I used the other to try and fan through the fog. The cloud coverage broke up slightly, and I managed to make out a dim light on the back wall. Below the light was Hooper's cart.

While swimming through the nastiness of the last twenty-feet, I pulled on a brand-new pair of gloves. I was sure that I hadn't touched the bat or the gun with my bare hand since I used them back at Hernan's place. Besides being at the crime scene, there was no way any of the evidence could be traced back to me. I'd seen my share of murders over the years as a detective, and I was always careful to not make the same mistakes the other idiots made.

The closer I got to the cart, the worse the smell of the air became. It was nearly overwhelming, and I gagged behind my mask. Unlike the stink of the alley near the street, the stench of the end of the alley was unmistakably familiar. It was so strong, in fact, that the potency made my eyes sting and water. I tried to rub off the fragrance, but nothing prevented it from penetrating my tear ducts. I pulled the mask further up over my nose and mouth, so it rested over my bottom eyelids. It didn't help much, but at least part of the skin around my eyes wasn't getting blasted.

I took the bat bag off my shoulder and quietly rested it near the broken front left wheel. I lowered myself, trying to avoid being directly downwind from whatever disgusting shit was in Hooper's rolling treasure chest. I unzipped the bag and shoved The Slugger's bat and the gun in the bottom shelf by the wheels.

As I grabbed onto the top of the cart and started lifting myself back up, I contemplated waiting for Hooper to return or patrolling the streets of The Row to find him. Before I had that chance to decide, however, I peered into it. I needed to know what the smell was. As my eyes sharpened and I saw what was behind the steel grates, an unsettling tingle made its way from my stomach through my throat.

The cart was filled with rotten cheese. And not just a few pieces or packages of cheese. It was filled, from top to bottom, with nasty, greened, and unwrapped cheese.

I bent my neck back and tried not to inhale the awfulness. And at that moment, I heard an aluminum bat drop behind me.

Hooper's Rhode Island accent filled the alley and echoed off of the bricks. It seemingly cut through the fog and darted me in the head. "Did you make it to the cheese, Jimmy-Jimmy-Rat-Boy?"

As soon as he spoke, my head trauma returned. The wasps feasting on my brain spun out of control. I kicked the handle of the bat out from under the cart and snapped it back into my hands. I turned around, spun the bat with my wrist, and then bounced it on my palm ten times. I needed to ignore the excruciating pain booming from through the rest of my body. Everything tingled. Everything felt wrong.

He stood directly in front of me at the entrance to the alley. His grotesque body was lit by the single light as it bounced off the fog around us. He lifted his arms and pushed it all backward. He created a curtain of vapor behind him.

"I've got you, Slugger." I coughed as my body pain quickly became crippling.

"I don't think you do."

He snapped his fingers, and the bat was torn out of my hands from behind. Two massive arms pulled it against my chest and secured me to a body. The body behind me made wheezing noises. It was gurgling and burping like a clogged toilet. I tried to turn my head and escape the vice, but the thug was too powerful. I couldn't move. I tried to stomp the feet to shake myself loose, but I was locked against him, and I couldn't find my footing to shift my weight.

"I'd like to re-introduce you to some old friends, Jimmy."

"Fuck you, Hooper," I shouted back with what little breath I could get from my constrained chest.

A shadow appeared from the wall of fog behind him. The figure's head flimsily wiggled behind the rest of its body like a ball unsupported by a frail piece of string. The thing dragged a bat.

"Our first batter is Denise Brozik." Hooper snickered. "She is an immigrant from Czechoslovakia who lost her way and ended up on the street after her parents sold her into prostitution."

She began limping toward me. The dead creature used one hand to guide her because its eyes were facing the other direction. A bat hung from the second, leaping around uncontrollably as it hit different pieces of trash discarded on the street.

"You call her The Doll."

I bounced up and down to loosen the grip of the assailant behind me. "What the fuck is this, Hooper? Let me go?"

"Next up is Phil Donaldson. He is a narcotic addict from Orange County, California. After spending ten years in jail on a drug charge, he wandered to Skid Row when he was released. He always promised to kick the habit and make it back to society, but… he never did. You call him 'Bullseye.'"

Another figure pierced the fog. The victim had a six-inch hole in the middle of his face. Its eyes and hair stuck to the inside of the precision wound. As it walked by Hooper, bat in hand, I could see all the way through its face. It bent over as if to vomit, and a glob of maggots poured out.

It joined The Doll and headed toward me.

"I don't know what you think you're doing, Hooper, but you're in a lot of fucking trouble. The black and whites are on their way here, you fat piece of shit.

I've got you, motherfucker."

Two more figures burst through the fog.

"Thomas Elenore and his HIV infected lover Sondra Campbell. They met on Skid Row and were married right over there." Hooper pointed back behind him.

They grabbed each other's hands and tried unsuccessfully to embrace. The male-thing attempted to run its fingers through the female-thing's hair. All it found was emptiness and sludge. The she-thing then tried to rest its palm on the male-thing's heart. The hand disappeared through his chest for a minute. When it came back out, it was covered in garbage and slop.

Hooper's voice became inhuman. "I give you: The Egg and The Crater." Instantaneously, they turned toward me and raised their bats.

As the Doll and Bullseye made it a quarter of the way between Hooper and me, I started shaking furiously. I couldn't get loose. A clump of brain matter dripped past my right eye-line and onto my shoulder. My pants filled with piss, and I started choking on the stench of the rotten rancid cheese.

"Chester Johnson. A Skid Row street preacher who fought for the rights of those who lived in his community. He worked with the city to try to pass mental health laws preventing the ill from dying on the streets." He paused. "Jimmy. I give you 'Tomahawk!'"

Tomahawk patted the top of his head. All he came up with was a handful of mush, goo, and blood. It choked up on its bat and jogged a little. Then, it caught up to The Doll, Bullseye, The Egg, and the Crater. The entire pack was closing in on me.

"Rounding things off, please allow me to introduce you to Levar Coates. Levar spent most of his time trying to feed his friends while working at the Hospitality Kitchen on 6th. You know him better as… 'Thanksgiving.'"

The other horribles blocked my sight, but I saw the creature break free from the knots I tied in its arms and legs. Rather than stand upright, it scuttered inadvertently on its back like a mutated praying cockroach.

The monster behind me pulled me in closer, and I felt my ribs snap under the power of the bat that was restraining me. The smell of decomposition swallowed my head. I puked into my mask, and my hyper breathing sucked it into my nose and then back down into my mouth.

"You've already met my good friend Charlie. Or, as you called him: "Lucky Number Seven." Charlie was a war vet who came home to an unthankful and unloving world. His wife left him. He lost contact with his children. He fled to Skid Row to escape a world that deserted him."

Seven rubbed its cracked face against the back of my head as it continued to snort and hiss.

I started losing my voice as my lungs collapsed. "Please fucking stop. Please fucking stop. I'm sorry, I'm so fucking sorry."

"You're not sorry, Jimmy. You've never been fucking sorry."

The mob inched closer and closer to me. Before the monstrosities reached me, they all stopped and bounced their bats on their palms and waited. That was, except for Thanksgiving. As it slithered under the opening in my legs, Lucky Number Seven banged the front of its face against the back of my head, forcing me to look down. The insect-like atrocity stared up at me with its blood-filled eyeballs and bit upward toward my dick. Seven playfully lifted my body up and down as if it were fucking with a dog.

I mashed my eyes shut. Thanksgiving's tentacles curled and tightened around my legs. The cold touch of death made my balls retract and my skin freeze. It felt like shock, but the buzzing from the wound on my head pressed against the cold, fighting to keep me awake.

"This just in," Hooper announced. "We have an extraordinary guest joining us tonight. Ladies and gentlemen…"

The victims turned away from me as their attention diverted back to Hooper.

"She was The Skid Row Slugger's very first victim. He raped her after breaking into her apartment, and then he had some Nazi eels beat her to death."

All I could do was beg. "Please, Mr. Hooper. Please, God. Please."

From the fog, she came forward. She was staggering, and her grey skin cracked and fell off her once beautiful face. Hooper handed her a bat. She spun it with her palm.

"Introducing: Detective Jennifer Carman Diez."

One-by-one, the horde of victims turned back to me. As if they were doors being pushed open by a gust of wind, they all moved aside as Jenny walked directly through the middle.

A piece of my barf whistled in and out of the space between my nose and my throat. I pissed myself again; I shit myself. Seven's wheezing turned to silence, and Hooper yelled, "Play ball!"

"Jenny. Jenny." I continued pleading for my life. "I loved you so much. Why didn't you love me back? You made me what I am. You made the Skid Row Slugger. Not me. I'm the victim." I addressed the whole crew. "I'm the victim of you all. I'm the one who pays my fucking taxes. I'm the one who risks my life every day while you shit in your beds and piss on businesses. I'm the fucking victim. America is the victim of your lazy, pathetic fucking lives."

And, then, with that, Jenny pulled her bat back over her head. Seven released me, pushing me forward. I lost my balance, and Thanksgiving's arms jerked me down to the ground. The awful crew born from the gutter of Los Angeles all followed Jenny's lead and lifted their bats, as well.

"You're the rat," Jenny snarled at me.

Then, the force of seven baseball bats pounded on every limb, every bone, every organ in my body. They furiously unleashed blow, after blow, after blow. The ones who had mouths laughed. I cowered, and I heard nothing but everything inside of me bursting and cracking.

In an attempt to escape, I rolled over on top of Thanksgiving. He crawled out from under me and began gnawing on my skull. I couldn't lift any of my appendages, so I tried to move away from them by rocking on my chest. The bats continued to slam into my back, completely demolishing all the vertebrae of my spine. I felt one all-powerful blow crack my tailbone. I was determined to make it to Hooper's cheese cart to pull myself off the ground and out of the onslaught but, before I reached it, I blacked out.

I woke up in a pool of water with my face buried into the foul streets of Skid Row. My body couldn't move, but I continued to drag myself slowly by rolling back and forth on my obliterated torso. It was raining again, but it was daytime. The monsters left me to die in the middle of the street.

Bent and nearly broken in half, I looked up as much as I could.

In front of me was a gigantic mountain of shit. An actual mountain of shit. A fireball fell from the sky and landed right next to my face, nearly singing it. I saw a covered building across the street. If I was to escape the nightmare, I needed to reach it. But, before I crawled any further, I felt a sharp pain dissect my already broken tailbone. I tried to look back and see where it was coming from but could barely move my neck. I tried to cry for help, but no words came out. I attempted to push myself toward the building, but I was pinned down. Seconds later, a gigantic shoe pummeled me in the ribs and kicked me toward the building.

It wasn't a building like I initially thought, and I'd been there before.

"You're the rat, Jimmy." Hooper laughed. "You're the fucking rat."

After I dangled on the edge of the sewer for a few last moments in Skid Row, I tumbled down the storm drain to my death… landing, eventually…

In Hell.

# The Poser

Drew Stepek

"Fuck this bitch."

I read through the brief on my phone for the third time before I went in. It was filled with the standard shit like, "The slut fired me", "A complete fucking cunt", and "Trying to steal the rights to—"

There was also a bold note that read. "Don't kill her or disfigure her in any way. Just ruin her. Get this bitch canceled by her fans."

In all caps below her picture, it also read: BE CREATIVE.

As if I needed a picture to remind me who Chastity O'Neill was. She grew up outside of Philly in a town called Bethlehem. Since I was born and raised in Philly proper and was around the same age as her, it seemed impossible to escape all her praise as a "hometown hero."

I visited Bethlehem once with my old man. I wasn't too impressed. It seemed like another town crushed by the steel mill closings statewide. Sure, they tried to fancy it up with hip bars and expensive boutique hotels, but all that was just putting a blanket over a dead dog on the side of the road.

Chastity managed to climb out from under her abusive mother's cage as her star began to rise at 16. In other words, with the support of her manager, she legally emancipated herself from her shitty past and left for Hollywood. The young starlet became Philly's favored export, over steel, and she quickly became a money-printing machine.

Her manager was this guy named Ty Shepard. He was my client.

He paid to record her first demo and all her future hits, footed the bill for her emancipation, moved her to Hollywood, and, most importantly, turned her into the biggest star in the world. And, how did the little PA cunt repay him? By firing him and then suing him for back royalties and the publishing rights to, what she considered, *her* music and career.

The law is in screwball LA where the courts usually side with the artists, even though legally binding contracts are in place. The artists typically get a ton of support from other artists, creating sympathetic fan campaigns on social media. If that doesn't move the needle, they accuse the other side of inappropriate conduct and/or serial harassment. The latter was the case between Chazzy O and Ty Shephard.

Ty sought me out because I have a unique gift. I can read minds. The technical term for what I am is "psychic." That term, though, is so limited compared to the scope of what I can do.

When I was a teenager, I figured out how to amplify my psychic abilities between two Bluetooth receivers. Since then, I've been able to transcend reading minds. I can enter people's consciousness and take control of their bodies. While I'm posing as them, I can turn them off and do whatever I want with and to them.

The law of numbers suggests that I'm not the only person who can do this, and although I suspect others can, I've never met anyone else. Sure, I've seen other postings on encrypted message boards for professed "posers." Still, I've never investigated it beyond reading their classified ads.

My clients all come to me through referral, and Ty Shephard was no different. They contact me through cloaked VPNs using burner phones. Those are the rules of engagement. The thing is that other than a way to distance themselves from my work and pay me using cryptocurrency, the precautions are somewhat overly strict. No one who hires me can be fingered for a crime that someone else was caught red-handed committing. Besides, who would believe some crackpot ramblings of body and mind infiltration as a legitimate legal defense?

Earlier that day, Ty told me that Chastity was eating on the patio of The Ivy in Beverly Hills, as she did every Tuesday and Thursday around noon.

I got there at 11:30 to get a table outside.

The host looked me up and down. "All these tables are reserved for lunch," she insisted.

Turning toward the outdoor dining area, I pointed out. "I don't see any reserved signs."

She looked down at the reservation book, hoping the conversation was over and that I would leave. "We have regulars, sir. They have regular tables."

I spun my hat around so the logo on the front was facing her. "What? Youse not a Phillies fan?"

Waving me away like a gnat, she let out a deep breath and added, "I don't know what that means. You've not dressed appropriately for The Ivy."

"Surely, you can make an exception just this once." I laid five crisp hundies on top of the reservation book and winked at her. "I'm in town for the week from Philly, and I've heard this is *the* place to get some chow."

"I hope you're enjoying your visit." She stuffed the money in her pocket, grabbed a menu, and showed me to my table.

"Can I get you a drink to start things off?" She asked politely.

"Can I get a Yuengling?"

She angled herself over my shoulder and studied the drink menu. "I'm not sure we have that."

"I'm just fuckin' wit youse. I'll have a Crudweiser.'"

"I don't know what that is, either," she said, regretting seating me.

"Just get me your cheapest beer," I finally said.

"Stella okay?"

"Sure."

Fucking LA. The only thing that talks in this shithole is money. It's Mecca for self-absorbed, no talent snobs. It's a cliché, but every waitress is an actor, and every barista is a writer. They're all pretty much garbage people.

I nursed the beer while I pretended to look through the menu. The prices were utterly outrageous. Since I already spent five bills on the job, I had no intention of actually eating anything.

That was the problem with getting paid to do illegal business with crypto. If I wanted to exchange the money for cash, I had to sell it, then transfer it to an offshore account. After that, I sent cash to several different wiring services, where I used a fake ID to collect the money. I never opened a bank account, and I never opened any lines of credit. Cash was always king, even in the make-believe world of Hollywood.

As far as the government and the cops knew, I didn't exist outside of Philly. I paid myself a freelance salary through a shell company that was just above poverty. That money was enough to pay for a studio apartment in the hood and its utilities.

In LA, I paid for everything with cash. Saying it took a while to get paid was an understatement. It was a good thing I had rich clients. These pricks were always so fucking desperate. They were always willing to pay just about anything for me to take care of their problems.

At around 12:06, Chastity O pulled her Tesla up in front of The Ivy and threw her keys to the valet, who I guessed she knew from going there so often.

She walked up the front path, through the gate, and directly to her reserved table, tucked away in the back corner of the patio. Sure, she wanted to be seen, but she didn't want to be bothered.

"Another Stella?" my waitress asked.

"Sure."

Chastity wore gigantic sunglasses and a terry cloth bucket hat to cover her signature rainbow-colored hair. There was no mistaking who she was, though. These stars put all this time and effort into haphazardly disguising themselves. The thing was, they thrived on the attention of being out in public. They lived for the spotlight. She should have stayed at her gated house all day. That way, she wouldn't become a victim to predators.

Like me.

I dumped a handful of receivers from a punch into my palm. It amazed me how small tech had gotten. I purchased a hundred thousand of these Bluetooth "fleas" from a Chinese company when I did my one and only corporate espionage gig a while back. They had a certain amount of navigational AI in them that led them through hair and to the skin. When they reached the skin, they flattened and attached to the head. Then, I could connect to the receivers through a parasite device that I wore over my ear. It was never a hundred percent, but usually, two or three of the fleas would connect. They didn't navigate through hats, though. So, more often than not, I had to get creative. And Ty Shepherd wanted me to be creative.

I walked over to her table and acted nervously. "Excuse me, Ms. O'Neill?"

She slid her sunglasses down the bridge of her nose and gave me a once over. Then, she pushed them back up over her eyes.

"Can I get a selfie wit you to show my boys back in Philly?"

"Go away," she whispered as she pulled the menu in front of her face and continued to ignore me like I was a pile of dirt.

"I'm from Philly… see? I pointed to the Phillies logo on my lid. "How about a quick pic with a hometown boy?"

Annoyed, she pounded her fists down on the table, then snapped her fingers to get the host's attention.

I had to act fast.

"What? You too good for Philly now, Mrs. Fuckin' Bigshot?" I leaned around her and pulled my phone in front of us. While doing that, I tugged the bucket hat off her head and then sprinkled the handful of flea glitter over her head. Without wasting a second, I snapped the picture.

"Get the fuck off of me," she screamed while pushing me to the ground.

Two waiters and the hostess picked me up and carried me off the patio.

"You got no idea where you're from, you fucking sellout," I shouted at her as I started retreating up Robertson Blvd. "You fucking cunt. Too fucking good for Philly."

I was putting on a show, but the fact was celebrities like Chaz were a dime a dozen. The only thing that they all had in common was that they felt they were better than everyone else. That pissed schmucks like me off.

When I got to my van, I sent the pic through to Shephard's burner to let him know that the mission was a go.

The receivers that I used only had a three-mile radius, making parking my van difficult in gated communities. Also, since Chastity lived in Agoura Hills, you never knew how the mountains would disrupt the signal.

Thankfully, Shepard gave me her wifi name and password. People are so fucking stupid. You could probably go to anyone's house, act like you can't check your email, and they will happily give you their password information. Chastity made the mistake of giving it to someone who she was eventually going to fuck over. I never share that shit with anyone. It's not like anyone would want to come over to my home/van and hang out anyway.

This is how the system worked in a nutshell.

I parked within visible virtual distance to the host. I hacked into their wifi network using a VPN. That wifi signal floats around in their home like smoke. Eventually, it locates the fleas that I dump on their head, and then I pair the one with the strongest signal to the parasite on my ear.

With a mattress and a colossal wifi extender stuffed into the back of my van, there was very little room to move around. Although I didn't own some shitty, rusted molester van, a suspicious van parked near a gated community filled with celebrities was a red flag to security and cops.

Yes. I said mattress. I needed the bed because once my consciousness left my body and latched onto the host, I practically fell into a coma—the combination of questionable connections and distance made for dangerous circumstances. Besides, I only had around an hour of connection time inside the host. The VPNs' stability, even the cloned and roaming shady ones I used, made for sometimes bumpy rides.

I needed to get in, get my job done, and then get the fuck out of Dodge.

I promised myself if 'Project: Chastity' was a success that I would try to track some more powerful equipment the next day. I knew someday someone was going to find me in the back of the van. When that day came, I was sure they would try to get my body to the hospital. Then when they ventured outside of the two-mile tether, the connection would break, and my consciousness would remain floating around in my host's house for eternity. At least until I found a way to escape. I was never sure what would actually happen if the connection broke.

It made me wish people liked me because the missions would have been much safer if I had a spotter.

When the seventh inning of the Phillies game ended, and my boys were getting their dicks handed to them by Boston, I turned off the game and got busy.

Using my laptop, I hardwired into the signal extender and began searching the area for Chastity's network. She named it after her first big hit, "N2U"—the year she was born, 92, and her dog's name, Grover.

So, combined, it was "N2U_92-gr0ver!".

It wasn't the worst network name. But, if I lived down the street from her, I would have known it was her network immediately. I was pretty confident that the moron who installed it helped her come up with it. When it showed up on anyone else's available networks, I'm sure they got that shitty song stuck in their head. It's a *really* shitty song.

The network came up almost immediately. So, using the password Shephard hooked me up with, I logged in. It was literally that easy. I'm sure if there were more psychics in the world—as in-tune with their abilities as I was—we wouldn't have a planet anymore. Some psycho would have blown it up a long time ago.

I paired the ear parasite with my computer and the signal extender. I started searching for the fleas that were, hopefully, attached to Chastity's scalp. The little bugs auto connected to the nearest network as soon as the host came within range of the nearest wifi signal after I pre-configured them with the network and passwords. The flea set-up wasn't easy to do, and it always required a magnifying glass and a small pin. I used the magnifier to locate a button on the device's side and then the pin to press the button and transmit a signal. These things were as small as tiny pebbles and lighter than a grain of salt, so the process of configuring twenty-five of them took an unreasonable amount of patience.

The fleas were also waterproof to about two meters and an hour submerged. So, for the most part, I never had to worry about the host taking a shower between first contact and connecting.

While waiting for the devices to work together and for the fleas to start popping up on the dashboard, I looked at the score in the Phillies game. They were getting murdered by the Red Sox. Since the two teams met so infrequently, only facing each other in rare interleague play, it would have been nice to grab a W. I hated Masshole bigmouths and all their cheating sports teams. Fucking cheater pricks. The problem with the Phillies was that they always beat themselves because, just like everything else from my town, the team still had a chip on its shoulder.

A ding popped up on my laptop. Followed by another. And, then, by six more. The fleas were in Chastity's network.

Before choosing one to pair, I ran diagnostics on all of them. For the most part, the fleas all seemed stable enough for the journey, but the first and second had the best tether to the network. I always paired with the second strongest flea that came online. It wasn't that I chose second place all the time because I didn't feel worthy of number one. It was just a habit—a ritual.

I turned all my equipment, including my phone, to night mode, laid down on the mattress, and pressed a button on the side of the parasite. I searched outside myself for the consciousness of the host. When I located her, I pounced hard, instantly putting Chastity to sleep.

Looking into the wall-to-wall mirrors of Chastity O's enormous bathroom, I pulled a robe over her naked body. Before I invaded, she was going to take a bubble bath. She probably wanted to cleanse herself after the unpleasant incident with the Philly fan at lunch. Fucking big shot. The truth was that I was pulling in a ton of money, too. Just because I didn't dress in some fancy disguise didn't mean that I wasn't rich.

To every piece of shit in Philly, getting the opportunity to get a look at Chastity O naked was a dream come true. She was our hometown hero and our choicest piece of ass. Even though I would have loved to snap a selfie of her in the buck for the boys back home, that wasn't in Shephard's job description. A lot of money was on the line here, for both him and me.

In as much as I was a scumbag and would have killed to fuck her under different circumstances, I never messed around with any tit or pussy when I was inside a girl. Raping their minds and ruining their careers was shitty enough. Actual rape wasn't part of my resume. I was asked once to take an ex-girlfriend to some scumbags house one time so he could fuck her brains out one last time as revenge for taking custody of their mutual bulldog. And even though I really needed the money, I declined. The guy ended up blowing his brains out in front of her and the dog instead. Fucking loser. The chick and the dog both survived. So, yeah. I wasn't one hundred percent a piece of shit.

It always felt strange to be inside a woman, though. The curvature and body make-up is so different. It was like walking into a room that you're familiar with, and new owners changed out all the furniture and painted the walls. Since I'm the type of person who spends a lot of time adjusting and readjusting my nuts, it's alarming to habitually reach down and find nothing hanging in my pants.

I bent closer to the mirror and ran my fingers through Chastity's rainbow hair. All the years of bleach and dye to maintain her signature look left the hair dry and damaged. I guessed I would be doing her a huge favor when I shaved it all off.

Despite early wrinkles and bags that came with working as hard as a pop star does, Chastity managed to hold onto her youthful and striking girl-next-door looks. She had enormous, ice blue eyes, a freckled little nose, and a pouty set of lips. Her face was tailor-made for makeup endorsements. And over the years, she had several. That's how rock stars make most of their money these days. Endorsements. As long as you are hot, it doesn't really matter how much talent you have.

She wasn't frail, by any means. Her arms were shredded, and her thick thighs were toned. I rolled her shoulders. Even though she was thin, I could feel the musculature of someone who worked out obsessively. Finally, I dragged my finger up her six-pack and peeked inside the robe, keeping my no-touch policy. She also had amazing, natural tits.

I definitely admired O'Neill, and I suppose I felt honored to feel so close to her. That still didn't excuse her from being a fucking bitch at The Ivy. I'm a hometown boy, and no matter how big of a star you think you are, you should always remember where you're from and who got you to where you are.

Since the clock on my occupancy was ticking, though, I had to get busy doing my thing rather than debating whether I was a super fan or a mind controlling troll.

After throwing on some clothes and grabbing her purse and, more importantly, her phone, I went to the hallway table where Shephard told me she kept her car keys. They were there, so I grabbed them and threw them into her purse. I used the alarm codes that Shephard had also given me to exit the house. I made my way to her garage that contained the Tesla SUV she drove to The Ivy, a G-Wagon, and the whip detailed in the job brief: a brand new purple Lamborghini.

It was purple in some lights. But from others, it reflected every spectrum of the rainbow and represented Chaz's hair and her rise from rags to riches. I doubt that she could have driven that car 50 yards back home. Either her fans would mob her and strip it to the bone or steal it from her and execute her in the middle of the street. Philly isn't the kind of town that appreciates show-offs.

I unlocked the doors using the fob attached to a Rainbow Bright keychain. The scissor door on the driver's side automatically unlatched from the car, whirling like a power drill as it opened about six inches. Finally, it spun upward like a lever. It seemed like quite a lot of bravado for a Philly—I mean Bethlehem—chick to get into her car. It was fucking cool to me, nonetheless.

Hoping in like an excited kid on Christmas, I stomped on the break and fired it up. As soon as the engine ignited, it growled like *all* of the Hells Angels just kick-started their Harleys at once. Before I opened the garage, I revved the engine a couple more times, feeling the Italian sportscar's power send an earthquake through Chastity's body. Had I been inside my body, I certainly would have had a boner.

Before I shot the car into drive, I savored the euphoria for a few minutes. Then, I gunned it out of her driveway.

Speeding through her neighborhood, taking turns at 80 MPH, I turned on the radio. Of course, she had been listening to her own music. Her public persona suggested that she wasn't as vain as I knew she was. It felt good to be right.

For the most part, Chastity was known as the good girl, despite her over-sexualized music and slutty look. Shephard inferred otherwise, though. He said she was a nasty drunk who said shitty things about people she deemed dirt after becoming a celebrity. As a matter of fact, her mother got sober and begged for her forgiveness on some shitty talk show. Although Chastity said she forgave her mom to the press, she also said she'd never forgotten. So, Chaz got some of her producer friends to make a series of viral videos where clips of her mother crying on the show were auto-tuned and looped together into a song. After a few weeks, that video became a meme. The mother, unable to live with herself anymore, pounded a bottle of Drano.

Shephard said Chastity laughed at the news and responded with an, "Oh well." She neither paid for the proper disposal of her mother's body nor attended any type of ceremony to honor her life. I suppose she didn't think risking showing up in Philly was worth her time.

After I slowed down, I waved to the guard at the gated community's perimeter. Feeling like making that poor jerk's night, I dragged Chastity's tongue across her lips and flashed her boobs. Then, I crept to my van and started putting the project together.

It was always unsettling to look at myself when I was inside someone else . The strangest part about looking at yourself through someone else's eyes was that you didn't look anything like how your brain processes your reflection in a mirror. All the features that you try to ignore and conceal scream out at you.

I bent down to my mouth and checked my breathing. Everything seemed okay.

One of Chastity's hoop earrings got caught in my long greasy hair. As I untangled it, I studied my scrawny body. I was always a wiry little fucker that could hold my own in a fight. I wasn't a disgusting looking fella. Just a normal blue-collar kid raised in the City of Fucking Brotherly Love.

My full name was Brandon Kelly Sullivan, but I went by the name "Sully." The more I was forced to see myself, the more I realized that I looked like a Sully. It was a pretty popular nickname in Philly.

I didn't return to my van because I needed to establish a better connection with the host. As soon as I chose my flea, that was my only connection inside. If the link broke or if I attempted to jump to another flea, the pairing became disrupted. The last thing I'd ever want is for one of my hosts to wake up, confused inside my "command center."

However, I did grab a signal scrubber off the van's dashboard and installed it into her phone through the USB jack. This was my guarantee to get out of the host if anything started going south. In other words, it built a corruptible mesh network between the parasite and the fleas. When I pushed the volume button on the side of her phone up, it unraveled the structure, my consciousness was sent back to the van, and all of the fleas in-network dissolved. That left no evidence of any type of technological influence on the host. As if the cops were ever going to be looking for that anyway. As far as the malware being discovered on the phone. Well, once I was safely back inside my head, I initiated a complete wipe of her phone and all network activity from my laptop. No evidence.

The timer above my body said that I was about fifteen minutes into the mission. I grabbed a pair of scissors and a gram of coke and put them into her purse. I also grabbed a couple Xanax pills and stuffed them into the small pocket of her skirt. Then, before I left, I patted my comatose self on the shoulder and said, "Sorry I was such a fucking bitch to you today at the restaurant."

Exiting the van, I made sure that no one was around the mountain path where I parked. The Lamborghini stuck out like a sore thumb, even in the darkest corners of the earth. I pressed the fob, the door opened in the same "way too cool way" as it had the first time. As I plunged into the driver's seat, I snorted a quick fingernail bump of blow. Before I headed to a liquor store that was a safe three-mile distance from the parasite receiver, I used Chastity's phone to check the score of the Phillies' game. Even though Shephard had also given me the security code to turn on the phone, I already had the two best security devices in the world: her face and her thumb.

The Phillies were still losing as the game headed into the 9th inning.

On the way to the liquor store, I did a couple more quick bumps of the cocaine and lined my gums with a freeze. Judging from how her body was responding, I guessed that my girl hadn't done a ton of coke, at least in the last few years. Her heart was thumping away like a fucking bongo drum, and her brain was telling her that she could beat Mike Tyson in a fight. That was a sign I needed to chill out. If I lost focus on the job, something cocaine frequently does to people, I wouldn't get paid. If I didn't get paid, I was fucked.

As I neared a half-hour of my occupation, I drifted into the front of Liquor Chest. Like the wasted and entitled celebrity Chazzy was, I made sure I parked sideways, taking up four of the five spots.

The coke was making her body start to shake and twitch.

After jumping out of the Lambo, I left the doors open like I didn't have a care in the world. Yep. I knew how to act the LA thing.

I entered the store in an overly frenzied state. A chime rang out from the door as I plowed through.

"Who wants to fucking party?" I screamed while beelining toward the whiskey section.

"Good evening," the stunned cashier returned, not knowing how to respond to the rainbow-painted and loud ass train wreck that just flew off the rail and into his store.

Taking a sarcastic and mocking tone, I said, "Good evening."

He watched me snatch up two bottles of Jack, and politely asked. "Can I help you with anything?" Then, as if he was alerting me to the store's security measures, he nodded his head toward the camera behind the counter.

I took one of the whiskey bottles and threw it on the ground, smashing it. "Fuck you, you piece of shit. Don't you fucking know who I am?" Then, I unscrewed the cap on the other bottle.

Somewhat stunned but not entirely surprised, he quietly confessed, "I know who you are, Miss O'Neill."

"Damn fucking right you do, you stupid, little fucking man." I flashed Chastity's tits for the second time that night and took a giant belt out of the second whiskey bottle. "I bet you'd like to fuck me, wouldn't you, you disgusting old perv?"

He stood silent. He didn't trip any alarm, and he didn't make a move toward his phone.

"That's what I thought, you dirty, disgusting goblin." I threw Chastity's entire wallet at him. "Keep the change and go fuck yourself. Creep."

I stomped out of the store as if I was wronged by the shopkeeper. I hoped the cameras in the store captured that meltdown. In a wealthy neighborhood like Chastity's, you never knew if the security cameras were actually recording.

Continuing to put a dent in the bottle, I wobbled across the lot and flopped her ass into the Lambo. I pushed the seat back a little bit and nabbed the scissors and phone from her purse. Acting quickly, I rested the phone on the steering wheel and opened up the Instagram app. As soon as the record light was done ticking off seconds, I began.

"Hey, you pieces of shit!" I yelled, pulling from the whiskey bottle, making sure that there was no mistaking its contents. "It's your fucking girl, Jazzy Chazzy O!" I put her nostrils right up to the camera and snorted another bump of coke.

While taking in the instant adrenaline that filled her head, I shook her trademark hair and continued. "You all love my hair, don't you?" I licked her middle finger, aiming it at her hundreds of millions of followers. "All you fucking disgusting loser little girls. You fucking horrible, filthy cunts." I held up the scissors and rubbed more coke onto my gums. "Do you like this?"

Without missing a beat, I pulled all the hair together and lopped of a huge chunk. Laughing from the cocaine, I continued to chop off long strands of hair haphazardly. At one point, I dropped the scissors and pulled strings of hair directly out of her scalp. When my hand was full of strands, I tossed them at the phone's camera and to the fans.

Satisfied that the haircut was batshit insane, and not want to chance disrupting the fleas, I left the scissors down and stared grimly into the phone.

"I want to talk to you fuckers about the Jews." I tilted back her head and flared her nostrils. "My ex-manager Ty Shephard is a fucking slave to the Jews. He steals my money because Hollywood and the recording industry is run by an elitist cult called Judaism.

"Even though he wrote, paid for, and produced all of my songs, I know the reason you assholes buy them is that you worship me. Not him. You want Chazzy O. Not the disgusting, Jew-lover, Ty Shepard. He says he owns the publishing rights to *my* music. It's mine because I sang it. I deserve *my* songs."

Before I pressed stop on the recording, I drunkenly sang the chorus to Chasity's hit song "N2U", only I replaced the words with "No To Jews."

I noticed that hundreds of thousands of people were watching Chaz live. From what I gathered, they weren't happy with the performance. At all.

Near the conclusion of my live stream, an older man and a preteen girl came out of a laundromat connected to Liquor Chest to see what was creating all the ruckus.

The whiskey made Chaz's vision blurry, and it started dropping frames. Her body was in no way prepared for the amount of liquor I dumped into it. I barfed a little bit into her lap and then ran her fingers through what was left of her hair.

Keeping their distance from the Lambo, the man asked, "Are you okay, ma'am?"

The little girl tugged on the sleeve of his coat. "Daddy, that's Chazzy O." She cocked her head sideways, seemingly confused. "I think."

I took a final gulp of the whiskey and whizzed the bottle over the top of the car. It landed short of a garbage can in front of Liquor Town. "Fuck you, ya little whore," I shrieked as the bottle collided with the brick wall behind the can.

"Go get inside," the man instructed his daughter. Shaken, she did as she was told.

Once the glass door closed, she remained behind it, watching them.

The man turned toward Chastity and took off his jacket. "I don't know what you're on but, you WILL NOT use that language around my daughter."

I stared at the trembling little girl illuminated by the bright lights inside the 24-hour laundromat. She was alone inside. There wasn't even an attendant on duty. I gave her the finger.

"Don't look at her! I'm the one talking to you."

As I fired up the Lambo engine, I began recording another Instagram video. I looked at Chaz's reflection on the phone. "I bet you thought I was done." I placed the phone on the dashboard and threw the car into reverse, backing it out, so it was eye-to-eye with the nosey, old man.

"Get back here, young lady," he insisted.

I left the car in reverse, and it continued to slowly roll backward.

"I'm talking to you, girly."

I grinned, baring as many of Chastity's teeth that could be seen, and threw the car into drive. I gripped the steering wheel, digging my nails into the leather. Without warning, I smashed my foot onto the accelerator pedal and peeled out.

Confused, almost as if the man didn't realize a car, not a person, was barreling toward him, he instinctively put up his dukes.

Seconds later, I plowed the low front of the car into his shins. I was whipped forward, bashing my teeth against the steering wheel. For whatever reason, there was no airbag deployed from the wreck. As the car came to a halt, I was thrown back to the seat with Chastity's teeth flying out of her face.

My eyes, which were jammed shut by the collision, reopened. The man was folded and wedged between a metal support beam of the laundromat's facade and the car's hood. As he tried to crawl toward the windshield, he let out agonizing, brain-melting howls. I grabbed the phone off the dash and made sure the entire show was in frame.

"Y'all like Jazzy Chazzy O's latest hit?" I asked the fans.

I re-hammered the accelerator. The back wheels spun, and the stench of burnt rubber filled the car.

I heard a massive crack that I imagined was the sound of the top of his body, separating itself from his calves at the shins. Now, free from the trap of the front of the car, he clawed his way toward Chastity's windshield. Unfortunately for him, the legs were the only thing stopping his body from getting squashed between the support and the hood. In a finger-snap, his butt rolled under the mount. As the car trusted forward, the support caught his tail bone. The force of the V12 engine didn't stop, and the support began shattering his vertebrae one-by-one. All the skin from his back also slid forward, bunching up around his neck. Once he was fully fileted, the flesh flapped over and his head. Now turned sideways, crunched, juice squirted in every direction. The head then deflated under the strength of the metal support.

I threw the car back into reverse and released it from the body and the beam. What was left of the man's lifeless body dripped off the front and unfolded into the laundromat's broken lower window.

Knowing that I was getting scarily close to disconnecting from the host, I felt around behind my seat until I found the scissors. I staggered out from under the half-closed car door and hopped through the front window of the laundromat. I used the pile that was the man as a stepping stool to get through the window.

"Little girl," I slurred as I hopped inside.

She whimpered quietly from the other end of the building. Rather than wasting any more time, I stumbled over to a hamper where I found her, hiding under dirty clothes. I grabbed on to her collar, and as I dragged her out of the hamper, it knocked over.

"You need to see this," I told her as Chastity's dizzy, wasted body struggled to walk twenty feet.

Right before we reached what remained of her dad, I opened up the hair shears and started carving up the little girl's face. She didn't put up a fight but man, did she shake and wail. I wanted to snip off her eyelids, forcing her to look at her father's corpse. Unfortunately, Chaz was way too drunk to successfully pull off a procedure like that without blinding the kid.

When I was done sufficiently disfiguring her, I threw her into her father's remains.

"Don't you ever forget this night," I whispered.

Before I got back into the dented and damaged, purple rainbow Lamborghini, I added, "Thank you for being a fan."

After a mile of driving back toward Chastity's mansion, I felt that I was about to pass out. So, I pulled the car into a ditch and took the handful of Xanax stored in her pocket.

Her eyes became heavy. Right before everything went black and I checked the Phillies game's final score—they lost 8 to 1—I pressed the volume button on her phone and untethered from the host.

That was the thing about posing. I got to live out my sickest homicidal fantasies and never had to answer for any of them. Since I was never technically killing anyone as Derek Sullivan, I also never felt any guilt.

While licking some nacho cheese dust from a bag of tortilla chips off my fingers, I responded to an encrypted message from Shephard. *You told me to be creative.*

*Homicide isn't creative, asshole,* he wrote back.

I turned on a multi-news channel feed and dragged the browser over to a separate monitor mounted above my mattress. All anyone was talking about was

Chastity O'Neill. There was a different story montage on *all* channels. Although they were each put together with a unique finesse, each contained security footage from inside Liquor Town, Chastity's antisemitic Instagram video, and crime scene shots of the Liquor Town/Laundromat parking lot. One of the better pieces also had bodycam police footage of the starlet being pulled out of the trashed Lambo that I drove into a ditch. In the corner of the video was her batshit crazy looking mugshot. What was left of her hair was all over the place. Makeup and blood were smeared crusty all around her mouth, and her front teeth were missing. She sure didn't look like America's rags to riches sweetheart anymore. I almost did a spit-take at the photo. Man, did I do a job on that cunt.

One element that all of the stations shared was the use of Chastity's music and music videos.

*You still have the rights to the music, don't you*?

Shepherd paused on the other end. He was deep in thought. At least that's what the three "please hold" dots implied in the messenger window.

Finally, he responded with an anemic, *Yes*?

*Turn on your fucking TV, dummy. I typed away. Every news report around the world is playing it today. They will tomorrow. They will all year. Then, when people start making documentaries and movies about her and her now fucked up legacy, you get paid. I'm sure her songs are all riding high on the streaming platforms right now, too.*

*You didn't have to kill that guy and slice up his daughter, you fucking psycho.*

I bit into a chip and ran a search for Chastity's name. Some sites were running the horrific crime scene photos, and "too soon?" memes were popping up everywhere. The most popular video on YouTube was a bootleg of the first Instagram video. No one had the second video posted. I'm sure that the censorship hounds on social media were on high alert trying to bury that one.

*You still own the catalog, right? That's what you fucking wanted. If her lawyers decide that they need the rights to the music back to help support her legal battle, which they won't, you set the price now. Yesterday you were getting close to surrendering those rights to her for free to save your career.*

The three-dot "thinking" animation came up in the messenger window again. This time he took longer to take in everything I told him.

I flipped my Phillies hat on backward and waited.

*The press won't leave me alone*!

*What the fuck did you expect? This is the biggest story of the year. It might even be the biggest story in the history of pop music. Guess what? You're not going to be poor anytime soon. As a matter of fact, you're going to become richer.*

*You didn't have to kill anyone. I specifically told you to "cancel" her. Don't you know what that means? Cancel doesn't mean kill other people. It means, make her wish she was dead.*

*That was just me being creative. You never have to worry about any of this tracing back to you. Who, besides a bunch of conspiracy loons, would ever believe someone else was in Chaz's body when all that shit went down?*

The three dots came up two more times, but he didn't say anything else. He got what he wanted.

I sent him further instructions for payment and logged out. I also added a little threat in case he decided not to pay me for my services. Since I never shared the ins and outs of how I pulled off the poses, I tacked on a pretty standard bluff that I told all my clients.

*Don't even think about not paying me. I can get inside of you whenever I want. What a shame it would be for you to commit suicide in a room filled with dead, sexually abused kids.*

Ten minutes later, I got an alert. Shephard paid me in full.

Usually, after a big job like the Chastity O'Neill gig, I treated myself to a little bit of pampering by getting a room for a week at the Chateau Marmont in Hollywood. I would never get treated like an LA heavyweight because they all saw me as a slob with my ripped-up jeans and my Phillies hat. That didn't mean I didn't have the money to live like them every once in a blue moon. It was great to live the high life as Derek Sullivan, rather than through the minds and bodies of the people I stepped on to make money. In my own skin, I was invisible to those fame whores. When I was in them, I was them, so even though I could do all their drugs and live in their house and shit for an hour, that was never me. Walking in a celebrity's shoes for an hour a day, though, was better than being an invisible nobody forever.

Over the years, I thought about how to take a host indefinitely. The fantasy of becoming a rock star or movie star always eluded me, though. Besides the logistics involved in networking and constant connection, the parasite and the fleas could never remain stable for more than a few hours. Beyond that, both devices only retained a ten-hour charge.

On top of that, *my* body would likely wither away in the van, and if something went wrong, there wouldn't be a body to go home to.

I'm not saying that I wouldn't take all precautions to try to keep *my* body alive in the home of the rich host. And, as much as it would be great to be somebody, the tech wasn't there to make that dream a reality. Besides, I didn't dislike who I was; I just didn't like seeing myself through other people's eyes. Seeing myself in a coma was a constant reminder of the bad shit I did when I was inside the host... even though they fucking deserved it. After a few more jobs, I would be just as rich as all those assholes anyway. Chaz O wasn't the only rags to riches story out of Philly.

I'd never met another poser, so I have nothing to compare my experiences and equipment, though. Of the seven and a half billion people on earth, I figured that someone else had the gift and figured out how to use it like me.

That night I watched the news coverage about a butcher pop princess in my plush robe. I had done some pretty fantastically sadistic jobs in the past, but Chastity's was going to be hard to top. It had so many elements to it. The drugs and booze. The insane haircut and the racist rant on Instagram. The recognizably unsubtle Lamborghini mangling an innocent bystander. A little girl seeing her father get torn to pieces by her favorite singer. The same little girl getting slices up and permanently disfigured.

It was a masterpiece. Unfortunately, Derek Sullivan would never be credited with the incredible story. It sucked to never get recognition for such great work because my "creative" was a million times better than the shit that the Hollywood writers were getting paid to pump out.

"Cheers, Sully." I raised my beer. "You've finally made your mark in La La Land."

After tying one on, I scoured the dark web for any possible leads on new equipment. Maybe it was the suite at the Chateau or the booze giving me dumb thoughts but living the high life 24/7 as someone else didn't sound too fucking shabby.

"Sorry about the other night." The fat man put an attaché case on the antiqued Chateau hardwood floors and extended his hand to shake. "Call me, Hoop."

Caught off guard, thinking maybe he was talking about the Chastity incident, I blurted out a confused, "Huh?"

He pointed at my Phillies hat. "My Bo Soxs tore your boys a new asshole."

Figures, a Masshole. They always want to brag when their teams win and hide when they lose. Fans from Philly just got drunk, talked shit, and beat the shit out of people who don't root for their teams.

Rather than smashing this fat fuck's glasses, though, I grabbed his hand to shake. "I never could have guessed you were from Boston." I relaxed my shoulders.

He hit a button on his case, and a rolling handle popped up. "I'm actually from Rhode Island."

"Even fucking worse."

"What? Oh!" He erupted in laughter, popping one of the buttons on his shirt. Noticing the button in flight, he pointed at it and started slapping his knee. "Look at that, we have a runner!"

Laughing, I invited him into my suite, closed the door behind him, and motioned for him to turn around with my finger. He looked at me perplexed, so I pulled out the gun I had concealed in the back of my pants.

"Ah," he said as he lifted his arms and turned around. "Nothing to hide here." He smelled the soggy armpit of his white Oxford and made a somewhat disgusted face. "That is unless trying to disguise my glandular issues is hiding a weapon."

I patted him down. Other than a candy bar in his back pocket, he was unarmed. And, even though his case could have been filled with grenades, I felt I could take this guy to the ground and put a bullet in his head before he unlocked it.

After I gave him the signal that he was clear to put his arms down, he pulled his long greasy hair back into a ponytail and brushed some crumbs out of his goatee.

He cleared his throat. "I usually don't meet clients face-to-face. You can meet some pretty unsavory characters online."

I pointed to two chairs and a table on the other side of the suite. I didn't want to make too much small talk.

He continued to ramble on as he waddled across the room. "I figured since I was in Hollywood, and since you seemed like a serious buyer that I might as well demo the hardware here."

While cramming his blubbery body into the chair and shuffling around to try and get comfortable, he started unlocking the case.

"How did you know I was in Hollywood, anyway?" I asked.

"Oh, come on, Mr. Sullivan," he looked up from the case. "I tracked your location the second you inquired about the receivers."

Raising the gun between his eyes, I asked, "How the fuck do you know my name?"

"They call you 'Sully,' right?"

Moving in closer to him with the gun still fixed on his brain, I grabbed the TV remote off the bed and turned down the volume.

"You can put the gun away. I'm not here to rob you. If that's what I wanted, I would have cleaned out all your crypto accounts last night." He nudged his head toward the TV. The news was still covering the Chastity rampage. "Was that your work?"

"What do you mean?" I waved the gun at the screen. "I had nothing to do with her… or *that*."

"Come on, Sully. I can spot the work of a good poser a mile away." He slid the candy bar from his pocket.

My trigger finger started to tremble, and I was speechless.

"After all, I'm the one who makes the equipment you use." He started tearing into the candy bar wrapper with his teeth. Once he got it open, he peeled it off the candy like it was a banana. "What are you using right now? The 2500xlf parasite and the unstable Chinese nanoflea PGS5X?"

"I… I'm not sure." I walked over to the room safe, unlocked it, and threw him over a bag of the fleas.

He caught the fleas, opened his briefcase, and pulled out a jeweler's loupe. After he took off his unusually thick glasses, he tucked the monocle around his eye and looked closely at the bag. "Oh, ho ho ha. Good God. No. These things are counterfeit, Sully. Chinese black market garbage."

"How do you know?"

"Who do you think I am? I already told you that I make the tech." He put the candy bar on the table and waved me to throw him the parasite. "You're lucky you didn't die while pairing with the host."

I threw him the parasite.

Fumbling to catch it, he dropped the fleas. Thankfully, they were in a zip lock bag. I guessed at that point it really didn't matter anyway if they spilled all over the floor. He picked the chocolate bar up again and took a massive bite.

"I knew it!" he shouted proudly while studying the device. "The 2500xlf. This was the breakthrough that Phillips and I worked on for five years."

I secured the safety on the gun and placed it on the second shelf of the safe. "Phillips?" I asked as I closed the door and locked it.

"Yeah, Phillips." He looked away from the parasite. "He *was* my partner. After we had stable prototypes, he stole the devices from my garage and tried to sell them to the Chinese military. I'm sure that's how the black market devices came to be."

"Where is he now?" I kicked at the safe door to make sure it was secure and then made my way over to the other chair.

"Not sure." He rolled the parasite around on his thumb lovingly. "He's probably dead. If I had my way, he'd be in Hell." His face went red as he exploded into laughter, causing his stomach to roll around like a waterbed in a porno. A peanut from his candy bar shot across the room.

"Well, Hoop," I said, interrupting the hideous laughter. "What else do you have in the briefcase?" I tried to peer around his leg to get a closer look inside.

After a minute or so of chomping on the candy and calming from the fit, he dropped the loupe into his palm. He took a deep breath, grabbed his glasses off the table, and cleaned the lenses with the unbuttoned cuff of his shirt. He picked up the briefcase and placed it between us on the table. "This, Mr. Sullivan, this is my greatest triumph."

He pulled a small steel case out of the attaché. Using a thumb sensor on the side to unlock it. The cover retracted like blinds and folded into the back. If the actual equipment was anywhere near as stellar as the packaging, Hoop was walking out of the Chateau Marmont with a shitload of crypto.

"That's the parasite. It's codenamed the Firebeetle." He pointed to a device that looked kind of like a cockroach. "Check this out." He rubbed the top of the machine three times, and it stood up in the case. It looked like it had a thousand legs. They pulsated, causing the bug's torso to move up and down in sync with the single blinking red light in the center of its head.

All I could muster up was, "Holy fucking shit."

"You ain't seen nothing yet, Sully." Hoop placed his index finger on another print sensor in the case. A smaller compartment retracted horizontally, similar to the cover. As if being pushed up by hydraulics, a smartwatch appeared from that compartment. Once the elevation was complete, he picked it out of the case and handed it to me. "Put this on."

I studied it. It didn't look all too different from any other wearable I'd ever seen.

"Tap the screen twice."

I did. The screen faded on, and a message said, "Setting Up. Running DNA Diagnostic." I felt a small prick on my wrist.

Hoop bit into the candy bar. "Don't worry about that. It's building preferences and customizing the ecosystem to you. No one else can ever use this equipment."

"Are you that sure I'm going to buy this from you?"

"Beatle. Pair with Derek Sullivan."

The parasite shot straight up out of the case and quickly started crawling toward me.

Astonished by the tech, I whispered, "What the fuck?"

The metal beetle crept up my fingers and onto my forearm, then paused, waiting for further instructions. In a matter of seconds, another message popped up on the display. It said: "Pairing Complete."

The insect continued up my arm. I could feel its legion of microscopic legs brush against my arm hair. When it reached my shoulder, it stopped and began pulsating like it had in the case.

I looked at Hoop in shock and awe. "Bro. What the fuck? Is this thing alive?"

"Not entirely." He belly laughed again. "It is part AI rolled into biological nanotech."

I looked into the flashing red eye on top of its head. It stared back at me, waiting for further instructions. "So. It is alive?"

He shrugged his shoulders. "Now say, 'Beetle. Lock.'"

I hesitated and looked into the case that this creature called home. I was anxious to see what miracle was inside the third and final compartment.

"Come on, Sully. Say it. The Beetle already recognizes your voice. And only your voice."

"Beetle," I began. "Ummm."

Hoop sat up in his chair a little bit and waved his hands, signaling me to get on with it.

"Beetle. Lock," I finally repeated.

The device stood up straight. It crawled from my shoulder to my neck and circled like it was wrapping a ribbon around a pole. When it reached my ear, it made a faint initiation sound. The legs wrapped around the outside of my ear, and the belly suctioned itself inside. I felt it pair with my body and subtle electric signals ran from my inner ear down to my big toe, creating a numb feeling as it traveled.

Confident that we were about to be in business together, I pointed to the device's cage. "What else do you have in your magic box, Hoop?"

He smirked and pressed his middle finger onto the third compartment.

After they paired with the smartwatch, or the "Nest," as Hoop called it, three miniature receivers hovered in the air a foot or so in front of me. Much like the Beetle, that waited patiently for a command, they throbbed.

"I call them hornets." Hoop got up from the chair and handed me a pair of sunglasses. "Put these on."

I did as requested. A display came on in the right lens. It said, "Pairing with Nest," then "Pairing with Beetle," and, finally, "Pairing with Hornets." A loading bar reached completion, and the same foreign operating system from the Nest took over the entire right lens.

Hoop adjusted his glasses a little bit. "Can you see the display?" he asked.

I swatted his bloated fingers away. "I got it. What do I do now?"

"Say 'Hornets. Engage.'"

"Hornets. Engage." Instantly the right lens split into three similar screens. I saw myself on each screen, and as I waved my hand in front of my face, the hornets followed it back and forth.

Grinning ear to ear and in utter amazement, I asked, "How do I control them?"

"The glasses use a combination of motion sensors, voice commands, cameras, and augmented reality. Essentially, the inside of the lenses is a mirrored camera that follows your eye movement. Closed your eyes for three seconds and then reopen."

Excited to see what other tricks Hoop had up his sleeve, I mashed my eyes together like I was making a wish and blowing out the candles on a birthday cake. When they reopened, the Hornets spun around. Now all three were looking at Hoop. He waved at me.

"Bro," I screamed. "How in the fuck did you get cameras small enough to fit inside these things? They're almost as tiny as the fleas I use."

Laughing, he said, "Trade secrets. Everything is smaller these days.

"How do I fly? How do I fly?"

"Everything is controlled with your eyes. You can throttle them by the intensity of how far your eyes are open. Move your eyes side to side and spin them to control movement. Start slow and have hornets swarm my head. Your pupils are the joystick."

I lightly opened my eyes and guided the hornets up over Hoop's head. When they were over his scraggly hair, they continued flying toward the wall I was facing.

"Close your eyes again for three seconds."

I did. When I reopened, the Hornets reversed direction. They began gravitating back toward the back of Hoop's head.

"See the bald spot on top of my head?"

"How could I miss it?" I joked.

"Ha," he fired back. "Focus on the bald spot."

As I continued to do as instructed, a target site came upon each of the glasses' screens.

"Choose which target you think would give you the most stable connection and say that, Hornet's number and 'Pair host.'"

"Hornet two. Pair host."

The bug flew onto the crown of Hoop's head. An alert came up inside the left lens of the glasses that said "Pairing." After a quick load, it confirmed the connection and then said, "Host Locked." Immediately, the other two unchosen Hornets retreated back to my wrist and hovered above the Nest.

My heart thumped away. "Holy fucking Christ."

Hoop snapped his fingers, and Hornet number two unpaired from his head. It joined the rest of the squadron.

I took the glasses off. "I… I…"

"You don't know what to say," he finished for me.

I studied the sunglasses and rolled the watch around on my wrist. "What are the connection constraints?"

"There are none. Each unit is a two-way receiver. And the ecosystem runs across cell towers. It constantly clones the signals as it bounces from one to the other. Its sole mission is to create a stable connection. The hornets flood the cell signals with a pairing request. It works like two magnets and usually takes milliseconds to unite."

"Which cell carrier?"

"All carriers. All speeds."

Reluctantly, I handed him back the glasses and the Nest. The Hornets followed the devices. "How long does the connection last?"

He broke out into a laughing fit. "Indefinitely. The Hornets have no known shelf life. On top of that, they run on solar power. If the poser chose to stay in the host, there would be nothing stopping them from doing so."

I took off my Phillies hat and wiped sweat from my forehead. "Get out of here."

"I'm not kidding. Let's say you were posing inside some celebrity and you decided that their lives were better than yours. Well, you can burrow the Hornet directly into the brain. All you would have to do is press a series of promos on the Nest to transfer your consciousness, permanently."

I became dizzy and retook my seat.

Hoop fanned me with his hands. "I know. It's a lot to take in."

I chugged some water. "So. What you're telling me, in not so many words, is that I could live forever if I jumped from host to host?"

Hoop took the seat next to me."Yes."

"If that were the case, why are you… you?"

"I like me," he answered, somewhat offended.

"I'm sorry. I didn't mean it like that."

"Besides, I'm not psychic and can't take over a host," he confessed.

I slugged down more water. "This all seems too good to be true."

He handed me back the Nest and the Beetle.

"You didn't think I was going to leave without giving you a test drive, did you?"

Hoop placed his phone next to the Beetle and swiped sway at the screen. "You're going to want to lie down, Mr. Sullivan?"

"What are you doing with your phone?"

"Running diagnostics and pre-pairing you to several Hornets I have configured around the world."

"What do you mean?" I relaxed my head on a pillow as I refined onto the bed.

He pressed one last link on his phone screen and said, "I mean, this is going to be a wild ride. You're going to see that there are no distance limitations with my equipment. I have several posers in the field, waiting inside different hosts. Once you enter the host, your mesh will boot out the other poser. They have attached Nests to each of the hosts' wrists."

"Why?"

"The hosts are set up in a chain of exhilarating events for you to experience, but you're going to want to get out. In other words, you're going to jump from one host to the next. He manually put a Beetle over his ear. "I am going to be able to walk you through each experience." He rubbed his Beetle three times on the back. "I won't be in your hosts' consciousness, but I will be paired to all their devices through a Bluetooth network."

"What's the voice command to jump?"

I closed my eyes.

"Nest. Jump." He patted me on the shoulder. "Don't forget."

I gripped the comforter tightly on top of the bed. "Let's do this."

"Nest. Initiate," Hoop whispered.

Instantly, I was on a ledge of a tall building.

*Welcome to Shanghai, Sully.*

Unable to balance on the ledge, I slipped and began plummeting to the busy street below.

"What the fuck, Hoop?"

The city's lights blurred around me as the host's body went into cardiac arrest and shock. I felt every single moment of the host's fear as his heart ripped through his chest. I started losing my ability to breathe as the pavement grew closer and closer.

*You better get out of there, Sully.*

"Nest. Jump!" I screamed with what little voice the host had left.

With the streets of Shanghai feet from my face, I blinked and was transported to a warehouse. There was a tire around the top of the new host's upper body, making it impossible to move. The stench of gasoline made it challenging to keep the host's eyes open. I was out of sorts, finding it impossible to stabilize the connection.

A man in a tracksuit bent toward the host's face and spit.

*Introducing: the Russian Mafia*, Hoop said.

The Russian guy stepped back from the host and lit a pack of matches. Then he threw them to his feet. Gasoline on the floor ignited and raced toward me. I shook, trying to escape the trail of fire. Unfortunately, the tire was fixed around the back of a chair that the host was sitting on.

The flame singed up the host's legs, burned through the guy's dick and balls, and engulfed the tire. I felt all the skin on the body melting off. The tire flames torched the host's eyeballs. The orbs liquefied and started streaming down his face. I started hyperventilating spastically. The chair collapsed, dropping the host to the ground as smoke bellowed into his lungs. The torture continued, but before the tongue burned off and I was unable to speak, I managed to spit out, "Nest. Jump."

*Let's douse those flames, Sully. Welcome to Finland.*"

Instinctively, I made the new host cough, clearing the smoke from my lungs. As soon as my connection to the host was established, she was rolling a massive cinder block over the side of a fishing boat. The cement crashed through the ice, tugging a chain behind it into the water. I looked down to see that the chain was handcuffed to my ankle. I bent over to grab the chain, but it was unraveling so quickly that it was impossible to hold onto.

"Hoop? What the fu—" Before I finished screaming, the chain pulled tightly around the skinny host's leg, flipping her backward and nailing her head on the boat. The force whiplashed her spine on the way down as her body was pulled through the hole in the ice. Right before her head submerged in the frozen water, her left eye snagged on an icy shard from the cracked opening. It broke open, and the socket filled up. I screamed, only managing to flood the lungs with the cold death of the water.

*Oh, shit*, Hoop gasped. *I forgot that you can't use voice commands underwater. Sending through an emergency jump prompt on the Nest now.*

I struggled to swim upward back toward the hole in the ice and the path the previous poser had forged to get out to the middle of the lake, but the host was too light, and the cinder block was too heavy. I felt a faint buzzing from the Nest. The inside of the girl began icing up and taking on more weight. I waved blood from the eye wound out of my face and tried to read the face of the watch. No luck. Just as I felt the cinder block hit the bottom of the lake, I repeatedly mashed the Nest screen, hoping to hit Hoop's emergency escape.

And, right before everything went black, I opened my eyes to see the ceiling in my room at the Chateau Marmont.

My body was filled with the sensations I had just experienced in a matter of seconds. Adrenaline caused my body to tingle from the jump in Shanghai. I was sweating, and a burning sensation covered my body from the mafia torture in Russia. And, although I felt like I was burning, my teeth chattered from struggling to escape the icy suicide in Finland.

Hoop handed me a beer as I cautiously sat up on my hands. I grabbed the beer and rubbed the same eye that the ice ripped out of the Finnish girl's skull. As I felt my face to make sure I was back in me, I noticed that I was balling.

I dropped my head into my hands and let out a huge, ugly, and loud cry. The misery and terror of the three hosts beat me into a state of exhaustion.

"I felt *them*. I felt their terror."

Hoop put his hand on my shoulder again. "I know. It's not as pleasurable an experience for everyone.

I used the back of my arm to wipe snot off of my nose. As my voice quivered from shock and sadness, I asked, "How much?"

Hoop bent to my ear and said, "All of it."

And Hoop did take it all except for enough money for me to live and remain a semi-permanent fixture at the Chateau Marmont. He also connected me to a dark corner of his network reserved for posers and those looking for them.

It wasn't easy parting with all the crypto I had accumulated since moving to LA.. But Hoop's offer was too good to pass up. The Nest ecosystem ran on an endless and powerful worldwide mobile network. And the promise to live forever...

Not just live forever. I could live forever as the wealthiest and most influential people on earth. You couldn't put a price on that. Well, Hoop could. Sometimes things happen in life for a reason. Me checking into the Chateau, getting drunk, and then somehow managing to connect with Hoop in Hollywood—where he happened to be staying on business. It was almost too good to be true.

I ran several multi-million-dollar jobs in the three weeks since our demo in the hotel suite. It didn't seem like work anymore. I wasn't prepared for the shock of experiencing a host's emotions. However, I quickly grew addicted to the thrill of partaking in the hosts' dread and fear. Hoop told me the emotional exchange was a glitch with the Nest, but I disagreed. It was a blessing. I was finally getting the opportunity to walk in a celebrity's shoes for the entire day.

The first job using the Nest was a studio head that blacklisted a bunch of actresses for not wanting to fuck him. They pooled their money together and asked me to plant a bunch of child pornography on all his computers. I was "creative" again and kidnapped a twelve-year-old prostitute. As the fat cat, I sliced up the hooker and then called the cops, crying and confessing. When they showed up, I got into a standoff with them and started firing a gun out the host's front door. After taking a couple bullets to the chest, I unpaired from the studio executive right before he bled out. The guy was an emotional wreck of a human being and definitely looked down his nose at someone like me.

After the job, the actresses all changed their phone numbers and ISPs and shit. Apparently, they didn't ask me to involve or cut up a little girl. And even though they claimed to want the guy dead, they insisted that they never instructed me to get him shot. Whether they would admit it or not, they were after his money more than they were after revenge. With him dead, they wouldn't get shit.

It goes without saying that the actresses tried to stiff me. So, I got inside one of them and walked her hot little body in front of a moving truck. I did the entire thing at a cafe on Beverly Blvd. and it only took around ten minutes. I went to the cafe where a paparazzi I was greasing told me she hung out. I got a table near hers. Flew the Hornet onto her head. Went and sat on the restaurant's shitter with the door locked. Paired the Beetle and the Hornets. Stood up from her meal and walked her into the middle of the busy street.

That's right. I killed that bitch. With Hoop's equipment and the ease of voice commands, I could actually kill the hosts. I can't even imagine what she felt for the millisecond after I left and just before she got flattened. It was risky as fuck. If I miscalculated in any way, or the Beetle malfunctioned for some reason, I would have been floating around on the world's cell network forever.

Well, the others lost their shit and paid up immediately. The tabloids latched onto the story. The chick I killed actually had a resurgence in popularity after her suicide. I guess you could say she was worth a lot more dead than she was alive.

After that job, I became thoroughly addicted to the power of sharing the emotions and terror with the hosts. That feeling of certain death was fantastic, and it added a new level of adrenaline to posing. It made sense to ensure I was enjoying what I did for a living.

As fun as all that was, though, I came to the decision that I was going to permanently vacate the shell of Derek Sullivan. I had been living on borrowed time for far too long, and I wanted to buy a new house because I was sick of renting. It was too uncertain.

My plan was to begin my journey by pairing with a hot and rich young actor. I would fuck models, live his life, and spend his money. I didn't plan on actually doing any work. Once the money ran out, or I decided to use my power to ruin the poor fucker's career, I would jump to my next host and leave that asshole in the gutter.

The whole chain would be much easier than you would think.

I would use my paparazzi pal to track down the first actor. and connect the Hornet. Then, park the old van in some neighborhood and pair from there. Once inside the actor, the plan was to return to my van, grab all the Nest equipment. And then repeat the process. I figured I might run into some snags jumping from one celebrity to the next every couple of years. Still, there would be nothing weird about one star going to the home of another to pick up the equipment.

Once I was in the new host, I figured it would also be smart to return briefly to have the previous host publicly commit suicide. That way, there would never be any question or suspicion placed on the new host. I also planned to do it for kicks. In other words, I had no plan to stop posing. I wouldn't do it for money anymore, though. I would do it for pure entertainment value and the thrill of death. That is better than any fucking video game or movie.

I knew there would be a lot of tricky massaging to ensure everything ran smoothly. Maybe once I took over the first actor, I would try to find Hoop again to buy a couple of backup units. God only knew how much that was going to cost me.

I started checking off a "to-do" list on my phone before syncing it with the Nest watch.

Message Hoop to tell him the plan. √

Find a new host. √

Pair Hornets. √

Destroy all old equipment. √

Stabilize signal. √

Say goodbye.

Live forever.

I reached out to similar avatars in the poser network to find Hoop and tell him I would take the big step into immortality. I never heard back. I wasn't too concerned, though. After I bought the Nest system, he ran me through everything, including the full conscious dump. For something that had such high stakes, it was a simple and relatively intuitive process. There was even a failsafe that gave me an hour on the other side before I completely disconnected from my body. I would remain in my coma-like state until I returned to my van to pick up the equipment and untether forever. With the body no longer supported by the Nest, and the conscious gone, the organs would shut down.

I reached the second to last item on the list, "Say goodbye."

I took a minute and then opened the video camera in selfie mode on my phone. I used the camera as a mirror to adjust my Phillies hat and then pressed record.

"This is the last will and testament of the body of Derek 'Sully' Sullivan," I said. "Not a bad looking kid. Went from being dirt ass poor to successful in his own right. Truly, a self-made man." My eyes began welling up. I wiped them off and continued. "Nobody thought that Sully would ever amount to shit. And, even though they should have been right, he was gifted and used his abilities to beat the odds. And, now Sully is going to continue to prove them all wrong. He will live forever and always be rich." I nodded my head in prayer. "May God guide him through this next chapter of his life."

Before I pressed stop, I looked back into the camera. "See you on the other side, Sully, my boy."

I closed the camera app and synced the Nest to my phone from a root directory using a VPN.

Wrapping the Nest's watch and around my wrist, I delivered my first voice command.

"Beetle. Pair."

The Beetle crawled out of the open unit case, over my fingers, up my arm, and around my neck. When it reached my ear, it latched on using its thousands of little legs.

After loading, the interface opened on my phone. I navigated to a menu link that was called Evac.

I looked around my van for the final time as Derek Sullivan. My phone made an alert sound, followed by a pop-up message that just said, "Sure?"

"Nest. Pair with Hornet 2," I commanded. The watch vibrated seconds later, telling me that I was paired with the actor.

I pressed the 'Sure?' button and closed my eyes. After waiting for a beat with nothing happening, I opened my right eye and held the phone in front of my face.

"Please agree to the Terms and Conditions," it read.

"Jesus fucking Christ."

I accepted the terms and then...

The face of a broken Chastity O'Neill stared back at me from a foggy prison mirror. She rubbed her gums, where her front teeth used to be. She ran her other hand across her head. The rainbow-colored hair that I had chopped was now completely shaved off.

As her face filled with her tears, I suddenly realized that I wasn't in control.

A familiar New England accent entered Chastity's mind.

*Hey, Sully. It's Hoop. Just checking in on you. Got your messages about the Evac plan. In case you haven't noticed, I redirected your call.*

Chastity took one last look at herself and then bent to her knees. She picked up a bed sheet-wrapped noose that was secured to a line pipe under her sink.

I felt every second of her misery. Her desperation. Her hatred for herself.

She pulled the noise over her head and adjusted it tightly around her neck.

*Every forty seconds somewhere in the world, someone commits suicide. Your eternity is living out every single, painful death. Do you feel that pain, Sully?*

Chastity turned away from the sink and forcefully lunged forward. I could feel it. I could feel all of it, but I was utterly helpless in stopping it.

Her windpipe snapped.

*Nest. Jump*. I kept repeating in her head.

*Voice commands don't exist here, Sully. Besides, you aren't even talking. You're not even paired with the host.*

As Chasity's head lumped over from suffocation, her eyes closed permanently, and everything went dark.

Immediately, I entered another body. This host set a shotgun between his legs and recited the Lord's Prayer. He was filled with so much sadness. He lost his entire family to a drunk driving accident.

*Oh. Another thing*. Hoop laughed and coughed. *One of my associates disposed of your body. You were cut into pieces and will be buried somewhere out in the desert. Even if you could cheat your way out of Hell, which you can't, you have nowhere to go back to. Besides, you accepted the terms and conditions when you decided to evacuate your pitiful fucking life. You should have read that shit. People should always read that shit.*

The man pulled the trigger on the shotgun.

*Enjoy eternity, Sully.*

From that point on, I jumped continually from one suicide to another. I felt all the awfulness of the hosts. I felt all of the pain, remorse, and sadness that they felt.

With no way to beg for salvation, I was lost in the misery of humanity forever, never able to return to Derek "Sully" Sullivan.

# KAREN

LUCY LEITNER

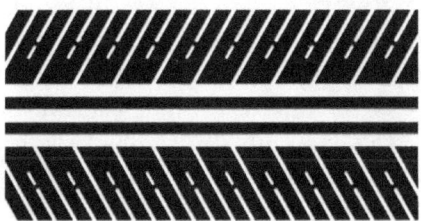

It was hard to believe that just last week, payments on the BMW X6 were the cause of most of my worries. Now, the car was the solution to all my problems. Aside from the moonroof, heated seats, and the wireless connectivity that an interim project director like me needs to multitask, the little SUV was strong enough that I could drive into 300-plus pounds of blubbery flesh without cracking the grille.

It's black. Basic bitch, I know, but so am I. The thing is the dark color makes it a lot harder to see any blood. Not that there was any visible carnage after I ran over my boss Monday night. If there were, Blake the agency president wouldn't have given me Kyle's job as a chance to prove myself while they search for his permanent replacement.

If the X6 could take out a man like Kyle who wore the same belt size as Saturn, it wouldn't have any trouble with the jiggling mass of lumpy flesh that was waddling down the lane of the gym parking garage this morning. The little SUV sat higher than her low center of gravity, leaving the perfect angle to crack her skull on the ground without throwing her massive carcass through my windshield.

I stomped on the gas, and the woman who cut my time short on the treadmill hit the grille with a satisfying thud. Her multiple chins bounced off the hood, rippling as her head flung back with such force that her neck snapped before she landed in a heap on the concrete.

The engine was barely more than a purr, letting me hear the bones crunch under the tires, the fatty tissue squish, the flesh tear, and the organs explode and spew bile from brand new openings in her bloated body. The mass of semi-flattened blubber on the concrete parking garage floor would have destroyed the Mini Coop I traded last weekend. Six-hundred dollars a month was a small price to pay. I finally had the promotion I'd deserved long ago, and now I had ensured a treadmill every morning exactly when I wanted it.

Maybe last week I would have waited for the woman to finish weakening the machine while somehow shedding zero pounds in the past few months, then hopped back on to complete my distance goal for the day. But that was before I took over running the daily status meeting, Creative Update Nine to Ten. A full half hour went into preparing the C.U.N.T. Because of that churro chomper, I had to cut my run seven-tenths of a mile short of my distance goal. Never again. Running a little farther and consuming a few less calories a day is how I've kept the weight off, as I tell my follower on Instagram. The first fat-ass I ever killed was me. I starved her to death. That bitch was in my way.

Unfortunately, I couldn't stop to admire my handiwork. I was in a gym parking garage after all, and 7:30 a.m. is a busy time to leave. Even though no one was walking down the aisle, it wasn't worth the risk of taking a look. But I bet she resembled a gingerbread man that exploded after rising too much. Whatever. The treadmill hog was now just another corpulent corpse, and she was out of my way.

I left the garage and drove down the road about a mile to Starbucks. The coffeeshop in the gym complex is locally owned, but they just don't have the same accountability for their staff. A barista gives you foam on your latte, management does nothing. Same with the supposedly "boutique" gym I belong to. The whole plaza—hell, the whole neighborhood—could benefit from a corporate takeover. It was coming, thank god. The BMW dealership where I bought my car had once been a concert venue. Head shops were converted into ink cartridge stores, bringing in a more productive class of people. The East End of Pittsburgh was slimming down, becoming leaner and more agile like our agency, and hopefully the residents would follow. Everyone knows cankles lower property values.

I pulled the X6 into the parking space and got out of my car, spitting my gum behind the Tahoe in the next spot. The hood was fine, not a scratch on her. No hair either like that urban legend says. If I avoided cameras, maybe I could run down an entire Golden Corral loyalty club.

A car honked. Did it really need to be so loud? Jesus, she should have it moo; would be more fitting.

"Hey! Could you please get your car into one spot? The lot's full," the cow said, her window down to reveal jiggling jowls. She probably had one hundred thousand Instagram followers, all telling her how amazing she was for never saying no to a cookie. What about me? No thanks, no likes, no fire emojis for telling those Girl Scouts they were perpetuating a culture of fatness and suggesting to their organization they introduce calorie-free options.

Obviously the car could handle another cow tipping this morning, but the C.U.N.T. is better with caffeine. So I pretended not to see her or hear the incessant honking as I walked into Starbucks.

They should reward loyalty at Starbucks. Buying a venti latte every day should let you jump the line, but instead, you have to wait with all the average customers—plus, they allow any slob off the street to use the bathroom. When it was finally my turn, I told the barista, who had apparently never heard of concealer, that I wanted a venti quad half-oat/half-almond milk latte with six pumps of sugar-free vanilla syrup and absolutely no foam under any circumstances. I watched my cup make its way down the assembly line. Oat milk, almond milk—good. One, two, three, four, five pumps syrup. Um, no. She slid it across the counter, and I intercepted it before she could call my name.

"Excuse me, miss," I said. "I deliberately requested six pumps. I saw you pump only five times."

"Oh. Sorry. I'll get you another pump." She took my latte back to the syrup station.

Before handling it, I slid it through a sleeve. Still no response from Starbucks corporate to my many emails about the temperature of the drinks. I took a sip. Yuck.

"Excuse me, miss. This is not half-oat/half-almond milk."

"I put both milks in."

"Oh, I know. But the ratio is all wrong. I taste way too much almond milk and, believe me, that is not a good taste."

"Fine. I'll make you a new one."

She didn't dare try to estimate the measurements this time with my eyeballs on her. She brought back my new cup. I wrapped it in a new sleeve and took a sip.

"That'll do."

"You're welcome," she said.

"Excuse me..."

"I thought it was fine."

"It's just that you spelled my name wrong."

"I can't make you another latte just for that."

"Oh, I know. It's for next time, so I don't have to speak to your manager. My name is K-A-R-E-N."

I parked in the lot outside of the single-story agency office. We should upgrade soon. A high-rise downtown. That'd better capture the image we need to project for an advertising agency on the up and up. It would be a great excuse to upgrade our staff to the type of people you expect to see downtown, not in this low-rent suburb. Kyle left me with a team of fluffy misfits who were consistently incapable of doing more than eight hours of work in an eight-hour day.

I tossed the Starbucks cup at one of the pigeons at the edge of the lot. It was right there, in the street that wound through this ancient office park, where Kyle finally got out of my way. He'd led the team to missed deadlines and angry clients for years, only keeping his position because he'd been with the company since the beginning. Unlike Starbucks, they rewarded loyalty at Young Isaac Norton Zimmerman, Y.I.N.Z. And as long as he was alive, he'd be project director, and I'd be under him.

Running him over wasn't the plan. I was just returning to the office to pick up my laptop so I could W.F.H. the next day. But then Kyle, with his big gut hanging over his jeans, stepped into the road. He was walking home after a late night, so committed to pulling the long hours necessary for an agency director that he sacrificed just about everything else—not that it did any good. All his meals were delivered to the office, he obviously skipped the whole getting ready for work process in the morning, and his only exercise was his ten-block walk to and from the office. And we still missed every deadline.

He was just another fat ass standing in my way.

Getting my own fat ass out of my way should have been enough. One hundred pounds gone in six months. Blake never noticed my dedication to finishing what I started, to setting goals and meeting them. I was the exact opposite of the over-promising-and-under-delivering issue he consistently berated our young account managers about. I promised *and* I delivered. And what happened? Nothing. Fat Kyle stayed in charge and the same mistakes happened again and again. Guy couldn't say no to a potato chip; how was he going to make tough decisions for the future of the agency?

So, when he stepped into the street three nights ago, I stomped on the gas. His beady little eyes went wide behind his glasses and his T-Rex arms reached as high as they could in fear. The grille smashed right into the hoodie pocket that he seemed to think obscured the General Tso's chicken and sweetened iced tea gut. The thump was satisfying, like one of those TikTok videos of someone slicing into bread. His bulbous head hit the ground, making a sound like an egg cracking. It reminded me of Easter egg drop contests in elementary school when no amount of padding could protect the delicate, raw egg as it plummeted off the roof.

His fat face crunched under one tire while the other flattened his calves that had grown enormous to support his weight. I drove off, monitoring the tire pressure on that handy digital gauge on the dashboard. There was no change. His layers of insulation must have kept any sharp edges of shattered bones from piercing the tires. They never quite cleaned him all up. Apparently, the impact sent parts of him flying from the street to the lot. Last week, Christine the intern came in with a tooth stuck in her shoe.

In the light of the next day, the X6 was as pristine as it was Saturday afternoon when I'd driven it home from the dealership after I hit the big hundred-pound milestone. No one else celebrated. No raise, no promotion, not even any new followers on the 'Gram. So I bought myself a present, just like I bought the condo when I hit the fifty-pound mark. I deserved it.

After the cops left Tuesday morning, Blake Zimmerman, one of the agency partners, had called me into his office.

"Kyle's death was tragic and we'll be grieving forever, but this is an agency. If we sit *shiva* for Kyle, we lose. You know the processes, the team, the clients. Congratulations, Karen. You're interim project director," Blake had said, reaching over his desk and shaking my hand. "Our headhunters start the search for the permanent replacement today, but you're in the running. And you've got a lead.

Don't drop the ball."

The raise, even for the interim position, would be enough to pay for the car and the condo and keep my bank account in the black. The credit card debt from all the new size-zero clothes I had to buy could wait. Maybe Ann Taylor would finally understand that they were ripping me off anyway, building the fabric costs for the A-frame dresses into the costs for the A-line ones that I bought. Hopefully, someday, corporate would acknowledge my many messages and Instagram ad comments and I'd receive a well-deserved refund. Since I'd become accustomed to not getting what I deserved, I wasn't going to hold my breath. To keep the collections' agents at bay, I had to get my team to finally start meeting their deadlines.

Some members of the team weren't in the office when I arrived. Typical. Artsy people claim they're night owls, that they can't be productive in the morning. Based on the login data of our inter-office messaging app I've been collecting since I took over, they're not too productive at night either. I ran three miles on the treadmill and over 300 pounds in my car before 8 a.m. You can't get here on time? All you need is four shots of espresso anyway. Breakfast was an invention of Big Cereal. And don't get me started on lunch. Invention of the labor unions to get paid for taking a break.

At 9 a.m. sharp, I started the C.U.N.T. By then, the designers, writers, and developers had gathered in the conference room. Including me, it was just eight people, but it felt crowded. That was mostly the developers' fault. Funyuns and pizza will make you a puffy group. Even when I was fat, I wasn't puffy. Doctors could hang photos of the developers in their offices and forego pre-diabetes screenings. If you look like this, you're in trouble. I was saddled with three pear-shaped men who swapped their testosterone for glucose. No wonder clients were always finding bugs.

I read off all the projects from the Project Management System, P.M.S., along with the latest comments. As usual, the status according to the team in the conference room differed from their last posted updates. They said they hated being in this room for a full hour every morning, but how was I supposed to cut it short when they saved all their updates for the C.U.N.T? If their posts in the P.M.S. were up to date, we wouldn't have to run through it verbally here. They say constantly updating about their progress impedes their progress. I say, how long do you want to be in this C.U.N.T.? As they relayed the status, I wrote the name of the developer, writer, or designer who was holding up completion on the whiteboard. It helped them be more accountable to see how much their slacking off affected others. When I pitched this idea to Kyle, he shot it down. He didn't like the idea of "public shaming" as he called it. If public shaming didn't work, why have my one-star reviews gotten so many waitresses fired? And in the two days since introducing the system, it appeared to be working.

If Charlotte didn't do the layout, Jess couldn't write the copy, and Juan couldn't develop the site. It all rested on Charlotte. It always did. You tell me excess weight doesn't slow you down? Blake told me I couldn't say that to her; that I could quote Lean Six Sigma all I wanted, but it didn't mean my team had to slim down. He also told me to keep everyone on deadline. Well which is it, Blake?

"Charlotte, today you have due the design for the Pro-Well print ad, which you estimated at four hours; the layouts for the secondary pages of the Champion Capital site, which you estimated at ten hours; and the retargeting ads for Chatter at three hours. You have seventeen hours of work to complete by the time the account managers must deliver these files, which is in eight hours. How are you going to accomplish this?"

"I'll get the Pro-Well ad done since that's got a third-party deadline. Then I'll bust out the Chatter and spend the rest of the day getting as far as I can on Champion," Charlotte said.

"But you won't finish Champion."

"Not unless you can bend time." She's a real smart-ass for someone with an ass that big. Her 12K Instagram followers always comment how witty her self-love posts are. They're not.

"So, it will be late."

"Yes."

"OK." I wished I recorded these meetings, but a roomful of witnesses is enough. An email to Blake that Charlotte admitted she'd be late on the Champion project would let the boss correctly assess on whose ass the blame lay.

You're just so much more productive when you replace food with caffeine. All those calories are weighing you down. If I put that in the caption of a selfie holding my latte and my laptop, I should get a hundred new followers for sure. People love useful tips with photos that bring it to life.

Back at my desk, I turned on the Pandora Cardi B station. It was kind of a tinny sound coming out of my computer speakers, nothing like the crystal clarity of "W.A.P." blaring out the windows of the X6. Jess sighed and made a big scene out of putting in her ear buds. She has tattoos. She only likes that awful tattoo music. Some of those freak bars she hangs in actually ask her to DJ sometimes. I had to turn off her playlist at the agency summer party. A favorable song about "Fat Bottomed Girls." Down seventy-three pounds at the time, it was triggering to hear that man she said was called Freddy singing about fatness like it was anything but a disgusting state of being that was dragging us all down. It made me uncomfortable, and I should never have to know another uncomfortable moment. I'd had enough of them when I was one of those fat-bottomed girls. When you're fat AF, every moment is uncomfortable. And this Freddy Jupiter fraud was normalizing it! In 2021! When he should have known better. Ugh, just the thought of that song was putting me in a bad place. Not to mention that man could use some auto-tune.

"Hey, Jess," I said from my desk six feet away from hers. The bland office was an open floor plan because we crammed in too many people to have cubicles. We were growing so fast that Blake said we didn't have time to move. Some said it was crowded, but it offered advantages for me. I could observe everything. When I took over for Kyle, I rearranged the room, gave myself a central location, a 360 view. When they slacked off, Blake got a message.

Jess pretended not to hear me while she typed furiously on her laptop.

"Jess."

"What?" she said but didn't take out her earbuds or look at me.

"Where are you on the Champion copy?"

"Same place I was fifteen minutes ago," she said.

"We need it by E.O.D."

"I'm aware. It's in the P.M.S. and on the board and now you're telling me. I have multi-dimensional deadline awareness." She looked straight ahead at her computer. So moody, that one. Probably listening to more Queen. That'll put anyone in a bad mood.

Commercials played on the Cardi B station. Trying to get me to pay for music. That's something Jess would do. It didn't work on me. I was always looking for more products to buy.

I pinged Charlotte for status updates in the P.M.S. She didn't answer.

I opened Instagram and scrolled. No new followers. No likes. No comments. Not even on my post about how starving yourself is the only way to kickstart your metabolism. Or my video about how cutting protein is key to getting over a weight-loss plateau. That one deserved all the Yaasses for sure. I scrolled through the accounts with the inspirational quotes that I would copy later, and there was Charlotte's big, fat face. @designdiva was holding a bagel and smiling.

"Fueling up for a long day at work. Got a lot of tough deadlines to meet, but it's important that I face the day with the right attitude. #selflove always!" Posted only forty-five minutes ago and already 312 likes. Forty-five minutes ago, 9:25 a.m., when she was supposed to be paying attention in the C.U.N.T., my C.U.N.T.

I took a screenshot of the post and circled both the time posted and the time shown at the top border of my phone. When Charlotte inevitably blew the deadline, Blake would be getting that screenshot.

"Charlotte," I shouted across the room.

"I haven't answered my messages because I'm trying to cram seventeen hours into eight," she said.

"What's your status?"

"A half hour less than at the meeting."

My computer dinged, interrupting the Biebs.

The message was from Blake: "New client coming in at 3 p.m. Need you in the conference room then."

"I'll be there with a smile on my face," I replied, adding a smiley emoji.

I leaned my phone against my open laptop and set it to selfie mode in Instagram. Which filter today? Ooh—one that draws attention to my hair. I just freshened up my bob with new blonde highlights when I hit the 100-pound milestone. Pursing my lips, I snapped the photo. Perfect. I typed my caption.

"I don't know who needs to hear this, but if food restriction wasn't the best way to increase productivity, the Nazis wouldn't have used it in the work camps. #healthytips #weightlossjourney"

I closed the app and waited for the new followers to flood in.

Two hours passed with several unanswered pings to the team and one message from Instagram about how my latest post violated community guidelines.

Charlotte stood up from her desk.

"Charlotte, are you heading out?" I asked.

"Yeah," she said. "I didn't bring lunch today, so I've gotta pick something up. Bad day for it, huh? But, working late last night, I didn't get to meal prep."

Meal prep. The biggest scam in the weight loss industry. The real key was no meals.

"I'll grab you something," I said. "I'm running errands anyway."

"Really? Oh, that would be amazing."

She sat her big ass back down on the chair. It squeaked in pain.

"No probs."

If it wasn't for the old lady in the Target toilet paper aisle, I wouldn't have had to complain to the manager.

I was filling my cart with toilet paper. Word was there was still a bit of a shortage. I originally stocked up with168 rolls at home but started getting nervous when I neared 150. Seventy-two more rolls were in the cart.

"Excuse me."

I turned to see the old lady behind me, one of those Quasimodo types.

"Can you tell me where to find the milk of magnesia?"

"Do I look like I work here?"

"You have a red shirt on."

"Do I have acne? A muffin top? A mustache?"

"No," she said. Oh, suddenly she was meek, after so casually hurling insults.

"I don't know where it is, but if you're looking to take a dump, try the cafe."

I left her in the toilet paper aisle. Going to that part of the store must have been wishful thinking on the constipated old bat's part.

If it weren't for the assistant manager's failure to understand how an "old lady's innocent mistake" related to his ability to staff the store, I would not have been so absent-minded that I forgot Charlotte's lunch. But, since I'm soooo committed to my team, I risked breaking my allotted hour lunch break to run back into the store and purchase her meal. The only real luck I had on that excursion was the spot next to the X6 being empty, so I could leave my cart in it.

The shortcut back to the office avoided the highways, but the narrow residential roads came with their own risks. Like the school bus in front of me, stopping every block to roll another kindergarten dough ball out to their front doors. When it stopped for the third time in about a mile, there was only one woman on the corner. I mean, the lone woman's T-shirt could have fit three of me, but technically she was only one human.

They say you are what you eat. She must have eaten a lot of ice cream cones. Standing with her feet together, her body widened up the lumpy legs of her sweatpants to the opening of the cone at her waist. Her pants squeezed the first gut-scoop over the waistband, on the sides, front, and even the back. The second scoop of monstrous breasts sagged like melting dairy over the first, and her neck-less head was the maraschino cherry on top. She waved and grinned, pinning her head back, her neck flab jiggling. Three normal-sized children walked off the bus. Must be a nanny. Like the most disturbing part of that Queen song. The fat nanny that made a bad boy out of him. Ew!

The bus reeled in its signs and its lights stopped blinking. It pulled away, leaving the ice cream cone and her three wards. The kids ran across the street. She waddled behind them, waving at me to thank me for letting them cross.

I smiled and slammed down the gas pedal. Her legs cracked against the grille. Did it actually sound like biting into an ice cream cone or was her shape influencing my imagination? The double scoop top of her body hit the pavement. The X6 bounced over her. By the way the tire sank, it must have been the midsection, the round and drooping bottom scoop. The kids screamed, tears running down their little faces. In my rear view, I could see the gulch in her belly, blood soaking the tarp she wore as a shirt like she was becoming a strawberry sundae. That must have been quite a sight for the kids. Enough to scare them out of eating ice cream cones for sure. That may save them in the future from heart disease, diabetes, kidney failure, cancer, Alzheimer's, and a BMW X6.

"Here you go." I set the Diet Coke bottle on Charlotte's desk.

"I thought you were picking up lunch," she said.

"This is lunch. I'm having the same thing. See." I raised my half-drunk bottle. It wasn't like I was subjecting Charlotte to some experimental regime. This had been my lunch every day for six months! And look at me now. Visible collarbone. Thigh gap that would make an Olson Twin jealous. 32AA. If Blake wouldn't let me run my weight loss challenge, I would have to slim my team down on the sly.

Charlotte looked disappointed she wouldn't be expanding today. I flashed her my best Instagram smile. She would have thanked me if she knew how badly I wanted to run her down with my car. I wanted to hear her bones shatter under the tires, the sharp, splintered ends piercing through her bulbous flesh. Drink your Diet Coke, Charlotte. It's for your own good. Being fat will kill you. Sooner than you think.

I scooped up my laptop and headed to the conference room. Lucky for me, Megan—my direct report—had forgotten to erase the morning meeting notes, again. At least it would let Blake get a clear look at who was holding up the projects. Maybe he'd finally give the OK to start interviewing designers, and as soon as I found one without the tonnage, Charlotte would be facedown on the pavement, just another statistic in the casualties of the obesity epidemic. I sat down at the table, popped my laptop open, two minutes early.

Blake entered the room. Hip guy, always well-dressed. If he'd just shave the mustache… we must lose clients because they think he's a child molester. Behind him… ugh, that must have been the client.

Did we have no standards anymore? We were supposed to be going for an image; young, slick, agile. Definitely not this slob that took a seat across from me and placed a black gift box on the table. His gut tested the buttons on his short-sleeved, button-down shirt. He just needed a name tag and he could rent me a pair of bowling shoes. The shirt stretched so tight, I could see his cleavage. His receding hair hung back in a greasy ponytail. Ew, please don't make me take him out to lunch.

Sweat stains under his arms. Fur over his arms. I could fit a knitting needle in his pores. My god, he'd be a lovely, temporary hood ornament on my BMW. And how did he button that collar without asphyxiating? He had a distinct chin, which made his neck flab's forward puff all the more pronounced.

"Karen, this is Sonny Hooper from Bug Wireless," Blake said.

Against my will, I reached over the table to shake his soft, fleshy hand. Mine came away wet. Fat people. You can get a staph infection just from meeting them. Far more likely than from sitting on the ab machine at the gym after I left without wiping it down.

My purse was under the table. While Hooper blabbed, I reached into it and squeezed the sanitizer into my hands.

"What do you think is the apex of wireless communication devices?" Hooper asked, his lunch still in his teeth. That man ate spinach?

"Um… 5G?"

"5G lets you upload stupid dancing videos to TikTok faster. Useful, sure. Disruptive, no. I'm talking about a device that changes the way we communicate. Like the iPhone did back in the aughts."

"AI?" I asked.

"No need for that," Hooper said.

"This is amazing," Blake said. He's giddy. Tech nerd. "You have no idea how excited I am."

"I give up."

Hooper removed the lid from the shiny, cardboard box. Blake grinned like he just ran Hooper over with his car.

Some sort of black, plastic object sat in the crevice of protective foam. Hooper pried it out and placed it on the table.

I jumped out of my seat. It wasn't a device. It was alive! I backed away from the table as the black thing crawled on its uncountable legs toward my laptop.

"Oh my god, it's a bug!"

"That is the company name," Blake said, laughing.

It must have had a million spindly legs. And they were all moving the horrible thing that was closing in on me. Hooper scooped it up and put it back in the box, replaced the lid. I stayed away.

"It's not an insect," Hooper said. "It's an earpiece. You wear it; you can communicate with other wearers by thought."

"You're messing with me," I said.

"He's not," Blake said.

"You put it in your ear, you speak just by thinking. This technology will change the world."

"And they came to us." Blake beamed. That smile under the mustache is enough to keep him at least five hundred yards from a playground. "To evaluate our potential to deliver the message to the world. I'm about to jump out of my skin here!"

"What do you need from me?" I asked, sitting back down. "You need the word out fast? I've got the fastest team in town."

"You're going to be the first non-Bug employee to try the device," Hooper said. "We need more real-world perspectives, beta users, if you're familiar with the concept. Try it for a day, so you can explain it to your team. In my experience, with a category-of-one product like this, that is much more effective than a creative brief."

"Karen, we pull off this spec work, we get the launch," Blake said. "I don't have to tell you what that would mean for the agency. Or the project director position."

"Me?" There was no one more qualified in this place to assume such an important role in the future of the agency, but still... I'm not an account manager; I rarely got first contact with new clients. As someone who manages and coordinates, I never got credit for my role in creative projects. I had to run over my boss to get a well-deserved promotion.Was it finally my time? Would Y.I.N.Z. give me the recognition that was long overdue?

"Hoop asked for you specifically."

I looked back at his ruddy, lumpy face. Ugh.

"I'm familiar with your work," he said. "Philips, an associate of mine, talked you up quite a bit. There is no one more suited to using this device."

Phillips? No doubt another disgusting Carl's Jr. customer of a client I'd blocked out of my mind the minute after the job was done.

"So, I just put it in my ear?" As I reached for the box, Hoop's hairy hand slid it away.

"Yes. But not until tomorrow morning. I'll be the other user who you'll think too, and I'm done for the day after this. Taking the wife to a matinee." Hoop smiled, the green strings hanging between his grimy, corn-kerneled teeth. He pushed the box across the table to me. "Tomorrow morning, place the Bug on your ear. It will lock in place with its legs. I'll be communicating with you throughout the day and you with me."

"So, I'm the first person outside Bug to try it?" Recognition. Finally. Fat Karen wouldn't have been considered. Good thing she was as dead as Kyle.

"Yes," he said. "We'll just need you to sign this N.D.A." He reached into his breast pocket and pulled out a folded packet of papers. Six pages of legalese. Whatever. I skipped to the last page and signed, careful not to touch the wet, sweaty spots that blurred the ink.

"So, how does it work, Mr. Hooper?" I asked.

"Call me Hoop. Just think, 'Hoop,' and I'll be in your head."

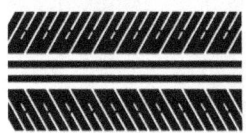

The X6 wasn't so powerful it could ram through all the cars that prevented me from traveling home at my desired speed, but it sure could handle the super-sizer in the crosswalk. I was only a few miles from home on my shortcut through the still-standing parts of the 'hood that Champion Capital hadn't yet razed to expand my condo development. The two worlds of the East End are my before and after pictures. Six months ago, I was like a burnt-out squatter pad with boarded up windows. Fat rolling over my desk chair armrests, necklaces strangling me, foot flab bursting out of my Birkenstocks. Having to slide the seat all the way back to fit behind the wheel of the Mini Cooper. Running out of breath walking from the car to the office door. Everyone assuming I was always the one who farted.

Well, look at me now! Like my new construction, standalone condo home. One bedroom with an attached garage and open floor plan. And just like me, the neighborhood shows no evidence of the transition, of those tough months of buying a new, smaller pair of jeans every week. Size ten, eight, six—so tempting to call my progress good enough. But I didn't. I had a goal. The East End does, too. It wasn't happy with the tattoo shops and art galleries that brought people with at least some expendable income to the squalor. Those freak shows were all gone now, replaced by banks, Starbucks, Chipotle, Target, civilization. Soon, the neighborhood will purge all memory of its ghetto past like the old photos on my Instagram account.

There was no traffic, even at rush hour, because few people lived in the hovels anymore. Except, apparently, this one, who just had to waddle out with his walker as I was approaching the stop sign.

I stomped on the gas. The walker flew into the stoop of one of the boarded-up slums and the flabby body collapsed with a thud. The X6 maneuvered over it with more ease than it did the potholes on this road. This one made a good squish sound as the tires rolled over the blubber. How would a skinny corpse feel beneath my tires? Would the bones pierce through the meager flesh and slash my tires? Maybe I'd find out, but the sad truth was thin people weren't as often in my way. A, they moved faster. And B, they took up less space, so the odds were just lower that they'd be blocking where I needed to go. And they weren't responsible for making me spend more than I earn. All those new clothes. You're telling me Ann Taylor doesn't factor the costs of the extra yards of fabric for the XXL into size zero? It does not cost the same in raw materials for pants that use twice the denim, and yet the costs earning interest on my credit card bills are the same. The fat asses, all of them, are preventing me from getting out of debt. I could run down a skinny woman texting in the road if she was blocking my way to work, but it wouldn't do a thing about my health insurance premiums that I know damn well are inflated to take care of the inflated people and their glucose monitors.

Ugh, just thinking about them and their diabetic feet so swollen they couldn't fit in shoes were the worst. So slow. They had no chance of getting out of the way of the X6 with its horsepower and cylinders and turbo-whatevers. And they shouldn't have been in the way in the first place. When their feet are eventually amputated, would those people still count as pedestrians even without peds?

I cranked the Yung Baby Tate back up and sang along. "I am healthy, I am wealthy, I am rich, I am that bitch." I rolled down the windows so my neighbors could hear some real music for a change. "When I count up them hundreds, they blue. Bitch, I'm the shit on the internet too, ho." Ugh, now I was home too soon, rolling into my garage before the song was over. I sang while carrying one of the twenty-four-roll packs into the house. "I am gonna go get that bag and I am not gonna take your shit."

Entering through the garage took me into the kitchen. I placed the toilet paper on the granite counter for a momentary break. It was so heavy! How did those middle-aged lard buckets carry the extra weight around and do nothing about it for so long? I'd had enough at thirty-one. After giving my arms a break, I carried the toilet paper the rest of the way through the galley-style kitchen down the hall to the closet. It was getting tight in there.

"Rosé!"

My French bulldog was in the living room crate where I left her this morning. She was the perfect dog who looked great in photos, but with my OCD I just couldn't bear the thought of her leaving little turds on my brand-new hardwood floors. She was happy to run out of the crate and out the front door for our walk.

Rosé and I strutted around the block of matching, modest, modern homes and their manicured lawns that the condo association mows. She was such a good little doggie, she didn't need a leash. And she knew not to shit until we were a couple blocks from our door. That way, it could stay there on the sidewalk and I wouldn't step in it. You just can't get dog crap out of Uggs.

"Here, little angel." I knelt down and Rosé walked right into my arms after doing her business. I set my phone to selfie mode, made a kissy face, and snapped a photo. One from the left, one from the right. The question wasn't which was my good side; it was which was my better side?

"Hey!"

A woman was running down the walkway from her house to me, her thighs rubbing together in her tight jeans. How did they market "skinny" jeans to size infinity?

"Hey! Are you gonna clean up after your dog? This is the third time you've left turds on the sidewalk this week!"

My phone was already out, the camera already activated, so it was a quick switch to video mode. I hit "record."

"Oh my god, why are you threatening me?"

"I'm not threatening you. I'm asking you to be a responsible pet owner and act like you're part of this neighborhood," she said, her shaking cheeks filling the frame. She had one of those faces that looked like a mask because the fat pinched under her cheekbones.

"Help! I'm being attacked!"

"You're not being attacked. You're leaving biological waste on the sidewalk. It's dangerous, not to mention gross."

Duh. That's why I didn't pick it up. I didn't own a HAZMAT suit. What did she want from me?

And talk about gross! She was getting too close, so I kept the camera on her. There were horror stories of thin people accidentally crushed to death beneath rolls of adipose tissue at buffets. A Jack-in-the-Box fart can knock you unconscious. This woman's aggression was getting scarier, the possibility of catching whatever fat person infection was in her saliva increased the closer she intruded into my space. The CDC should have forced them to keep wearing masks after the rest of us could finally throw those things away, to protect us from their spit and their jowls and their chocolate-smeared teeth. No one should have to see that. I didn't have my car, just a French bulldog and my phone. I was literally naked.

"You're harassing me! Help! Help! This woman is physically intimidating me!"

"Jesus, get it together," she said. "And pick up after you dog."

She stormed away, her ass wide and flat in the tight jeans. She disappeared behind her door, I snapped a photo of the house number.

Wait until the condo association management hears about this.

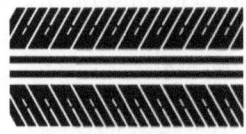

Rosé was back in her crate and a glass of rosé was in my hand. I alternated sips with nibbles of white bread. It was fortified, like my wine. I had all my vitamins covered. Dinner at my desk in the living room while *The Masked Dancer* played in the background. It was a shame I couldn't see the dancing, but I had multitasking to do.

At 6:48 p.m., my entire team had logged off the chat. They were done for the night. I took a screenshot. When ProWell fired us, all those grayed out names would be to blame. I stayed logged in while I moved onto the evening's priority project.

It wasn't hard to track down a name by a house number on the condo association website. Hilary Spencer. No other name on the home register. It was a little more difficult tracking down her social media. There were a lot of Hilary Spencers. Luckily, I had her on video and could match the enormous, menacing face to the Facebook profile pic. She looked thinner online, but the bland, brown curls and padded cheekbones were a definite match.

She liked to cook—shocker—and watch true crime shows and tell her friends all about both hobbies. A week ago, she and her team had won trivia night at Stout Brewing Company. Heh. They'd won two weeks ago as well and taken third the week before that.

I knew where Hilary Spencer would be tonight. And it was in walking distance. For her. I'd be in my X6.

I parked across the street from the brewery. Like anyone follows handicapped parking rules. I cut the lights and the engine and waited. This was fun. Kyle and the three pedestrian pachyderms today were spur-of-the-moment societal liposuctions. Was I up for this challenge? Could I really be both planner and executor of such an ambitious project? Yes, I could. Those doubts were just the imposter syndrome talking. I couldn't let the self-doubt dominate my thoughts. That was the same type of negative self-talk that made the first ten pounds so difficult. What got me through then? Aside from eliminating all non-caffeinated liquids, it was the fantasies, all the things I would finally gain when the weight was lost. The project director title, the upgrade from my crappy studio apartment, the prince to show off on the 'Gram. He hadn't arrived yet, but it was only a matter of time before the perfect man swiped right on that bikini shot that showed off my ribcage.

To escape my anxiety, I started fantasizing. Running down Hilary would be beautiful, the sounds like ASMR. That soothing thump of a heavy torso flopping onto the hood for the briefest moment before dropping back, the head cracking on the asphalt. Maybe some brains would leak out.

It was a shame I was in too much of a hurry earlier today to inspect the carnage. Maybe tonight was the night. The darkness provided a cover and who was out at 10 p.m. on a Thursday? No one in our condo complex. Not even when I drove the three-fourths of a mile to get here half an hour ago. We'd be alone. And as long as I kept the car slow, we'd have quiet.

Though the brewery was close to home, it was in that *other* East End. Champion Capital would soon be converting these old warehouses into lofts. Maybe a Hollister would move in, or a North Face, and a 24-Hour Fitness. But, for now, the area was dark, and didn't have a lot of foot traffic. Stout Brewing Company was the only attraction at this time of night.

Hopefully Hillary was trying to walk off the beer calories. If she'd driven, this whole excursion would have been a complete waste of time.

Since nothing was going on outside, I multitasked. With Hilary's rude interruption monopolizing my evening, I didn't have a chance to edit my Rosé shots. They would bring in the followers for sure. Everyone loves dog photos! All the pics were so perfect, I was having decision paralysis. I selected one of Rosé and me, our faces mushed together.

I typed my caption: Sorry not sorry!

Post!

I refreshed and refreshed for twenty minutes. Still no one tapped the little heart. The five other posts that used the same caption this afternoon all had at least one hundred likes. And there's Charlotte on my feed again. A big plate of chicken with some sort of disgusting green vomit drizzled on top.

'Long day at work. Treating myself to an old favorite. #selflove #healthyliving #balance'

That was it! I'd forgotten hashtags. And I was usually such a good multitasker. I was deleting and re-uploading the post when beer bellies started bouncing out of the brewery.

And there she was. I'd recognize those fat cheeks anywhere. No, wait! There was Hilary in the red sweater and a growler in her hand. No, it wasn't! That was her, hugging a friend. Those "skinny" jeans still on from earlier. She'd probably have to cut them off. That one. Those sad, bodiless curls that could have used some of the fluff from her face. She waved her friends goodbye and started walking toward the abandoned warehouses.

I wouldn't have much time. If I wanted to get her in the desolation, I'd have to hope no one else was on foot. The warehouses only spanned a couple blocks before she'd cross the busy Fifth Avenue and would be back in the development. But I wanted it. I wanted to feel her bubbly body burst under my BMW so bad.

She rounded the corner. No one followed. Except me. Her thighs rubbed together so hard I thought they might ignite and she'd become a flaming human torch. I turned off the headlights as I turned the corner. As long as I kept my hands at ten and two on the wheel, I'd stay straight and hit her in those friction-filled thighs.

What luck for me. No sidewalks in this abandoned industrial area. I slammed my foot on the gas and barely a second later came the thump. But the car continued smoothly. No satisfying lumpy bump. No crushing bones. No splat. I flicked the headlights back on. No one was behind me. Where was she?

I kept driving down the dark block until I hit the red light at Fifth. My heart started beating like I was on treadmill mile two. I jumped out of the car and ran to the front. Oh, thank god. She wasn't stuck to the grille like that urban legend my old friends—that an introvert like me lost touch with—told at childhood slumber parties. Where was she?

There was no point driving back to look for a fat corpse that may or may not have been on fire. There was only one place she could be. And the best thing to do was drive home.

The tunes were way down, and I kept one eye on the rear view to make sure I wasn't dragging a whale behind the car. No screams. No body in the street. I couldn't even feel the extra weight of her trapped in the undercarriage.

I pulled into my garage, shut the door, and turned on the lights. I got down on my hands and knees and peered under the car. Yep, there she was, that AIDS quilt she wore as a top was stuck to some sort of machinery under the X6. Of course it did; the thing was about as big as the fifty-something-ton one they made for charity. She was face down and her blood was pooling on my garage floor. Ew!

I went into the kitchen and grabbed a pair of scissors. I slithered under the car, contorting myself around her bulbous body, and cut the quilt loose. Her globular body hit the floor with a squishing fart.

With her chin on the ground and her eyes aiming straight ahead, she looked like one of those dead animal rugs that weirdos with beards keep in their foyers with their deer heads and other trophies of their kills.

Well, I guess I had one now. But who'd want to step on a cellulite rug? At least it didn't look like the blood was gushing or anything like that. It was likely just scratches from being dragged a half-mile over gritty asphalt.

The garage cleanup would be easy. But what to do with Hilary? Rosé wouldn't eat her. I didn't have sharp knives to cut her up. And, anyway, ew! Where would I even buy vats of acid? Adulting is hard. Tomorrow night, I'd put her in the backseat and kick her into one of the rivers. Damn. Hilary and her fat fucking carcass would be in my way on a Friday night, which I was keeping open for a swipe right, not corpse disposal. In my way, just like the rest of them. I removed over a thousand pounds today and this one comes back to be removed again tomorrow. Must be how Jillian Michaels felt when one of her Biggest Losers made the wrong type of gains between seasons.

I left the corpse face down under my car and sprayed some Febreze, just in case she started to stink. Like stink even worse than people her size always do.

It was late, but I was wired. The glass of rosé wasn't doing its job. The X6 had let me down. Maybe I needed a car that sat even higher off the ground. Hilary wasn't nearly the biggest I'd run over. If the X6 couldn't handle her… And who knows what damage she did to the car. What could I get in trade? I'd need another raise for a down payment.

The black box sat on the coffee table, containing the device that could make that happen. Hooper said to wait until morning, but he also set today's meeting for three and didn't complain that I was there at 2:58 p.m.

I opened it, and the legs wiggled. Ew! I slammed the lid back on. I'm supposed to put that on my skin? Yuck! I opened it again, and this time I touched it. Plastic. Thank god. No furs like a spider. Hmm, it must really be a piece of tech, not an insect. I pulled it out and its million legs crawled around my hand. It felt good, kind of like one of those pin art things. What's the worst that could happen if I put it in now? It would give me time to acclimate before jelly belly started thinking at me in the morning.

As soon as I placed the bug over my ear, the legs started to crawl, some locking over the cartilage. Oh! The other little legs crawled into my ear. It tickled, then it stopped. It was fixed to my ear, covering the whole thing, but not uncomfortable at all. Light. After a minute, it was like it wasn't even there.

OK, that was enough for now. The slick plastic made the half-sphere hard to grip. Using my nails, I tried to pry a leg from the cartilage, but it didn't budge. I tore through the box, tossing the foam rubber on the floor. No instructions. No branding even. No warnings. Bug Wireless must be real paranoid about this tech getting into the wrong hands. Maybe it *was* as revolutionary as Blake claimed.

Well, at least it didn't hurt when I finally laid down in bed. So much better than a CPAP machine.

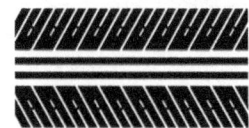

Between the Bug in my ear and the body in my garage, I was up until 3 a.m. I'd even scrolled through Instagram until there wasn't a single post from the past two days I hadn't judged, and it still didn't put me out. When my alarm went off at 5:15 just two hours after my eyes finally closed, the struggle to get out of bed was real. But, when you have a poor night's sleep, the best thing you can do is work out. When I shared that tip on the 'Gram last week, a couple trainers disagreed. What do they know? I saw trainers like them, working with the same clients for months, and guess what—those clients still look like they're in danger of being pursued by Captain Ahab.

Not me. I was currently at 2.8 miles on the treadmill. The Bug wasn't even slowing me down. Hooper must not have been awake yet. Not that I'd have expected a Slurpee slurper like him to be an early riser.

A third of a mile left and Drake blasting out of my phone speaker when a tap on my shoulder nearly sent me hurtling to my death.

I jumped off the belt, onto the stationary sides, and jerked my head around. A human bowling ball was standing beside the machine.

"Excuse me, but could I please use the treadmill? You've been on for thirty-seven minutes," she said.

*I couldn't take a time limit seriously until the gym implemented a weight limit.* I hopped back on the belt and resumed my run.

"Excuse me?" she said. "What did I just hear you say?"

"Nothing. I have 0.2 miles left." *You know, the circumference of your waist.*

She yanked the emergency string and the treadmill stopped. No time to anticipate, I lurched forward into the console and bounced off the machine. The elliptical on my right broke my fall. Ow! My ankle twisted under the footrest. I was on the ground, wailing in pain, and that Twinkie muncher stood there starting at me.

*What? You've never seen someone fall for any reason besides something under them breaking*?

A trainer ran over.

"Miss, are you all right? Are you hurt?" he asked.

*Yes, I am hurt. And some meathead can't fix me.*

"Meathead?" His face scrunched, almost like he was annoyed by having to do his job. "I have a masters in kinesiology."

*And I have a Ph.D. in gibberish.*

"What?"

"What?" I said, pushing myself to my feet. The ankle wasn't broken; I could stand on it. But taking a step caused a searing pain to pass down to my toes. I held onto the elliptical. "It's her fault. She pulled the emergency string while I was running."

"She was on it for over thirty minutes and was playing some god-awful profanity out of her phone without using earbuds."

"Miss, you know both those things are against policy," the trainer said, his obnoxious biceps flexing as he talked.

"Well, I can't exactly put in earbuds with this thing, can I?" I turned my head and showed them the Bug.

"You can always listen to the music on our speakers," the trainer said.

Ugh. "I want to speak to the manager."

"All right." He waved his big, muscly, stupid arm—which he couldn't use to help me up, apparently—over at the big man in the black polo. The man looked uncomfortable, not with the situation, but with existing. Like one of those ex-jocks who didn't stop eating when his athletic career did. He lumbered over to us.

"She wants to speak to the manager," the trainer said.

"I'm Paul. What's the problem?"

*He was the manager of the gym? A man who clearly couldn't manage his own weight was managing a gym*?

"I manage my weight just fine," he said. "What is the problem?"

Was I so tired I didn't realize I was speaking?

"I was assaulted by this woman and I've sustained major injuries." I pointed at the tub of lard.

"From what I've seen, she provoked it," the trainer said.

*Like a meathead who teaches fatsos how to pick up a dumbbell can solve anything.*

"Kinesiology is about a lot more than bicep curls," he said.

"Wow, she's nasty to everyone," Harriet Tub-woman said.

"Look, we've had complaints about you for months. Taking selfies in the locker room where other women are in all stages of undress. Hogging treadmills. Never once wiping down a piece of equipment. Far as I'm concerned, you've had more than three strikes. You're out."

"I'm out?" I tried to walk forward, but the pain shot from my ankle up to my thigh like a bolt of lightning. I stumbled back, grasping the machine for support. "I was attacked!"

"Just take your bag and leave before I call security." The manager shoved my bag at me, knocking me into the machine.

I was off-balance already when Miss I-Have-A-Thyroid-Problem tossed my phone from the treadmill console into my forehead. The two gym employees apparently thought what I could already feel growing into an ugly bruise was funny. I shoved the phone in my bag and pulled myself up on one of the elliptical machine handles. I hobbled away, each step sending a stabbing pain that dissipated into throbs for the split second while the left foot gave it a reprieve. It erupted again on the subsequent step.

"I'll be speaking to your manager," I said as I passed them and limped to the door, past those idiots wasting their time with the free weights.

Everyone else at the agency had the luxury of staying home if some psychotic whale attacked them. It wasn't their C.U.N.T. The entire fate of the agency wasn't on their shoulders. Blake hadn't told them they needed to get the Bug kickoff meeting done ASAP due to the tight deadline. I ran my fingers over the Bug. Luckily, it survived the assault. But what was I supposed to tell the team about the device?

*Where was Hooper? Did he snore his fat ass to death?*

I dragged my injured foot to the X6 like a zombie. Whatever. It was less painful than trying to use it like a regular foot. Pressing the gas sent spasms up my leg and shivers through the rest of me. Would I even be able to run down a burger biter if his motorized scooter stalled out in front of me? The pain blinded me at times, but I made it to Starbucks. America's bathroom would at least let me change out of my Lulus and into my office attire. I swung the car into a spot and limped out with my bag.

"Hey! This is a busy lot. Could you please try to stay in one spot?"

*I'll park in one spot when you buy two airplane seats.*

"What did you just say to me?" the woman asked. *FEMA could use her dress to house a family of five.* She's holding her Starbucks cup, leaving, why does she care about parking spaces?

"Nothing." I tried to limp past her, but she put her bulk in front of me. *This must be how Earth feels, having to circumnavigate a giant mass of gas.*

She flicked her wrist and I went blind.

My face was on fire. Was I melting? I squished my lids shut, tears coming to save me from the scalding, spicy mess in my eyes. Who knew hippos drank tea? My skin burned, bubbled, I could feel little blisters forming over my pores. I blinked my eyes open. My assailant was gone. Blurry-eyed, I limped into the Starbucks.

The line almost reached the door. It wouldn't reach that far if the customers could resist the call of the Frappuccino. I managed to squeeze through the line, without my bag catching on the bulbous bellies. The ankle was screaming, the pain so much worse. I hopped the last five feet to the bathroom door, elevating the injured foot like the doctors say. I turned the handle and, on one foot, used what little weight I had to push it open. It was early, so no one had shat out a bag of Doritos yet.

That meant the smell was coming from me. Ew! Drying sweat. I set my bag on the toilet; it was gross but reaching down to the floor on one foot was too difficult. I tried to block out all the cottage cheese asses that spilled over the sides of the seat and the lumpy legs straddling the cracking porcelain.

Bending down with as little pressure on the right foot as possible, I dug out my perfume. Twenty-three spritzes total from feet to head. When it hit my neck, the skin sizzled, like pouring salt on a slug. Aaaaah! But worse. The slug would die, but this didn't stop. I hopped to the sink, splashed water on my burnt neck, rubbed the foam soap on it. And I looked at my reflection.

Red rashes smeared my face and neck, concentrating at my chin where the blisters bubbled. So many of them, pimpled across my jaw like a teenager who ate too much chocolate. The tiny lumps formed a terrain on my face. A touch and they could erupt, and it would feel like burning lava.

I splashed cold water on my chin and ran my fingers over the delicate little volcanoes. Something thicker than water lubricated my fingertips. Pus. My face was oozing pus. I blotted the water and discharge with a paper towel. Even with the bubbles and lesions and scorched skin, I looked better than anyone who dipped their pizza in ranch dressing. That could not have just been tea. Did that Fanta fanatic in the parking lot blast me with a shot of pepper spray as well? That would explain the burning upon burning, and the bubonic plague breaking out on my jaw.

My face stung, and peeling off my leggings on one leg was a challenge. My right ankle was purple and swollen. At least my cankle would only be temporary.

Putting on my pumps made me realize my foot was swollen too. Balancing on stilettos was tough, but if Lizzo could do it, so could I.

A knock on the door.

"There's someone in here," I shouted. Fifteen minutes is lightning speed for this before and after.

I took a last look at myself in the mirror. It's not fair that I'd be the only one to see how I'm really pulling off this injured chic. Selfie time! The shot captured the whole look, from my new highlights to my pearl earrings to tie-neck blouse tucked into my high-rise capris. I uploaded the full-body shot to Instagram, playing with the lighting so the blue tones of my ankle and red blisters on my face really popped.

'Burn victim vibes this morning. I've been attacked by two large women before 8 a.m. I can barely walk and I'm pretty sure the second-degree burns on my face are infected. #bathroomselfie.'

Shared. Gotta be authentic. That's how you make it on the 'Gram.

The line didn't stretch to the door anymore, but that may be due more to the customers themselves shrinking. The extra-belt-hole crowd apparently received their whipped cream-covered calorie bombs and went about pushing us all closer to the center of the Earth. The line moved quickly, since I multitasked, running through the points for the morning meeting. I was so late by now I wouldn't have time to review the P.M.S. I could just assume Charlotte was holding back the project, like she would a relay team. My phone buzzed. Instagram. @mulva liked my post. So did @gina832. @realness87943 followed me.

Finally some recognition!

When it was my turn to order, I didn't even speak and the cashier said, "Venti quad half-oat, half-almond, five-pump sugar-free vanilla latte, no foam" like she was repeating what was in my brain back to me.

"Yes." She wasn't familiar; how did she know my order?

Hoop, I thought. *Come in, Hoop.* Nothing. Did he give me a lemon? I should have trusted my instincts. No real revolutionary company would have someone with moobs as a representative.

"Karen?" The barista said. Was that a question or was that how he ended all his words? He was new, and more flaming than my scalded skin.

I took a sip. It wasn't right. Only four pumps. Ugh. No time to send it back.

"How did you know my name?" I asked.

"Wild guess."

Everyone was seated around the conference room table when I limped in. They couldn't hide their shock. I could pass for anyone in Starbucks, but Y.I.N.Z. knew better. My team knew I never came in without makeup, my short bob perfectly puffed in the back and my bangs swept to the side.

"Karen, are you all right?" Megan, my direct report, asked.

"Just a bit of a mishap this morning, and believe me, the people responsible will be held accountable."

I was already planning my one-star Yelp! review of the Starbucks for serving psychos weapons they could use to attack fellow customers. And the gym? Well, that manager would be managing debt more sizable than mine by the time I was done lodging my complaints. And that trainer would have to go back to fantasy school for another made-up degree. Plotting my revenge had taken my mind off the pain on my drive here while the ankle throbbed and changed colors. And Hoop better hope I suffer no permanent damage from these injuries, because I'm damn sure they've got something to do with that Bug in my ear. I seem to be able to think to everyone except him.

Based on my horrific treatment at the gym and Starbucks, it appeared this Bug joke was projecting my thoughts outward, or forcing me to verbalize them. If that happened in the conference room, my C.U.N.T. would be out of control. I concentrated on remaining upright in my heels first, then controlling my thoughts. Think only of work. Deadlines. Projects. Clients. How Charlotte was delaying everything by prioritizing eating over work. No! How the whole team was signed off last night by dinner time. Yes, that was much better.

Pus was seeping down my face. It was an opaque yellow when I checked it in my car mirror, so I assumed it was the same color that dripped from my chin to the floor now. *Deal with it, you slobs. I've been dealing with your B.O. and your fat rolls and your F.U.P.A.s for months.* Oh shit.

"No one has B.O. here," Jess said.

"What's a F.U.P.A.?" Christine the intern asked.

*Jesus, they didn't teach anything in college these days, did they? May as well go to kineso-whatever school. She can't be worse at that than she is at production artist work.* No! Stop it, Karen! Pro-Well website!

"Hey, Christine's doing a great job," Charlotte said.

*Oh, of course, one fat ass stands—or sits—up for another fat ass. Solidarity. An impenetrable wall of blubber. Where are the harpoons*? Dammit, my brain's multitasking talents were sabotaging me.

"Char isn't fat," Jess said.

Did I put the Bug in backwards? No, Hooper said just to place it on my ear and the tech would do the rest. Where was he? And why can everybody read my mind? No, Bug Wireless, your technology isn't going to disrupt anything. Anything except my life.

I squeezed one of the Bug's slick, plastic legs between my fingers, trying to pry it up again. If I could break one, I'd get the rest. It didn't budge. I kept trying.

"What is that on your ear?" Juan, the developer with the hideous, third-world hairlip scar asked. "Looks like a beetle. Why do you have a beetle on your head?"

*Of all people, he should know what a beetle is, considering they eat them where he's from.*

"We don't eat beetles in the Bronx," Juan said.

"It's not a beetle. It's a Bug, and it's going to change how we communicate. We'll be meeting about it later this morning."

Brian sneezed. Then he sneezed again. He was turning redder than my burned face.

"I'm sorry, that perfume is killing me." He sounded like he had a clothespin over his nose and ran out of the room.

I continued trying to break the legs. They were stronger than any plastic I'd ever encountered.

"Karen, what are you doing?" Jess asked.

Did that bitch look amused? Yes, she did. *Is this what I ran over Kyle for? To get saddled with defective technology and mocked by these losers*? Oh shit. Think something else, fast!

*I got my peaches down in Georgia.*

*Thank you for coming to my TED talk.*

*Rosé all day*!

"You ran over Kyle?" Juan's jaw dropped.

"I heard it too!" Jess said. "You killed him. I knew it! I fucking knew it."

"I'm calling the cops." Charlotte started tapping on her phone.

I lunged at her and knocked the phone from her hand, my cankle turning over in the process. The pain was so bad it made me scream.

I straightened myself up, and my team surrounded me—that group of seven misfits that were allowed to be unkempt freaks because they were "creatives."

"Kyle was nice," Megan said. "If he was still around, I would have gotten a raise. Instead, you told Blake I didn't show the necessary commitment to the agency, that I spent too much time filling my water bottle at the cooler."

She stepped toward me, holding her rollerball pen like a prison shiv. Jess raised her laptop over her head, ready to strike. Juan and Ken crushed their near-empty Red Bull cans in their hands, brandishing the sharp corners toward me.

Charlotte recovered her phone, but she didn't dial, just stood there, staring at me. I didn't have time to duck when she threw it into my forehead, right where the bruise from my phone at the gym was already turning brown. Blisters popped, sending viscous pus and blood into my eyes. I blinked, trying to form tears, but they just mingled with the gore to form a red, translucent filter over my vision.

Something cold hit my arm. It didn't hurt. Oh wait, yes it did. I knew blood was warm, but it felt cold as it gushed from my forearm. Squinting, I could see Juan pulling his hand away. Ken swiped at me with his matching aluminum-can knuckles. He scraped my arm near the gash Juan had left, but I got the better of the altercation. Blood flew from my arm into his face. He should have thanked me. The spatter covered his pimples.

A horrible pain erupted in my leg, like my team of Judases were driving in the first nail. It sounded like a pop and a zipper at the same time as it ripped through the flesh and muscle and whatever else held my bone in place. I jerked away. A pen stuck out of the side of my leg. Blood and black ink ran down my thigh.

I left it there, keeping at least some of the blood in my leg, and started my run from the conference room. It took one step, shifting my weight on the right leg, to know it wasn't a flesh wound. With a hole in the muscle, every movement sent a searing pain impaling my thigh. The ankle throbbed. But it wouldn't stop me. My purse over my shoulder, I clenched my teeth and pushed past Christine. Jess stood between me and the open door. She tossed her laptop on the conference table and reached down. I knew she was a psycho! Those tattoo people always are. She plunged the pen deeper into my leg and I screamed. She moved it around, doodling on my bone like she did in my C.U.N.T.

I kicked, freeing the pen from her hand and knocking her back, but also opening the flesh and sending more blood gushing down to the floor like Niagara Falls. As Jess crawled back to her feet, the felt tip of a dry-erase marker slammed into my forehead. Charlotte dragged it across my face. Blisters popped, sending a cascade of mucous-like pus down my nose. The fat designer was all that was blocking my escape. She smirked, that smug expression that gets all those fire emojis in the comments.

"You're done," she said.

*You're fat. But not so fat, I can't push past.*

"Charlotte isn't fat!"

"You're going to prison!"

"Call the cops!"

My ankle throbbed and the pen still jutted from my leg, but I didn't stop hobble-running from my team that had apparently been bitten by rabid dogs this morning. Blood and pus and tears puddled beneath every step like some sort of a prison slop. The cleaning lady would finally have to do her job tonight.

Outside, I stumbled to my car. My ankle rolled again. Fuck! Fuck the heels. I threw them at Blake's Charger. The alarm went off, honking morse code or something. Fuck you, Blake, for getting me involved in this fraud with that pig Hooper. A rock implanted itself into my good heel. It dug in deeper and deeper as I dragged my bleeding leg behind me. Another pebble lodged between my toes. I was almost to the X6. I could stand the pain a little longer. It couldn't have been worse than the neuropathy those Blizzard lickers with diabetes felt before the merciful doctors sawed off their swollen hooves. I'm still better than them. With the rollerball tattooing my bone, blood and green ejaculate oozing from my face and leg like a merry celebration of bodily fluids, I was still better off than 70% of the population.

Back in the X6, I excavated the rocks from my feet. They left dents, but not much blood. And my French pedicure wasn't even chipped. I snapped a photo of the tie-dyed ankle, uploaded to the 'Gram.

'If you can't handle me at my worst, you don't deserve me when I'm slaying. #thatswhatsup'

I tossed my Starbucks cup out the window and stepped on the gas. Who knew it would wiggle the pen tip in a way that felt like how nails on a chalkboard sounded. The torment pulsed from the leg and the ankle, making the road in front of me momentarily black. Driving wasn't ideal. An ambulance would have been more appropriate, but there was no time for a hospital detour, not with the mess in my garage.

I had a plan. After Charlotte reached for her phone, I started multitasking. While fending off their stabbing and clawing and marker attacks, I was thinking about disposing of a corpse. I'd have to expedite. If I was good at anything, it was getting things done fast. The cops were my deadline. Hilary's fat ass would be in the river before they arrived at my place. Hey, my team did me a favor by their callous attack. I wouldn't have to explain the garage blood. I'd still file a complaint with HR obviously though. And Bug Wireless. Even if I had to track down their investors.

I cranked up the tunes. Miley took my mind off the pain. The roads were clearer at 8:45 a.m. than 5:30 p.m. Maybe I'd be able to get home without any obstructions, no one in my way. I rolled down the windows as I hit a goddamn red light. Moving my foot to the brake pedal repeated the whole flood of pain and cloud of blackness. Miley needed to be louder to drown out that awful guitar sound coming from the Hyundai next to me. The light turned and I floored it. Just three more lights until I could turn onto the winding residential road leading to my house. Roll the skinless carcass into the river and get this parasite out of my ear even if I had to pull a Van Gogh to do it.

I flew through the next three greens, but when I turned down the homestretch, my luck changed. A kid, a fat one like most of them are these days, was challenging the structural integrity of a bike. He wasn't riding fast. Of course not. His heart would explode. He pedaled right in front of my car and I so badly wanted to see his puffy little body bounce off the hood. The pain rippled through my ankles and the plugged hole in my leg when I slammed down the gas, but it would be worth it when that Cheeto chomper soared through the air. Would he bounce? Of course he wouldn't, but who would blame me for wondering based on his ball shape?

The kid was within inches of the front bumper when he swerved into the empty opposite lane. I followed his lead, but he swerved back. I wanted to kill that kid so bad, wanted to see his fat little corpse go *splat* on the asphalt. I wanted to see his warped bike in the street as a foreboding sign for what would be found next. His fat parents would come waddling into the street, see his mangled body. And I wanted to back over him as they watched, their little dough boy looking like he'd had some trouble rising.

But I couldn't. Every time I zigged, he zagged. It was like he anticipated my every jerk of the wheel, like he could read my mind… Fuck! This goddamn Bug!

My street was the next turn, but I was tempted to keep driving, to chase down this human pinball. Maybe my luck was changing; he turned right. I followed. This was where I'd get him, on the straightaway. After the turn, he hopped onto the sidewalk.

Oh well.

Then, standing in the street, forming an offensive line (like, offensive to the eyes) of blubber must have been fifty of the fattest bacon biters north of the Mason-Dixon line. Beer bellies and muffin tops ballooned over the extra-hole belts around that arbitrary point that they considered their waists. T-shirts stretched to near transparency. Blubber against blubber, nowhere for air to pass between them. An hour earlier, they could have blocked out the sun. The kid was gone, out of my way. This line of hypertensive adults was standing in front of my house. I'd have to get through them to reach my garage.

Shit. I shouldn't have idled. They were waddling closer, shuffling footsteps almost synchronized, the labored breathing of this minuscule movement audible from yards away. I started to open my door to make a run for it, but the line was curving. They were surrounding me. I pulled the door shut and stomped the gas, sending a knife through my thigh. The car picked up to 40 mph and collided with the wall of flab.

That's not possible! The X6 should have plowed them over, but my head slammed back into the seat, then forward. The airbag deployed, pinning me back. The engine was quiet, but this time the bones I heard cracking were mine. The airbag deflated. They were all still standing there. How were they doing this? They should be on the ground, their bodies flattened and covered in tire tracks. But they didn't show a scratch, and they were moving in. They were against the bumper yet getting closer. How? The ominous sound of bending metal. The X6 was compressing.

As the moon roof glass shattered, I squeezed my eyes shut and ducked my head. The tiny glass pebbles cascaded down my back and into my shirt. The steering wheel pressed closer, pushing my spine into the seat, the glass burrowing into my back.

The car was getting smaller, like it would have felt six months ago. I unfastened my seatbelt and pressed my hands on the wheel to leverage my body up and around it. As I stretched, what felt like a nail stuck in my lung. My breath was short, and it made a pathetic sound. I pressed as hard as I could and my abs made it over the wheel. I lifted my right leg, trying to stand my foot on the seat. With the right height I could escape through the moon roof.

The car kept shrinking as the donut munchers pushed their bulk into the hood. Before I could slither out the window, the steering wheel pressed into my injured cankle, pinning it against the seat. I jerked it, but the swelling made it too thick to escape. My left foot was like a swimmer's on a starting block, my hands holding tight on the door where I'd thankfully left the window rolled down. I flexed all three and tensed myself, yanking my right foot. One, two, three, now! The bones cracked. I couldn't tell where. The foot? The ankle? Who knew and who cared? It seared and stabbed and throbbed and I wished it was off my body, but it was free. Mangled beyond recognition, in all colors but skin tone.

I stood on the seat, balancing on my good foot, my midsection draped over the roof. The car was compressing, my only exit shrinking fast. I hopped, scraping my stomach on the glass shards. They were now embedded front and back, stinging and dripping blood. I slithered toward the edge, reaching as far to the ground as I could. I was a couple feet away, but I went for it anyway, jumping to get my hips in line with the roof, then folding my torso down and slowly easing myself to the ground, hands first. They hit the asphalt and the burning of ripped palms was instantaneous. The rest of my body tumbled out, my destroyed right leg hitting the pavement. The angled pen plunged deeper into my leg, the tip scraping my bone. The right foot flopped on the ground, the impact finally drawing blood. I tried to pull myself to my feet, but even my meager weight was too much. The right ankle snapped and sent me back to the ground. The jagged bone pierced through the skin and my foot was hanging off by a ligament or a tendon or whatever that creepy bloody string was.

I dragged myself across the ground on my stomach. The fatties weren't coming after me. Their work was done. They couldn't get in my way anymore.

Each crawl scraped my bleeding palms, loose pebbles implanting themselves in the open wounds. It hurt worse than any belt buckle digging into my gut six months ago, like nothing I could ever imagine, but I was so close to home. It was like those final few pounds last week. My stomach felt like it was eating itself but stepping on the scale made it worth the pain. My hands reached the grass, the damp blades cooling them. Then a wet, squishy warmth further soothed the raw flesh. I raised my hand. It was brown. Dog shit. At least it wasn't causing more pain. I kept crawling, sliding through the wet feces toward my house. It smeared on my shirt and down my legs. I reached the single step to my front door.

My keys were still in the car.

*Hoop. Hoop.* I tried one last time to make the Bug work. It was the only thing still working on my bloody, pus-oozing, shit-covered, broken body.

As I left a turd handprint on the step, pulling myself into a cobra position, the front door swung open. There he was. The Bug worked. Hooper.

"Oh dear, let's get you inside," he said.

I slithered through the door. There was no point in getting in a position other than horizontal. In my living room, I rolled onto my back and it was like sleeping on a bed of nails. The shit started hardening on me, but I didn't care.

"Let's have a look at you," he said, standing over my supine body that still looked better than his. I couldn't see his face from this angle with his gut in the way. Hair peaked through the gap in the fabric where the buttons barely fastened. "Blisters on the face. A broken pen in your leg. Bloody shit-covered hands. Now I'm not a doctor, but I don't think you want to get shit in open wounds. And your foot! Would you look at that! I've never seen anything like that before."

*Please help me*, I thought.

"I will," he said. "But first, let me take a selfie." He pulled a phone from his pocket and angled it so we were both in the photo. "Now that that's out of the way, let me get some supplies and I'll fix you right up."

*No, don't leave.*

"I'm just going to the kitchen."

I was cold, not like it was winter. It was coming from inside me. Inner cold. Chills. I would have shuddered, but I couldn't move. Weak. So weak. Too weak to feel the pain anymore.

Thunderous footsteps and Hooper was a blur above me. A bottle in one hand, a silver blade in the other.

He spilled the bottle over my ankle. It stung. I wasn't too numb for pain. I screamed, wailed, nearly choked on a sob. It was easier to do that than speak. He lowered my bread knife to my throbbing ankle and everything turned to black.

The blackness dissipated. My Live, Laugh, Love poster taunted me from across the room. I was seated now. Upright, on my couch, staring straight ahead. It smelled like the office bathroom after Charlotte left it. Some awful guitar music played softly; I had to strain to hear what passed for vocals. And when I did, ugh! And my ears had been the only parts of my body that weren't in pain. Not even the one covered by the Bug.

*Put on the Cardi.*

"Oh, you're out of luck there. All our Cardi B is in use right now on some Nazi punks. Queen wasn't going to have the right effect on them, like it will for you. Listen to Mr. Mercury sing about how there's no escape from reality. Fitting, isn't it? Considering your current situation."

I stopped focusing on the awful noise. The pain rushed back like a tsunami. Pins and needles in my foot, throbbing in my leg, burning face and hands, a thousand tiny knives stabbing me in the back.

"It was probably good you passed out for that," Hooper said. "You didn't have vodka or whiskey or anything, only rosé, so I had to use that to sanitize the wound. And since you don't really eat, you don't have any sharp knives and so the procedure didn't go quite as smoothly as I'd hoped." The fat man was sitting in my chair, at my desk beneath the poster. Rosé was on his lap. He stroked her pretty little head.

*What procedure*?

"Your foot, of course! As I said, I'm not a doctor, so I fixed you up the best I could. Take a look."

I tilted my head forward and the whiplash from the crash sent it right back. Raising my leg, still painful, was more successful. But I still couldn't see my foot. I raised my leg higher.

"Looking for this?" Hooper asked.

No. It couldn't be. He dangled it over my face. My foot with its little infinity symbol tattooed above the middle toe. I kicked up my leg, the pain searing. It ended in a stump, crude black stitching sealing in the blood and bones. I opened my mouth to scream, but a garbled whine was all that came out.

"Hey—you finally hit your goal weight. You're under a hundred pounds. Congratulations! Only thing is I see you've got one of those fancy scales that's activated by bare feet. That's gonna be a problem for you now. I suppose you could place this on the other sensor, but after a couple days it's gonna get a little mushy. Unless... unless we preserve it! You got any embalming fluid?"

*This is your fault*, I thought, glaring at him. It was all I could do. *You put this in my ear and now everyone can hear my thoughts. It doesn't fucking work. Your bullshit technology doesn't work.*

"It works exactly as it should," Hooper said.

*I can't hear anyone else*!

"You're not supposed to. It says so in the agreement. It's not my fault you didn't think you needed to read the NDA."

*You tricked me. Because of that thing, you know everything about me and you destroyed my life.*

"I don't know about you because of the Bug. I gave you the Bug *because* I know you. This device, it is revolutionary. And exclusive, only available to people who deserve it. And I can make it exactly what those people need. For you, it worked exactly as I intended."

He knelt down in front of me, his disgusting mayonnaise breath even worse than the poop.

"I know everything about you. I know who you are, what you've done. But you know all that. So let's talk about what happens next. You're a cripple. No more running. Your car, that you couldn't afford anyway, is crushed. Your job is gone, after that C.U.N.T. fiasco. Your colleagues already called the cops, but I'm half-tempted to have my people clean up your garage so they don't have anything tangible to take you in for. Disfigured face. That thing in your ear projecting all your horrible thoughts. Good luck getting through a job interview."

I grabbed the Bug, but my blood and shit covered hand slipped away, not that I had the strength anyway.

"You'll be here, eating your way through your depression. Real depression. Not the self-diagnosed OCD you like to claim as an excuse for being a cunt. Getting fatter and fatter until you're fused with the couch and they'll have to use a crane to get you out when the bank forecloses."

*No.*

"Oh yes, but I do have good news. Your Instagram is heating up. Three hundred followers today! Keep posting your life here, you'll be an influencer in no time. I keep an eye on those, so I know what works, and Karen, you are on your way to Instagram stardom. And, of course, you'll have your friend."

*You*?

He laughed. It sounded more like a cough. "No, I have meetings. I'm a busy man, a very busy man. Many departments to oversee, people to manage, you know the feeling. You met my human resources department outside. I'm talking about her." He pointed to my right.

It hurt to turn my head. The sight was worse than the pain. A body that's been run over by a car and dragged a mile on blacktop then left in a garage overnight is a lot yuckier than it sounds. The face, or what was left of it, was flattened like it was shaved off by a rusty razor. The nose was gone, only a hole in the open wound. Black pebbles stuck in the deep red viscous blood.

The front of her shirt, or poncho or revival tent or whatever it was, was gone, revealing craters where parts of her sagging breasts had shredded. The remaining flesh hung like frayed ribbons. What was left of the gut pooched over her skinny jeans. They must have fused with the cellulite beneath them; aside from some holes, they were mostly intact.

I looked away. Ew! *Hilary isn't my friend. Get her out of my house.*

"Hilary? That's Matilda Bennet. Oh, you thought that was Hilary Spencer? Your neighbor who didn't like your dog shitting on her walkway? That's not the girl I pried off your axle in the garage. We all really look the same to you, don't we?"

I pushed myself off the couch onto my feet, but I only had one of them, so I fell flat on the floor. My cheek pressed against the hardwood. Tears mixed into the blood and pus.

"Welcome to Hell, Karen," Hooper said. "Where, as you've seen, you don't want to speak to the manager."

# SKIN DEEP

LUCAS MILLIRON

I wiped the juices off my dick with a blue rag, then used it to clean my patient's mouth and pussy. It was an accident, of course. I wasn't trying to make such a mess. Although, seeing creamy strands of semen across her unconscious face made me ready for round two. I pulled out my phone and took a few pictures, wishing I'd remembered to film it this time. I like taking souvenirs and mementos. With seconds to spare, I pulled up my scrub pants before Roy, my anesthesiologist, came back.

"How's the patient holding, Mark?" Roy asked.

"All vitals normal." I threw away the evidence in the biohazard bin.

"Thanks, Doc," Roy said as he began reviving the patient. "I didn't expect to be talking to Felicia for so long. Once she gets started—"

"Don't mention it!" I patted him on the shoulder. "Took me five wives to learn that marriage ain't for me."

"Think you'll ever settle down again?"

I looked him up and down.

"Ha! Never. And it seems to be working out quite nicely for me."

"You haven't even had a steady girlfriend since I met you. Wait, not true. There was Rachelle. What ever happened to her?"

"Didn't like cats."

"You broke up with her over a cat?"

"It's a deal breaker. No one comes between me and old Uncle Frank."

"How long have you had that cat?"

"Franks gotta be going on, about…I dunno…twelve years now."

"You let your geriatric cat come between you and a relationship?"

"Only monsters and serial killers don't like pets."

"Yeah, but Rachelle was cute. Wasn't she some kind of constitutional lawyer too—?"

Anajeli, my COMT—certified ophthalmic medical technician—entered the operating room. Girl was a walking hourglass, all hips and tits with a waist you could wrap both hands around.

"Dr. Irvin," she said in her thick Cuban accent. "There's a patient waiting for you in the lobby. No appointment, but he says it's important."

"If I have to." I gave an exaggerated groan, smiling and laughing as I winked at Anajeli.

I headed toward the lobby, stopping in my tracks when I saw the person waiting for me. My blood boiled against my cold, clammy skin, and I was thankful the room was empty except for Steven. The last thing I needed were witnesses if I bashed the man's skull in.

"What the fuck do you want?" I asked, walking up to him.

The man looked like shit, smelled like shit, was shit. His nappy gray beard was dreadlocked around his jawline. The wrinkles in his face were drawn deeper with motor oil and grease. If I'd lit a match in front of his mouth, he'd have barked fire from all the cheap vodka on his breath.

"That any way to greet your father?" Steven adjusted his MAGA hat.

*I'm sitting in a bedroom at Steven's trailer. I hear the aluminum can crush in his fist.*

*"God damn it, Mark!" he yells. "I told you to pick your shit up!"*

*My body's shivering. There's no where to run. His steel-toe boots sound heavy on the hollow trailer floor. The door opens. I see the wooden paddle in his hand. My heart's ready to explode. Sweat runs down my face. If I cry, he'll only hit me harder. Why did I forget to pickup my toys? Mommy says Daddy loves me. But why does it have to hurt?*

Steven had lost weight since the last time I saw him and the stretched-out camo shirt now fit him like socks on a rooster.

"We have to talk," he said.

"I ain't got any money."

"I don't want money."

"No drugs either."

"I got that covered."

"Then what the fuck do you want?"

"I'm dying."

"No shit. You've been using that line the last ten years. First the colon cancer, then the brain tumor. What's it this time?"

Steven tried handing me a manila envelope. Maybe I was too pissed off to notice he'd been carrying it in the first place, but I didn't give a shit.

"Uh-uh." I shook my head. "No fucking way."

Steven took off his sunglasses. His eyes were a deep, piss yellow. He pulled down his lower lid to make his point before putting on his crooked, coke-bottle thick wire spectacles.

"Hepatitis got real bad." He averted his jaundice eyes from mine. "Doc says I don't qualify for a liver transplant. Addicts don't get second chances."

"Fuck you they don't!" I barked. "You piece of shit. How dare you come into my place of business and tell me about second fucking chances!"

I felt my neck and forehead throbbing as my heart pounded against my rib-cage.

"Son…" Tears fell down the man's cheeks.

"Don't be so pathetic." I rolled my eyes. "I'm not paying for your sins. You're the junky who couldn't figure out what a clean needle looks like. You screwed up your own life well enough with me out of it."

"I'm sorry I hurt you," his voice quavered. "I couldn't help myself. Life wasn't—"

"No, no, no," I cut him off. "Don't give me that 'life isn't fair' bullshit. You've been feeding me that excuse since I was kid. You brought this all on yourself."

"Please," he begged. "All I want is to spend time with you. I don't have much left."

I sized the sniveling fuck up and down. He was a cockroach, a kernel of dogshit stuck to the bottom of my shoe. The man was beneath me.

"Get out of my building before I call the cops."

"Funny thing about second chances," Steven said as he turned around, "sometimes you don't notice, even when you're staring it in the face."

Soon as he stepped out the door, I picked up and slammed one of the hot yellow waiting room chairs into the ground. The sound it made as the recycled plastic shattered into a dozen pieces was satisfying. Still, all things considering, I'd say I kept my cool.

I went to the bathroom and stood in front of the mirror. I stared at my reflection. Parts of Steven's anatomy glared back at me. We shared the same hairline, same nose and eyes. If I ever grew a beard, it'd probably look a lot like his. I was nothing like my father. The fact that I shared his physical likeness disgusted me.

Of course, I thought about plastic surgery, of removing Steven's nose and brow, but his contamination was more than skin deep, it was genetic. My heart raced. I cocked my arm to punch the mirror but stopped myself short, instead pounding my fists into the marble countertop.

I needed to slow the fuck down, to find some kind of release. Pulling out my phone and cock, I started scrolling through my photo gallery. Not all the women were unconscious or sedated, but it sure as shit made taking pictures a lot easier. Sometimes scrolling through old photos is worse than finding meat-beat videos on Pornhub, you know what I mean? When you've got twenty windows up and you're not sure which one is gonna make the final cut, so you keep on scrolling? Usually it takes me half an hour before I find something I can rub one out to, but I was still reeling from Steven's visit, and all I needed was to bust a nut and release some tension.

I stopped on a photo of Mrs. Parks. She was a cute broad, and technically a GILF since her sixteen-year-old daughter got knocked up. Didn't take me long. Seeing my jizz rolling between her crow's feet made me harder than Chinese algebra. Jerked off for about five minutes before I blew my load into the sink. Humiliation is such a powerful aphrodisiac. I washed off my meat and potatoes in the sink, dried them with a paper towel, and went back out to finish closing shop for the evening.

I passed Roy and Anajeli still in the recovery hall on the way to my office.

"Everything okay?" Anajeli asked me.

I pointed back toward the lobby. "Next time you see that ass hat come here, you call the cops!"

"Hey, whoa." Roy held up held up his hands. "What happened?"

"Sorry." I smacked my forehead with my fist. "I just can't stand that guy."

"Who is he?" Anajeli asked.

"Not important."

"We gotta know something." Roy shrugged. "Especially if you wanna put a trespass notice on the guy."

"I don't wanna talk about it, alright?" I huffed and rolled my eyes.

"I'm really sorry, Dr. Irving." Anajeli rushed over and grabbed my arm. "It was my fault. I should have asked more questions. I just assumed he was a patient. He looked so sick…"

She looked at me with those puppy dog eyes.

"It's alright." I rolled my eyes. "It's my biological father."

"Oh." Roy nodded.

"He's a piece of shit," I replied, before remembering I was in the company of one of my techs. "Sorry, didn't mean to swear. He's been trying to guilt trip me into a relationship with him since I was twelve. I'm constantly telling him to back off, but he won't get the hint."

"I'm so sorry." Anajeli frowned. "I'll be more careful next time."

"You couldn't have known." I patted her on the back. "Alright, we've just about finished. Why don't you go ahead and start closing up. I'll deal with charts tomorrow."

"Alright." Anajeli waved and headed toward the nurse's station. "Bye, Doc!"

Roy's eyes dropped to her ass as soon as she turned around. Everyone knew he had the hots for her, everyone except Anajeli, of course. She was out of his league though, and a good fifteen years his junior. But I couldn't say I blamed him for wanting a piece of that fine Latin ass.

I cleared my throat and looked at Roy.

"Here." I handed him a blue surgical towel.

"What's this for?"

"To cover that boner."

Roy's face blushed like a tomato. "Is it that obvious?"

I laughed. "Everyone knows you got the hots for her. Except Anajeli."

"Shit! I'm such an asshole! I'm so sorry, me and Felicia…well…we haven't exactly been intimate in a while."

"Relax." I slapped his back. "I'm kidding. How long's a while? More importantly, what's got you in pussy time-out anyway?"

Roy sighed, wiping his receding hairline with the towel. "Well, it's been a about a year and a half."

"Holy shit! A year and a half??"

"Yeah. So I've been…watching porn. She caught me and that only made things worse."

*"Porn?"*

"She's weird about stuff like that."

"Weird how?"

"She says it's cheating."

I about busted a seam laughing.

"You shitting me?" I asked, trying to catch my breath.

"I know, it's weird." Roy blushed again.

"Fuck if it's weird! It's absurd! Jesus fuck, no wonder you can't keep your eyes off Anjeli."

"I'm so sorry, I don't wanna make things awkward around her."

"Don't sweat it, pal." I wrapped one arm around his shoulder and waved my other as I spoke. "Perhaps, I can help you. Not with Anjeli, of course, but every man has needs. Fantasy is healthy. And sometimes, we have to be a little…indulgent."

"What are you saying?"

"I'm not saying anything." I unwrapped my arm and stood in front of him, counting his problems on one hand. "No sex with your wife in over a year. You can't watch porn. What I'm asking is: when's the last time you've busted a nut?"

"Oh jeez." Roy hesitated. "I guess…"

"Stop right there. If you're guessing, it's been too long."

"Well how long has it been for you?"

"Fifteen minutes. Why does it matter? I'm not the patient here, Roy. You need some attention and your wife's not tending to her marital duties. How about you come out with me tonight?"

"I'm sorry, but I'm not sure I follow?" Roy sized me up.

"I didn't say I'd fuck you!" I wrapped my arm around his neck again, pulling him away from the door. "Listen. I have some friends who can help you out. All I gotta do is make a few calls. I'm sure these girls would just love to get to know you!"

"I don't know, Dr. Irvin."

"Dear God, Roy!" I smacked my forehead for effect. "Six years we've been working together now? Call me Mark."

"Mark, I'm just not sure I can do something like that. Porn is one thing but—"

"If your wife cared, she'd be riding you like a Ferris wheel!"

"Felicia would kill me if she found out. Forget no sex. She'll never—"

"Don't worry." I put my hand on his chest. "Tell her we're pulling an all-nighter. I'll even keep ya on the clock incase she checks your pay stubs or something."

"You sure this will work?"

"Trust me. I'm a doctor!"

I drove, promising I'd drop him off as soon as we'd finished having our fun. The problem with Roy's brand-new Tesla was the tracking feature. His wife kept him on a short leash alright. She even bugged his phone with a spy app to keep tabs on him at work. We left that back at the office, too.

I was still heated from Steven's visit.

"I am nothing like that man! I mean, nothing!" I punched the steering wheel.

"I hear ya." Roy sank in his seat. "I had it out with my old man once."

"Not like this fucker." My knuckles were white hot as I gripped the wheel.

"Walk out on ya?"

"Best thing he ever did was get arrested. Then the fuck had to go and find Jesus…"

"Whatcha mean?"

"I mean the bastard turned into a born again. Said it's his mission to earn my forgiveness. He's a fucking Trumper! A racist, backwoods, redneck, republican ass hat. Douche bag can burn in hell."

"What'd he do to you?"

*I'm sitting on the floor in my stepsister's—Heather's—room. The pink wallpaper is pealing like lizard skin. I can feel the dead glass eyes of her dolls and teddy bears watching us, a gang of stuffed voyeurists.*

*"Lay down," Heather tells me.*

*I do as she says. I'm only four, and she's six. You always listen to your elders. My father is standing at the door. Heather unties my shoes.*

"I don't wanna talk about it."

"I didn't know your friends lived near Biscayne Bay?" Roy pointed out the window of my Land Rover. "Felicia and I were thinking of getting a small condo in this area. Maybe when we retire."

"That's nice," I snickered.

The houses in Biscayne Bay were like Botox lips on a stripper. Massive, beautiful houses adorned the intercostal, but Roy had no idea what was hidden just beneath the surface.

Once we entered the gated community, the houses just kept getting bigger. When we pulled up to the driveway of the seven-thousand-square-foot mansion, his eyes lit up like a kid walking through the gates of Willy Wonka's chocolate factory.

The exterior design was modeled after Villa Vizcaya in Miami, though much more modernized. As we approached the front door, a woman opened it. She was blonde, wearing only a pair red Calvin Klein panties. Her breasts hung heavy, nipples pink and hard with dark areolas shaped into hearts.

"Hello, Doctor." The blonde leaned against the door with one hand while rubbing her tit with the other.

"Hi." I looked at Roy, his jaw dangling open. "Roy, this is Alexa. Alexa, Roy."

"Pleasure." She proffered a hand to Roy.

Roy's handshake was about as meek and clammy as a dead fish. He was grinning like a boy about to lose his virginity. A whimper squeaked out from the back of his throat. It could have been a "Hi," or just as easily some indigestion. The last thing I needed was him to bust a nut now and have second thoughts. So I pushed him into the house.

"Welcome to my home away from home!" I said as he stumbled into the marbled foyer.

"Shall I prepare the usual?" Alexa asked, following us inside.

"Usual?" Roy looked at me.

"Make it a double." I smiled. "It's my friend's first time."

"I'll have the girls ready." Alexa kissed my cheek and made her way up the spiral staircase.

"This isn't a cheap street corner whorehouse," I whispered to Roy. "This is the Ritz-Carlton of high-end sex, with clients ranging from news anchors and political influencers to high end bankers."

The house was furnished with the finest whores in Miami and Dade County. The air was perfumed with lavender, cinnamon, and sex. Spectacular oversized terraces, accessible from almost every room, ran along all three levels overlooking downtown Miami and Biscayne Bay.

Roy followed, his head craning to see all the sights and sounds. Music of all kinds thumped and popped into an amalgam of electronic noise peppered with the sounds of pleasure. The walls were black and red with paintings of dicks and pussy mounted in elegant picture frames as if they were works of Rembrandt or Picasso. Marble statues of Greek Gods posed in every hallway, hung with horse cock boners.

Sodom and Gomorrah might have blushed at the kaleidoscope of pleasures available in every size, shape, and color imaginable. Bitches built like line backers oiled their hulking biceps, while fat whores sucked off dick-shaped lollipops. Beautiful exotic woman massaged clients' shoulders while they waited for private rooms.

Blowjobs were given out like popcorn at a ball game. Whores unzipped their Johns and serviced their cocks out in the open, unabashed by the crowds of other waiting clients stroking their meats as they watched. Men screamed in hideous climax behind closed doors, while others fucked right on the Calacatta gold marble floor.

Roy's eyes bulged when he saw the oiled, muscular black man, his massive slab of beef swinging like a tree branch as he walked by.

"What can I say?" I smirked, smacking his chest with the back of my hand. "They're an equal opportunity employer."

As we walked toward the staircase with black oak banisters, I caught sight of a man out of place amongst the crowd. The guy leaned against a wall with an Asian broad servicing his eggroll. He was a white dude with about as much sex appeal as a toad. His fat, pale belly distended over his unbuckled jeans, glistening with loose hairs and sweat.

The gelatinous mess jiggled and slapped the bitch's forehead as his legs buckled beneath the ecstasy. He ran his pudgy fingers through his greasy ponytail, then whipped the slathering of drool from his mustache and goatee. His metal wire glasses fogged as he panted.

For once, I felt bad for a whore. I could smell his yeasty musk from across the room. Roy didn't seem to notice; his attention was fixed at the threesome on the banister. A white girl dressed like Daphne from Scooby Doo was being pounded in the ass by a black dude, when the scrawny white guy in her pussy pulled his dick out and licked her oozing creampie clean.

I grabbed Roy's shoulder to get his attention, then sniffed and tapped my nostril. "You like nose candy?"

"Excuse me?" Roy looked at me as if I'd slapped his face with my dick.

"You like blow?"

"I don't—"

"You're right." I snapped my fingers and pointed at him. "Drinks first."

We made our way up the stairs and to the playroom. The room itself was a sprawling master suite separated with a large ornate pocket door. On one side was a massive California king bed with leg straps chained to the bedframe and a Saint Andrews Cross mounted in the corner.

The focal point of the second room was a large liquor cabinet glistening with fine spirits and a mirror on its countertop along with few baggies of blow. There was a massive couch overlooking a large plush rug. Bookcases filled with shimmering sex toys lined the walls.

As I made my way toward the liquor, I stopped when I noticed Roy wasn't behind me. I turned around and saw him standing outside the room, fixated on something going on down the hall. I went over to see what it was. One of the hookers was riding a ball player we knew from the Florida Marlins sitting naked in a chair at the end of the hall. Her back arched as she cursed in Spanish, bucking the chair with each thrust like a mechanical bull.

I clapped in front of Roy's face.

"Focus, focus, focus!" I said in rhythm to my clapping. "Don't be square."

"Sorry." Roy blinked himself out of his trance.

I closed the door behind us, and Roy followed me to the liquor cabinet. I cracked open a bottle of Glenlivet 18, pouring two glasses, neat.

"Cheers." I clinked my glass to his and knocked it back.

Roy took a sip.

"Don't be a little bitch." I rolled my eyes at him and filled my glass again.

Roy huffed, then took a long swallow before choking on the whiskey's cool burn.

"That's better." I smiled, pouring him another.

"This is all a bit much. I've never…I mean…"

"Don't get all prude on me." I downed my glass and filled it again. "I told you. It's perfectly normal to live out a few fantasies."

"I can't afford this! Felicia's gonna find out as soon as I take out the money!"

"Don't sweat. My treat. I need this as much you do."

"How long have you been coming here?"

"It's best you don't ask questions."

I pulled out a credit card and a hundred-dollar bill, then chopped the coke waiting for me on the mirror.

"You're really doing this?"

"What does it look like?" I licked my finger and rubbed off the coke from the credit card, then rubbed it in my gums. "You sure you don't want any?"

"What the fuck? I didn't know you were serious. Fucking no! I'm not having any!"

"Suite yourself." I shrugged. "I don't know about you, but I couldn't possibly fuck all those girls without a little help from snow white."

*"All* those girls?" Roy licked his lips.

"If you gotta pace yourself and only have one bitch at a time, I understand." I slipped a baggy of coke into my pocket. "At least a guy your age can be proud that he can still sport wood without a blue pill."

"What?"

I glanced down at the boner shooting from inside his scrubs. Roy tried to cover himself with his hands, blushing red.

"Seriously." I chuckled, rolling the hundred-dollar bill into a straw. "That's like, what, five boners in one day? Bless your heart."

I leaned over and snorted two rails of nose candy. It didn't feel like coke. The powder was a little brown and gummy, but man it got my heart beating like a stuck rat.

"What the hell am I doing here?" Roy smacked his forehead.

"Relax. Felicia's never gonna know." I sniffled and sat up, rubbing my nose as the back of my throat went numb.

"Just cause I'm in the doghouse doesn't mean—"

"Don't give me this sanctimonious crap, you're miserable!" I slid the mirror toward him. "Don't make me celebrate alone."

"What are we celebrating?"

"The death of a tyrant!" I held up my glass before guzzling down the whiskey.

"You mean your father?"

"No, Donald fucktard Trump. Of course, my father!" I poured another glass, killing the bottle.

"Did he say how long he has?" Roy sipped his glass.

"Bastards always dying of something. One week it's colon cancer, the next is diabetes, then his bad heart. He didn't say how long, but this time…I'd guess any day now."

"I get it, man, he was a piece of shit." Roy took another heavy gup of whiskey. "But that's kinda messed up to wish on anyone."

"No!" I slammed the bottle against the counter.

Glass exploded like a hand grenade, sending shards everywhere and cutting the back of my hand. I felt its impact but not the pain. The drugs and liquor deadened my senses, and I was glad for it. If I'd been sober, I'd have been furious. I welcomed the numbing intoxication glazing over me.

"No," I said softer, watching the blood run down the back of my hand.

*My heart beats faster as I hear Heather washing her hands. I can feel the weight of the room crushing me as I look up at the ceiling, still lying on the floor. Everything is spinning. Sweat stings my eyes. It's not my sweat, it's Heathers. I can't feel my toes.*

*I drop my head to the left, tears falling down my cheeks. My pants are crumpled on the floor, curled up like a scared puppy. Steven is standing in the doorway, fixing his buckle and wiping his nose with a crusty red shop rag. My heart feels like glass shattered across the floor. I'm four years old. I want to die.*

"You don't get it." I snort a wad of metallic tasting phlegm, holding back the tears brimming behind my eye lids.

I glance over at Roy. His face was buried in the mound of snow. I smiled. Free will is an illusion, for we are slaves bound by genetics and circumstance. After all, a man has needs.

There was a light knock on the door. I grabbed a couple more baggies of coke and stuffed them in my pocket, then cracked open another Glenlivet 18 and took a long pull from the bottle before answering the door. A redhead and a blonde stood in the threshold.

The girls were naked, aside from their signature red and black Calvin Kline panties. They were lean with heavy tits and curvaceous asses, smiling with perfect teeth. Their bodies were impeccable, not a single blemish on their soft, supple flesh.

I invited them in, and they made themselves comfortable on the couch, their flesh glistening, and every orifice moist and wanting. They groaned as they started tasting each other, fingering holes and licking gossamer threads of pussy juice as it dripped down their digits.

Roy was already naked by the time we sauntered over to the couch, suckling the redhead's tits like a pink baby piglet. God, I hoped I'd never look that pathetic.

I grabbed a leather flogger draped over the armrest while Roy buried his face in the redhead's pussy. The leather creaked as I tested its grip and weight.

I snapped my fingers. The blonde stood up and followed me into the bedroom area, closing the room divider behind us. Before we got started, I set up my camera phone on the dresser by the bed and started recording—there's something sexy about watching yourself pounding the fuck out of a hot blonde. It's a different experience to the unconscious girls back at the office, more of a challenge humiliating them.

I let her unzip my fly and pull out my cock. She got on her knees and spat on her hand, using it as lubricant as she jerked it. I took another pull from the bottle, feeling it burn as it ran down my throat.

"That's right," I spat as the bottle left my lips. "Daddy's had a hard day."

"You like it rough?" the girl cooed.

"If I wanted yapping—" I leaned over and grabbed a fist full of hair "—I'd have bought a Pomeranian. Shut the fuck up and come to Daddy."

Blondie cocked an eyebrow and licked her lips. I swung my flogger against her ass. It hit with a crack. She moaned as the leather bit into her soft pale flesh, stinging it with lines of pink. Blondie took my old boy all the way, kissing my pelvis. Snot bubbles spat from her nose as she deep throated it, her tongue cradling my balls. I swung the flogger again, harder. I could feel her grunts resonating against the base of my cock.

I hit her again, and again. Her cries matched my intensity. I hung the flog over my shoulder and grabbed her by the chin, lifting her to her feet. Tears smudged her mascara as she gasped for breath. I wrapped my flog around her throat and kissed her, tasting the salt of my seed on her lips. Blondie worked my shaft with unabated enthusiasm.

I looked at the wall and saw the giant mirror hung in a black ornately carved frame. It wasn't my own reflection I saw on the receiving end of the blow job. It was Steven. The way his moist, flabby flesh sagged against his bones repulsed me. His crinkled brow furled with sinister delight, the same look he'd given me while standing in the doorway of Heather's room.

"I don't have much time left, son." His words echoed in the room.

I threw Blondie onto the bed. She giggled as she rolled on her belly and pressed her ass into my pelvis. I spat on her asshole and rubbed my dick up and down her shitter, then shoved it inside her. She screamed, unprepared as I stretched her colon.

"Shut the fuck up!" I shouted, smacking her with my flogger.

The leather hit hard, tearing into her back. Thin strands of blood peppered the raw flesh. Her sphincter clenched around my dick as she screamed again. I leaned over and grabbed her by the throat to shut her up. The girl bucked and kicked. I felt her heart beating in my hands, felt the blood rushing through her neck, feeding her brain with life.

My dick throbbed for release, but I wasn't done. I yanked my cock from its brown sheath and finished taking off my pants, then fished around my pocket for the little bag of coke. Blondie scuttled up to the headboard and curled into a ball. I stuck my nose in the bag and breathed deep. Dust trickled off my nose as I sniffled. I couldn't taste the scotch anymore or feel its burn.

"I'm dying." Stevens words were like gnats in my ear.

"What's it this time?" I said aloud. "Cancer or brain shit?"

"What are you talking about?" Blondie asked.

The bottle exploded against the mirror before I realized I'd even thrown it.

The blonde was screaming, but I couldn't hear. I dragged her to the edge of the bed and fucked her good. Steven was breathing down my neck, laughing as I pounded the whore. The room was spinning. All I saw was red. I heard the smacking of meat against meat, felt my balls release and dick hardened afresh at the sound of heavy sobs.

I turned to look at Steven, felt my fingers at his throat. Terror contorted the hard lines in his face into a silent scream as my hands snuffed out his cries. I slid my fingers along his face. He coughed and called my name, begging me to stop. He said he'd do anything, just begged me not to kill him. He never once said he was sorry. Never once asked for my forgiveness.

My thumbs traced the dark bags under his eyes. They slid higher, touching his gray lashes. He smelled like piss and cheap hootch. I smiled as I dug my thumbs into his eyes. The delicate tissue popped like zits. Vitreous fluid oozed into his beard in strands of chunky snot.

I laughed. I laughed and laughed and laughed. Steven fell to his knees, sobbing blood. I felt the warmth of his skull swallow the tip of my dick as I slid it inside the gapping wound. My body clenched as I fucked his brains out, edging my way to climax, then jizzing all over his grey matter.

Exhausted, I fell to the floor. The room was a red stain spiraling out of control. I felt the weight of the world pulling me harder onto the ground like roadkill. I closed my eyes, but the starlight and nebulous galaxy behind my lids offered no reprieve from the roller coaster inside my head. My stomach wretched. I rolled on my side and felt vomit ooze out of my mouth and nose. It burned like razor blades and lemon juice. I puked until there was nothing left.

My muscles clenched and body shook. I couldn't breathe. Darkness swallowed the stars as they extinguished like candlelight. As the coldness washed over me, my heart began to settle, and I felt myself drift asleep.

My dreams were vivid technicolor, an acid trip down the yellow brick road on my way to Oz. Street lights burned with sulfur, home windows glowed with red, blue, and purple light as the occupants festered in front of their worship boxes. The adults had televisions, the children their iPads and Cellphones. The sounds of night were different in the city, especially when I was walking next to a corpse.

"You're such a fucking asshole," Blondie scoffed as we waited for the bus.

"Eat shit, bitch." I rolled my eyes.

The bus pulled up and we got on, and that's when I knew this whole thing had to be a dream. I immediately recognized the fat guy with the ponytail driving the bus. He smiled at me with bright red and yellow eyes, beckoning me on board with a nasty clawed finger. People on the bus scoffed and snickered at Blondie and I as we took our seat near the front. An old broad with her hair tied in a bonnet got up with her Pomeranian and waddled to the back of the bus, her fat ass barely able to squeeze between the aisles.

The bus was a kaleidoscope of sights and sounds. The colorful advertisements for health insurance and antismoking campaigns glowed like a nuclear rector in full on meltdown. The black man across from me wore a red suite so bright, you'd have thought he was on fire. The woman next to him was covered in dragon tattoos that crawled along her skin like geckos. The passengers were whispering, talking amongst one another. All about me and the dead girl.

The bus slowed down and pulled over for its next stop. My heart sunk as Steven climbed on. I was at his throat in no time. His eyes were wild with terror, his beard a knotted mess of gray steel wool scratching my arms. I punched his face, heard his nose break, and felt as someone tried to lift me off him. I thrashed around until I broke free and looked at the guy holding me back.

The man looked like Steven's clone. I glanced up. Everyone on the bus had become Steven. Everyone, except the driver. He grinned at me and stepped on the gas, running red lights and swerving around traffic. The gang of clones fell back into their seats as I found my balance and stood up. The Steven on the ground tried to crawl away, but I grabbed a fistful of hair and smashed his face into the floor.

I reached in my pocket and grabbed the glass shard. Didn't remember taking it from the whore house, but how else could it have gotten there? I reached around and slit Steven's throat. His plead for mercy drowned in a flood of crimson drooling from the gaping wound. I rolled him over and Blondie screamed. His eyes were wide open, his mouth dribbling blood. I ran the glass around his face and peeled it away. I'm such a good surgeon, it only took three cuts to remove the bastard's face. Blood gushed like tomato paste.

"Now I don't have to see your face in the mirror," I whispered in Steven's ear. "You sick twisted fuck."

I never put much thought into dreams or nightmares, but anytime I can kill my father again and again, must be a good night of sleep. The bus driver blew the horn as we flew through another red light. He cut the wheel, and the bus toppled over, flinging everyone like clothes in a dryer. I felt the stomach-churning effect of zero gravity as I tumbled end over end. Everyone was screaming, the bus scrapping the asphalt until it came to a sudden stop, smashing in a concrete powerline.

Blondie and I climbed out of the wreckage. The people inside groaned like the aftermath of some perverted orgy. I smelled gas, saw a puddle of the stuff creeping toward the sparking powerline. Blondie and I jumped off the bus and ran across the street just in time to watch the fuel ignite. Flames raced across the gasoline trail and engulfed the bus, roasting everyone inside. The flames were so beautiful, orange and red illuminating the streets bright as daylight.

"We gotta go!" Blondie pulled my arm.

She was right. I could hear police sirens in the distance. I looked around. We were back in Boca. My office wasn't far, if we ran, we could make it. And so we did, the surgeon and the corpse outrunning the cops, flames biting our heels.

Uncle Frank woke me up, meowing and licking my ear.

"What?" My throat was hot and sticky. "I don't wanna get up. You can't make me!"

Frank meowed and rubbed his face into my forehead. His soft coat brushed my eyes, tickling my lashes. I peeled open my eyes and found myself back in my apartment, laying on the floor by the front door. My head was pounding, my nose and throat burning like napalm. Frank kept on meowing.

"Forgot to feed you," I groaned, "didn't I? You're right, I'm an asshole."

I felt dampness around my upper lip and touched my fingers to it. Of course my nose was bleeding. I could taste the blood in the back of my throat. My whole body was shaking as I got to my feet.

My apartment's modern and simple. I don't have time for frilly furniture and shit. Homes are meant for two things: sleeping and fucking. I have a bed, couch, entertainment stand, and an office. My place is about a two-hour drive north of the whore house. I'm off of Climates near downtown West Palm Beach. I have no idea how I got home, so I figured Roy must have dropped me off.

*How the hell did I get that fucked up?* I wondered, knowing Roy would never let me live it down.

I checked my watch. It was already a quarter past eleven. Must have slept through my alarm. The first patient wasn't until twelve, but I was hung over. I should call out. Should just crawl into bed and say fuck all to the world, but it was boy's night last night. Didn't know if Roy was coming in or not, but I couldn't let him hear that I didn't show up to work, especially if he'd dropped my drunk ass off.

Uncle Frank kept on crying.

"Alright." I rolled my eyes and rubbed my temples.

First thing I did was go to the kitchen and open the last can of tuna flavored cat food.

"Come to Daddy." I gave Frank a few kissy faces as I crossed the kitchen.

Frank circled my legs while I walked over to his bowl, nearly tripping me twice. I fed him, gave him fresh water, scratched his back while he ate, then hopped in the shower without so much as looking in a mirror. I knew I looked like shit, so the last thing I needed was to see how bad. Standing in the shower, I felt dizzy, my stomach twisting into knots. I only puked twice, but each time was nothing but bile and stomach juices.

I sat on my knees under the showerhead and watched the brown, murky water wash down my body and spiral into the drain. My dick was sore and stung a little under the water. It looked like a couple of friction burns, but nothing worse than usual. After toweling off, I stopped in front of the mirror. My stomach churned, not at the sight of all my bruises and scrapes, but because for a split second, I thought I saw Steven staring back at me.

I shook off the heebie-jeebies, then dried off and put on a clean pair of scrubs. My nose was killing me. It felt stuffy and itchy. I blew it over the sink. Pink snot rockets splattered the white marble like Kurt Cobain's head, post shotgun. My nose started bleeding, so I stuffed a tissue in each nostril. It was already a quarter to twelve, so I rushed to the kitchen and filled my thermos with coffee and Jameson (hair of the dog that bit ya), then grabbed my sunglasses.

"Alright, Uncle Frank," I said, putting a few cat treats on the counter. "You behave."

Frank jumped on the counter and started mawing the fish-shaped treats. I scratched his rump, said my goodbyes, and made my way out the door, hoping my car would be in the resident parking lot, and not still back at the whore house. It was, but that is where my luck ran out. Between traffic and my splitting headache, it was almost an hour and a half drive to Boca.

It was already gearing up to be a shitty day. By the time I got to work, my nose stopped bleeding. I could still taste something metallic in the back of my throat, but at least it wasn't running down my face.

I didn't see Roy's car. I could only imagine the hell he got from Felicia walking in so late last night. Poor Roy didn't have a chance. His wife would have sniffed the pussy on him soon as he stepped through the door. Lucky for me, Roy wasn't my problem—although, imagining his day being worse than mine was a little comforting. The only thing on my mind was making it through my next eight-hour shift without puking my guts out…again.

I walked in the front door, sunglasses on as I rushed through the lobby. My nose was burning, head still spinning. It wasn't as busy as I'd expected. A fat man in a cheap suit was at the counter. There was something familiar about him, but I couldn't put my finger on it. Maybe it was the yellow sweat stains around his collar and armpits, but I couldn't stop staring at him. Imagining being stuck in a cramped exam room with him stinking like musk and cornstarch sent my stomach tumbling.

"I have an appointment with Dr. Irvin," the man said in a thick Boston accent.

*Great*, I thought.

"Your name?" Beckie at the counter asked.

"Hooper," he replied with a grimace of browning teeth. "Sonny Hooper."

I sat in the doctor's chair by the computer with the lights turned down. One of the perks about being an eye doctor is working in dimly lit exam rooms. Made nursing my hangover a lot easier. The room itself wasn't much, just a desk with a sink, cabinets full of eye solutions and drops, the exam chair with all its accessories, and a phoropter—the thing your eye doctor puts up to your face and asks which is better, one or two. There were some frame adjusting tools, like screw drivers, and a hot box full of salt used to heat up plastic frames for adjustments.

I was dozing off when Anajeli knocked on the door and began opening it.

"You can have a seat in the exam ch—" She stopped talking to the patient when she saw me half asleep in front of the computer. "Oh! Dr. Irvin, I didn't see you come in this morning."

I peeled myself outta the chair and fixed my scrubs. Of course the fat fuck would be my first patient of the day. I put my hands in my pockets and tried to act casual but felt something crinkling under my fingers. I pulled it out just enough to see two baggies of coke from the night before.

*How the fuck did that get there?* I thought as I pushed them back in my pocket.

"Patient suffering discomfort with contact lenses." Anajeli handed me the guy's chart. "If you need help or anything…"

"Nope, I'm fine."

"Sure you're not coming down with something?"

"No," I said a little firmer than I'd meant. I stopped, cleared my throat, and repeated slower, "I'm fine."

"Me too!" the fat guy snickered. "Fine and dandy."

I shot him a look. Even in the dark I could see how red and swollen his eye was. I hate people who sleep in contact lenses. Worse, people who don't fucking change them out as instructed. Dick heads like that always got what was coming to them, pink eye, ulcers, and corneal abrasions. All those cheap fucks ever wanted were more free sample trial lenses. I was not going easy on this guy.

"I'm sorry, Anajeli. Just had a hard time sleeping last night. Thank you, though."

She smiled and touched my shoulder. My arm tingled with pins and needles.

"Page me if you need anything." She winked before leaving me to the patient.

I sighed and went back to the fat fuck.

"I'm Dr. Irvin." I took a seat in my chair and rolled toward the patient.

My heart did summersaults as I looked at the guy's face. He was the fat fuck from the night before, the one getting the Asian special at the whore house. A second longer, and I remembered the weird dream I'd had. He was the bus driver, too. Goosebumps prickled along my arms and neck.

The last thing I wanted was someone recognizing me from a place like that. I kept the lights dimmed so he couldn't get a good look at my face. My head was spinning. I couldn't think straight. Then I remembered the baggy in my pocket. More hair of the dog.

"Excuse me," I said before standing up and going to one of the tall cabinets on the other wall.

It was a storage cabinet we used for contact lenses. I opened the door and hid behind it, pulled out the baggy, and took a quick bump off my pinky nail. My eyes lit up and I felt my shakes start to subside. I took a deep breath, pocketed the rest of the coke, and went back to the exam.

As I rolled my chair closer, the man's smell hit me. It was a noxious funk of piss, sweat, and vomit. His white buttoned shirt was matted to his fat tits with perspiration and a spattering of coffee stains. The gross fuck must not have showered after the whore house.

"You look familiar," Hooper said in his Boston accent.

"This your first time to the clinic, Mr. Hooper?" I asked, rubbing my nose behind the paper chart in my hand.

"Yep. First time here. And please, call me Hoop." His breath stank like rancid butter.

I felt my guts doing summersaults. I needed to get this exam over with or I was gonna throw up.

"Sorry—" I cleared my throat. "I've never been to Boston."

"Rhode Island," Hoop corrected.

"Haven't been there either." I shook my head.

"What's your father's name?" he asked, fingering one of his three chins.

"Excuse me?" I looked up from my paperwork.

My stomach cramps vanished. In its place was a wave of hot sweats and elevated blood pressure. My hands were shaking again.

"Your father?" Hoop repeated. "What's his name? You look like this guy I drink with at the bar. Steven."

"Did he send you here?" I stood up so fast, I knocked over my chair.

"Wow!" Hoop held up his hands in surrender. "Take it easy! Seriously, I'm here for a fucking eye problem!"

Hoop pointed at his swollen red eye. I apologized as I bent over and fixed my chair.

"Plus," Hoop went on, "kinda hard to be sent anywhere by a dead guy."

"What?"

"Steven died last night. Bus accident. No survivors. I knew he was sick; thought he might have made a comeback the way he was talking a day ago. Sad shit, real heartbreaker. Hey, Doc, you alright?"

"Huh?" I blinked a few times, felt tears running down my cheeks. "I don't talk to him much."

I sat back in my chair. Hoop leaned back and fixed his greasy hair into a ponytail.

"No kidding."

"Let's focus on your eye problem." I cleared my throat again.

"You look just like him."

"Can we not talk about Steven?"

"Sorry. Him and I go way back. Brushed elbows with him in the Navy days."

"Yeah, I still don't care."

"Uncanny how alike you two are."

I threw his chart on the keyboard to my right. "Get out!"

"What?" Hoop waved his hands again. "It's alright, kid!"

"If you bring his name up again…" I gritted my teeth. "I swear to God I'll kick your ass out myself."

"Okay, okay!" Hoop swallowed.

"So what happened to your eye?" I sat back down in my chair and settled into the exam.

"Slept in my contacts."

"Obviously. How long have you been wearing them?"

"Not sure. Couple months?"

"You don't even know?"

"Look, Doc, times are tough. I just need to see."

"If you have a corneal abrasion or edema, you can kiss contact lenses goodbye."

I set myself up in the slit lamp. It's kind of a microscope for the eye with a really bright light. Hoop placed his chin on the rest and his forehead against the bar. I always start with the unaffected eye. Allows you to focus the equipment and give you a benchmark. Right eye looked fine, so I went to his left eye. The inflammation was awful, the tissue around the contact so enflamed it looked like a tree growing around a fence.

"Contact lens is on there pretty bad." I leaned from the slit lamp and let Hoop do the same.

"Well, no shit."

"You're the one who's been sleeping in old contact lenses." I got up and went to the cabinet.

"Ayuh, I get that, but what do I do now?"

"Try to flush the sucker out. If not, I'll have to remove it manually."

I felt my hands trembling. I didn't want this prick to think I was losing my game. While Hoop leaned his head back, I grabbed a bottle of saline and tried flushing it out. After killing off a fresh bottle, the contact lens didn't budge. Wasn't surprised. Figured at the least it would moisten the fucker enough for the next step.

"Nothing?" Hoop asked.

"Nope." I grabbed optical forceps and a foreign body spud—a small tool with a sharp head like a spade. "Gonna have to pull it off."

I put Hoop behind the slight lamp one more time and looked at his eye under magnification. The redness and swelling around the contact lens was worse. I first tried to use the long-pointed forceps but couldn't find any grip without damaging the soft tissue around the lens.

In one hand, I used the sharp edges of my foreign body spud to press against the cornea, prying just enough space to slip the forceps under the lens. I breathed heavily through my nose—I could smell the metallic tinge of blood in my sinus, could taste it dripping on the back of my tongue. Was a lot better than Hoop's stank ass. I sighed out my frustrations to steady my hand. Less than a fraction of a millimeter, and the tool could puncture his eye.

Hoop's eye began to twitch a little.

"Stop moving," I barked.

"I'm not," Hoop said, trying to keep his chin still.

He was right. I glanced at my tools. My hands were shaking, but I was so close. Sweat stung the corners of my eyes. I could see part of the forceps vanish beneath the murky contact lens. A fraction of a millimeter more. I held my breath, and with the gentlest push my jerky fingers could muster, slid the forceps under the contact lens.

I let out a sigh of relief and began to lift the lens. Hoop winced. I stopped, put down the foreign body spud, and increased magnification. The lens was really stuck on there, I could see vascular tissue trying to grow inside the contact lens like tree roots into a sidewalk. Again, I tried to lift the lens, and Hoop grunted.

As the contact lifted, the cornea began to tear like orange zest. I moved the tool to the left and to the right, trying to pry the lens at different angles. The more I tried, the more his cornea began to split. If my hands weren't bad enough, my heart pounded my ribs like a prize fighter. I leaned back a little so I could rub my nose again and take a breath to calm down.

Hoop's eyes watered. He was going to blink at any second. If he did, his lid would press the contact lens back into place, and I would have to start all over again. I took a deep breath, and like removing a stubborn band aid, yanked off the contact.

Hoop grunted and squinted as his cornea ripped off. I gasped as vitreous fluid spilled from his eye and down his cheek. I wanted to look away, to flinch in the face of disaster, but something caught my attention. It wasn't my patient quivering in pain—he deserved it. Something inside his pupil was moving. I increased his magnification. A long, wiry leg with thick bristled hairs and sharp barbed feet reached out of his pupil.

I stumbled backward.

"What's wrong?" Hoop asked, still sitting in the slit lamp.

I didn't reply. I got back on my stool and looked through the eyepiece again, watching as another leg pulled itself out of his eye. It was impossible, there's no way anything that large could get inside the eye. I increased magnification again and saw eight unblinking eyes and two long dripping fangs as a spider tried to free itself from inside Hoop's eye.

My brain was so high on coke, terror, and fascination, I'd forgotten to breath. Hoop didn't even seem to care, just sat there staring, unblinking as the tiny little insect tugged against his lid. Its head slipped free, but its bloated abdomen was like pulling a watermelon through a hole the size of a lemon. With a pop, the rest of its body came out, sticky with vitreous fluid like afterbirth.

I coughed choking on air as I watched the spider crawled along Hoop's sclera, taking in its new surroundings. It turned, staring through the slit lamp lens directly at me. It jumped onto the lamp. I tumbled backward again.

I cried out as I hit the ground. The room was even darker than before, with only the slit lamp's thin beam to illuminate the room. Hoop didn't move, didn't make a goddamn sound. Ripping off his cornea should have been agony, not to mention the fucking spider!

Something else was wrong. The room was too dark. It was as if the shadows were swallowing the air around the sliver of light from the lamp's beam. I got to my feet and went for the light switch. Nothing. I went to the exam chair, which powered both the slit lamp and the overhead light attached to it. I clicked it on and swallowed my scream.

It was Blondie from the whore house, topless aside from her red Calvin Kline panties. Her face was peeled off like a grape, her eyes missing. Gossamer threads of pink dripped out of her gouged sockets and fleshless nostrils. Her chest looked as if it'd been ripped open by a wild animal. Ribs were cracked and turned the wrong way round out of a gapping creator between her breasts. I got to my feet and examined the body closer.

"Have a heart, son!" I heard Steven behind me.

I turned around. Steven was standing there, naked, offering the bitch's heart. Blood covered his arms, face, and crotch. His jaundice eyes glowed in the dark like rotten eggs, his breath was nauseatingly sweet with rot. Steven smiled with a mouthful of maggots and stepped toward me. I tried to back away but fell into the dead whore's lap.

The corpse slumped over and fell on the ground. I turned for a second to see the mess, but when I looked back at Steven, he was gone. For a fleeting moment, I thought I'd imagined the whole thing. My heart sank when I saw Blondie bleeding all over the floor.

Someone knocked on the door.

There wasn't time to think things through. I was alone with a dead hooker, my DNA oozing out of every orifice. In Florida, they give you the chair for murder. I picked up the body and propped it back up in the chair.

Light spilled in as the door opened.

"Everything okay?" Anajeli asked, about to poke her head into the room.

"Yeah." I rushed over, stopping the door with my foot. "Could you do me a favor and bring the janitor cart?"

"What's wrong?" She tried to look over my shoulders.

"Mr. Hooper had an accident," I whispered. "He got sick and...well...crapped his pants."

"Oh Lord." She shook her head. "Need me to grab one of the nurses?"

"Nah." I puffed my lip. "I got it. Just bring me the cart and some heavy-duty gloves. Do you mind keeping the other staff outta this wing for a bit? He's kind of embarrassed and wants some privacy on his way to the restroom."

"Okay." She nodded. "Give me like, five, ten minutes to clear everyone out."

"Don't forget the cart."

"Oh, I wont."

Anajeli was quick with it, too. She knocked and told me it was outside the door when I was ready. In the meantime, I had to figure out how the fuck I was going to get rid of Blondie. After a minute, I grabbed the cart and rolled it into the exam room. It's one of those plastic things with the yellow mop bucket on one side and the big garbage can on the other.

I looked at Blondie, then at the cart. My brain was steaming trying to figure the logistics. There's no way I could hide her whole body in the bag, not without cutting her up first, and there's no way in fuck I was about to butcher a hooker in my office. Even dead, this bitch was still fucking me.

I tried to pick her up under the armpits but lost balance the second her legs slid out of the chair. Funny thing about movies, they always make carrying a body look so damn easy. I'm not fat, but I'm not a gym rat either. Sure I go for a run once and a while, and I watch what I eat, but holy shit that hooker was heavy! My back almost gave out twice as I tried lifting her up a second and third time.

After that, I let her slide onto the ground. My arms and chest were soaked in the whore's blood. I felt my blood pressure rise the more pissed off I got. I tried again, lifting her about waist high off the floor and dragging her toward the cart. Both her arms were bobbing and flailing around. As I was about to throw her on top of it, her wrist smacked the cart and pushed it out of the way.

"Damn it!" I grunted and dropped her.

Blondie collapsed on the floor like a wet rag doll. I ran my hands through my hair and paced around the room. My nose was burning and hands were shaking. I kicked Blondie square in the ribs. It felt good, so I kicked her again. One of her ribs crunched behind my foot, and I was sad the bitch couldn't feel it.

My face was covered in sweat, and the room was starting to smell like shit. One glance as the broad's crotch, and I could see that her ass was starting to leak. For the first time in my life, I regretted rough anal sex. The way the whore was folded up reminded me of the way fire fighters carry unconscious people down ladders in the movies, which gave me an idea.

I crouched next to the body and threw her arm over my neck hoping I could carry her on my shoulder. It wasn't easy, her limp arms swinging this way and that while I tried pulling her on top of me. After a minute, it felt like I had her. I stood up, carrying her fireman style, then flung her on the cart with a wet smack. She looked like a drunk college slut in a sorority hazing.

I peeked my head into the hallway. Coast was clear, so I rolled out the janitor's cart and made my way around the corner to the bathroom and brought her inside. She was starting to drip a funky brown sludge that ran down her toes. As I picked up her legs to throw them in the trash, the fucking cart started moving! I put my foot in the way, but it only pushed the cart further.

"Shit, shit, shit!" I tried to steady the cart and not get any of the colon bile on me.

The cart hit the opposite wall, and I used that for support to get her legs in the trash bag. I grabbed some cleaning supplies—the mop and detachable bucket, a couple rolls of paper towels, some bleach, and heavy-duty cleaning gloves. Just to make sure no one walked in on her, I used my master key to lock the toilet from the outside and grabbed an 'out of order' sign from the cart and hung it on the door handle.

Lucky for me, there wasn't any shit on the floor, so I went back to the exam room and cleaned up my mess. Washing coagulated blood is miserable work. You spend half your time smearing the shit everywhere before it starts to clean up.

Someone knocked on the door. My heart stopped a second.

"Dr. Irving?" Anajeli said from the hall. "Did Mr. Hooper leave?"

"I let him go out the back exit," I said, opening the door a crack and sticking my head out. "Don't worry about his copay, we're not charging him."

"I wanted to talk to you about something else…in private."

"I'm not—"

"Please?" She looked up at me and bit her lip. "It's important."

"Alright. I'm almost finished."

I threw a few bloody rags in the bio-hazard bin, then took another bump from the baggy in my pocket. Bloody water sloshed around in the bucket as I kicked it into the corner, hoping the room was dark enough that she couldn't see the rest of the mess. I peeled off my bloody scrubs and tossed them along with the rubber gloves behind the chair as Anajeli opened the door and came inside. I was still wearing an undershirt, and the blood stains on my scrub pants looked almost black in the dark light.

"What's up?" I said, hands on my hips, trying to catch my breath.

"There's some things I've been keeping to myself for a while now and I need to tell you." She looked at her hands, fidgeting with a ring on her pinky finger.

All I could think about was the dead hooker in the bathroom, and this girl was about to get all mushy on me about something that didn't matter.

"Alright…" My heart was beating a thousand miles a minute.

"Roy is starting to make me uncomfortable." She looked at me with sad kitten eyes.

"Roy?" I wasn't surprised, but I faked it well enough.

"He keeps staring at me," she confessed, "and when I look at him, he always looks away and acts like nothing happened. It's weird."

"I can talk to him." I put my hand on her shoulder.

"I know you're both friends, and he's super nice. I don't wanna give him the wrong impression. You've always been easy to talk to."

"Hey, no problem. I'll talk to him." I don't know what I was thinking, the next words just slipped out. "You're one of my best COMT's. You're invaluable to my practice and I want you to be comfortable here."

"That really means a lot to me."

She grabbed my hand from her shoulder and held it. I could feel the softness of her fingers stroking my palm. My skin tingled with pins and needles. I felt my cock stiffen, but I kept my cool.

I cleared my throat. "I can definitely have that talk with Roy. Was there something else you wanted to talk about?"

"Maybe." Her voice was a soft purr. "You seem very…tense, though."

"I just found out my biological father died."

"Oh, no! I'm so sorry." Anajeli gave me a hug. Her scent assuaged my stinging nose with coconut oil.

"Don't be." I wrapped my arms around her. "He was kind of asshole."

"Yeah, I remember you were saying something like that."

"I don't know how to feel." I pivoted my hips to keep her from the poke of my boner. "I'm just, conflicted, ya know?"

"I know exactly how you feel." She pulled from the embrace just enough to look into my eyes again. "Is there anything I can do to help?"

"I dunno." I swallowed hard.

"When's the last time you read the employee handbook on harassment?"

"We never made an employee handbook."

"Then there's nowhere in the rules that say I can't do this…"

Anajeli put her hand on my cock, and I forgot all about the dead hooker. I felt Anajeli's fingers tug out the knot in my scrub's drawstring. I rubbed my nose and swallowed hard. She grabbed my other hand and placed it on her breast. It was heavy and firm, the way a real tit should be. My dick popped out of my fly like a flagpole. She pulled me close, jerking me and moaning.

I slid my hand in her shirt and grabbed her tit from under her bra. It was cumbersome, so she helped by taking off her scrubs top. I licked her neck and chest. Her caramel skin tasted as sweet as it looked. She moaned, stroking my meat faster, only stopping once to lick her hand for lubricant.

I clutched her throat. She gasped and looked deep into my eyes. They burned with passion, her lashes fluttering. She put a finger over my lips as I leaned in to kiss her, then went down on her knees and sucked my cock. My grip melted away as I felt her tongue caress my glands.

Anajeli was a goddamn blow job savant. She could have suck-started a firehose. I felt her throat vibrate as she rolled her R's as if to stay something in Spanish. I grabbed a fistful of hair as she gagged on my meat like a damn porn star. She pulled it out, gasping as she worked my shaft with her hand.

I pulled her to her feet and kissed her, tasting my salt mixed with strawberry lip balm. She dropped her scrub pants and sat in the exam chair, positioning her ass on the edge. I slid inside her with ease, wetness gushing from her swollen twat.

Girl was tight as a nine-year-old. I couldn't help it; less than three pumps and I was about to burst. She responded to my throbbing meat by bucking harder. I closed my eyes, trying to chew back the orgasm, but you can't stop a train. At the last second, I tried to pull out. The bitch wrapped herself around me like an octopus and held me in tight. Anajeli's nails dug into my skin. I didn't care though. Not until I felt the blood running down my back.

I opened my eyes.

Steven was naked in the exam chair, my dick and balls deep in his hairy fucking ass. I could feel his swollen cock slapping my stomach. Without a thought, I punched him in the face and broke his nose. My dick pulled out with a slick *pop* as I shot jets of semen all over his dick and belly.

Steven tried to stand, but I grabbed him by the throat, choking him before he could make a sound. His dick pointed like a spear, smacking my own wilting vegetable. The sensation of meat-on-meat action made me furious, and I squeezed his throat harder.

Steven's face turned purple, then blue, then the whole fucking thing exploded. Bits of brain and skull showered my face like hot, chunky syrup. I let him go and backed away, rubbing the muck from my eyes. His dick fell off, revealing a massive vaginal cavern dripping with goo. Flesh around his twat split like a fissure up his chest and ass crack. His skin peeled away like a banana, exposing glistening red musculature with yellow strips of fat like sticky cottage cheese.

"Fuck!" I screamed.

Strips of Steven's flesh writhed around like grizzly slugs, leaving pink and crimson trails as they undulated toward dark and shadowy corners. Steven walked toward me, smiling with meaty, skinless lips. Blood smeared over his fetid teeth like cheap lipstick. I felt a draft waft across my dick and fumbled to put it away as I backed into the computer table.

"Don't you love your father?" Steven asked, his voice wet and gooey.

"Fuck you!"

"We're the same, you and I." His cheesy fat giggled as he laughed.

"Like shit we are!"

"It's not what's on the outside that counts, son. Beneath the flesh, we are the same."

I looked around for anything I could use to defend myself. There were a few screwdrivers on the other side of the counter, but the closest thing to me was a box of salt for the hot box. I ripped open the top and grabbed a fistful. When Steven got close enough, I tossed the handful in his face. He shouted in pain as the tiny crystals stuck to his wet musculature. He tried to rub his eyes, but the salt only stung his skinless hands.

I threw another fistful of salt, then another. Steven backed away, screaming. I pushed him into the exam chair. He fell into it with a wet thud, knocking the swiveling slit lamp and phoropter into the wall with a hard crash. I poured the entire box of salt right over his face and jumped on top of him, rubbing it in. Steven tried to buck me off, but I punched him in the ribs. I heard the bone snap and saw a piece of cracked marrow sticking out of his side.

I got up and rushed toward the counter, digging through the drawers looking for anything I could use to defend myself with. I found a scalpel.

Steven rocked back and forth, falling out of the chair and onto the floor, crying like a little girl. I walked over, scalpel in hand, and slashed the fucker in the chest. He belted a pitiful howl as I dragged the blade against soft musculature. It cut like butter.

His windpipe swelled with each of his labored breaths like a throbbing cock. I grabbed his throat and started sawing through the meat. His screams died in my grasp as the blade lacerated his voice box. Blood bubbled out of his windpipe like chocolate milk. I watched Steven's eyes roll up and into the back of his head, watched his chest fall as he exhaled his last dying breath.

Standing up, I took stock of the mess I'd made. The room was a bloody fucking disaster, again. *I* was a bloody fucking disaster. I grabbed my shirt from behind the doctor's chair and used it to wipe most of the coagulated blood and sticky fat from my arms and fingers, then threw it on top of the corpse.

Now I had two bodies to get rid of. I grabbed a trash bag from under the sink and started wrapping him up before scrubbing the whole mess down again. By the time I finished, I was exhausted. I pulled out the baggy, took another bump, then peeked into the hallway. After I made sure the coast was clear, I dragged Steven's body into the bathroom with the hooker.

After a bit of work, I threw Steven on top of Blondie. Blood oozed from the trash bags, flooding the top of the cart with slick fluids. I threw in a bunch of rags to soak it up, but there wasn't much I could do at that point. My main focus was making sure I kept the blood off the floor. There were some more heavy-duty trash bags in the janitor cart. I wrapped up the bodies as fast as I could, then made my way out the side entrance.

It was raining, which meant I didn't have to worry about the bags springing a leak. Figured the rain would wash the shit away, plus there wasn't anyone walking or standing around to see me. I left the bodies by the dumpster for a minute while I went around the building to grab my Land Rover, parking next to the cart.

Steven was lighter than I expected, but the wet bags started slipping as soon as I grabbed them. I got my arms under his legs and lifted him into the back of my car. Blondie went in with little trouble. I threw in a couple bottles of bleach just in case. To keep my car from smelling like a corpse, I tossed a bunch of urinal cakes and air fresheners on top of the bodies before closing up and making my way back inside.

After I finished cleaning the bathroom and the detail work on the exam chair, I took off my scrubs and threw them in the biowaste, then grabbed a clean set from the storage closet next to the bathroom. I went to the front to talk to Beckie.

"Everything okay?" she asked, from behind the nurse's station.

The station was pretty typical, just a semi-circle counter with computers, fax machines and file cabinets overlooking the front lobby. A few of the other COMT's and office staff tried to keep busy, but the girls kept glancing over their shoulders at me, noses crinkled. The stink of whore shit must have seeped into my pores. Beckie looked like she was trying not to breath through her nose.

"I think I'm done for the day." I leaned on the counter, not trying to hide my exhaustion.

"You don't look too good." Beckie cocked an eyebrow and nodded. "Want me to cancel your appointments?"

"Sure. I need a hot shower after all that."

"I guess it was a lot more than puke."

"You saw the guy, he was disgusting!"

I turned to leave when Beckie stopped me.

"Before you go," she said, "Roy called. Something about wanting to talk about last night."

"I'll call him later."

I sat in my car for a long while, trying to get my heart to slow down. It was a hard after all the coke and sickly-sweet smell of chemical deodorants and rotting bodies in the back.

"Calm down," I told myself. "Calm, the fuck, down. You're going to dump them in the Everglades, go back to the house, and sleep this shit off."

The plan sounded good. They always sound good until your brain kicks into high gear.

*My Daddy's sick. He needs to take his medicine. I can hear him in the bathroom. His tummy hurts real bad. I have to use the potty, but Daddy's still in there. I knock on the door, but he doesn't answer, even when I call his name. The door isn't locked, so I open it and peek inside.*

*Daddy's sitting on the floor between the potty and bathtub. His face is sweaty, and his lips are blue. His mouth looked like Lucky after he got in a fight with a squirrel, wet like whipped cream.*

*"Daddy?"*

*He doesn't answer.*

*I walk into the bathroom, my bare feet slapping the warm tile. He's not wearing a shirt. He's got cuts and boo-boos on his chest and shoulders. His arms look like ant bites. I want to touch him, to push him awake, but I see the needle. I'm scared of needles. It's still inside his arm, stuck inside the ant bite.*

*I run out of the bathroom and into the kitchen. The phone is too high on the wall for me to reach, so I grab a chair and climb up. I think real hard, trying to remember the phone number for the police. I stand on my tip toes and press the numbers 9-1-1. It rings two times before someone answers.*

*"911, what's your emergency?"*

*"I'm scared," I tell the woman.*

*"What's wrong?"*

*"Daddy won't wake up."*

I was bawling my eyes out when the roar of thunder snapped me out of it. My heart was running a thousand miles an hour. I could still smell the burnt plastic and mildew-stained bathroom, could remember how musky and damp Steven's trailer always felt, even above the rotting meat in the back of my car. Somehow, the memories of Steven's trailer made me feel even dirtier than cleaning up corpses.

I turned on the ignition and drove west toward the Everglades. An hour later, I was right on the edge of civilization and swamp land. The horizon was long, flat, and wet. Not many places I could hide an SUV to dump a body. I kept driving until the end of Loxahatchee RD, which led to the dirt road right into the everglades. Normally this area was sprawling with kayak and airboat tours, but with all the rain the area was completely deserted.

I kept driving deeper into the scrub, pulling off the dirt road into the brush a couple of miles in, and found a good spot to dump the body. It was near the water in a patch of endangered mangrove trees. I backed up to the edge of the of water, popped the trunk, and dumped Blondie on the ground.

The rain was beginning to let up a little, so I went and grabbed the bottles of bleach, and doused her face to wash off my DNA from her eyes, nose, and mouth. I took another bottle and pored it right down her snatch.

One thing my dumbass forgot, gloves. My fingers were red and burning by the time I finished, but it was a small price to pay for keeping out of jail. Satisfied, I rolled up the legs of my scrubs and took off my shoes and socks, then dragged her toward the water and half threw half rolled her into a patch of mangroves. She snapped a few roots, but eventually settled into the thicket.

Steven's body was remarkably light, but I was in too much of a rush to care. I grabbed the bag around his shoulders and threw him right on top of the hooker. I filled the bottles of bleach with sand, then tied them around some extra garbage bags to make sure they wouldn't float or fly away if the rainstorm picked up again.

I put on my socks and shoes, then drove home.

My head was killing me as I stepped through the front door. As soon as it closed behind me, the whole mess of the day caught up all at once, and I puked right on the floor. My abs burned as I upchucked nothing but bile and coffee. I wiped my face on my sleeve and stepped over it, went to the kitchen and threw a dishcloth under some hot water, then laid it on top of the mess for me to deal with later.

Uncle Frank meowed his usual greeting, twisting himself around my legs as I walked through the house. I knelt down and pet him before stripping off my clothes. It wasn't until I started going through my pockets that I realized I didn't have my phone.

"Fuck!"

Uncle Frank hissed and darted into the kitchen.

"Shit," I said looking in the direction he'd ran. "Not you! Sorry, fucking lost my goddamn phone!"

Uncle Frank continued to meow.

"What do you want?"

Frank meowed.

"I already fed you this morning."

Again, that low angry, hungry meow.

"Fuck it, fine!" I went to cabinet and grabbed the last tin of tuna-flavored cat food.

I stopped for a second and looked at the can. I couldn't help the weird sense of *déjà vu*, but I was all over the place, so I just dumped the food in his bowl and put the thought aside.

My mind scrambled trying to think when and where I last saw my phone. I didn't use it at work or have it on me when I was dumping the bodies. Anajeli was saying something about Roy trying to call me. My heart sank when I remembered. It was back at the whore house.

*What if someone finds it?* My mind spun out of control. *What if they unlock it, see what I did to the patients? Oh, God! I'm fucked!*

"Somebody once told me the world is gonna role me, I ain't the sharpest tool in the shed." I heard my phone's ringtone: "Allstar" by Smashmouth.

It came from the living room. I was up and on it before the first chorus. The phone was sitting face up on the counter. No idea how I missed it. Maybe a coke comedown? I was feeling kinda shitty and lethargic. Didn't matter. I grabbed it and looked at the caller ID. Roy was calling me.

"Hello?"

The line went dead in my hands. I checked the screen. The low battery light flickered with less than 3%. Roy must have hung up, but I didn't care. I needed to see what happened last night. The last thing I remembered was polishing off a bottle of scotch and a couple lines of coke before fucking the shit outta Blondie. I fast forwarded the first three minutes before the phone died.

"Damn it!" I threw the thing across the room.

My nose was burning and my body ached. I ran my hands through my greasy hair, trying to collect myself. Took a deep breath and sighed it out before I went over, picked up my phone, and plugged it in. I felt a pull in my bladder and went to the bathroom to take a piss. I washed my hands, looking at them for the first time since the night before. The sight of them sent an uncomfortable shudder down my spine.

I really fucked up. My knuckles were split and swollen from shards of glass and punching the shit outta Steven. It was too much, and I looked up at the mirror. As bad as my hands were, my face was worse. My eyes were gaunt and cheeks' pale, making my nosebleed look red as marinara sauce in comparison. I looked as shitty as I felt.

"Do you know what you did?" Steven's voice asked from behind.

I turned around. The apartment was empty.

"Where the hell are you?" I asked the empty space.

"Never far."

A chuckle rippled through the bathroom.

I raced through the apartment, turned on all the lights, opened all the windows, searching for the bastard. Uncle Frank followed me from room to room, sitting in the doorway watching with intense curiosity.

"Get outta my head!" I grabbed my pounding skull as gravity dragged me to the floor.

Blondie's mutilated face flashed in my head. She stared at me through hollowed eyes with bits of cream-colored skull peeking through the mess of meat, her teeth bared like a feral animal in a lipless grimace.

*What the fuck did I do to Blondie?* My mind spiraled out of control. *Where did Steven come from anyway, and why was he lighter when I dumped him in the*

*Glades? Did I hallucinate everything with Anajeli? What the hell was happening to me?*

I got to my feet and made my way to the living room to check my phone. There was just enough battery to turn it on. I waited for the screen to load, my hands shaking, sweat dripping down my nose and chin. When I went to unlock the home screen, it fizzled and pixelated.

"The hell?"

The screen cracked and the phone sparked in my hand. I dropped it and jumped back as it smoldered on the ground. The lock screen returned. The numbers clicked as if someone was pushing in my code. The home screen came up, swiped over to the photo gallery, then opened my videos.

My skull was a throbbing mess. A culmination of pain from my pounding heart, burning sinuses, and a coke headache rattled my brain. I didn't recognize the video that played. Not until I heard Steven laughing. The picture was grainy, like something filmed on an old RCA Camcorder. It was his ex-wife's house. The same house where my stepsister Heather lived.

The image focused as someone adjusted the lens. I saw myself lying on the ground, saw Heather walk on scene toward me. Before anything else happened, I turned away and threw up. I heard Steven's heavy breathing. My stomach wretched, and all I could muster was an ounce of acrid bile. Everything hurt.

Someone knocked on the door. My body was shaking in the worst comedown of my life. Each knock battered my skull like cannon fire. I ran toward the front door and forgot all about the towel I'd left on the ground. As soon as my foot hit the damp washcloth, I slipped and cracked my head on the tile. Lights out.

"You look like shit." Roy was standing over me.

Looking at Roy's face was like staring into the sun. My eyes were on fire.

"How the hell you get in?" I grumbled, my head facing to one side.

"Door wasn't locked." Roy tapped my cheek. "Come on, big boy."

Roy slipped a hand under my armpit and helped me to my feet. My legs were jelly. I leaned on him as I hobbled toward the kitchen, taking a seat on the barstool at the large marble island. Uncle Frank meowed his usual greeting, which Roy obliged with a gentle petting.

"You actually went into work today?" Roy asked.

"Tried to." I grunted.

"That was stupid." He snickered.

"Why are you here?"

"I talked to Felecia." Roy turned his gaze away from mine. "About what we did last night."

"You did not!" I wasn't surprised, I was furious.

"I can't keep secretes from her."

"So you tell her we went to a fucking whore house?"

"She's my wife!"

"And that makes her the LAST person you tell!"

"It's okay. She promised she isn't leaving me."

"Lucky you." I shrugged my shoulders.

"But I have to tell the police."

"Excuse me…What?" My ears were ringing, the pain in my head intensified.

"I was talking about it with her last night." He kept digging dirt from under his nails, fidgeting with his hands. "And I was feeling guilty."

"Skip it." I crossed my arms and puffed out my chest. "I wanna get to the part where you go to the police and tell them about an illegal whore house your friend frequents."

"We have to go to the police. What if some of those girls are slaves from human trafficking?"

"You ate the redhead's fucking puss! We did blow there! You're in this shit just as much as I am!"

"Yeah, but I didn't actually go through with it! I didn't even kiss the girl."

"You don't kiss whores, you dumb fuck! And I don't give a shit! The owners find out you went to the cops, and I'm the shit ass who brought you, what do you think they'll do to me?"

"I'm sure the police can help. Don't they have like, witness protection or something?"

"You're a fucking idiot!"

"I've already made up my mind." Roy got up to leave. "I promise I won't say anything about you."

I saw something sticking out of his jeans front pocket. It looked like my phone.

"What's that?"

"What's what?"

"Your pocket." I snatched it from his pants. "Why do you have this?"

"Oh, yeah." He smirked like an imbecile.

"What the fuck are you doing with my fucking phone in your pocket?"

"You left it at the place last night."

"No, I didn't."

"Yeah, you did." Roy looked at me like an idiot. "Why do you think I called the clinic? I was telling you I had it and was still handling the shit with Felicia."

"I was just fucking using it! You fucking called me, you liar!"

"Why would I call your phone when I have it?"

I clicked the power button, and the home screen came on—the phone was unlocked.

"You looked in my phone?"

"What?" Roy shook his head as if to feign disbelief. "No! You just unlocked it!"

"You little shit, this was already unlocked! What did you see?"

"The hell are you talking about?"

"WHAT THE FUCK DID YOU SEE?"

"Wh—"

I grabbed Roy by the throat, surprised at my own strength. My barstool crashed, and Uncle Frank retreated to the bedroom. Caught off guard, Roy and I fell to the ground, me on top. He tried slapping me and grabbing my hands, trying to pry off my fingers. I was too furious to care.

"You fucking snitch!" I felt his heartbeat in my grasp. "You rat fucking bastard! All I wanted to do was show you a good fucking time, celebrate some shit with a friend!"

"I do—"

"Shut up!" I cut him off. "This is the thanks I get! You trying to frame me! Trying to ruin me!"

Roy didn't answer. His face was turning purple, lips blue and eyes wild. I felt sweat dripping down my nose, saw pink droplets land on his cheeks. My nose was bleeding, but I didn't care. I had to plug the hole.

Roy's hands fell to his sides as he stopped struggling, but I didn't let go, not until I felt his heartbeat die in my grasp. His head smacked the ground when I let him go and got to my feet. I grabbed the bar stool off the floor beside him, then used it to bash in his fucking head. His skull crushed like a melon, spilling red across my white tile floor. I swung it again, and again. The metal legs broke on the third swing, so I used its sharp edge to stab the fucker in the heart.

I felt hot blood splash across my face like a warm shower. My body shuddered in delight as my cock stiffened. I kept going, kept stabbing and smashing his face into an unrecognizable pile of ground beef. My hair was matted with sweat and bits of flesh and skull as I panted over Roy's mangled body.

"Shit," I spat, tasting more blood in the back of my throat. "Fucking shit, Roy! Why'd ya have to go and do a stupid thing like that! You can't take another man's phone."

I collapsed on the floor, sitting by Roy's body.

"What the hell am I gonna do about you?"

I rubbed my nose. Only place I could put him for now was the bathtub. I went to the bathroom. Uncle Frank poked his head around the corner, watching me.

"Don't give me that look," I said. "He was gonna snitch! I've already gotta figure out what to do when they realize their hooker's gone. Him calling the cops only complicates shit further!"

Uncle Frank let out a low grunt and went back to the closet.

"Fine." I threw my hands in the air and continued my business.

I took down the plastic shower curtain, then laid it out beside Roy's body. I rolled him on top of the curtain, then used it to drag him into the bathroom without getting anymore mess on my tile. He went up and into the tub with little issue. Either he wasn't very heavy or I was getting used to moving dead bodies.

"Alright," I sighed, observing the mess. "What's next? Am I gonna have to chop a fucker up?"

Indeed, I was. I don't even change my own windshield wipers, so of course

I didn't have any fucking tools around my place. So I went to the kitchen and grabbed a chef's knife from the cutting block. There I was, using a six-hundred-dollar handmade Japanese damascus steel chef's knife to carve up my only friend like a rotisserie chicken.

My hands were hot and shaky from the chemical burns, so I started with something easy, the shoulder blade. I let the knife do all the work. The razor edge glided through flesh and muscle with ease. It was a little work, but I pulled and rotated his arm in the socket until it cracked. With a little weight and pressure, the knife cut clean through tendon and cartilage. I removed his arm and placed it in his lap. Blood was running everywhere, so I turned on the shower and let it wash the mess down the drain.

As I was about to move the body to get to his other arm, someone knocked on my door. Again? Fuck my luck. I was a bloody mess and thought about pretending I wasn't home, but the person at my door only knocked harder.

"Fuck!" I rubbed my nose with my forearm, trying to keep blood from smearing across my face.

I couldn't take the knife out there with me, so I stabbed it in Roy's chest and went to the sink. I washed my face and wiped my body down with a towel, then put on a clean shirt and sweatpants before making my way to the front door. Whoever it was, was relentless.

"Hold the fuck on!" I shouted as I threw the lock and opened the door.

"Oh, hi, Mark!" Hoop said, pushing me aside and entering.

"What fuck are you doing here?" I shouted, wishing I still had my knife.

"Came to pay my respects." Hoop sauntered into the living room.

"Get the hell outta my house!"

"Whatcha gonna do?" Hoop saw the blood on floor. "Call the cops?"

I went to the kitchen and grabbed another knife from the cutting block. Hoop drew a small revolver and pointed it at my stomach.

"What the hell do you want?" I dropped the knife and raised my hands so he could see them.

"Funny you should ask." Hoop smiled. "Have a seat."

He pointed at the couch and I did as I was told.

"How's your head?"

"Excuse me?"

"You're head, numb nuts."

"Hurts."

"Ayuh? No shit. How much PCP do you think you've done the last few days?"

"I don't do that."

"Don't give me that crap. You've been pounding Angel Dust as if ya like the smell. Why do you think things got out of hand at the whore house?"

"I thought that was coke!"

"Dumb as fuck."

"Just take whatever the fuck you came here for and leave!"

"Oh, don't worry." Hoop came out of the kitchen with a glass of water. "I always get what I want."

Hoop winked at me before downing the glass in one gulp.

"Anything else?" I asked.

"I want whores." Hoop waved his arms. "Murderers, drug pushers, rapists, pedophiles, those bastards who can't use a fucking turn signal! I want scumbags like your father. Like you."

"I'm nothing like my—"

"Shut up!" Hoop fired a shot, missing my foot by inches. "You are the same, and worse."

"What are you talking about?"

"You don't remember? Enough of the rose-tinted glasses bullshit."

The walls moved as if ants crawled under the wallpaper. A single black hair sprouted from the pristine white. I looked closer. It wasn't a hair, it was a scratch of ink. In fact, the whole wall looked fake, like a painted movie set. More scratches emerged. They wriggled like worms forming a rat's nest of scribbles.

The room exploded with a meaty splat, a reptile shedding its skin. The wall's flesh hit me like lukewarm gristle. The house was meat, a living, breathing structure. Beneath the white walls was a vast network of arteries and musculature glistening with blood and sweat.

"You were so fucking easy," Hoop said. "Once your dumbass mistook the PCP for coke you were all mine."

I tried to stand, but a skinless hand reached out from the couch and grabbed me. More hands erupted from the furniture; their skin sloughed away like a burn victim. The sofa was a beast of stolen body parts, a coked-out Frankenstein's nightmare.

"What did you do to me?"

"Not a damn thing. You killed Blondie and stole her face. You murdered Anajeli and ripped off her skin. You killed your father, again, and again."

"No!" My head was swollen with terrible memories.

I remembered Blondie and the terror in her eyes. My hands felt the glass bite and slash her flesh with ease. I fucked her brains out. My meat was throbbing in her ocular orbit, dripping with semen as I draped her face over my own. I gazed into the shattered mirror, glad to see I looked nothing like Steven. Next was the bus ride. The fear in the other passengers' faces when I dragged the corpse onboard. The look of terror in the old woman's eyes when she saw me, still wearing Blondie's face.

Steven was on the bus. I killed him. Slashed his throat in front of all those people. The bus driver—some black guy I didn't recognize—looked away from the road for only a second before colliding into a semi-truck. We spun out, knocking everyone to the ground before slamming into the concrete powerline. I escaped with Blondie's corpse before the bus caught fire and dragged her back to my office.

Anajeli's screams stopped at my hand as I choked her out. The scalpel slid across her skin, parting it like Moses and the red sea. Anajeli slipped out of her skin, and I stood their wearing her flesh like a father in his daughter's pajamas. I looked myself over and sighed with relief that I saw nothing that reminded me of Steven.

"I'm not the man you say I am," I pleaded.

"Bullshit." Hoop laughed. "I knew your father very well and the apple never falls far from the tree."

"But I'm nothing like him!"

"You spent all your time avoiding the monster; you didn't notice the one you'd become. Just look at yourself."

Mirrors appeared out of thin air, filling the room. I saw myself cast in a thousand reflections. Everywhere I turned was a new angle, every painful detail, of how similar Steven and I truly were. From the wrinkles in my brow to the rolls of fat around my back and sides, his likeness was everywhere. I couldn't look away, couldn't even close my eyes.

"If you don't like the skin you're in…" Hoop grimaced as he picked up Uncle Frank and stroked his coat. "Allow me to change it."

My skin was on fire. I saw smoke billowing out of my pores as a light sparked in my chest. It started as indigestion, but soon the burn was beyond description. The flesh around the glowing spot began to crinkle and smolder. The hole burned brighter, hotter, then erupted like a welder's torch in a flurry of sparks.

My body burst into flames. I drew breath to scream, but only sucked in a mouthful of fire. It scorched everything on its way down, burning as if I'd swallowed a smoldering brick of coal. My skin smelled like pork, the fat around my belly sizzling like bacon grease. Hoop laughed as my flesh fell away in scorched chunks. The muscle beneath looked like well-done steak.

Uncle Frank leapt from Hoop's arms and onto the meaty countertop, licking its bloody surface. Hoop approached me from behind holding some sort of robe. He draped it over my shoulders. My exposed nerve endings screamed with pain.

"There you go," Hoop said, stepping back to judge his work. "Now you look as ugly on the outside, as you are on the inside."

The robe began to move, undulating like slugs across my naked meat. It stretched and pulled as it covered my body. It was soon apparent this wasn't any fabric, it was skin. Steven's skin. I saw familiar moles and patches of hair, wrinkles and rolls of fat as the living organ dressed me. My hands felt like they'd slipped into gloves stuffed with lukewarm butter, my cock felt flesh sliding over it like a second foreskin.

Steven's face bent and contorted as if laughing deftly. His face stretched over mine, a gross mask still dripping with fat. Steven's skin fit like a wet bathing suit, glistening with blood.

"Like father, like son," Hoop said, picking up Uncle Frank from the counter. "Welcome to hell, Dr. Irving."

# PINK

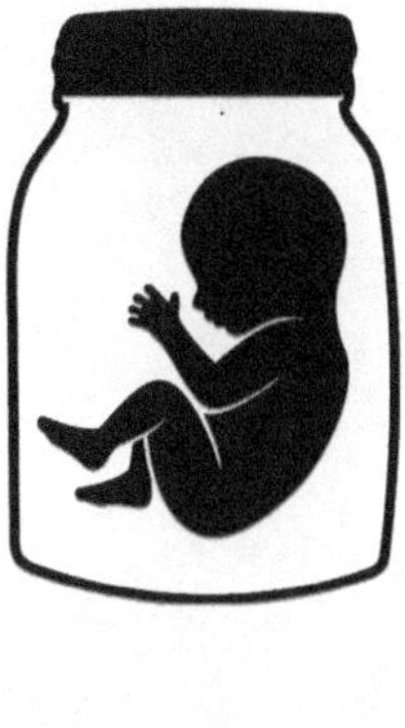

JOHN SHUPECK, JR.

My name's Theo, and I'm a sex addict.

Ever since coming into maturity (no pun intended), all I could think of was the next big thrill that might come my way. Guys, girls, it didn't matter. Don't get me wrong. I wasn't some nymphomaniac who would spread my legs for just anybody. But if it was a sultry Friday night and the drinks were flowing, let's just say I was the kind of barfly you'd want to run into.

My body was okay. Nothing really to write home about, though I suppose I could fill out a pair of jeans well enough. My biggest assets were my boobs. All I'd have to do is throw a tight halter top on and do my face up a little bit, and they would swarm to me like flies (though I admit my reputation may have also had something to do with that). In fact, my reputation almost got me into trouble a few times.

"Did you fuck my man, you bargain basement whore!?" some floozy in a sundress once screamed at me from the post office across the street.

"What? I don't even know who your man is!"

"Bryan, ho! You know who my man is!"

"Sorry, honey. Don't know who your man is, and I wouldn't give him the time of day if I did!" I chuckled as I walked to my car. Bryan's wallet was lying on the front seat. He'd left it at my apartment the night before and I was planning to stop by the tire shop and drop it off after running errands. Guess we'd have to set up something a little more private.

It wasn't that I went out of my way to make people cheat on their spouses; I just went by the "Don't Ask, Don't Tell" policy. If he (or she) wasn't wearing a ring, I didn't ask. If he (or she) *was* wearing a ring…well, I still didn't ask. I figured if their SOs could satisfy them at home, they wouldn't be out looking for a piece of ass like me at the local Moose club. Love me or hate me, that was my policy. As long as they could keep up with me and make sure my proverbial bean was properly flicked, what the fuck did I care?

Truth be told, I *liked* the way I was. Sure, sometimes I'd have a scare. A couple times, I even had my uterus scraped at the local baby killer's. Once, when I was in the middle of jilling-off, the remains of a fetus just dropped out, right onto my fingers. Unable to stop myself from a good cum, I flicked it into the heating vent and finished. That's when I decided I'd make the guys start wearing protection.

No, a few wriggly worms getting torn from my snatch didn't bother me at all, nor did the blurry mornings, forgotten nights, and even a short bout with Hepatitis C. These were all risks that came with the game, and when you're in the moment, doing what God has created you to do…well, foresight kind of goes out the window. What brought me to that little church basement on 4th Street was something I would have seen as relatively innocent under normal circumstances. Jacob and Jessica. The two Js. The couple I fucked to death.

Not right there in the moment, of course. That night, we'd had the time of our lives, with fingers and mouths and bodily fluids going every which way. Truth be told, at least up until that point, I don't think I ever came as hard with anyone else as I had with them. The two Js, Jacob on top, Jessica on bottom, licking our slick taints whenever they'd touch together after a good thrust. My friends used to make jokes about me being a squirter. After that night, I could finally tell my friends they were right.

I'd had threesomes before; in fact, I'd get them whenever I could. I'd torn apart a few relationships and even a couple marriages. Some shit-brick couple decides they want to expand and try out something new, never thinking of the consequences that could come afterwards.

"Sure," the cooze says. "What would you want: another guy, or another girl?"

"Um," the asshole says, trying to pretend like his decision wasn't made the day he found the Hustlers hidden in his daddy's sock drawer. "Well, I thought it might make sense to try it with another woman first. You know, just to be careful and see how it goes."

Yeah, okay, buddy. Blood would be flying the very second another man's pecker came close to your old lady's taint, and you know it. Two tacos for the price of one, though, that's perfectly fine. A-Okay. We can become dykes on demand, but don't you dare ask a guy to fondle another stud's ball sack to help *you* get off. Men are such fucking hypocrites.

No, the two Js hadn't had any regrets in what we did, at least initially. We made an agreement, we enjoyed the time we had together, and we stayed in each other's good graces afterwards. We had to, after all. That was part of the agreement. It wasn't until later, when the *big* cum came. That's when the relationship started to sour a little. It got better after they were dead, but it wasn't quite the same. I needed to move on. I needed closure. I needed more of them.

I was standing outside the church smoking a cigarette when someone approached me from behind and touched my elbow. Just the mere sensation of human skin making contact with my own sent a small jolt of pleasure through my body. Wow, was it really that bad?

"Excuse me," a woman's mousy voice squeaked. "Are you here for the meeting?"

I turned around. The sun was just beginning to set, but there was still enough light to see the pathetic creature standing before me. She couldn't have been over five-foot-tall. Her face was bookish, with a nose so smooshed in it could barely hold the wire-rimmed glasses perched on its bridge. Her black hair was pulled into a messy bun with renegade strands hanging this way and that. She was tiny…so, so tiny, without a mountain or a molehill of a tit to be seen through the oversized hoodie blanketing her. Though the black sweatpants she wore were just as comically massive, it didn't take a rocket scientist to see the sad truth: no ass.

*This would be me if you sucked all the fun stuff out and replaced it with rat shit.* I smiled a little at the thought.

"Yes," I said, taking a final drag from my smoke. "You're...um, here for the meeting, as well?"

Her alarmingly pale cheeks suddenly turned an equally alarming crimson red.

"Yes," she said, looking down at the sidewalk now. "I just started coming a few weeks ago. I missed last week's session, though. Dr. Sharma really is the best. She's already helped me so much."

"Well, I'm very happy to hear that. My name's Theo. What is your name?" I glanced at my watch. 7:55 p.m. We'd have to get in there soon.

"Well, um, I'm Casey. Twenty-one days clean, ha-ha-ha."

Clean? What the fuck were they teaching in there, to be totally abstinent while singing Kumbaya to your dildo?

"Well, I think it's about time I meet the rest of the class. You wanna show me the way?"

Casey's head snapped up. She looked as if someone had just forced her fingers into a live toaster.

"Oh, yes! Yes, it's starting soon, and Dr. Sharma doesn't like stragglers. Follow me!"

She turned and pulled open the door leading to the basement steps. I followed closely behind, wondering what the hell I was getting myself into. I was in awe once we were downstairs. Every few feet or so was the door of a Sunday school classroom, with colorful pamphlets and crudely drawn crosses pasted all around their frames.

'Jesus Saved Me Before I Was Born!' one banner proclaimed proudly in a shaky child's scrawl.

'And Lead Us Not Into Sensation, but Deliver Us From Evil. Amen!' another poster shouted as we turned the corner and passed by the basement's lone water fountain.

"What kind of church is this, anyway?" I asked Casey as we approached the only room with the lights on.

"Oh, um…actually, I don't know. Not Catholic, I don't think. One time, they were doing renovations down here and we had to hold the meeting in the chapel. There weren't any water holders or anything at the entrance. Maybe it's Presbyterian."

"Aw, okay," I said, as if I had any fucking clue what that meant. I was surprised my head hadn't burst into flames the moment we crossed the threshold.

We were at the door leading into what appeared to be a conference room. Since deciding to do this, I hadn't felt one ounce of reservation. Now the butterflies were beginning to flap their wings. In my stomach…in my nether regions. Fear never felt so good.

*Okay, no turning back now, Theodora. New hunting ground…lots of fresh fish in there. Don't fuck this up.*

Casey pulled open another door. We walked around a big refreshment table and took our seats. There were about a dozen other people in the group, sitting on wooden folding chairs in a semi-circle. Soon, we would speak of our lurid backstories, telling some asshole about our "struggles" with sucking cock or shoving vibrating action figures up our asses. All the while, the rest of the group would sit there silently, nodding along with their hands clasped over their laps, ardently trying to hide their wet spots and boners. Therapy? Give me a fucking break. This was one big mental suck and fuck without any meaningful payoff at the end. Well, until now that is. That's what I was there for—to give them all a happy ending they'd never forget. One by one. Or maybe even two by two. Freaks like to get freaky, and I had hit the freak motherload.

We sat there for a while, talking about anything but sex. Casey was the librarian of a place a couple towns over (I knew the one; I used to fuck around with a trustee board member there). Casey was a single mother of two who had lost her husband just recently. She didn't give me the full story just then, but I was astute enough to guess the rest.

Little sad freak bitch home all alone, two tots in bed, no fun to be had. Sure, vibrators and the shower nozzle had tided her over for a while, but it wasn't enough. She wanted to lie in someone's arms; for them to pet her hair and tell her all the nice things even though they both knew all the nice things were a lie. It didn't matter. She could at least have someone for a night. To make her feel pretty.

*Try a dating website!* one of her more attractive friends had probably urged. *You need to start looking out for yourself, Casey. Your husband's dead, but that doesn't mean you are.*

So, Casey starts browsing all the major sites, putting her best picture first, which still requires about twenty pounds of makeup and a selfie filter. Suddenly, the boys come calling, telling her she is the most beautiful creature walking God's green earth. Meanwhile, these same guys have another tab open, talking to some raven-haired cam girl for $3.49 a minute and squirting into the crusted-over macaroni and cheese underneath the desk. Hell, the raven-haired cam girl could have been me. Probably was.

Then little miss Casey starts going on dates. At first, she's shy. She feels guilty for moving on from the man she had promised to love and obey for the rest of her miserable existence. Then, after a few tequila sunrises, there's a handy underneath the table. Then two. Before you know it, little miss Casey is getting bukkaked four nights a week, three guys shooting their loads onto her nerd glasses while her two tots snore the night away in the next room.

Did she become careless one night? Did she pass out before one of her gentleman suitors had finished? Did one of the children come out in the middle of the night for a glass of milk, only to find mommy spread eagle on the carpet, head bouncing off the floor with a string of saliva hanging between her mouth and the pillow?

That's what I would have done if mommy passed out. Double-sided dildo, no lube. That's the best way.

A few more minutes, and finally, the door opened. The sex counselor had arrived.

"Wow," I whispered to Casey. "Dr. Sharma really let herself go."

"That's not Dr. Sharma. I don't know who that is."

"Oh, okay."

"Hey, hey, everyone," the rotund stranger said as he took his jacket off and hung it on the rack. "So sorry I'm late. Dr. Phillips was in a car accident, so I am taking his place for the night."

The group looked at each other, puzzled.

"Who's Dr. Philipps?" Casey said. "Our counselor is Dr. Sharma. A woman."

"Hmm…the team upstairs must have gotten their wires crossed. In any case, your regular doctor could not be here tonight, so I am in charge. Now don't anybody worry, because he…I mean, *she,* is doing just fine. Just a minor fender bender. If anyone wants to grab refreshments, please do so now. I don't want grumbling tummies interrupting the meeting."

*This* was supposed to be a sex addiction expert? The guy had sweat stains around the collar and armpits of his dress shirt, which didn't fit him anywhere near properly. The buttons looked like they might explode from their threads with every step he took. When he sat down, his bare stomach showed through the slit near the bottom of the shirt. I wanted to vomit just at the sight of him.

Casey got up, saying she wanted to grab something from the refreshment table. As a joke, I asked her to grab me a Boston cream donut. I did love my filling.

"Tonight," he said, "we'll start with a clean slate. You can tell your stories to Dr. Hooper. But no formalities here. I find that makes the process a bit awkward. So, just call me Hoop."

His hair…that long greasy ponytail, so much like my own when I wouldn't wash it for a few days. I imagined that if you grabbed it, it would slip out of your hands on its own accord, like a cobra slicked with shit. The thought of boiling pepperoni rolls sprang to my mind. I had to audibly hold back a gag.

"Miss?" Dr. Hooper said with concern. "Miss, is everything okay?"

"Yes," I said, composing myself. "Sorry. I'm just a little nervous."

"*Ho-ho-ho-ho-ho!*" Hooper's laugh sounded like a fucked-up Santa Claus from hell. "I'm assuming this is your first time. Don't worry, we *all* get nervous our first time, isn't that right, everybody?"

The group tittered together and nodded. Every single one of them. Even me. Maybe this wouldn't be so hard, after all. We trusted each other. That was the easiest way to get in.

They all told their stories. One by one, each one of them poured their guts out right there on the church's basement floor. They spoke of curiosity, loneliness, inability to control themselves once they bit the hook and got dragged in.

Charlie was a successful accountant who spent his evenings dressing in his wife's underwear and heading down to Harrison Hills Park to cruise for young black men walking through the woods. (Of course, these young men were *always* of legal consenting age, wink.) Shelly was a marital counselor who got caught by her assistant with a steno pad in one hand and a client's rod in the other. And Kelly? Well, Kelly was a delicious young black girl who got sucked into the game, giving blowjobs for rocks until she realized she'd much rather suck a skin pipe than a glass one. I fucked around with a black girl once. It was fun, but not an experience I wanted to repeat. Too sassy.

On and on it went, the next orator seemingly trying to top the last one's tale of depravity. You could probably stick a fork straight up and grab a piece of the decadence floating in the air; it was that palpable. Just one giant cake of perversion, the layers separated by the oozing brown sludge of each participant's trespasses. I knew right then that I belonged there; that this was the place I had been drawn to by some inexplicable force. These were my people, and I would have them all.

The most interesting story was Casey's. Feeling neglected by her husband, she had taken on a new job at the library. Eventually, she befriended an older man. He'd asked her to come to his house one night. Unbeknownst to her, the man and his girlfriend were swingers. After consuming copious amounts of wine, she'd had sex with the both of them.

One encounter turned to two, and eventually, she found herself in a full-out affair, hiding her phone from her husband and leaving the house at odd hours to meet up with the couple. As time went on, Casey's husband, like all good husbands do, found out. After many late-night fights, threats of divorce, and even a few physical altercations, they had both decided she should be here, among of group of people who struggled with similar problems.

"He died just a few days before I attended my first session," Casey said, struggling with all her might not to start blubbering. "So, here I am. Even though he's gone, I still feel like this is something he'd want me to do. Thank you."

The group clapped. Such a sad, sad story. As I clapped along, I decided it: Casey would be my first.

"Well," Dr. Hooper said, wiping a tear away from his own eye. "I'm proud of every single one of you for standing up and telling your stories so boldly…so genuinely. But I think we missed out on one. Perhaps a mouse in the corner of the room who might be a little shy? So, tell us all, mysterious black-haired stranger: what brought you here?"

I had been in a daze, wondering what I could do with the opportunity laid before me. It was only when the room became silent that I realized all eyes were on me. I had to take a few seconds to compose myself before I spoke.

"Well…first of all, my name is Theo, and I'm a sex addict."

*"Hi, Theo."*

"Well, uh…this is the first time I've ever talked about this, but…my sex addiction led to the deaths of two people. I had a threesome. With a husband and wife, and, and…"

"Theodora, we are here for you," Dr. Hooper said. "Really, don't hold back. Let it all out. You're amongst people who are the same as you. No judgement. Anything you did or do in the future, you've already been judged. We are just here to assist in the journey."

"Okay," I said, feigning hesitation. "Okay. So here is the story. I was working with a girl. We became friends. Eventually, she started inviting me over to her house to watch movies. Her husband was there a lot of the time. We also became friends. Then, eventually, we made a plan."

"What plan was that, Theodora?"

Hooper was erect in his seat now, that streak of belly flesh nowhere to be seen. He cared about me…he wanted to hear my story. The rest of them…there was no redemption, no conquering of demons. They would keep coming and telling their stories to impress each other, and then they would go home and shove a stick of anal beads in the microwave, sodomizing themselves to their heart's content. They'd wake up in the morning, sore, ashamed of themselves, swearing they'd never do it again. Wash, rinse, repeat. Back here the next week, trying to portray themselves as heroes overcoming some incurable disease. I knew better. I liked who I was, and I would proclaim that pride without batting a single PBT-infused eyelash.

"We had the greatest time ever. He came in me, and I came on both him and her. It was the first time I ever squirted. They'd been having problems with their marriage. Arguing with each other all the time. They couldn't make a baby. That was what they really wanted. So, I came between them. I let them be able to take out their frustrations without hurting each other in the process. And then…"

"What, Theo? What did you do, sister?" Casey placed her hand in my lap and clenched her fingers around mine.

"I told them…I would be a surrogate for them. If Jacob could get me pregnant, I would carry their baby to term and give it to them after it was all over. Jessica had some reservations, but she agreed in the end. The only thing, I told them, was that I didn't want to be inseminated. I wanted a little bit of fun to make the process worth it. No money, no consequences. I just wanted them both, for one night. I could do whatever I wanted, and he could cum in me at the end. That's it."

I pulled my arm down a little bit and start rubbing the knuckle of Casey's thumb against the top of my clit. I'd intentionally wore the tightest jeans I owned, along with an equally tight black t-shirt from the Pink brand. Pink. That was the perfect phrase to describe me.

"So, I'm assuming they went through with the agreement?" Dr. Hooper had to have seen what we were doing, but he didn't seem to care one little bit. No judgements. I liked that.

"Yes," I said. Casey had now opened her hand and was pushing her thumb and index finger inside my panties. "We set up a weekend in a cabin Jacob's father owned. Anything went, as long as I was pregnant at the end. We intentionally set it during the time my ovulation cycle was in full swing. And…"

"What happened, Theo?" Dr. Hooper said. "Did you get everything you wanted?"

Another hand had joined Casey's now. Charlie, the crossdresser. I felt as his and Casey's fingers wrapped around each other, pushing and grinding, teasing and tickling. I was moaning. Soft sighs, right there in the middle of everyone.

"Yes…uh-huh. Yes. In my ass, in my mouth, in between my tits. She sat on my face while he stuck me. In and out, in and out. The old in out, in out. She tasted like strawberries. I don't know if she freshened herself up with some weird spray beforehand, but it was like sweet fruit. Gushing down my lips, dripping down my body onto his dick. Yes, yes, yes!"

Hoop was all ears. Despite my initial disgust for the man, I wondered if he was hard. The fabric of his ketchup-and-mustard-stained dress pants wouldn't tell.

"Do you like this, Theodora? What's happening?"

I looked around me. They were all doing it. Hands in each other's pants, stroking, rubbing, playing. Casey pushed Charlie away and got on her knees. She licked her lips, then shoved her face into my crotch.

"Yes," I said after a prolonged moan. "Yes, I love this. Can we do this every week? I think…I think I'm going to squirt again." My body began gyrating violently.

"And what about *him,* Theodora?" Dr. Hooper was oblivious to the surreal insanity going on all around him. He was looking at me, and only at me, eyes opened wide.

"What?" I said, struggling to concentrate. Charlie had joined Casey in licking me. I leaned back and began pushing myself against their hungry mouths. "Who? Jacob—?"

"The baby, Theodora? Tell me, did he cry?"

*Jacob Jr!* my mind screamed. *He knows about Jacob Jr! What else does he know?*

"I'm cumming, I'm cum—"

I snapped open my eyes. The hands were gone, the faces just phantoms behind the veiny screens of my eyelids. It was just me in an empty seat, staring ahead at another empty chair. The group was gone. Dr. Hooper was nowhere to be seen.

I looked at my phone. 10:23 p.m. Over an hour had passed in the span of a couple minutes. What had I done? What had I said? What the fuck was going on? Had I told them everything…about the bodies?

I waited for a long time, rubbing my hands together and waiting for someone, anyone to walk in and let me in on the joke. No one did. At some point, I realized my pussy was aching. I looked around, then unbuckled my jeans and checked my underwear. Flowery blooms of blood dotted the white cotton between my taint and lips. My period, already? I could have sworn my last cycle had ended just a few weeks ago.

Still not completely together, I grabbed my handbag and made my way up the stairs, ready to breathe the cool night air and leave this all behind forever. No more meetings, no more spilling my soul in front of everyone. I blacked out; it was that simple. I blacked out, and they had all left me there, none of them caring what would happen to me. Even Dr. Hooper. Well, let's just say a certain "therapist" was about to get his license revoked. I fuck around plenty when it suits me, but don't you dare think you can fuck with me. Because no matter what, in the end, I will fuck you, whether you like it or not.

I was getting ready to cross the street to my car when I felt a familiar hand touch my elbow. My legs immediately turned to jelly.

"Hey, sis, you okay?" Casey sounded so nonplussed, so normal. It was as if the giant semi-orgy in the conference room had never happened.

"Huh?"

"Look," she said, still holding onto my elbow. "I know you said you'd be fine, but I figured I should wait up for you and make sure everything's all right We are all struggling the same way. You're never going to get past this if you don't let someone in. The group is a safe space for people like us. I want to be a safe space for you. Okay? Do you understand?"

I wanted to pull my arm away, to get her to stop touching me. Not because I didn't like it; my underwear was already sticky again. It was because of *him,* what he'd said to me before the darkness took over.

*And what about* him, *Theodora? Did the baby cry?*

Quickly, I darted my eyes around, trying to see if maybe that fat fuck slimeball was in one of the cars waiting to pull out. Nothing. As a matter of fact, my car looked to be the only one on the block. He was gone.

*Fuck!*

"Can you come with me?" I said to Casey without thinking. My back was still turned; for some reason, I didn't want to face her just yet. "That is, if your babysitter doesn't mind watching your kids for a little while longer. I can drive you back."

Casey tightened her grip on me.

"Of course, honey. Group ended a little early tonight, and I always go for coffee afterward. I could spare an hour or so."

*Sweetheart,* I thought as we crossed the street and got in the car. *An hour is all I need.*

Turns out I was wrong. It only took about twenty-five minutes.

Casey's head was in the crook of my elbow, her dismal excuse for a body pressed closely against mine. This was the part I always hated, when the cum was drying and the other one wanted to cuddle and spoon for a while. The dreaded after-fuck. I'd learned to bite my lip and deal with it after so many times, but that didn't make the act any less ridiculous. I equated it to a lion shoving food down the ripped-out throat of a zebra, making sure the kill was well-nourished after the fact. I got mine, now let me digest in peace.

"I had a good time tonight," I said, blowing out a ring of smoke. That much was true; Little Miss No-Ass sure knew how to scarf down a beaver.

"Yeah…I had a good time, too." Still shy, still unsuspecting. No, I hadn't said anything when I blacked out at the group session. My secret was safe.

"So," I said as casually as possible. "I noticed lots of guys in the group. Hopefully, they don't get tempted as easily as we do."

Casey kissed the inside of my arm and giggled. It sounded like a bird trying to chirp with a mouthful of worms.

"Yeah…I always say to myself, 'No, no, no. We need to resist. It's not right. We need to fight it, sweetie.' Well, look at how well I fought it tonight." She let out a sigh. She was ashamed of herself.

"It's okay. There's nothing wrong with what we did. Just a little hiccup. Hey, you have two kids. Can I ask you a question?"

Casey didn't answer. It seemed as if the weight of her mistake was finally pressing down on her. Good. Her pain made the situation a little more bearable. Sexier.

"Your kids. Were they, you know, cut out, or did they both have vaginal births?"

"Umm… Both natural. I did have an epidural the second time just because of how bad the first one hurt. Why?"

I lit up a new smoke and blew a few circles into the air. My nipples had been hard as ice whenever we first entered the bedroom. Now they were back down to little pink dots on my chest. Casey's nipples, however; those girls were standing loud and proud. Even through her disgust, Little Miss No-Ass was still horny.

"Nothing. Doesn't matter. Say, I couldn't help but notice your fancy shmancy clit ring. That thing really help?"

Though an intentional topic changer, I *was* interested in where Casey had bought it. It resembled some kind of spider or mite, with dozens of black legs clamped around either side of her clit. There was a little red dot in the center, which I assumed to be an LED light. As I'd wrapped my lips around her pussy and sucked, I couldn't help but notice how it would vibrate against my tongue every time she moaned. Motion-activated? Is that how it was done?

"Oh, sweetie, you wouldn't even *believe*!" Her spirits seemed to suddenly lift. "It's on twenty-four hours a day. Even when I'm not thinking about it, it just starts going off. Dr. Sharma gave it to me as a form of therapy so I could resist whenever temptation was strong. You might want to ask Dr. Hooper about it. It's all the rage within sex therapy circles right now."

A clit ring that could react on-demand? How was such a thing even possible? Not that it would satisfy *my* urges…nothing could. But something to hold me over until the next main course? I was more than interested now.

"That's hot. I mean, not that I would misuse it. I'll ask Dr. Hooper about it next week."

She nodded in agreement.

I was about to get up when Casey ran her finger through my pubic hair and pressed down. Say what you want about her looks; that little whore knew exactly how to get your attention.

"Not yet. Let's play again."

"What about your kids?"

"Fuck 'em. I'll pay overtime. You ready to go into overtime?"

"Fuck yes, baby. *Fuck yes.*"

I was just starting to cum for the second time when there was a loud bang in the other room. Casey snapped her head up from between my legs, an alarmed look on her grease-smeared face.

"Theo?" she whispered. "Theo, what…what was that?"

"Oh, I'm sorry, honey. Probably the bookshelf in the guest bedroom. It's been falling apart for ages now."

I tried to speak as nonchalantly as possible even as the cold grip of panic steadily clutched itself around my throat. Had it fallen? I had to go check.

"Oh…okay," Casey squeaked. "Hey, it's getting late. Would you be able to take me home? The babysitter's probably wondering where I'm at. Then I'm gonna have a long talk with my accountability buddy, ha-ha. Don't worry, I won't mention your name."

"Okay," I said, not giving a solitary flying fuck about Casey's dick-nosed babysitter or her shit-headed accountability buddy. "Okay, I'll take you home. Can you just give me one minute? I want to make sure nothing important broke."

Casey agreed, taking the opportunity to get dressed.

I half-sprinted to the other room and flung the door open, expecting the worst. No, he was still up there in his normal place. I scanned the room, finally finding the source of the noise. A piece of drop ceiling above the shelf had cracked and fallen. There'd been a leak up there for a while that I hadn't taken the time to fix yet. The water must have eaten through the tile and caused the cork to crack and crumble.

I chuckled, then let out a sigh of relief. It was safe. All was well.

"Theo, do you think we could stop for an iced tea along the wa—"

I spun around quickly. Casey was standing behind me in the doorway. Her already pale cheeks were now dead white, her mouth open in a wide frozen O. Her gaze flicked back and forth—from me, to the baby in the mason jar, to the blood-stained chains hanging from the ceiling, and then back to me again. The light in the room was dim, but the choking noise emanating from her throat made it clear: she'd seen everything.

"Theo…what…what did you do?"

Casey stood like that in the doorway—frozen, mouth dropped to her chest like some kind of retarded ape. Her hands were wrapped around her own throat as she kept making that disgusting dry heaving noise. No judgements, huh? Well, I was feeling pretty judged just then.

Already planning on killing her before we got to the front door, I pulled the shoelace out of my pocket and lunged at her. She clawed, bit, hit, but let's be real: that little ninety-five-pound bitch was dead the moment she got into the car with me at the church. As we struggled, she managed to shove a hand up my shirt and wrap her fingernails around my nipples. Unphased, I rammed my knee into her side over and over again until she finally stopped. When I saw she had no energy left, I grabbed hold of her shoulder and rolled her face first onto the floor.

"Plea…please! Can't…breathe…Theo…My baby…"

"I'm sorry, honey," I cooed gently into her ear as I wrapped the shoestring around her throat. "But you make me cum like crazy. You're uglier than sin, but boy, do you know how to get a girl off. Take this as a compliment."

I sat down on the flat of her back and leaned backward with all my weight. She put up a hell of a fight, I'll give her that. Even when I yanked with all my strength and crushed her windpipe, she still managed to claw my hands all to hell before finally dropping her feet to the carpet and letting out a loud, disgusting fart. For having no ass, she sure could rip one with the best of them.

Finally, I let the shoestring go lax. I made an attempt to stand, then decided it would be better if I just sat on the carpet and rested for a while. I'd only done such a thing once before, and with a far less physically capable opponent.

Finally, after catching my breath a little, I looked across the room to my baby and smiled.

"Don't…worry…" I managed to gasp out. "She's…just…a…toy. I'll…dump her after a few days. There'll be more."

Just as always, Jacob, Jr. remained quiet. Except for his eyes. His eyes never left mine. It looked like he was condemning me. Good.

"So, sweetie," I said as I leaned forward and ran my fingers through Casey's greasy hair. She was lying in the same spot the two Js had laid just before I used them up and dumped their bodies in the river. "We never finished part two. What do you say? Wanna see if the sequel's just as good as the original?"

She didn't protest. Turns out, part two was just as good as part one, and then some. I made sure to turn Jacob Jr.'s jar so he was facing the wall. This was not something a baby should witness.

A week passed by without incident. They'd made passing mention of Casey's disappearance on the news a couple times, but nothing major. Apparently, she had been bipolar and was prone to episodes of mania where she'd leave for weeks at a time without any notice or explanation. Her disappearance might be taken more seriously a month from now, but by that point Little Miss No-Ass would be long gone, floating down the Allegheny River with a pocket full of Xanax and half her face missing. There might be questions about that latter detail, but I couldn't worry about it now. I'd gotten a little out of control on that first night; sloppy. No matter. Only men did the kind of shit I did. They'd never suspect someone like little old me of being able to commit something so heinous, so depraved. And hey, no cock, so no DNA tracing. Women truly do have it better.

Sometimes, I'd look at Jacob Jr. and think of Casey's own two little shits. Kids. You birth them, bathe them, feed them, and yet they still keep sucking. Just sucking and sucking and sucking, hanging off your teet until it feels like the nipple's going to snap off and your tit fat will fall to the floor in a bloody cascade. I would never allow myself to be in that situation. Given the chance, I'd walk right into the nursery ward of a hospital with a baseball bat and start playing bloody pineapples, smashing each and every infant into oblivion as their parents watched from the other side of the glass, crying their eyes out and asking why.

*Indeed, why? Weren't you a baby once? Didn't your mother love you?*

The fucking whoremaster should have killed me when she had the chance. She gave birth to the devil, and I was more than willing to live up to my title. And as far as Casey went…well, in my eyes, I had done her a big favor. At least I could appreciate her without sucking her bank account dry and upchucking banana yogurt all over her shirt. I'd keep her for around a week or so—play with her until the odor became unbearable—and then she'd be floating. It was a perfectly miserable ending to a perfectly miserable existence. Wash, rinse, repeat.

The group gathered again on Thursday. I'd wrestled with the idea of finding another meeting, perhaps somewhere deep in the city. One local SAA member had already gone missing, and more were sure to follow. Sure, I'd have to take off the training wheels and go out into the real world eventually, but this was new hat for me. The two Js had already been dead when I moved them from their shack on Pitt

Street to my little love palace, meaning I'd technically only ever killed two people: Casey, and a newborn. I needed to practice with the vulnerable before moving onto more self-aware, better-equipped targets.

I pulled up to the church just as the meeting was about to begin. There was a water leak in the basement, meaning we had to meet upstairs in the worship area. Just like Casey had said, there were no ceremonial bowls of virgin piss to dip our fingers in. No, definitely not Catholic.

This time, there were no strange blackouts or mass jerk-off sessions. We talked, we gave our stories, we ate cheap chocolate brownies from Giant Eagle, then we made our way to exit. Strangely, no one mentioned anything about Casey's disappearance. That was perfectly fine with me. I certainly wasn't going to bring the hideous little whore's name up, especially when she was still in the apartment, hanging against the wall with a banana stuffed inside her. There was still enough flesh there to get my engine cranked.

I was in the middle going up the stairs with Charlie the crossdresser when Dr. Hooper called out to me. Damn it. I was just getting ready to give the invite to go out for coffee. I wasn't going to take him home yet. Casey was still too fresh.

"Theodora! Hey, Theodora! Would you mind staying behind for a couple of minutes? There's something I want to talk to you about."

Feeling uneasy, I turned around and took a seat a few pews down from Dr. Hooper. Even though we were the only two in the room, I couldn't quite allow myself to get close to him. Even from a distance, he smelled. I couldn't quite put my finger on what the source of the aroma was—balls, ass, armpits—but there was definitely something coming off of him. Something rotten.

"Theodora," he said after everyone was out of the room. "Have you heard from Casey at all, the girl you sat with last week?"

He was wearing the same outfit as the week before: a red dress shirt with giant pools of sweat underneath the arms and neck, along with the same pair of baggy black dress pants. Could that be where the smell was coming from—the unwashed clothes?

"What?" I said in my best it-wasn't-*me*-who-took-the-last-cookie voice.

Dr. Hooper shot a glance around the room, as if to make sure we were indeed alone.

"Theodora, I talked to Casey last week after the session ended. I...saw that she left with you, so I gave her a ring to make sure everything was kosher."

My intestines immediately turned to dry ice. When would she have been able to answer him? We'd been in bed together the entire time.

*No, Theodora. Not the* entire *time.*

When I'd ran into the other room to check on Jacob Jr. That was when he called. But less than a minute had passed before I caught her looking over my shoulder. Could they really have had a conversation that quickly?

"But...how? You just started here. How would you have her phone number?"

He chuckled and reached down into his left pocket, producing a Hershey's bar. He ripped it open with his two fat thumbs and tossed the wrapper carelessly onto the floor. The chocolate looked warped and runny, as if half of it had melted off into the wrapper.

"I had all of you write down your numbers last week, Theo. I also gave you my number. Don't you remember?"

No, that's not right; he didn't say it like that. *I also gave you my NUMBA. Don't you REMEMBA?* That's the way he said it, like some kind of uneducated asshole from up north. Maine, Rhode Island? Definitely not New York. But somewhere up north…maybe Boston.

*BOSTON! Don't you REMEMBA?*

"Oh. I guess my mind was on other things then. Anyway, we just went out for coffee, then I dropped her off outside her house. What's the problem?"

Dr. Hooper regarded me for a minute, then took a big bite out of the chocolate. A little bead of brown crested over his bottom lip and dropped down to his chin, eeling its way toward the wiry hairs poking out of his shirt collar.

"She told me where she was, Theodora. At your apartment. You wanted to help each other. So, what about it? Did you help each other?" He took another chomp from the candy and giggled. His jowls flapped back and forth against his skull; his belly jiggled in the same way that old poem said it would. Santa Claus from hell, yes. Only, was it hell? Maybe he was Santa Claus from New England. Same place, right?

"Yes," I said, barely hearing the words coming out of my mouth. "I was still nervous about the group, so she came to help me understand things and get my mind straight."

"Did you fuck her?"

"Um…excuse me?" The question came so swiftly, so matter-of-factly.

"Theodora, come now. Well, I guess you did already, didn't you? *Ha-ha-ha-ha!*" Now that belly full of jelly looked like a waterbed full of pudding spread. If he didn't stop, Dr. Hooper's tits would fly into his neck. That would be good…at least that trail of melted chocolate would be wiped away.

"Okay," I said. "Okay, yes. I was fresh off the wagon, and she was there for me. So I fucked up. So did she."

"Theodora, Theodora," he said between chortles and asthma-strained hisses. "I'm not judging you, dear. In fact, after that little story you told during our last meeting, I would have expected nothing less. You're a dirty girl, aren't you?"

"Last session? What story did I tell during last sess—"

Dr. Hooper slopped up the last bit of chocolate. In horror, I watched as his tongue slithered out from his mouth and ran up and down his fingers, trying to pick up any remaining residue. Normally, such an action would have turned me on. Seeing Dr. Hooper do it made me sick to my stomach.

"Listen, honey, I'm going to tell you exactly how it is. You're fucked up. More fucked up than anyone else in the group. After all those despicable things you said—"

"I…don't remember. I think I blacked out."

Dr. Hooper waved a dismissive hand in the air.

"No matter. The point, darling Theodora, is that I know what you need, and I know exactly how to give it to you. But I can't help you if you keep killing my patients. It's against my code of ethics, don't ya know?"

"I saw something," I said quickly, not knowing what else to say. "On Casey. Something Dr. Sharma gave to her. It was a…" I felt nauseated even thinking of saying the phrase in front of him.

"A clit ring?" he finished for me, nonplussed. "Aw, yes. I prescribe those myself. Unfortunately, Dr. Philipps…errrr, I mean, *Sharma,* was still giving out the older model. Very obsolete compared to the one I offer. Were you thinking of asking for one?"

"Well…"

Dr. Hooper started cackling again. He reached out and slapped a chocolate-stained hand on the knee of my jeans.

"Theo, Theo, Theo. This is what these little get-togethers are for. No shame here. It's a safe space. I wouldn't be doing my job if I wasn't providing what you were asking for. So, let's get you what you need. Give me one minute, my darling little necrophiliac." He tipped me a sly wink, then got up and went to a storage closet across the room.

I wanted to say more, but I was flummoxed. I *told* them? Every single one of them *knew* my secret? How could have I been so careless, so mind-bogglingly *stupid*? Had I been drugged; had Casey slipped something into my punch? But that didn't make any sense. I'd only lost my memory for maybe forty-five minutes—an hour, tops. What kind of date-rape drug could be so effective for a limited amount of time and then provide zero side effects after it wore off? And then what had happened before it all went blank…everybody practically fucking right there on their seats. Could date-rape drugs make you hallucinate like that? Dr. Hooper… *Hoop.* Had he hypnotized me? But how? When? And he was helping me now, even though he knew about the two Js, about Jacob Jr., about Casey.

Dr. Hooper poked around in the storage closet for a minute before producing a black leather bag. He placed it on the table beside him and rummaged around, finally finding what he was looking for. With a clasped hand, he walked back across the room and reclaimed his seat near the doors.

"Here," he said, pushing his arm out toward me. I flinched in response. He laughed. "Theodora, *calm down.* This is the bug we were talking about. It's self-attaching and self-activated. All you have to do is spread the old tree trunks open, and it will crawl right in there. Adam & Eve don't have shit on this."

I held my hand out and Hoop dropped a device into my palm. If I hadn't seen Casey's own special little friend, I might have jumped in revulsion. It looked like a large tick with hundreds of legs. In the center of its body was a flashing red LED light.

"This will…help me?" I gulped.

If I had truly told them everything the last time, then he would surely know this plastic-coated plaything couldn't provide anything near the satisfaction I needed. It's like a soldier killing a hostile enemy for the first time; once you get a taste for human blood, it's not like you can go back to sticking pins in cats or drowning frogs in a bucket outside the outhouse. You're on a higher level now. Going down would do nothing except make you want to go back to the top.

Dr. Hooper chuckled again.

"As sure as Boston rain helps a mountain pine grow. Well, how about it, Theodora? Take her for a little test drive. I'll turn my head. Wouldn't want the doctor to see the goodies now, would you? That would be unethical."

He turned his fat ass on the pew until he was facing the wall. I did a triple take to make sure he wasn't watching, then unbuttoned the top of my jeans and pulled my underwear open. I was just sliding my hand inside the waistband when the device came to life, skittering back and forth across my palm. I screamed but remained still. The toy made its way to my navel, then ran down to where my clit and urinary opening met. I felt a slight tickle as the legs pressed down against my skin. I let out a pleasurable shriek as the bug spread the top of my labia open and clamped down. Then the vibrations started.

"Oh my…Oh my *God!* This is…this is amazing! It feels like it. Really, I *feel* it!"

Sweat was pooling around my eyebrows within seconds and my fingertips felt numb. Dr. Hooper was turned around now. I still hadn't buttoned my pants back up yet. I didn't care. Let him watch. The sick bastard. He knew what he'd given me, so let him enjoy the fruits of his labor.

"Oh, Theodora. It seems like you're wearing a Wednesday on a Thursday. Naughty girl." He pushed his unnaturally long tongue out again, licking some of the chocolate away from his chin.

"Make it…make it stop," I said, even though I *never* wanted it to stop. "How can I…how can I go to work like this, or, or, or grocery shop? I'll be fff..fucking cumming my brains out in aisle 3."

"Clean up in aisle 3!" Dr. Hooper yelled joyfully, the folds in his belly rippling at full blast. "Better get some clerks down there to clean up that number!"

*We need to clean up that wicked pissa of a numba! Rememba, Theodora? Rememba the Alamo? Three clerks! Three friends! The three Js! Rememba them!? Come on, Theo! Rememba, rememba, REMEMBA!?*

"Oh, fuck! Fuck, fuck, fuck!"

It happened quickly, and yet felt like it took hours. Electric jolts running through my spine; legs turning into muddy puddles; fierce tickling from my belly button to my groin, spilling out from between my thighs. Without thinking, I reached my hands under my shirt and viced my nipples between my fingers, pulling them every which way as the thunder reverberated through me and made the world go black. Somewhere in the recesses of my mind, I heard a baby crying. As the big moment came closer, so did the sound of the baby, increasing further and further until it was one loud, ear-shattering shriek.

*MY BRAINS ARE BLEEDING OUT OF MY SKULL! MY FUCKING BRAINS!*

Then, just like that, it was over. I had practically capsized out of my seat by time the orgasm had run its course. My hands were on my knees. I was hunched over, panting like a dog.

"What did…how did…where did…that's *impossible*. What did you just do to me?"

"Well," Dr. Hooper said with more than a hint of pride in his voice. "After your story last week, I knew you needed something with a little *kick* to it. A little extra *oomph* to get the party started, if you will. Now you have it, and it won't put you in federal prison for the rest of your life. Simple. Effective. *Orgasmic*."

"You won't…you won't tell anyone, will you, Dr. Hooper? I promise, I'll never do it again. Not after this. I promise."

"Oh, Theodora, you misjudge me. The purpose of what we do here is to provide a place you can spill your guts to without having the world come down on your head. What happened, happened, and there's no way to erase that. All you can do now is move forward and be the woman you were always meant to be. So, again I ask, are you ready to be the woman you were meant to be?"

"Yes," I said with a small whimper. "Yes, Dr. Hooper…*Hoop*. Thank you so, so much. I need to be going now. I think I'm ready to move forward."

"Good. So don't kill any more of my fucking patients, okay?"

I stood up, almost sliding out of the pew as I did. The puddle I'd squirted out was massive. It looked like someone had spilled a bucket of cooking oil on the hardwood. Legs wobbling underneath me, I carefully made my way to the doors, never looking back to see if Dr. Hooper was watching. My jeans looked like I had pissed myself, and I had no intention of letting him see my embarrassment.

"Make sure to come back next week, Theodora. Oh, and say hi to Casey for me. I know she's still there."

Now I did turn around, but where Dr. Hooper sat was another vacant pew among rows of many. He knew… He knew, and he didn't care at all. Perfect.

Briefly, I considered going back to clean up the puddle I'd left. Just as quickly, I decided against it. Maybe some church prude would unknowingly sit in it during the services on Sunday. That would be pretty funny.

The bug vibrated in response. He knew what I liked.

The new clit ring worked exactly as Dr. Hooper said it would. When I was out and about, not a peep. When I was at home, though… When I was at home, it would go off just when I needed it to. Soon, I had to place towels over everything I sat on. The bed, the easy chair in the living room, the floor of the bathroom. The first time I showered, I'd tried to take it off so I didn't get any water in the wiring, but no matter how hard I pulled, the legs wouldn't budge. Part of me was worried. What if I couldn't clean off all the gunk underneath and developed a yeast infection or something? As if triggered by the thought, my new friend started going to work, almost like it was letting me know it would take care of me. Take care of me it did, and it took care of me very, very well.

I skipped the next week's meeting. I didn't need them anymore. As a matter of fact, I didn't need anything. I tried going online a few times just to see if the itch could be tickled the old fashion way. However, my new friend seemed to be a jealous one, wanting me all to itself without any outside interference.

Once, when I was in the middle of a cam show, the bug actually shocked me, as if trying to say I didn't need this scrubby sleazeball on the other end, rubbing Vaseline on himself and wiggling his tiny dick on the screen as if I was supposed to be impressed. I told him I had something I needed to take care of, then turned the cam off. As soon as I was offline, Dr. Hooper's miracle device went to work, satisfying me in the only way I could appreciate.

Sometimes in between fuck sessions I would go to the guest bedroom. Casey was still there, but I felt nothing when I saw her. The smell was getting pretty bad now, and I knew the neighbors would start complaining if I didn't get rid of her soon. They had before, with the two Js. But I'd been thinking more clearly then; more aware of my surroundings. The bug had me slipping. Slipping and sliding, oh yes.

*Tomorrow,* I'd say to myself with full confidence. *You'll get rid of her tomorrow, Theo. Whether the bug allows you to or not. Get a grip on yourself.*

While Casey was indeed a problem, these visits were not for her. I went in there to see Jacob Jr., my one and only baby. I wanted to remind myself of the situation that had led me here, to this unending euphoric bliss.

*REMEMBA, Theo! REMEMBA how it all STAWTED!?*

The look on their faces, the two Js, when I had told them what happened. I didn't spill the beans all at once, of course. If they knew the extent of what I'd done, that initial phone call would have ended with a knock at my door twenty minutes later and me being hauled off in handcuffs. No, I'd been subtle about it. Slick. They needed to know the truth, but not the whole truth. Not yet. Not until they had seen.

"Hey, Theo, we want to ask you a favor."

"Oh, sure. Anything for you, Jessica."

"This isn't easy. Understand that. The other options are really expensive. We would never even ask you if we weren't so desperate. I'm barren, and…we really want a baby. Can you help?"

Desperate? Like I was the last choice? Who the fuck did they think I was, some machine they could just inject cum into without any questions asked? I needed more. If they wanted me to be their local pump and dump, that meant I would receive something back in return.

"I want to fuck you. Both of you. I'm not going to accept any other answer. Take it or leave it. If you leave it, good luck finding someone else."

Jess didn't care. She was already an admitted bisexual. They'd had threesomes before. Really, it was no big deal, except for the part where Jacob nutted inside me. In out, in out. Job well done, wait for the cheese to ferment. I said as much. They agreed.

After the night at the cabin, I began to feel weird. Then the weight began packing on. Then I had a sonogram. A few months later, I was lying across my velvet sheets, pushing another human being's head out of me without anyone else in the world knowing it was happening.

At first, there was pain; massive amounts of pain. Then came the ripping, then the screaming, then the laughing. The cum. So much cum. I remember having to reach down and pick the baby up just to keep it from being drowned. My water had broken just a few hours before that. What flowed out of me now made that look like a small bucket sitting next to Niagara Falls.

Orgasmic births were rare, but not unheard of. Fewer than 1% of women experienced them, which made me happy to be in the minority. To have missed out on such an experience...as a matter of fact, the orgasm was the only reason baby Jacob had been able to experience a few minutes of life before I regained my composure and suffocated him with a pillow. Like Casey, he had tried to fight. Unlike Casey, he was gone within minutes, dead to a world that had never known he existed at all.

"Look, Jess...um...I went to the hospital last night. I didn't want to alarm either of you."

"WHAT!? OHMYGOD, IS EVERYTHING ALL RIGHT!?"

"Listen, um...we lost the baby, Jess. Still-birth. I just got home right now. Please, come over as soon as you can." I was looking up at Jacob Jr. as I talked. I'd put him into an old pickle jar filled with formaldehyde. He was staring at me with his cute glazed over eyes. I couldn't wait for them to see him.

"Yes," Jess said, trying to hold back her sobs. "Yes, we'll be there as soon as Jacob can get out of work. Oh my God...ohhhh my God..."

But they never did show up that day.

And then...and then...

I was sitting on the loveseat reminiscing of these things when my cell phone lit up. The number wasn't one I recognized, though I had a gut feeling of who it was. After all, I'd given him my *NUMBA*, hadn't I?

"Hello?"

"Aw, Theodora! So happy to hear you're alive and well. How have you been?"

"Very well, Dr. Hooper. I don't know how I can ever repay you. I'm basically cured." Well, not completely. If I had been completely cured, I would have tossed what remained of Casey out a week ago. I needed to come back to reality.

"Hmm...well that's encouraging to hear. I trust there haven't been any...slip-ups since the last time you were with us?"

Slip-ups? Like what? Did he think I was some kind of serial killer?

*Well, you are up to four, Theo.*

"No, Dr. Hooper. I haven't even really left the house except to get groceries." I didn't need to feign genuineness; this was the absolute truth.

"Marvelous, marvelous. Say, I couldn't help but notice that you haven't been to group in the past two weeks. Any reason for that?" He was smiling. Even though I couldn't see him, I knew the Porky Pig-faced bastard was smiling.

"Oh, no reason. Things have been pretty busy for me. I've been picking up overtime at work, so evenings have been pretty booked. Is everyone doing okay?" I hadn't been to work in almost a month. Probably fired for all I knew.

"Theodora," Dr. Hooper said sternly, though I somehow knew that smile was still there. "Charlie hasn't been to group in a week. Neither has Kelly. Their families are searching for them."

I was shocked. The sheer coincidence…that I could kill Casey one week, and then two other members of the group would go missing so soon after.

"I didn't…I mean, I couldn't have. Why would I need to do tha—"

"Are they there?"

"Excuse me?"

"Don't play dumb with me, Theodora. Are they there? Kelly and Charlie."

I…" I hesitated for a moment, not knowing what to say. Casey was still there. He knew that much. The motherfucker was just toying with me. "Yes. I mean, no. I swear to you. I never even talked to them after group was over."

"Just like you never went anywhere with Casey that first night…"

"Dr. Hooper," I pleaded. "I swear on my mother's grave, I don't know what you're talking about. I didn't go near Charlie or Kelly, and I don't know what happened to them. The bug has been taking care of me this entire time. Why would I need anything else?"

"The *bug*? What bug?" He sounded perplexed. Still smiling, though. I would bet my soul on it. No matter what he said, no matter how concerned he sounded, I knew he was sitting there on the other end of the line, sucking down a candy bar or some other sugar-loaded treat, just smiling away.

"Listen, you son of a bitch. I don't know what game you're playing, but you know exactly what I'm talking about. The bug. The one you practically shoved into me. The reason I haven't been able to leave my apartment for days at a time. What is this, blackmail?"

"Theodora, listen—"

"Stop calling me that! My name is Theo!"

"Okay, Theo. I don't have any clue what you're talking about. I never gave you any 'bug.'"

"Oh, right, right," I said sarcastically. "Just like I never told you about the two Js, or how I'd been dry humping their corpses for almost a month and a half, or about the baby. You also don't know I murdered Casey, right? None of those conversations ever happened?"

Blackouts. I'd blacked out during the first night; hallucinated things. Is it possible I'd done it again?

*AND LEAD US NOT INTO SENSATION, BUT DELIVER US FROM EVIL.*

*AAAAAAAAAMEN!*

"Theodor—I mean, Theo. It seems like you have gotten yourself into a lot of trouble. Please, come to the church as soon as you can. I can help you. Please, we need to talk—"

"*Ohhhhh, no!*" I screamed. "You're not serving me any more of your roofie Kool-aid! You know what I'm talking about, and you better not try to fuck with me. I'm the one who does the fucking, you fat, mustard-stained walrus fuck! Go ahead! Try it!"

"Theo," Dr. Hooper said calmly. "I think you're very sick and need help. I'm not going to call the police or anything yet. But I really think you should come to the church. Please, before things get worse."

'Fuck you"

I threw my phone across the living room into the kitchen. With shaky hands, I pulled open the waistband of my pants and looked down. All that looked back at me was the bare skin of my pussy, an unusual layer of pubic hair covering my clit.

"Fuck! What the fuck!? Where is it!? Where is it!*?*"

I sprang up and flipped over the love seat cushions. Beyond a few stale cheese curls and a corroded battery, there was nothing. As I was on my knees searching, I felt an itch starting to grow between my legs. By time I stood up and ran to the spare bedroom, my crotch and thighs were on fire. I wrapped my legs around the door frame and grinded myself against it, trying to get the burning to stop. Finally, the pain abated a little. I grabbed the knob and flung the door open.

"What…no. No, no, no, no, *no!"*

Casey was gone. In her place were two decomposing corpses, their unidentifiable bodies hanging by their wrists from the chains. Both of them had been torn to shreds, with deep scratches running from their throats to their ankles. I looked down to examine my recently manicured fingernails, horrified to discover the previously long tips to be nothing but worn-down nubs. The skin on my fingertips was chapped and raw, as if I'd been digging into a scratching post made of steel wool.

The itch came back. I reached my hand down, scratching until the skin felt like it was melting. Warm liquid was now oozing through what was left of my nails, but still I couldn't stop. Everything in the room soon became something I could rub myself on: the doorknob, the empty bookshelf, the bodies hanging from the chains.

Desperate now, I reached up to grab Jacob Jr.'s jar so I could rub the lid against my throbbing cunt. I ran my hand along the shelf, expecting to find nothing there. Just when I thought I'd completely lost my mind, my fingers came upon glass. Hard glass. Yes, even though the other Js were gone, the most important one was still there, bottled up tight, just the way he should have been.

I pulled the jar down and held it to my face, so happy to see something *normal* in a world that had otherwise flipped upside down. I simultaneously screamed and fell to my knees, resuming the incessant scratching with my other hand.

GOLDBERG'S EXTRA-LARGE DILL PICKLES, EST. 1969

Where my baby once floated was now a small ocean of murky green and white. Not thinking, I opened the lid and reached my hand inside, retrieving a putrid pickle. I regarded it for a second, then shoved it down my pants, pushing it against me as hard as I could.

"What the fuck!? What the fuck is happening to me!? Oh, god! Oh, god! It burns…it fucking *buuuuuuuurns!*"

I whipped the jar against the door. It exploded on impact, sending thousands of glass shards to the floor in an unholy jingle. I crawled on my hands and knees to the glass. The pickle in my pants slid against the floor as I moved, leaving a snail trail of juice behind me. I arrived at the broken jar and reached down, retrieving the largest shard of glass I could find. I pulled the pickle out of my pants and dropped it beside me. This would take care of the itch, yes, yes, yes.

*No…no, no, no. Shit, no, Theo! What the fuck are you thinking?*

Glass. Itch. Of course, it would help. I might peel my clitoris away in the process, but at least that infernal fucking *itch* would be gone. I opened my pants and held the shard millimeters from my slit.

*No, Theo. No. Goddamn it, no. Drop the glass. It's not that bad…it's not that bad.*

An image popped into my mind of my pussy being sewn up after I'd smothered Jacob Jr. and made my way to the hospital. The birth had been both painful and exciting, but the aftermath had only been painful. Did I really want to mutilate myself like that again just because of some stupid rash?

*Yes. Scratch the itch!*

No. It wasn't worth it. I could damage myself in a way that could not be fixed. How could I fuck again with a mutilated muff?

Struggling with my decision, I dropped the glass on the floor and got up, shambling my way to the main bedroom. My pants were smeared with a mixture of pus and congealed pickle juice. Kneading myself against the dresser all the while, I dug through the drawers, finding a hoodie and a pair of sweatpants baggy enough to not rub against me and make the itching worse.

It was only then that I had a fleeting thought of what day it was: Thursday. The day of the Sex Addicts Anonymous meeting. They would all be there. Dr. Hooper wanted me to be there with them; to let them hear my story so they would know to abstain from such wicked behavior. Yes, I would go. Not because I gave a single drop of shit about helping the rest of them, but because Hooper had done this to me, and Hooper was the only one who could fix it.

*CALL ME HOOP, YOU DISEASE-RIDDEN NUMBA OF A PISSA!*

As I passed by the mirror on the wall, I was astonished. Not one bit of a curve could be seen through the sweatsuit I was wearing. My massive tits were gone. I'd never had the greatest of asses, but it was enough to get the job done. Now it was a distant memory, hidden by the sagging shroud of extra-large cotton fleece. I didn't even recognize myself. When was the last time I'd eaten?

In that fleeting glimpse, I realized my lack of showering had left my hair greasy and puffed out. I couldn't go to group looking like that. I snagged a tie from the dresser and quickly wrapped my hair into a bun. On my first night, Casey had shown up in an eerily similar state. I'd laughed at her on the inside and made a bunch of judgements that ended up being wrong. She'd made me cum.

As a sort of joke, I opened the top drawer of the dresser to see if Casey's glasses were still where I'd stashed them a couple weeks before. They were. I put them on. It was perfect; everything looked crystal clear and smooth, almost as if they'd been made for me all along.

Scratching all the while, I grabbed my keys and ran down to the car. I don't even know if I took the time to close the front door or the door leading to the kinky secret in the guest bedroom. Anyone coming up the stairs could just look in and see the bodies clear as day. I didn't care. All I wanted was to get to Dr. Hooper, to the group. He would help me; they would help me. Someone there would be able to scratch the itch.

I raced through town, swerving around traffic like a madwoman. When I made the turn that led to the church, I sideswiped a couple cars parked in front of a retirement home. Grannies and Grampas, laid up in their beds, thousands of fucks swirling through their collective heads. I bet they never did what I did, though. Soon, they would be bodies just like the three Js, just like the others. After enough time, they would rot and become unrecognizable. They would be sexy again. Anything can be sexy, as long as you're willing to drop your standards a little bit and become creative. The corner of an end table, the base of a parking meter late at night; piss, shit, blood, dead bodies. If it could lube you up, it was worth it. Sometimes there were consequences. Sometimes...you caught something. But only for a little while. Then it was right back into paradise. Take care of the problems when you could, indulge when the problems were gone. Yeah, all those oldies had been fucked, but had they ever truly fucked someone else? I'd fucked a lot of people, and I wouldn't take it back for anything in the world.

I skidded to a stop in front of the church and checked the time. 7:51 p.m. Most of them were probably inside already, waiting for that no-good son of a bitch to arrive and spread his venom through their minds like steaming spunk on a Finnish whore's areolas. He'd given me a bug; he'd given us all bugs. How had it manifested for the men? Self-activating cock rings; motion-controlled prostrate strokers? That's what happened during that first session; everyone had an itch that Dr. Hooper had given to them, and he'd let them scratch to their heart's content.

I gave my cunt a couple big rakes before getting out. This time, there was blood on my fingers when I pulled my hand out. Just a little while longer...then it would all be over.

I crossed the street and went around the corner to the door Casey had led me through just a few weeks ago. I stopped dead in my tracks at the sight I beheld.

A woman was standing there by herself, her back turned to me. There was an undeniable snake of gray smoke twisting itself above her head. Tight blue jeans and an even tighter black t-shirt. I scanned through my mind, trying to remember what I'd done with the Pink shirt from that first night. I could see from the side that she had big luxurious tits. An explorer like me? Could she scratch my itch?

I began walking toward her, unsure what I was going to do or say. Before I knew it, I was inches away, smelling the stink of Paris Hilton Fragrance Mist. My brand. The kind I'd douse myself in whenever I hadn't showered in a couple days. God, I just wanted the itch to stop.

With a shaking hand, I reached out and lightly touched her elbow.

"Excuse me," I said in a trembling voice that sounded foreign to my own ears. "Are you here for the meeting?"

"Yes," she said. The cherry of her cigarette was down to the butt. With the grace of an addict, she took one last hit and flicked the smoke on the ground. A lot of things had been in and out of those lips. "You're...um, here for the meeting, as well?"

I said I was. I went through the script from the very first night, only this time replacing Dr. Sharma's name with Dr. Hooper's. I told her I was twenty-one days clean. It was true. I hadn't killed anyone in twenty-one days. I felt proud of myself.

*Liar. What about Charlie and Kelly?*

*Fuck off. She doesn't need to know about that yet. She will, in time.*

She looked at her watch and said we should get inside soon. I agreed, pushing open one of the doors that led to the basement. Every step was torture. My pubic hairs were rubbing against the coarse fabric of my panties, making the itch come alive all over again. When was the last time I'd changed them—one week ago, *two* weeks?

*JESUS SAVED ME BEFORE I WAS BORN!*

Jacob Jr. hadn't been saved.

*AND LEAD US NOT INTO SENSATION, BUT DELIVER US FROM EVIL. AMEN!*

Amen, brothers and sisters.

We stopped at the conference room door, her butterflies flapping away in her stomach, mine digging deep down inside of my ovaries, destroying everything that made me woman. I told her to follow me and held the door open once again. Theo walked right into the trap, taking her seat next to Charlie. I sat down beside her, rubbing myself against the wood as we talked.

"I decided to start coming here right before my husband died," I said in my mousy little voice. "He really wanted me to get help, and his death just cemented the fact. My babies…how would they grow up with me going down that path?" I hated this, playing some helpless damsel in distress. I was an eater of worlds, not some fucked up looking shrew who allowed herself to be used as a dildo in the asshole of life. There was one redeeming factor, though: it made me forget about the itch for a while.

She bobbed her head along with my words, scrunching her eyebrows and pressing her lips together at all the right times. Sympathy. This was an indisputable bitch, and she deserved every single thing that was about to come her way. She didn't give a single shit about what Casey had been through. Not her loss, not her struggle, not her pain. She came here to take advantage of people; to hear their stories, then suck them in and spit them out as soon as all the good stuff was gone.

I ardently wished I had a mirror right then just so I could see the look on her face as she realized everything.

Eventually, the doors opened, and there was my old friend, Dr. Hooper, pit stains large enough to devour a planet, goatee combed to a jagged point so fine it could jab a fetus in the womb and still come back without a single hair out of place.

"Wow," she whispered to me. "Dr. Hooper really let himself go."

"Yes," I said, breaking script for the first and only time. "Yes, he certainly has."

He welcomed everyone, offering us refreshments before the session began. I grabbed myself a cinnamon roll and my guest a Boston cream donut, just as she'd requested. Fucking wench. She really did think this was all one big joke. We'd see who was laughing at the end.

Everyone told their stories: Charlie, the transgendered accountant who cruised the woods looking for black boys; Shelly, the marital counselor who apparently didn't give one lick about the binding vows of matrimony; Kelly, turning tricks for coke and then turning tricks for more tricks; Jerry, the Jerk-off King; Hailey, Dave, Staci, Tyler, and the rest, here on Gilligan's Isle! But the worst hadn't come yet; the one who broke the mold and would turn life as I knew it into a twisted cyclone from the darkest depths of Gehenna. Dr. Hooper was waiting for her. She was the entire reason for this get-together. The star of the show, waiting for the spotlight to shine on her so she could take her panties off and do the bald beaver Cancan for all the boys and girls. The light would shine on her, and she would do exactly what she'd been made to do.

*REMEMBA, THEODORA!? REMEMBA THE ALAMO!? HOW THEY SCREAMED!?*

My turn was up. I said it all: the neglect, the loneliness, the threesome, the ongoing affair, the fights. As I repeated Casey's words, I felt myself *becoming* her: working in a library no one was coming to anymore; going home to cook dinner for a man who would show up in the wee hours of the morning, disheveled, distant, disinterested. No one talked to me, no one understood me. I would call my sister sometimes, but she was little miss perfect, living with her boy toy hunk in a palace forty-five minutes up north, never a problem to be had.

The library job was supposed to make things easier, I thought. Give me something else to focus on. Fill my time, so the thoughts would go away. But they didn't. They persisted. One day, a trustee member decided to stop in and see how things were going. He was older, wearing an expensive black suit that fit perfectly around his tall, muscular physique.

Two weeks went by, then he came back, saying he needed to pick up some receipts for the accountant. One week went by, and he was back again, asking for a copy of the card catalogue for an upcoming renovation project. Three days later and there he was, this time asking if I wanted to have dinner. I accepted. Imagine my surprise when the door was answered by his girlfriend, a beautiful woman with huge jugs and a serviceable ass, eagerly inviting me in.

We'd done everything. We played with the Whoomph Bush, the Moss Covered Three Handled Family Gredunza, the old in out, in out, with a waiting mouth always there to catch every last drop.

"I...loved my family. But I was messed up. I needed something more. And I found it. But it was ruining everything. Poisoning me. So, finally, I told my husband."

"Umm-hmm," Dr. Hooper said, pretending like he was writing things down on his clipboard. "And you wanted to fix things, so you came here after your husband died. You're so brave, Casey. So strong. Thank you for your testimony."

Everyone clapped. Polite golf claps. *Tap-tap-tap*. Good job, Casey. You're doing the right thing.

*I am doing the right thing,* I thought. *I'm setting things right. Finally.*

Now it was the cunt's turn. Dr. Hooper thanked us all and said there was one person who hadn't given her testimony. Feigning shyness, she sat up straight, those gigantic tits pushing through the fabric of her shirt like two bald-headed babies desperate for someone to put their hands on them and sing a lullaby. Theo was the focus, the main attraction, the light at the end of a stinking, cum-covered tunnel. I could *smell* her. Sitting so close, there was a distinct mixture of raw fish and chlorine permeating the air. She needed to die. To scratch the itch. That was the only way.

The scene played out exactly as it had before: Theo began her testimony. I grabbed hold of her hand at the right cue, allowing her to push it down and masturbate herself. Charlie's fingers soon joined mine. We leaned across her lap and began kissing. Then we unbuckled her jeans and got on our knees, shoving our faces into her panties, sucking, licking, biting. As we did this, the itch in my own crotch subsided. For the first time in hours, I felt like I could touch myself without screaming in pain. I shoved my fingers into her as far they would go, hoping I could reach up and hook the cervix she didn't deserve to have.

"What happened, Theodora?" Dr. Hooper said. "Did you get everything you wanted?"

"Yes...uh-huh. Yes. In my ass, in my mouth, in between my tits. She sat on my face while he stuck me. The old in out, in out. She tasted like strawberries. I don't know if she freshened herself up with some weird spray beforehand, but it was like sweet fruit. Gushing down my lips, dripping down my body onto his dick. Yes, yes, yes!"

We dug in. Charlie and I were passionately kissing, wrapping our tongues around one another and grazing them against her minge. She was gyrating into our mouths, begging for it.

"And what about *him,* Theodora?"

"What?"

"Tell me, did the baby cry?"

"Yes," she said, gasping and moaning all the while. "He screamed. He didn't even know where he was. So small. I told them he was a still-birth, but that wasn't true. I wanted to see what it was like, to push one out. *AHHHHHH, AHHHHHH!*"

"You'd wanted to know for a while," Hoop said. "You'd had tests before, for pregnancy. In the course of receiving those tests, you were also given another one. The big one. You knew. You knew you had *it*."

*"Yes…YES! YES! YES!"*

"So, after one escapade or another, you started feeling under the weather."

*UNDA THE WEATHA*

"Yes."

I pulled her panties to the side and ran my tongue across the slit. It tasted like a greasy 9-volt battery.

"So, you finally took the big test. It was positive," Hoop said, that jolly Santa Claus tone back in its full hellish glory. "HIV. Eventually full-blown AIDs. But you didn't care, did you, Theodora?"

The rest of them had stopped at some point. They were gathered around the three of us now, cocks and pussies and tits exposed, the owners not showing a hint of shyness. They were all jacking and jilling, the spotlight on the star, as she'd always wanted it to be.

"No!" She screamed as I pulled my face from her snatch and began punching it as hard as I could. Soon, her perfect white panties sported scarlet patches of red. No matter how hard I punched, she just kept screaming and moaning, her itch being satisfactorily scratched.

"Even before Jacob and Jessica Lewis came to you, you knew you had it. You would pass it onto them. If you got pregnant, the baby would get it. That's why you killed it."

"*Uhhhhhh, uhhhhhh!"*

I was digging inside her now, using the nubs of my fingernails to tear out whatever I could. Scratching her helped me.

"So you spread it to the Js, and then… Well, what did she do, Casey?"

"*SHE FUCKING GAVE IT TO ME! HER AND HER SCUMBAG BOYFRIEND! THEY USED ME LIKE I WAS SOME DISPOSABLE FUCK RAG!"*

Charlie reached out and rubbed my chin with his cum-stained thumb.

"I'm sorry, honey. I didn't know. She got me, too. And my wife."

"And me."

I turned my head, seeing that Kelly the junkie had stepped forward, nipples hard enough to cut glass, vagina spilling a mixture of clear puss and blood to the floor.

"And me," Shelly the marital counselor chimed in. "She gave it to my husband, Charlie."

"Don't…stop…" Theo hissed out. "Please. Feels…so…good…"

"So, all of you, then? All of you died because of Theodora's nasty little secret?" Dr. Hooper was unwrapping a candy bar. Butterfinger.

"She fucking killed me!" I was still scraping into her flesh, so dearly wishing to rip her entire reproductive system out. "She fucked me, then she killed me! No matter what, she'll always be the one who fucks you at the end!"

"That's right, Casey," Dr. Hooper said, dropping a wink my way. "She always fucks you. How's your itch?"

Just then, I felt pressure down below. Reaching to the waistband of the comically large sweatpants, I undid the string. At first, it was nothing but the overgrowth of pubic hair, thousands of tiny black wires crisscrossing over one another. Looking closer, I noticed some of the wires were longer than the others, specifically the ones coming from the chasm of my pussy lips. Just as I noticed this, the long hairs raised up, fluttering around each other like tall pieces of grass being blown in a gale.

"It never went away," I said, watching in sick amusement as the hairs clamped down on both sides of my thighs and the pressure resumed. My lips swelled as the black body of the bug pulled itself out, regaining its place on the top of my clit. I pulled my hand away from Theo's blood-covered panties and began scratching myself again. The itch was back and worse than ever.

"I told you, Theodora. It's self-acting. It has a mind of its own. It's one wicked little pissa of a numba, that's for sure. Do you want the itch to stop?"

I looked all around me. They were all leaned over, the faces of my victims just inches away from my own. The spotlight was on me now: on the thing I was, and the thing I was about to become. I'd known I was going to die, and I made sure to bring as many of them with me as I could. Come they had, and now they were all here, in the place I'd brought them to: Gehenna.

I shot my eyes back to the Theo of the past. She was dead to the world, her own eyes rolled back into their sockets. Rivulets of blood dripped from her bleeding honeypot to her legs. I'd quite literally fucked her to death.

"I can make her come alive again," Dr. Hooper said. "I can resurrect her. Give her one last hurrah before the world goes black. Or you can just leave her dead. None of this will ever happen, and her victims can finally rest in peace. You'll never get fucked again, and the itch will be relieved forever. What do you want to do, Theodora?"

I sat there on my knees for a few minutes, thinking long and hard. I could break the cycle. I could just accept death and turn into nothingness, the transgressions of my past nothing more than forgotten dust floating through the cosmos.

"I won't feel anything?"

"Nope," Hoop said, taking a bite out of his candy bar. The trail of chocolate was back on his chin, though this must have been special chocolate, because it was red and syrupy. "No pain, no pleasure. You're just…gone. *Poof!*" He regarded me with his predatory eyes and began cackling.

"No," I said immediately. "No, I want to feel. I need this. I need the itch."

Hooper took another bite from the Butterfinger, which now resembled a real finger. A fresh tendril of blood spilled down his chin.

"So mote it be. Can't wait to see you for next week's meeting, Theodora. I think we made a lot of progress tonight. And now, without further ado…*VENI VIDI VICI!"*

Hoop clapped his hands and suddenly I found myself outside, huddled on the church steps. The sun was down now, making the buildings ahead look like abstract shapes in a gothic painting. She'd be coming out soon, dazed, confused, unaware that every decision she made from here on out wasn't hers at all. She deserved it. Fucking cunt.

Suddenly, the doors leading to the basement opened with a huge bang and there she was, taking in a breath of the cool night air, huge tits swelling and retracting with each exhalation. I felt the bug between my legs start to tickle me. The itch was back.

*A few weeks,* I thought with great relief. *I just need to be dead for a few weeks. Then I can see him again. My baby. I can rememba what happened. I can have the itch scratched.*

Accepting my fate, I stood up and made my way to the sidewalk as quietly as I could. I couldn't break the script. Theo needed me, and I needed her. To fuck that up meant it would all go away. My heart rose to my throat as I thought of Jacob Jr.

*JESUS SAVED YOU BEFORE YOU WERE BORN!*

*Amen, baby. Yes, he did. I'll see you again soon.*

I reached my hand out and grabbed her by the elbow. She jumped a little, then relaxed. She never turned toward me. I could be anyone. A stranger; some overweight devil, a candy bar in one hand, and a long list of transgressions in the other. And yet she knew…deep down inside, she knew. There was no reason to panic. She was in loving hands.

"Hey, sis, you okay?"

No one ever fucks me; I fuck them. Except for Hoop. He fucked me pretty good.

# HELL WEEK

LEWIS KELLY

"I'm not so sure about this, Tailor," Nicole slurred.

I think her name was Nicole. Maybe Naomi? Fuck if I remembered. Her name definitely started with an 'N'. Or maybe it started with an 'M'? To be honest, I was so piss drunk, I could barely remember how we met. All I knew was that she was my type of girl. Bit of a hog, but humble and innocent with great a pair of tits.

All the frat brothers were out enjoying Sunday Funday at the bars, and Nancy and I had started out in the downstairs Sigma Chapter Room, drinking and shooting the shit. She was an exceptional bore, yapping about true love, summer camp bullshit, and then… horses.

Fucking horses.

What dirt town was she from? I couldn't tell from the high school crest on the sweater, but surely it was some nowhere-inbred southern place with only a handful of graduates in her class. Dirt people like her made me sad, and they always bored me. But girls like that were always the easiest to manipulate. Leaving their podunk shitholes for big-city college life; excited for opportunities and adventures.

Most of these hogs were virgins when they got to college. For a hot guy like me, president of a fraternity, to ask them to hang out their first week on campus… Well, you can't put a price tag on that. Can you? It must have been like a peasant being invited to fucking Buckingham Palace. The only difference: I don't think people regularly get their asses destroyed in the royal circle! Not by my cock anyway.

Melanie—or whatever the fuck her name was—at least had a cute face and rocking tits despite the baggy sweater she wore in a vain attempt to hide them. I convinced her to come back to Sigma the same night we'd met, despite her having classes early the next day. I knew that to be the case because she kept buzzing about it like a gnat while I was trying to fingerbang her.

Imagine going to class, am I right? I never went to class and my professors never failed me. They kept their jobs and I slid by with a "C" average. Only commoners had to go to class.

She had continued to blabber on about school, missing her family, and her continued obsession with fucking horses—all the talk about horses was making her look like a horse to me. And I just kept on nodding, throwing in and a few "mhms" to keep the bitch drinking. In the span of a couple hours, I'd downed about triple the number of beers she had; and she must have said quadruple the number of words I had. Fuckin' blabber-mouth whores. If pussy wasn't so good, I'd never put up with that shit.

When she started slurring so badly that she was saying "horsles," I helped her upstairs to use the restroom and freshen up. When she stumbled out, I was right there to catch her and lead her back inside.

It was time to teach her how thoroughbred "horsles" were made.

Now, as she was trying to fight unconsciousness, she might have said that she wasn't sure. But a whore is a whore, am I right?

These kinds of girls wanted to be fucked and treated like dirt but would never admit it. That was okay by yours truly. There were multiple ways to get those panties down and my dick buried inside. The way I saw it, I was helping her. Really, I was a charity for closeted sluts. Charities need donations to operate, and I always left a hefty contribution in their drop boxes.

I propped her head on the sink so she could look at herself in the mirror while I started unbuttoning the front of her jean shorts.

"Don't worry, we don't have to do anything if you don't want to. Though, I did listen to all your horse stories. You *really* should repay me."

She giggled nervously and wretched a little bit. Her eyes rolled back in her head.

Right before my pants dropped to my ankles, she wheezed, "T-T-T-ailor! I… don—I don' wannado this." She looked at her drunk reflection. A tear streamed down her cheek.

I kicked the pants aside and in my best dirt-person voice, I mocked her. "Well heck, darlin', you d-d-d-d-don' wannado this? I reckon it's a little late for second thoughts. You can't leave the rodeo early. Pigs are the most important part of the show."

"I don' wanna…" Her face kept slipping off the sink as she continued to moan, so I planted it into the faucet with my palm. Then, I wet my finger and stuck it into her tight little ass, her hole puckered around my digit.

"Don't worry, just saddlin' ya up."

"No…" she moaned without much strength. "I don' wanna—"

"You don' wanna feel my horse cock inside you or you don' wanna talk anymore?"

Whatever came out of her mouth next was no longer words. Her eyes rolled back again and I knew it was showtime.

"Ride 'em cowboy!"

Out came my finger and in went my dick. Balls deep, showing her what a fucking thoroughbred stallion felt like. After a few minutes, I used her hair to wipe my forehead and nose.

She tried to say something again, but all that came out were pig squeals and dolphin clicks. Fucking Pig Dolphin. Could have been because of the drugs I slipped into her beer or maybe she was in ecstasy because it was the greatest day of her shitty dirt life. I'd lean toward the latter.

Turns out, I was so shit-house drunk that I couldn't cum. I must have fucked that Pig Dolphin for over an hour. Ass fucking was always great, but it doesn't self-lubricate like the old puss. So I started moving back and forth between her cornhole and gash. I even shoved my dick in her mouth for my specialty move: ass-to-mouth-to-ass-to-pussy—repeat as desired. But that was about as effective as jerking off with a piranha. She had fang teeth and eventually hooked my circumcision scar with those fucking gnarly choppers. Ouch!

Maaaaaaaan, I was really starting to hate Pig Dolphin.

And then, just as I'm starting to feel a little twinkle of hope in my balls, she started mumbling. More fucking animal noises from the Pig Dolphin. I shoved my cock into her pussy again and thrust with the might of Zeus, trying to bust a nut before she woke up. It was no use.

Her eyes bounced open, and she locked on to the edges of the sink countertop. Turning sideways, she slipped on the puddle of sex below us. As she slammed to the ground, my half-mast dick fell out of her and bounced around like a limp Baseball Frank. Still not completely realizing where she was or what the fuck was going on, she scrambled about the floor, unable to stand.

Man, that was funny. Pig Dolphin rolling around in a sty composed of my blood, juice, and some bile that seeped from her ass when I pulled my dick out. Fuck, this place was gonna need a deep clean. Thank the good Lord for pledges.

I put out my hand to help her up, and in a soothing voice, I said, "It's okay. It's okay."

Man, was she fucked up. That dumbass took my hand. I gently lifted her and then… *BAM!* I pushed that Pig-Dolphin ass back to the bathroom floor. Her bare ass landed with a slap that sounded like someone belly flopping into a pool.

"Get off of m—!" She tried to scream, but the shit in her mouth caught up with her. Liquidy, diarrhea-smelling vomit started spewing from her mouth. She covered her mouth with her hands, but the vomit just shot out of Pig Dolphin's nose, coating her and expanding the puddle on the floor.

"Gah, that's disgusting! You gross ass bitch." I grabbed her by the hair, stood her back up, and pushed her against the wall, hoping the change of position would get me closer to busting. I held her hands in place and continued ramming her ass like a dump truck into a Mini Cooper.

I just wanted to cum. Needed to cum! I did everything imaginable; I squeezed her melon-looking tits until they turned white, I clawed at her ass, I just about ripped her fucking pancake nipples off until my seed was finally ready to fly. All the while my ears rang with her Pig-Dolphin chokes, wretches, and sobs.

God, I fucking *hated* that sound!

"Shut the fuck up, bitch!"

To shut her up and cum in peace, I started slamming her head into the wall. Each crack against the drywall sounded like two bowling balls hitting each other. With a dull crumble, her head went through the cheap wall and into a steel pipe.

I didn't care; I could feel the elusive nut building in my sack. I slammed her head into the pipe and felt her skull crack. The pipe cracked a bit too and water started spilling from it, but at least she was finally silent.

I let go of her broken skull and her oversized body fell to the floor with a heavy thud.

A red foam oozed from a gash that had opened in her forehead. Strangely excited by her swollen tits and her gushing pink brains, I began jerking myself off. There was something beautiful about her gore-coated body that made my cock harder than a priest in front of a choir boy. The water spilling over her, mixed with the blood and whatever the hell was dripping from her head, created an oily substance that mesmerized me.

Boy, did I cum quick after that. My thick love juice sprayed like a firehose and hung on her corpse in strands like Silly String. The mangled, disgusting piece of meat that used to be a Pig Dolphin, now freshly glazed, was the most amazing thing I'd ever created.

I should have taken a picture. This was truly the craziest Hell Week fuck ever. And I wasn't sure any of the inner circle—or myself—would be able to top it.

I shook myself out of the post-nut haze, realizing I had a cock and hand covered in Pig Dolphin shit and this bitch was dead. Not just a little beat up, not just sexually assaulted. Her brains were all over the floor. Fucking dead. I hadn't planned it to go down this way, but now that it was done, I really had enjoyed myself. However, there was no way the regular brothers were going to understand.

I grabbed a handful of the girl's hair and wiped my hands and cock as best I could. Since she was dead, I couldn't exactly get pledges to clean this up, so I grabbed a towel and tried sopping up what I could of the foul-smelling mess that caked the bathroom floor. With water still spilling from the busted pipe though, that didn't do much good. I raced down to the basement to turn the water off—luckily, the downstairs was still deserted. I then went back upstairs to finish with Pig Dolphin.

Through the bathroom window, I saw the moonlight starting to wean. "Aw fuck!" My brothers were still out, but I knew I had to work fast if I was going to get rid of this whale before anyone got back from the bars.

Stumbling under the weight of the beers I drank, I grabbed the corpse by her feet and dragged her downstairs, her head cracking loudly against each step. All I needed to do was get her to my car before the boys returned and drive her to the quarry. All my problems would be solved, and I could share my "W" with the Sigma House inner circle—a fucking Hell Week hero.

On the way out, I grabbed my backpack stocked with a few handy gadgets. Never know when you may need a gun, drugs, duct tape, whatever. One of the only things my cocksucker of a father taught me was to be prepared for anything.

I had the fat bitch on the cement by the trunk of my Tesla when I heard someone behind me.

"Tailor? What the hell?"

I dropped the corpse's feet and reached into my backpack. In one motion, I pulled the Sig Sauer out and spun around like in an action movie. I may have stumbled a little in the footwork, but whatever.

I looked into the terror-stricken eyes of Brice, one of our newest pledges during Hell Week. He put his hands up and took a step back. "Woah, wait. What the fuck, Tailor?"

He was a standard-issued shit pledge. Khakis. White polo. I nicknamed him the fuckin' "Fairy Prince" when he *somehow* managed to not get blackballed. He always wore a stud earing in one ear like a queer.

I closed one eye because my vision was all fucked up and pointed the gun at the center of his face. "That's President Tailor, Fairy Boy. Why you creeping up on me?"

"I'm just coming back from my freshman calc study group." Rich white kids aren't used to looking down the barrel of a gun. His eyes moved to the Pig Dolphin disaster. "Is that girl dead?"

The corpse's head was split down the middle, only being held together by a few strands of muscle and syrup-caked hair. Her ass was a wet gaping mess.

As a Sigma pledge, it was Brice's duty to be my bitch. That said, he wasn't going to go along with murder. Sigma was owned by my father. Pledges kept the house thriving, but only my inner circle engaged in the "special" Hell Week festivities. I needed to make up something fast.

"This isn't what it looks like. This is all a huge misunderstanding." Forced tears rolled down my face. I hadn't cried since I was five and my mother told me that my parents broke up because of me. I was a fucking Sigma, not some crybaby turd. I wiped my nose on the back of my palm and steadied my gun. "You know me, Brice. It was an accident. I swear."

Brice rubbed his forehead and took a step back, avoiding eye contact with me and the corpse. "This is fucked up."

"I know, man. This is fucking crazy." I sat down on the pavement and sobbed into my trembling hands. "She slipped while we were fucking in the bathroom. Hit her head. I… What am I gonna do?"

"We can call the ambulance. Explain what happened." His eyes wide with fear.

"Ambulance?!" I lifted her face, then let it fall. "She's dead, not sick."

"Well, I don't see any other choice. You need to call someone. Now!"

I turned off the fake waterworks and stood. "No, Brice, you *need* to help me get rid of the body."

"What?" Brice was shaking in his boots. "I am not fucking helping you. This is your problem; not mine. I'm not going to prison."

Oh well, I gave him a chance to agree willingly.

I raised the gun. "You don't have a choice. You're going to help me or I'm going to kill you."

Brice let out an audible gulp.

"Finish putting her in the trunk."

His eyes darted around, dumbfounded. "What?"

"Did I stutter, pledge? Put the fucking corpse in the trunk and then get in the passenger seat or you're going to die right here, fag. Right fucking now!"

He took a step toward Pig Dolphin, breathing heavily. He grabbed her ankles, slipping twice and crying as he attempted to lift her. With all the might his little mayonnaise body could muster, he finally heaved her into the trunk.

That's right, little peasant. Do my bidding!

Once he was done, he held out his hands, gnarled as if they were in pain from the bodily fluids that soaked them. His face was twisted, nose scrunched, and eyes half-closed in repulsion and shame. It was like he'd never touched a whore covered in shit and piss before. Fucking pledges.

I slammed the trunk shut and then, using the gun, I guided him into the passenger side of my Tesla. I got in after him.

"This is a joke, right? Hell Week prank?" He tried to laugh, but his voice just cracked.

"Maybe. Maybe not. Just remember that I've got all my old man's connections. Think of this as a chance to be a part of the Sigma Brotherhood. Otherwise, after Hell week, you'll be voted out and just another bitch on the college scene."

The uncertainty of the prank shut him up and we sped away from Sigma house.

On the way, I pumped the pedal and tried to rev the engine, but the sounds the car returned were lame as hell. I hated this pussy ass car. When I was thirteen my father bought me a '65 Mustang fastback. With 225 horsepower, the thing was an absolute beast and the 289-4V sounded like a jet engine when it ripped down the highway. After I wrecked it on the night of my sixteenth birthday by slamming into a telephone pole, he got me the Tesla. He said it was "safer" and "more eco-friendly." What a crock of dog shit. A man that made a billion dollars in the coal industry didn't care about the environment. He was just feeding me shit. He probably got it in some bulk discount deal for the company. I would have wrecked it on purpose if he hadn't threatened to not buy me another car. What an asshole. Fuck him and his shitty electric car. If it wasn't for his money, I would have taken the old bastard out years ago.

Once we left campus and started heading toward the industrial part of town, Brice cleared his throat, never taking his eyes off the road.

"What's your plan, Tail—P-P-President Tailor?"

Now he was getting the picture.

"We're dropping her at the quarry. When they find her bashed to hell at the bottom, they won't assume she was murdered."

"So you're gonna throw her in there and hope the police think she committed suicide?"

"Yes, motherfucker. Are you that dense? Connect the dots."

Oh, Fairy Boy, if only you knew what dots I was connecting now. It was so beautiful even in my drunken state.

After that, he was quiet, and my mind turned to anger at Pig Dolphin. I was pissed, anxious, pitiful, and more pissed. Things at Sigma house had been so good for so long and then that dumb whore had to come along and mess everything up. I'd raped what, a hundred pigs? None of them had been stupid enough to put up that much of a fight. And none of them got killed.

You know what? The problem is women in general. With all this woman-power bullshit in the media, they've forgotten how to act. The inner circle of Sigma didn't follow the new status quo. We knew women were lesser creatures than us. Like a cow. Nothing more than an animal used for its meat. That's why the inner circle did what the others couldn't. If you wanted to join Michael, Nick, Dallas, and I, you had to be willing to commit the ultimate prank. Rape a bitch on camera.

Only us four were able to, and we rarely extended an invite to anyone else. Not after Richard. We thought he was a real man, but once he was actually balls deep in some passed-out chick, his conscience caught up with him. He left Sigma, but he never ratted us out because we had the video. No one ever truly leaves Sigma's inner circle. A circle that the rest of the brothers didn't even know about.

At long last, we entered the quarry complex. Passing by the final streetlamp, we nearly ran over a couple of busted-looking sluts. Being in this part of town felt like wading through a pool full of hot diarrhea. It was the perfect place to dump a dead whore.

I drove us to the deepest part of the quarry, which I imagined was at least fifty feet down. Various ledges rose every ten feet or so to the top. Each level was separated by a steep rock face and contained jagged edges which would be perfect for tearing a body apart. I started to get excited, running through what I thought was going to happen in my mind. Would she stay intact and then splat at the bottom like a bug? Would she rip apart like she'd gone through a cheese grater? Whatever happened it was going to be fun.

We got out and I popped the trunk. As soon as it opened, a gust of the dead bitch made me gag. The mixture of shit, blood, cum, and meat, all slosing in the trunk, made for some horrendous fucking stew. The shit, blood, cum, meat, all sloshing in the trunk on the ride over made for some horrendous fucking stew.

I poked Fairy Boy in the back with my gun. "Toss her in."

"Why can't you—" He peeked into the trunk. "This is a joke. That isn't human. Just some stitched-up animal parts, huh? Realistic Halloween prank?" He started laughing hysterically. I think I broke his fucking mind. "This is my Hell Week initiation before the vote on Saturday."

"*Yeah…*" I took the gun off him and scratched my leg. Halloween in fucking August. What a dummy. "We picked you for a very special initiation," I lied. "The inner circle."

'What's that?"

"You know who my father is. Only a few brothers of the inner circle are allowed to use his connections. Can write their fucking ticket anywhere they want after college. You just have to prove your loyalty. But you can't tell anyone I told you the corpse wasn't real." I gestured at Macy. "Ready to complete your initiation?"

Pride beamed in his stupid eyes, and he grabbed Pig Dolphin's corpse, dragging the whole disgusting package out of the trunk. Her head slammed to the ground and finally split completely apart, splattering the remainder of her brains on the ground. I'd always viewed these bitches as sex dolls, but now she really looked like one. Like a plastic, life-size sex doll that had been found at the bottom of a dumpster. The little Fairy Bitch pushed her body right to the edge of the huge quarry hole and then kicked her square in the tits.

She rolled over the edge and started tumbling. She struck the first ledge horizontally, bouncing up like she'd hit a trampoline, her flabby body rippling in the wind. Each level broke more bones, tenderizing her meat and destroying any recognizable features. On the second to last level, she left her skull behind, the now empty sack of head and face skin flapping about like a deflated balloon. When she finally hit the bottom, she was nothing more than a pile of meat. From the top, you couldn't even tell it had once been a human, maybe a large pile of mashed potatoes and ketchup.

Brice refused to look over the edge and see what *he* had just done. After a few seconds of wiping away his tears and sniffling, he asked, "What time is it? I think I left my phone in your car."

I glanced at my plain Rolex, then smiled. "Time to die."

Like a Spartan warrior, I drove my foot into Fairy Boy's chest. Brice gasped as the air was pushed from his lungs. He reached out wildly, grabbing at me for balance. All he managed to catch was my watch. The band popped from my wrist and Brice tumbled, smacking the ledges like an ungraceful ballerina. His clothes kept him together a bit better than Pig Dolphin on the way down, but by the final level, his limbs flapped around and wiggled like they were made of rubber and filled with jelly.

I watched this unfold in morbid fascination, just as I had with the previous body. My heart raced, my mouth dried up, my cock hardened. Fuck! This killing thing was a massive rush. Way better than anything I'd felt from weed, but maybe not as good as molly. I dunno. Maybe I'll try combining highs next time.

I looked at the Rolex tan line on my now naked wrist. Figures my dad would give me such a cheap piece of trash as a high school graduation gift. Should have been the white gold vintage Daytona Rolex. That wouldn't have broken in Fag Boy's grip.

Oh well. No real loss.

"See you later, Fairy Prince. Enjoy eternity with your fat girlfriend."

When I got back to the Tesla, I rummaged around and found his phone. It was a smaller brick-looking iPhone. I scoffed as soon as I saw it. Fucking poor people.

"How the Hell did that dirt farmer not get blackballed on day one?"

Luckily, he didn't have a newer phone that required a thumbprint or facial recognition. It took a matter of seconds to find his mom in the texts and compose a message:

My Beloved Mother,

It is with a heavy heart that I write this message to you. In my short time away from home, I have fallen for a beautiful woman. Due to circumstances out of our control, her parents have forbidden our love. Call it fairytale infatuation if you like, but to us our love is eternal. It is because of this we have decided to end our lives together so that we may be together in the afterlife. For eternity. I will miss you and Dad dearly but rest assured that your darling boy will be happy in the ether with his one true love.

Forever, Brice.

Once that message was sent, I powered down the phone and chucked it into the quarry as close to Brice's body as I could.

My cock was still rock hard from when I'd thrown the Fairy Rat to his death, so I started jerking myself off in the car. I think writing out that message only made me hornier. I jerked faster, having to switch hands as one got tired. Closing my eyes, I thought about Brice's mother reading that message. I wondered if they'd make her come by the coroner's office and claim the body? The look of sadness on her face when she sees her son's mangled corpse would be fucking priceless. As I came, I imagined splattering that old hag's wrinkled face with my seed. Right as she's starting to tear up, *BAM*, a shot of semen right in the eye.

I wiped myself with the Fairy Rat's backpack and then sped back to Sigma house to finish cleaning the mess I made in the bathroom. The entire time, I was riding the high from killing Pig Dolphin and Fairy Rat. Those two stupid fucking freshmen thought they'd bested me—a real fucking Sigma.

Fat chance, shiteaters!

The next morning, I woke up feeling like I'd been hit in the temple with a hatchet. I loved drinking, but hangovers sucked hairy nuts. Especially hangovers that involved a few tabs of X and disposing of two bodies. I'd learned something since starting college, though. The only surefire way to get rid of a hangover was to get shit-faced once again. So, that's what I planned to do.

As I headed downstairs for beer, I could hear the brothers running around and yapping like chickens. I stepped onto the landing amidst a fray of clones. Sigma definitely attracted a certain type of guy. Most were upper class. Some were athletes. Some were nerds. All wore nice clothes and had short hair. It was the whitest bunch of homos I'd ever seen.

After thinking about it, I realized that there wouldn't be this much of an uproar if it was just about the water being turned off. They must have known something. Time to act again.

Some loser wearing a sweater vest walked by the stairs and I grabbed him by the arm, pulling him over to me. I couldn't remember his name. There were too many pasty rich kids around here to remember them all.

"What the fuck is going on down here?"

He blinked at me wildly. "Oh, Pres. Tailor. You don't know yet?"

"Know what?" I said, shaking him.

"It's Brice. He and some bitch jumped into the quarry last night."

"Aw fuck," I said under my breath.

"I know, right? He was just a kid."

I mumbled Jesus's name a few times and tried to hold back my laughter. "Let everyone know that there's going to be a meeting in one hour," I said. "All Sigmas and pledges. Mandatory."

"On it, Tailor," he said.

My next stop was the fridge to shotgun a few beers. I needed to formulate my memorial for Fairy Rat. The beer would help me clear my head, which was still throbbing like a hard-on.

An hour later, I was standing in front of the entire Sigma brotherhood. There had to be at least fifty brothers and pledges sitting and standing, waiting for their fearless leader to make a statement. I really, really didn't want to be holding a meeting. I fucking hated talking to people, especially crowds. But it was my duty as president. There was no one else cut out for the job.

"As Hell Week draws to a close, I have some very sad news. One of our pledges, Brice… My fucking boy. He…" I stuttered a little. "He ended his own life in an apparent suicide pact with some fucking bitch."

Everyone was silent.

"I know we're hard on you pledges, but…" I took a deep breath and held up a finger, signaling that I needed a second. "We want the best, and I think Brice was just that. He would have been a brother. This tragedy cuts *really* deep."

After wiping away my highly convincing tears and drying my eyes, I continued through fake chokes. "Despite this tragedy, the Hell Week Kegger on Saturday will continue as planned and when we vote on everyone, remember Fairy—Brice. Let's throw the greatest bash ever for Brice, Boys!"

"For Brice!" the brothers chimed. Spineless followers, all of them.

"For the Sigma brotherhood!"

"For the Sigma brotherhood!"

Thank you, thank you. I would like to thank the academy.

With that, I resigned back to my room upstairs to call the maintenance department for the busted pipe.

The doorbell rang a few hours later and signified the plumber's arrival. By then, there were only a handful of Sigmas left in the house. I think they went to light candles for Pig Dolphin and Fairy Rat in the center of campus. How sweet… and fucking stupid.

I ran down the stairs as fast as I could and cut off some kid in tan cargo shorts and a university shirt who was walking toward the door.

"Don't open the door, deadbeat. Leave this guy to me," I said.

Behind the door was one of the ugliest tubs of lard I'd ever seen. He wore a mechanic's jumpsuit and had glasses so thick they could see into the future. The sheen from his hair and face made it look like he hadn't showered in a month. The greasy strings on his head were tied back in a ponytail.

He licked his fingers and flipped through some papers on a clipboard. "I'm looking for Tailor… Phillips?"

"Why hello," I said. "Welcome to Sigma. I'm President Tailor. Are you the repairman that the college was sending?"

The man looked me up and down, his watermelon gut rising and falling with each strained breath. "Phillips, huh? Are you from England?"

"Born and raised in the US? Why do you ask?"

He leaned into my face. I could smell the remnants of a tuna fish sandwich that dusted his heinous goatee. "You remind me of someone I know named Phillips. He's a Brit." The man paused. "Anyway. You had a leak or something?"

He sounded like a shitbag with a Boston accent, which was jarring. I hate Boston accents, or anything east coast for that matter. *Paak da caa in da yaad* and all that dumb shit.

"Yessir. A pipe burst upstairs," I said. "I can't imagine what could have caused it."

He took a step inside and scanned the room with gigantic eyes magnified by the gaudy glasses. I had the urge to punch him in his pudgy gut. He kept scanning and not saying anything, acting like he was casing the place or something. Who did this fat boy think he was? A fucking cop? That wasn't possible. This gross fucking jello-looking motherfucker was too obese to be a cop.

He licked his lips and then finally spoke up. "You got an old house. Shit breaks down."

"Very true," I agreed. "Anyway, the pipe is upstairs if you want to follow me."

He licked his lips again, grunted, and then started walking up the stairs without me like he owned the goddamn place.

With his fucking tree trunk thighs, it took him a good minute to get up the twenty-six steps to the second floor. I took the opportunity to rush by him and held my breath as I did so. I didn't even want to know what that guy smelled like this close. I can imagine it was a mix of wet farts and Doritos. *Go faster, Slow Jams*! I said to myself as he shuffled down the hall to the bathroom.

After what seemed like an eternity, I ushered him inside and pointed to the busted pipe.

"That it?" he asked, looking at the giant hole in the wall

No. It's the other broken pipe in the other room. I just brought you to look at this one for fun. Fucking retard.

"Yes sir, that would be the culprit. So, what do you think?"

He leaned in and got his face right up to the pipe. He was eying it up like a woman. As if deciding on whether to stick his little acorn dick into it or not. Eventually, he pulled a white handkerchief from his back pocket and wiped around the threaded part where it had busted. I knew I was fucked when he pulled the cloth away and I saw a patch of red hair. Pig Dolphin hair.

Okay, let me set this straight, I do not clean. Under any normal circumstances, I would never be caught cleaning anything. I'm the leader of the goddamn Sigmas for fucks sake, I can just make the peasants below me do that shit. These were not usual circumstances, however. I may not have done the best job, I mean, I somehow managed to get all that blood and shit off the floor, and I figured that was good enough.

Apparently not.

"What does this look like to you?" the fat man asked.

It looks like none of your business, lardass. Fix the pipe and get the fuck out of my house.

"Oh, I don't know. That's strange."

His big ugly eyes squinted at me. "How did you say the pipe broke?"

"I'm not 100% sure. It just broke last night and I had to shut the water off."

He turned back to the pipe. "It looks like it was hit by something. Hit pretty hard."

I looked past him. He was right. The once straight pipe was bent to shit. Goddamn Pig Dolphin and her mongoloid skull. I should have used her head to hammer the pipe back into shape before I dumped her.

"Total mystery," I said, pulling out my wallet. I held up a handful of twenties. "I definitely wouldn't know anything about that, sir."

As much as I wanted to kill that *fackin' Bawston pissa*, I didn't need any more blood on my hands in the span of twenty-four hours. Though it would have been so easy to ram my fist into the mirror, grab a shard, and jab him over and over and over in his pudgy gut, I had to control myself. That obese sack of shit's time would come.

He let out a huff of air like a heifer, "Stop with that 'sir' shit, buddy.... Call me, Hoop."

"Alright then, Mr. Hoop. Do you think you can fix this mess for us?"

He looked at the twenties and waved a meaty hand. "Money's no good here. Since your fraternity is enrolled with college housing and has good standing, they'll pay for it all."

I wouldn't say we're in 'good' standing per se. Our average GPA besides freshman is 1.5 and we don't usually go to college-run events, but we haven't done anything too bad to piss them off. Most of the shit we get up to happens right under their nose and those retards aren't the least bit suspicious. Well, except for this plumber guy. I patted him on his sweat-drenched shoulder. "Well, that's very nice of them. But surely I can give *you* something..."

"Yeah, those cheap bastards don't cough up money for shit. But since this was an accident…" He shot me a wink. "They'll cover the bill. But maybe there is something you can give me… I always wanted to go to a real college party…"

"Well, isn't that a coincidence. We're having our huge Hell Week Kegger on Saturday. You should totally come. We've gotta repay you somehow."

Hoop gurgled the phlegm in his throat, then hocked a fat loogie into the toilet. My new boy Hoop seemed like a no-wipe-after-a-shit kind of guy. In only that small time, he'd made the entire bathroom smell like a public gym locker room.

"Will there be beer and bitches?" He snorted, following up his joke by nudging me in the ribs with his fucking lunch lady arm.

"Only for those of us who are of age of course." I winked. "I might have to card you, you old devil."

"Alright then. I'll see if I can make it," he said as if he had anything better to do.

What? Gotta sit at home alone and eat Cheetos and watch kiddie porn, you pervert?

"I hope you can. We'd love to have you. But…" I gestured to the pipe. "How do we fix this today?"

"Got a tool in the truck to straighten that pipe out, then all you'd need is a new fitting."

I left Hoop in the bathroom, and in less than thirty minutes the water was back on. Interestingly enough, most of that time was spent hauling his fat ass up and down the stairs again to get his tools. He worked without saying another word.

When he was about to take off, I reminded him about the party. He may have acted like he was uninterested, but I knew deep down he was excited. Someone like Hoop knows what a loser he is. Of course, a fat, gross loser like him was going to jump at the opportunity to hang out with the cool kids. Hopefully that would be enough to keep his mouth shut.

Saturday morning, the pledges finished preparing for the Kegger and then we held the voting ceremony for the pledges—all but Brice. Michael my VP, Nick the Secretary, Dallas, and I stood there, smiling as the new brothers were admitted. None of them were inner circle material, but that was okay. We needed peons to survive because all the four of us cared about was partying.

God, the anticipation for that night was always like edging. But after lunch, the wait was finally over. We quietly retired upstairs to the Presidential Suite for our special Hell Week rituals while the newly initiated brothers began partying downstairs.

Michael, Nick, Dallas, and I passed a blunt first, then we each recounted our favorite fucks and crazy shit from the summer.

"... and then she fucking puked!" Michael said. "Not like some chunky shit, straight up liquid all over my new Jordans. I was pissed. Like, c'mon, couldn't you wait till we're not in the fucking dressing room?"

Nick fist bumped him. "Holy shit, I've been there M-Wagon."

"Some bitches just can't take a cock all the way down their throat. When she was finished barfing, I shoved that chili dog right back in her mouth."

The rest of us chimed in, "Fucking bitches."

No one understands you like your brothers, that's for sure. I mean, with who else can you share a story about choking a girl for so long she passes out, to then waking her up by pissing on her face?

"What about you, Pres?" Dallas asked.

"I've got a Hell of a story for you. But first…the next part of the ritual."

I pulled the small baggie from my sport jacket pocket. Inside was a small sheet of paper, perforated into tiny squares, each with the Sigma symbol printed on it.

"Remember, three tabs a piece. Don't be a fucking pussy."

I tore off three tabs for myself and then passed the sheet to Dallas.

We each placed the three tabs on our tongues and while preparing for the acid to kick in, I said, "This year I outdid myself, boys. This may be a new chapter in our brotherhood. *If* you think you can keep up."

"What did you do?"

I couldn't stop grinning. "Know that busted pipe that shut off the water?"

They leaned forward—

*Knock, knock, knock.*

"Ah, what the fuck?" I shouted.

"Sorry, Pres, but there's an old guy downstairs asking for you," someone said from the other side of the door.

"Tell him to piss off," I said, opening the door. The kid behind it had a buzz-cut and wore tacky jean shorts. Who the fuck was he to be interrupting our sacred inner-circle rituals? Then I remembered Hoop. "Wait, that fat smelly guy?"

"Uh, yeah," the pledge said. "But he's got…some friends you should see."

Friends. That piece of shit. I help him and he brings friends. No worries, maybe tonight we'll start a new tradition. Instead of raping bitches on camera, maybe we'd start killing fat fucks instead.

I looked to the inner circle. "If you will excuse me, boys, I have to get that. I'll be right back."

The acid started to kick in as I made my way downstairs.

*You got this, Tailor. This fat fuck doesn't know what's about to hit him. Dumb fucking plumber. He doesn't know shit! He ain't even ready. I'll show him. He'll learn not to mess with fucking Sigma right before he dies in a pool of his own piss! And my piss! Double fucking piss pool!*

I stopped at the landing. Hoop was dressed in a tacky Hawaiian shirt and a pair of equally gaudy madras shorts. He teetered back and forth in his faggey flip-flops.

"I hope you don't mind; I brought some friends."

Nudging his head, he signaled to his guests. There were three smoking sluts behind him. Not just smoking. These were real women. Not the dyke-looking college student body. They were all dressed in business pencil skirts and blouses. They were ripped right out of a Strippergram ad. What the fuck were these chicks doing with a shit-eater like Hoop? Did he hire them? Were they pros?

"Well, I wasn't expecting this, Hoop, but of course it's all right. Welcome in, ladies," I said, ushering them inside with a bow.

The three MILFs looked around for a moment before one of them spoke. "Seems kinda like a Peter Brady, Hoop."

"Peter Brady? What's that?" I asked.

She dragged her index finger across my chin. "It means no one is here."

"Huh? Oh, don't worry. There's a lot of fun to be had. There's a keg, whiskey, and bongs in the kitchen. I have acid, E, and blow in my Presidential Suite."

Another slut from the crew walked by me, dragging her palm against my bulge. "Hmm. I don't think we're interested in that kind of fun. We had something different in mind."

*Holy shit!*

"Say no more, ladies. If you follow me to the suite, we can have some *real* fun."

My boner led the way upstairs and Hoop's Slut Squad followed. Things started to get more interesting when the stairs turned into spaghetti about halfway up. *Who the fuck dropped a bunch of spaghetti on the stairs? Damn slobs always leave shit everywhere.* Then I remembered the acid. Thankfully it didn't seem to be affecting my cock. At that point, I didn't care if the room turned into a lasagna. Pussy is pussy. Getting laid is getting laid.

The walls upstairs were melting like ice cream. I glanced back at the sluts. They were following as if nothing was wrong, their plump blowjob lips curling into smiles. Obviously, reality wasn't melting for them. Fuck! This acid was fucking wild. I planned to ask the junkie I got them from if he did anything different with that batch. It never kicked in that quickly or was that sick before. Usually, my hands disappeared, or the room moved around and shit, but melting walls and spaghetti? Definitely a step up.

We finally got to my bedroom. Thankfully, the bed was just a bed. Also, a good thing, the inner circle was gone. They most likely would have suggested an orgy, and I wanted these whores all to myself.

The second we got in the room, the clothes started coming off. Well, it looked more like their clothes were sloshing off and then crawling away. *Fuck those living clothes,* I thought.

I usually didn't get mature pussy because the younger bitches were so much easier to spit game at and get fucked up. Instead of some big-mouthed kid hiding her freshman fifteen under a tent-sized sweatshirt, I was looking at bolt-on tits and tight *woman*-bodies. These bitches definitely did yoga because their bodies were fucking temples. On top of that, they were wearing sexy lace under their business clothes. Those didn't stay on long either. They crawled away just like the rest of the clothes, using their clasps as hands to drag themselves along.

I slapped myself in the face, trying to focus on these chicks, but the trip was getting weirder and weirder.

*Focus on the T and A, Tailor!* I kept telling myself. That would get me through this.

My shorts crawled to the door and stopped at Hoop's Fred Flintstone feet that were stuffed into a pair of Birks. "You like this, Tailor?" he said with a smirk.

I turned back to find that all three sluts were completely naked, rubbing their nipples, fingering themselves, and tossing their hair around like they were in a music video.

I whipped my cock out and shuffled my boxers down to my calves. They crawled away too.

I stood firm in the center of the Slut Squad and beat on my chest like a gorilla. One of them laid down on the bed in front of me. Before indulging in my animal instincts, I looked around at the full scope of these bitches that I was going to destroy. They all looked really similar, like they could be sisters or something. Maybe they were some kind of gangbang group that Hoop hired to butter me up. They couldn't have been his friends though! A fucking slob like him didn't know any women besides his mother.

As I slid my dick into the first snatch, it felt hot. It's usually pretty warm in there, but this bitch was on fire. I don't know if she had a fever or something, but it felt like putting my dick into a wood-fire oven. The other sluts crowded around, groping at us and moaning. Their hands were warm, too. And the room felt like it was getting hotter.

*Jesus Christ!* I was sweating like a fat girl struggling to get a tub of ice cream open and we hadn't even been going at it for more than a minute. Despite the heat, the whore I was drilling into was wet as shit. So wet, in fact, my dick was slipping all over the place. I could barely keep it in her for more than a few pumps. I wasn't used to that. Unconscious bitches didn't get turned on. So, I was usually chafing my cock's head in their dry pussies.

I wiped a gallon of sweat from my eyes as another squad member tagged herself in. She pushed me onto the bed and crouched over me. Her thighs were thick and muscular but smooth as silk. She held my hands down and gave me a searing hot kiss on the forehead.

"You bitches are really going all-in on this power dynamic thing, huh? Good for you. I can dig it," I said as the second MILF dropped down onto my cock.

The temperature in the suite continued to rise. Sweat dripped off me and accumulated in a pool in the center of my bed. No matter how uncomfortable I became, I couldn't stop pumping and thrusting. There was something about those bitches. I couldn't control myself. It felt like I would die if I didn't fill all of them to the teeth with jizz. And that's what I was determined to do. Whether I drowned in my own sweat or got heat stroke, I was going to give these sluts every single drop of semen in my sack.

But that's when shit started really getting fuckey. Like, more fuckey than crawling clothes.

As the bitch riding me peeled off and got down on her hands and knees, the walls stopped melting. There was black brick underneath now visible inside the suite. The clothes on the floor were gone, and the pool of sweat underneath me was bubbling, just about to boil.

I changed to doggie-style on the third. The others dug their long nails into my skin. Whether I was frightened or not, I just kept shoving my pelvis back and forth. I was exhausted. Dehydrated. Hot as a motherfucker. That's when I first noticed they were changing.

Something sharp poked me in the ass and puckered my cornhole, clenching in reaction. I whipped my head around to see the slut behind me raising a clawed-hand dripping with my shit. She pressed it up against her lips.

I remembered those bitches having long nails, but I didn't realize they had fucking badger claws. She licked the turd on the end of her finger and then scratched at my dick. With all that scratching, I was sure to lose my hard-on. So, I smacked at her claw.

She looked to the other and they both burst out into fiendish laughter. And, when she turned back to me, she smiled and hissed, revealing her reptile-like tongue and razor-sharp fangs.

All the while, I didn't stop fucking the slut on her hands and knees. I couldn't. I tried to pull out, I swear, but my dick was fucking stuck in her vice-grip pussy. If anything, her fire-cunt was sucking my cock in like a vacuum, pulling at the flesh around the head and the base. I felt pubes being tugged out of my skin.

She looked over her shoulder at me and smiled. She had transformed too. They all had sharp teeth and twisted-up tongues. Horns sprouted from their foreheads as pointy tails bloodily grew from their lower backs. Blood spurted everywhere. They continued rubbing up on me, slashing my body with their claws. Still, I couldn't stop fucking. In. Out. In. Out. Never very far out or else I'd feel uncomfortable resistance. In. Out.

It had to be the acid. That was the only logical explanation. I was having a batshit, bad trip and it was making me go fucking crazy.

"Try this on for size, Stallion," one of them whispered in my ear.

I felt a sharp pain in my asshole again. Behind me, one of the MILFs was rimming me with that sharp tongue and it felt like I was being stabbed with an ice pick right.

"Fuck no! I am not into that, you fucking freak! No fag shit!"

I grabbed her head, ripped it from my asshole, and threw her to the floor. She giggled in response and wiped the shit and blood from her lips. I got the sense something was very wrong; more than just the acid, and I needed to get out of there.

To get my dick free doggie-slut, I put both my hands on her ass and pushed with the power of Hercules. With tears now gushing from my eyes, it finally unlocked with a loud pop.

*Oh shit*, I thought as I stumbled off the bed. *No. No, that pop isn't good.* I closed my eyes, not wanting to look down.

"What the fuck did you bitches do to me!?"

I opened my eyes and screamed. Between my legs was nothing more than a bloody, hairy sack and a couple dangling veins.

"You ate my fucking dick, you cunt!"

My tears turned to blind rage.

They all laughed at me. In the corner, Hoop mocked me by covering his crotch with his hands and making a crybaby face. I darted at the monster bitch who'd eaten my asshole. I shoved her, sending her backward. Her body coiled around itself like her arms and legs were wet noodles and she looked like a snake.

I tried jumping over her, but she caught me with her fangs. Her neck elongated and she chomped the vein at the back of my leg, tearing it open. More blood sprayed the floor, adding to the boiling sex-sweat soup.

That's when I went berserk.

I knocked two of the Slut Squad to the floor and stomped their heads into the boards, squishing their ruptured skulls into the wood grain. I wiggled my toes and felt their warm, leathery skin and slimy brains between them. Before the other could react, I charged and close-lined her. She bounced off the bed and landed face-first on the floor. I then crouched down, grabbed her hair in my fist, and slammed her face into the floor twenty, maybe thirty times. I didn't stop until all of her evil demon teeth were scattered and her nose was inverted into her face.

I slid down the wall in the corner, trying to compose something dick-like from the scraps of meat, blood, and veins between my legs. I started to hyperventilate, realizing that my manhood was gone forever.

Hoop erupted in laughter. He slapped his knee and fogged up his glasses. After minutes of applause and delight, he took a few deep breaths, then removed his glasses and wiped the lenses with his awful Hawaiian shirt. After he put the glasses back on and let out an enormous final laugh, he said… "Fuckin' whores, am I right?"

He pointed to the demon-MILF corpses.

There were three ravaged bodies, but they weren't those of the Slut Squad. They were the bodies of my inner circle. Michael, Dallas and Nick, and their bodies were just as fucked up as I'd left the demon bitches. One of them, whom I'd squished under my heel, had a huge gaping hole where his asshole was supposed to be. I looked down. My cock was still there and intact even though I knew I had just seen and felt it ripped from my body. It was covered in shit and blood.

"*What the fuck*?! This isn't real!"

I didn't fuck and kill the bitches. I fucked and killed my brothers.

"*Oh, it's real*," Hoop said as he walked over to me. "I almost forgot." He slapped my wrist, then, taking his hand away, he revealed my watch. That shitty Rolex my dad gave me. "You lost this at the quarry, Tailor. Don't worry, I got it back for you."

My hands trembled. My breath staggered and I couldn't control my tears.

Someone banged on the door like they were trying to break it down.

"Time is up, Tailor," Hoop said with a wicked smile. He walked back to the door and stood behind it with one foot flat on the wall and his arms crossed.

The door to my suite flew open. Multiple men dashed in and shouted, "Get down on the ground, you piece of shit!"

They drew an arsenal of weapons at my head.

I put my arms up. "This isn't what it looks like, it was all Hoop—"

Before I could further plead my case, one of the cops shouted, "He's got a gun!"

I looked at my wrist. My watch was no longer there. Instead, my hand held the Sig Sauer pistol. And it was pointed at the cops.

I was interrupted by a chorus of gunfire. Bullets ripped through my flesh, opening a hundred warm, gushing holes.

And then, as I found myself in an elevator descending into the ground, I heard Hoop.

*"Fucking whores... am I right?"*

# FREAK FUCK

## PETER CAFFREY

The bright spotlight was focused on the princess, forcing her to squint. I could only assume princess was her rank as she had it tattooed across her rotund belly. The badly calligraphed and garishly-coloured word was split by the pink slash of an appendectomy scar and surrounded by stretch marks and a smattering of red spots with pustular heads. Above the cheap backstreet inking, her breasts drooped like a pair of bloodhound's ears. The nipples were little more than brown splotches, as if a tobacco-chewing grandpa had spat on her tits.

I lifted her left breast carefully with the end of my pen, before letting it sag back into its normal position.

"Uh huh," I mumbled and scribbled a note on the form.

"Can you do anything to help?" she asked, her voice fearful.

"Oh, yes. I can help."

I looked up from my notes with a choreographed shit-eating smile.

"When I'm finished, you'll have the bosom of an angel."

She liked that. They all liked that, the desperate cunts who came crowding through my door. They liked it despite never considering what sort of a bust angels had.

"And my nipples?"

"They'll be as perky as—"

I stopped myself before I said something that might give the game away.

"They'll be perky."

"What size will they be?"

The question triggered an image of her waking after the procedure to find her nipples the size of gorillas' thumbs. Horrible, gnarled black things with a rubbery consistency, protruding at least four inches from her massively over-inflated breasts.

"Doctor Oliver?"

I snapped to attention and glanced up. She was staring at me, a confused look on her face.

"Yes?"

"I was asking about my nipples. What size will they be?"

"What size would you like them?"

She held up her little finger and gripped it to indicate her expectations. I went to make a note on the form and realised it was obliterated by a frenzied mess of jagged lines and insane doodles.

"And this hair?" I asked, tapping the bruise-like nipple. "Would you like it removed? If you pluck it, it'll only grow back thicker. I could kill it from the root, and it'll never bother you again."

Glancing down, she looked shocked.

"Oh, no. I hadn't seen that before."

Maybe she needed something more than a breast augmentation; maybe she needed a fucking eye test. This wasn't a wispy hair which might be hard to spot unless in a certain light. It was like a thick black rope, the type knights use to climb towers and free real princesses, ones with firm tits and perky nipples.

I made another note and then put the clipboard down, ensuring the I placed the form face-down on the desk, so she didn't see the crazy scrawl.

Sadly, she didn't fit the bill for my *magnum opus*. In truth, she didn't even come close. She would be a great payday. But her body was too old, her skin lacking elasticity. The lines and stretch marks made her look like a faded road map, and her tattoos were ugly and poorly executed. Her body was riddled with scars and scabs. Some were from previous procedures, and others looked like they'd come about after altercations with disgruntled johns.

Moments like this made me wonder if I was being too selective. Five years, I'd searched in vain. But I needed perfection. Well, as close to perfection as I could find. There was no point in violating someone's beauty if they were fucked-up to begin with. Where was the thrill in that? So this one, this princess with a body like a wet sack of shit, was just easy money. Another medical tourist who thought she'd have the bosom of angel for a discount price.

"Thank you, Miss Smith. You can get dressed now," I said, picking up my scheduling diary. "How long are you in the country for?"

"Ten days; it's only a short trip," she said, trying to force her sagging breasts into her frayed bra.

"I understand. I do have a free slot which fits with your schedule. I could pencil you in if you like."

"Yes, please. That would be great."

Her voice bubbled with excitement. It was all too common amongst my clients. The thought of low-cost surgery and a quick turnaround meant they rarely questioned their own decisions. What they say about a fool and their money is just as apt for women teetering on the brink of decay. Offer them another year or two of youth and they'll throw their cash at you as soon as they'd drop their knickers for an elderly playboy with a yacht and a heart condition.

"As you've been informed, we require full payment in advance to reserve your appointment. Also, you won't be able to fly for at least three days following the procedure. During that time, you should adhere to the guidance provided. Should there be any issues, we are only a phone call away. The nursing staff is available around the clock. If you see Nurse Jenkins at reception, she'll take your payment and make the final arrangements."

The princess rose and held out her hand. As I shook it, I saw a tear glisten in the corner of eye.

"Thank you so much, Doctor Oliver."

"Don't worry, Miss Smith," I said, wearing my well-practised smile. "By the time you leave us, we'll have you looking fabulous."

With her name of the list, I'd achieved the numbers required to hit my financial target. It was time to cut and run. By tomorrow morning, the clinic would once more be the empty shell of a closed-down grocery shop, the clients' money would be in an off-shore account, and I would be on a plane with Nurse Jenkins, off to new pastures.

Doctor Oliver would cease to exist. I'd assume a new identity, set up another clinic, and the process would start all over again. We'd promote the new practice using the time-honoured trick of weight loss success stories, and once we'd raised its profile, other procedures would be offered. The inevitable tide of patients would wash up at our door, all looking to exchange a bundle of cash for another shot at youth.

Perhaps somewhere among them, I'd find her, the elusive perfect woman from which to create my *magnus opus*. Given that most cosmetic surgery patients were flawed in some way, I knew discovering her would be a long haul, but I had hope. One day, whether driven to me on a wave of anxiety and insecurity, pushed into procedures by the cruelty of others, or simply obsessed with incurable vanity, she will find herself walking into my clinic. And when she does, I'll be ready.

Belgrade was a miserable shithole, but it didn't bother me. I wasn't here to go sightseeing; I was here to make money. Once we'd cleared immigration, Nurse Jenkins headed to the clinic, anxious to check on the refurbishment. Once her inspection was done, she'd head into town, score some horse tranquilliser or whatever shit she was using nowadays, and do the rounds of the local nightclubs looking for new friends. It had become a routine, and deep down, I think it was the part of her job she enjoyed the most.

My taxi driver was old and haggard. He'd probably been around during the Balkans War and, looking at the reflection of his eyes in the rear-view mirror, I figured he'd fucked a few corpses while pinned down in the bomb craters. Why not?

It was better than letting them rot. A waste of good cunt, as my old Dad used to say.

He spotted me looking at him in the mirror.

"You want girl?" he croaked.

"I'm fine," I replied.

"I can get you fat, fat bitch. She'll let you do it ... how do you say ... up the anus."

He laughed, his dank gob hole opening and a solitary yellow tooth glinting in the reflections of the streetlights. The car filled with the stench of pickled fish as his laughter transformed into a bronchial cough. I cracked the window to let some air in and pretended to read messages on my phone for the rest of the journey. The last thing I wanted was anal sex with a fat, fat bitch.

Arriving at the hotel, I showered, ordered room service, and downloaded my email. My design guy had sent proofs of the marketing materials for the new clinic. With those approved, I hit the sack.

The next few days were spent arranging the clinic opening. Nurse Jenkins bore the brunt of the burden, but still found the energy to be out at night, combing the local nightclubs to expand her circle of friends. When we eventually got time to sit down, she fetched her tablet and scrolled through a mix of social media profiles.

"I've selected half a dozen possibilities that tick all our boxes," she said, her voice indicating she was pleased with the friends she'd made. "All are socialites past their prime, and they're active on social media. They're definitely the types to publicly boast about receiving a free procedure because they've befriended the nurse. Have a look. They all need some help."

I scrolled through the profiles, examining their photos. All had the tell-tale signs: the way they stood, how they held their handbags, the poses they struck were all designed to hide the extra few pounds they were carrying. They weren't obese; it was more a case of the midriff getting away from them. They were ideal. I didn't want drastically overweight women; the results had to come quickly.

"Do any of them exercise?" I asked, already guessing at the answer.

"They talk about it," Nurse Jenkins replied with a grin. "My guess, however, is that they're too strung out or hungover to get out of bed before lunchtime. It's the usual situation: too washed up to make the A-list, but too precocious to admit it."

"Okay. Reel them in," I said, flicking open the desk diary. "Try to make their appointments for next Wednesday."

"Very well, Doctor Oliver," she said with a grin.

"Nurse Jenkins, remember we're in Belgrade. Doctor Oliver disappeared somewhere in Budapest."

"Sorry," she muttered. "I wasn't thinking, Doctor Fairweather."

"Always think," I said. "Always fucking think."

The weight loss scam was straightforward. I'd take a woman with a bit of a belly paunch, introduce *Taenia Saginata* eggs to her intestines, and wait for the tapeworms to hatch and grow in her gut. They'd then devour a significant portion of whatever she ate. She'd shed the pounds, and before the infestation became detrimental to her health, I'd give her a dose of Praziquantel to deworm her.

There was nothing new in tapeworm diets. The Victorians used them, and the practice only fell out of favour when amphetamines became the appetite suppressant of choice. Tapeworm pills were available on the black market, but I knew if I handed out pills, some nosy fucker would steal one and have it analysed. I found a way to hide how I administered the eggs. It was smoke and mirrors, but it added to the theatre of the process. Women seeking easy weight loss loved a bit of theatre.

I didn't claim to be brilliant for using tapeworms to accelerate weight loss. If I were brilliant, I wouldn't have been scamming people for the cost of procedures I had no intention of performing. If I were brilliant, I'd have helped humanity, repairing kids with fucked-up faces or something noble like that. If I were brilliant, the General Medical Council wouldn't have struck me off.

The first of Nurse Jenkins's nightclub friends to arrive was Anja. She was a twenty-yard woman—at that distance she looked good, but every step closer made her flaws more obvious. Some women who think they're getting a favour because they're a friend of the nurse are overfamiliar, as if knowing her somehow bestowed on them a friendship with me. Thankfully, Anja was the quiet type, avoiding conversation for fear I'd raise the issue of a fee.

We went through the rigmarole of questions and answers. What did she want to achieve? Had she tried any other weight loss programmes? Was she active? Did she take any other medication, prescription or otherwise? She failed to mention the cocaine she'd obviously hoofed to get herself out of bed early enough for the consultation.

"And finally," I asked, "have you eaten anything in the last twelve hours?"

"No," she said, almost in a whisper. "I haven't eaten or drunk anything."

I looked at her, my eyebrows raised.

"You've been drinking plenty of water, surely?"

She shook her head.

"Nurse Jenkins should have told you to drink water. It's vital you're well hydrated."

I stood and went into a side room, returning with a glass and a bottle of water. She drank it down, draining the glass, eager to ensure the treatment wasn't delayed. She didn't notice the *Taenia Saginata* eggs floating in it. They never did. Then it was time for the theatre of the procedure, the smoke and mirrors to hide the simplicity of what I'd done.

"Anja, I need you to undress. The procedure involves a subcutaneous injection into your lower abdomen wall, just above your groin. The positioning is critical, so I must ask that you remove any undergarments. It can be painful, but the discomfort will only last for a few seconds. Are you happy to proceed?"

She nodded and started to disrobe. While she did, I prepared the syringe, loading it with a basic saline solution. Subcutaneous injections need not be painful, but I made sure they were. It wasn't just the tingle I felt when hurting people which made me do it; the charade enhanced the illusion it was a complex medical procedure. The women usually felt more entitled if they'd suffered for their weight loss, and that made them more willing to tell others what they'd achieved. These women were my advertising campaign, my social media influencers, and the pain of the injection guaranteed me a greater reach.

Anja's body was in decent shape, but the first signs of deterioration were there: broken veins, less than elastic tissue, and a paunch forming around the belly. Using a surgical wipe, I cleaned the area for her injection. As I did, I had a good look at her cunt. It had fared better than other parts of her body. She'd obviously washed it that morning. Some patients—and not just those getting a freebie—stank like a trawler's bilge pump. Anja was clean, fresh, and nicely trimmed. With my face so close, I fought back the urge to nuzzle into her vagina and take a long hard sniff.

"This might sting," I said, pushing the needle hard into her groin. She tensed, her body rigid. I enjoyed her reaction, so I pushed the needle in a bit further, harder than necessary. Her whimper made me throb. Pushing down the plunger, I released the saline solution into her muscle, before withdrawing the needle.

"All done," I said with my usual shit-eating grin. "You'll feel tender for a few days. Get dressed and see Nurse Jenkins on your way out. She'll arrange your next appointment."

After Anja, I saw Katarina, a moody wannabe model, Margaret, who was aloof and sullen, Caroline who suffered verbal diarrhoea and laughed at her own jokes, and Jana. Jana was twitchy; everything indicated she was ripe for a breakdown if the right buttons were pushed.

I had one more girl to see, Petra, and my work for the day would be done. After her treatment, I could return to the hotel and enjoy a single malt or three on the veranda before dinner.

Petra was late, which annoyed me. We'd extended a courtesy to her by offering a free treatment, and the bitch couldn't be bothered to turn up on time. Nurse Jenkins had an appointment at the printers to collect the brochures for the clinic, and rather than delay their use, I sent her off. If Petra arrived before I headed back to the hotel, I'd explain she'd missed her slot and would have to pay if she wanted another booking. If she didn't like it, she could go fuck herself. I needed people to talk about the clinic, but I wasn't going to tolerate rudeness just to get a few reviews.

I finished off some paperwork, collected my things together, and prepared to leave. When I went to exit through the waiting room, I realised someone was there. A woman, who I could only assume was Petra, was dozing on one of the sofas.

Younger than the other women and arguably prettier, she was slightly dishevelled. Her body was predominantly skin and bone, but the tell-tale rolls of fat and flab adorned her midriff. Her appearance screamed 'junkie,' but her exposed arms were free of track marks. I coughed loudly, but she didn't react. My patience was running thin, so I kicked the sole of her foot hard enough to jolt her awake.

"Can I help you?"

Struggling to sit up, she wiped a trickle of drool from her mouth with the back of her hand. Her eyes showed she was strung out; I guessed it was some type of opiate.

"I said, can I help you?"

"I'm Petra," she muttered. "I have an appointment."

"You *had* an appointment, but you're late."

"I guess I am," she replied, not apologetically, but more as an agreement of the fact. "I'm here for a treatment. I arranged it with the nurse woman."

"By the nurse woman, I assume you mean Nurse Jenkins?"

"Maybe." She shrugged. "So, what happens now? Do I need to sign something, or do we just get on with it?"

"Well, Petra, allow me to explain," I said with fake sincerity. "You had an appointment for a consultation, but you're late. You're not a few minutes late, or even a half hour late. Your appointment was over an hour ago. Nurse Jenkins has left for the day, and I'm about to do the same."

She sat up, a coquettish smile creeping across her face.

"Surely you can fit me in, Doc. After all, you're still here and it's not like you have any other patients."

"First, my name is Doctor Fairweather. I don't respond to Doc. I'm not one of the seven fucking dwarves. Second, there are no other patients because the clinic is closed. If you wish to make another appointment, feel free to do so tomorrow. I'm sure Nurse Jenkins will be happy to supply you with a list of the relevant fees."

Petra stood and leaned toward me, her icy blue eyes sparkling.

"C'mon Doc. I'm sure we can come to some sort of arrangement, can't we?"

I wanted to throw her out of the clinic, to tell her to grow up and treat others with respect, but I didn't. There was something about her, something which the other women lacked. She might have been a touch skanky, but her skin was good, her hair thick and lustrous, and from what I could see of her body through her tight clothing, she seemed to be well toned. She wasn't perfect, nor did she have a natural beauty, but she was good enough to justify a bit of experimentation. Perhaps I could use her as a sketch pad, a trial run for my *magnus opus*.

Something about her intrigued me, so instead of showing her the door, I glanced at my watch.

"Maybe I can fit you in."

"I have a feeling I could fit you in, too," she said with a lascivious wink.

I poured two large glasses of single malt. Into Petra's, I dumped the tapeworm eggs. I wasn't sure if the alcohol might inhibit their hatching, so I doubled the usual dose. Her lateness had annoyed me, so I added yet another batch of eggs. She wanted a treatment, and I was going to give her one.

When I walked into the consulting room, she'd already stripped. As I suspected, her body was in decent shape, but the bruises and pock marks on her skin gave an indication of her lifestyle. The tell-tale track marks were visible now, the scabbed puncture wounds dotting her groin.

Most of the women I treated would have killed for her figure, but something about Petra was repulsive: it was her sense of entitlement.

She took the glass of scotch and downed it in one. Wiping her mouth with the back of her hand, she grinned at me, a slutty grin. I smiled back. She had drank more tapeworm eggs than any other woman I'd ever treated. If they all hatched and grew, it wouldn't be long until her gut was distended, worm fragments hanging from her arsehole. I thought about fucking her worm-infested butt and started to get hard.

She pulled me close and I offered no resistance as she fumbled with my belt. With it undone, she unbuttoned my fly and let her hand wander inside. I kept fantasising about the tapeworms tearing through her gut wall and chewing their way through her organs, so her fingers found me rigid.

Laid on the treatment table, head hanging over the edge, she took my prick in her mouth. She wasn't the best at oral, so I fell into a rhythm of thrusting, jamming my cock to the back of her throat. She gagged and tried to push me away, but her discomfort only aroused me more. I retaliated against her resistance, fucking her mouth harder. As she struggled to push me off, I dropped on top of her, using my superior strength and weight to pin her down. The feeling of her trying to escape was a turn-on, the tension in her body a catalyst for my bestial nature.

My face was close to her groin, the stink of her unwashed cunt heavy in my nostrils. The odour was a mixture of sweat and decay, with a background whiff of yeast, a fungal stench both foul and vinegary. She clearly didn't stay on top of her feminine hygiene.

I pressed my face into her groin, breathing in the vileness as she shuddered beneath me, struggling to get air into her lungs. I sniffed deep, inhaling her filthy stench. I wanted to sink my teeth into her sex, bite her as hard as I could until I tasted the coppery blood.. But I resisted the urge to tear her flesh like a rabid dog. It would be unwise to destroy my sketch pad too soon.

As I mentally played out the procedures and augmentations I could inflict on her, I felt my peak approaching. Her struggling body beneath me, the stench of her rancid vagina, and the thought of things to come took me to the edge. I exploded, filling her throat until I had nothing left.

I drove Petra into the city centre. She didn't speak, glaring out of the window in silence like a spoiled brat for the entire journey. She wasn't pleased with what I'd done to her. Then again, she didn't know how much worse it could have been. The urge to tear her rancid cunt to pieces with my teeth had been overwhelming, but I'd deferred my gratification for the longer-term plan.

She'd whinged and whined that my actions had been tantamount to rape. The threat was implicit, but she dropped the act once I'd agreed to drive her to her dealer. I knew it would cost me, but at least it shut her up.

We waited in a backstreet car park while she huffed and puffed, theatrically coughing as if she still had a throatful of cum. I tried not to laugh at her sulking. Eventually the man arrived, and I bought several packages of smack.

While Petra slinked off into a dark corner to sort herself out, I pocketed one of the bags. If I ever needed to get rid of her, I could cut it with something nasty and give her a hot fix. It's best to plan ahead when dealing with unstable people.

With the crap circulating in her veins, she wasn't in the mood to hang around, which suited me. I headed back to the hotel alone. In the rooftop cocktail bar, I found a quiet corner and started working my way through their selection of scotches. There wasn't much else to do but wait. Once our evangelists were posting about their weight loss success on social media, the phones would start ringing and we could do the hard sell on other procedures.

The next week was mostly spent schmoozing potential contacts. Nurse Jenkins set up meetings with the great and good of Belgrade, and I turned up to drink their booze and smother them with my charming and witty repartee. As is often the case with the influential members of high society, they were all old and well past their prime. If they'd been meat, they'd be minced up for dog food, and not the premium brands. The haggard women took an interest in me, some openly flirting in the hope they might be able to swing a cut-price shot at a return to their youth. The men politely asked about the financial side of my business, probably trying to work out if they could hide the cost of a boob job for their mistresses.

After a week of schmoozing, it was time to bring Jenkins's contacts back for their follow-up consultations. If they looked good and were happy with the results, I'd deworm them. If their progress was slow, it'd be another dose of *Taenia Saginata* eggs.

Anja had lost a decent amount of weight and looked a touch more sculpted. She was over the moon, and her quietness from the first consultation had transformed into more flirtatious behaviour. The confidence inspired by weight loss is astonishing, but she had a long way to go before being fuckable. In fact, she'd need to invent a time machine and go back to before gravity dragged her tits and buttocks towards the floor.

I worked my way through the routine questions, pretending they had some relevance. In truth, she could have given any answer and I wouldn't have cared. The tapeworms were doing their work; she didn't need another dose. To keep up appearances, I injected her with more saline solution and sent her off for another week.

Katarina, Margaret, and Jana had shed a few pounds, but nothing significant. I figured they'd been less fastidious than Anja. As I prepared the saline shots, I asked if they'd been regularly hydrating. I didn't really listen to their replies; my standard response was to shake my head and caution it wasn't enough. They sucked down the egg-laden water and took the jab. I deliberately made it more painful to teach them the treatment wasn't an excuse to be overindulgent. I gave them follow-up appointment dates and sent them back into their artificial world of idiocy.

Caroline was the only one who'd gained weight. She swore she'd been controlling her calorie intake, but said she'd been badly constipated since the first treatment. There was probably a big old tapeworm coiled up in her colon, blocking the flow of faecal matter. The worms sometimes got through from the stomach, and if they latched onto the intestine wall they created a shit-plug which backed everything up.

The temptation to examine her sphincter, to stick my fingers up her backside and grope for the blockage, was huge. It would have been impossible for me to reach the worm, but the thought of greasing her up and shoving my hand into her anus aroused me.

Despite the urge, I decided to play it safe and told her to use an over-the-counter laxative. I just hoped she didn't examine her stool when it passed. The mental image of her pulling apart a solid lump of blood-streaked faecal matter was too much, and I struggled not to laugh as she waddled out of the office, her shit-pipe well and truly blocked.

Petra didn't turn up for her appointment. I hadn't expected her to, but I knew she'd come at some point. It was just a matter of time.

Six days later, while I was finishing off some paperwork, I saw someone moving around in the waiting room through the frosted glass. I knew it'd be Petra; no doubt snuck in again just after Nurse Jenkins had gone back to the hotel for the night. The woman was probably sick and unable to find another mug to pay for her fix.

She'd changed her look, no doubt in anticipation of her soon-to be svelte figure. Her hair now dyed white and cut into a bob, her makeup smoky and alluring. It was striking, but underneath the affected styling, I could tell she wasn't well. Her stomach was distended; the tapeworms were growing at a good rate.

"Petra, hello," I said wearing my cheesiest fake smile. "My oh my, you're looking good."

She patted her swollen gut.

"Is this supposed to happen?" she asked, her question accusatory.

I wiped my smile and went into sincere mode.

"It shouldn't, but can I ask something? Have you been indulging in unprescribed medicines?"

Her shrug wasn't necessary; we both knew she had.

"It could be because you didn't listen to my advice," I muttered. "I'll need to check you over. Come into the treatment room."

As she undressed, I leafed through some paperwork. It was an exercise in killing time. She needed to learn how to wait. Like a puppy who'd pissed on the rug, she needed to be taught.

Eventually I glanced up.

"Pop yourself onto the bed," I said, nodding toward the treatment table.

As she settled on it, I pointed at her.

"Stop right there."

"What? What's wrong?"

I sighed, a dramatic exhalation.

"Well, I just noticed … actually, forget it. It's nothing."

I rose and walked around my desk. I could feel the tension in the room. It was palpable; I could have sliced through it with a scalpel.

"Your new look is interesting," I muttered as I picked up my stethoscope, "but I noticed your nose is, well, a bit angular. It's not bad, but if it was straighter, it'd set your face off a treat."

I placed my hand gently on her distended gut and pressed, but she sat up, her swollen belly forgotten.

"My nose?"

"Yes, your nose," I repeated in a distracted way. "It could be straighter, and with raised cheekbones and maybe a rounder jawline…"

I pressed gently on her stomach, but she remained sitting.

"Lay back, please, Petra. I need to check your abdomen."

She didn't move.

"What the fuck can I do about my nose?"

I smiled my shit-eating grin.

"What can you do? I suppose *you* can't do anything, but I could work wonders with it. Now lie back and relax."

She didn't move. Her vanity had shifted into overdrive.

"How much would it cost to … well, to do it all?"

Placing my hand on her shoulder, I gently pushed her back, so she was lying on the examination table.

"It wouldn't be cheap, but we might be able to work something out."

She was silent for a moment, thinking, before she asked, "What would you want me to do?"

I feigned an expression of surprise at her tone, then laughed. It's all about the timing of the laugh.

"Nothing!" I said. "Well, nothing like you're thinking. I would have one request you'd need to agree to."

"You want to fuck my arse?"

"What do you take me for?" My tone signalled offense, but I didn't overdo it. After all, I'd tried to choke her with my cock the last time we'd met. "If I were to consider helping you, I'd want time to do the job properly. It would mean you'd need to be here, under my care, for a few weeks at least."

She hesitated, thinking it over, before saying, "I have things I need to do."

"Things to do, or things to buy?"

She shrugged.

"Don't worry," I said. "If you need anything, I can make sure those *things* are supplied."

"What's in it for you? Why would you put yourself out for me?"

I turned my smile up to maximum manipulation.

"I enjoy creating perfection. It's what I do. Pure beauty is all the payment I need."

She sighed and nodded. The vane, selfish, ignorant cunt had swallowed the bait. Before she could change her mind, I went to the drugs cabinet and fetched three vials of Propofol.

Under the cold glare of the treatment room lights, Petra's body revealed its secrets. It was in worse shape than I'd initially thought, but not battered enough to make me reconsider my plans. Before doing anything else, I checked her anus. The sphincter was distended, a mass of tapeworm segments bulging outward. It looked like a partially peeled blood orange. Sorting her guts wasn't an urgent consideration; I needed to start work on that nose.

She needed what most women of her kind needed: a snout. She was a pig, a dirty fucking pig only fit to be snuffling in the shit, and a snout would be her crowning glory. On a few occasions I dreamed of creating a perfect proboscis for a pig bitch.

I ran the scalpel down the bridge of her nose, peeling back the skin to reveal the top ridge of her septum. After removing small sections of the bone structure, I gripped the septal cartilage. Without a nurse to swab for me, there was more blood than I was used to working with. I toyed with the idea of cutting the cartilage back but remembered who I was working on. A grin spread across my face as I tore it free, ripping the gristle out of her skull.

I probably didn't make things easy for myself, but what can I say? I'm a fucking artist. The trauma of yanking out the cartilage created a puddle of blood in the middle of her face, and I had to swab to stop her inhaling the ichor.

Before constructing the snout, the wound needed to be cauterised. To do the job properly, I needed a laser device, but the clinic didn't have the necessary tools. With the exception of Piggy Petra, I was scamming my patients, not putting them under the knife, so there was no point in wasting money on advanced surgical equipment. I had the bare essentials to make people feel my clinic was legitimate: a few monitors, a couple of machines that made pinging noises, and a gas cylinder festooned with pipes from the local DIY outlet.

I figured I'd have to go old school. Luckily, my Dad was a fan of gritty western films, so I had a fair idea of how to improvise. The best makeshift solution I could devise was using Petra's Zippo and a scalpel. I pressed the scorched blade to the ruptured blood vessels. The wound was still weeping blood, but the flow slowed enough to get on with the reconstruction.

The hands on the clock crept around. The process took longer than I thought, but I was pleased with the way things turned out. The snout was very pig-like. I could have excelled at Rhinoplasty if I'd applied myself, but it didn't float my boat, nor did it pay as much as dishonesty. My time was too precious to waste taking a bump off here and straightening a bend there. A snout was another thing altogether, and this one was masterful.

As I admired my work, I couldn't help but think the rest of her face let it down. It was like a diamond sat atop a pile of pig shit. Whatever further improvements I considered would have to wait. The Propofol wouldn't hold her under for much longer and administering another dose might have implications. I didn't care if she died, but I would have hated to see that snout go to waste before I had a chance to enjoy it.

As I removed the suction tube from her mouth, I must have blocked her airway for a moment. Forced to breathe through the snout, she emitted a snort. It was beautiful, an echo of pig-like snuffling. Instantaneously, I felt a surge of pride and a rising erection. Was there a way to force her to breathe through her nose all the time? It would be a dream, the snorting snout a constant reminder of what I'd done to her.

I thought about sewing her lips together, but it would mean she'd be unable to eat or drink. A drip would sustain her as she snorted her way to a slow death, but the downside was it shortened my time for experimentation. Maybe I'd sew it up later, once I grew bored of her as my plaything. For now, I just needed to make it unpleasant if she breathed through her mouth.

I don't know too much about dentistry, but I do know the nerves are bundled together in the pulp, at the core of the tooth. With holes in her teeth, the cold air would deliver ongoing spikes of agony. She'd have to keep her mouth shut, snorting her way through what was left of her fucking miserable existence. The thought of it got me hard.

I didn't have any dental equipment, but there were still some tools the workmen had left in a cupboard after fitting out the clinic. There had to be something I could use.

A quick rummage armed me with a cordless drill and a rough file which I figured I could just about get into her mouth. I fitted the smallest drill bit I could find and headed back to the treatment room. The bit was rusty, but that wouldn't be an issue considering what I had planned for the coming days.

Drilling holes in her teeth was more of a struggle than I'd anticipated. The drill bit simply skipped off the surface of the enamel, cutting into her gums. The slick of blood made it harder to work, but I'm nothing if not persistent. I could tell the Propofol was wearing off, as when I did manage to bore through a tooth, she'd jerk with pain. I nearly dropped the drill the first time she did it, which resulted in the tooth breaking. I managed to drill a few more before another jerk of pain caused the bit to snap.

Getting the file into her mouth was awkward, and while it took chucks off the edges of her teeth, it also lacerated her tongue. If it became infected, I'd get to suck on the septic organ while we kissed. It was a win-win scenario.

Breathing through the nose, her snorting made me laugh so hard I couldn't maintain my erection. I cleaned her up, set the suction hose in her mouth to suck off the blood and spittle, and prepared a hefty dose of Phenobarbital. It would hold her under until the initial wounds from the procedure had settled.

Once everything was done, I stood looking at what I'd created. It was glorious. The snout would be with her until the day she died, and that thought reignited my arousal. As she lay, drifting out of consciousness, I stood at the side of the bed and jerked off, shooting my seed onto her belly.

I woke later than usual, the euphoria of building the snout still buzzing through me. I luxuriated in the glory of my creation for a while, before showering and enjoying a leisurely breakfast. Afterwards, I drove to the clinic. When I got there, I was shocked to find the place locked. Where the fuck was Jenkins?

In all the years I'd known her, Nurse Jenkins had never let me down. Ours was more than an employer-employee relationship. We both brought something to the party, and I respected her for that. We'd met when … well, to be honest, how we'd met was a bit hazy. My memory was of us sharing a few lines of marching powder at a party in London, although whenever I tried to replay the event in my head, it all seemed wrong.

She was from Whitechapel, a shithole in East London best known for pox, villainy and murdered prostitutes. She said all her family were long dead. It didn't surprise me; nothing good ever came out of Whitechapel. However, after we'd been working together for a few years, she'd denied being born in the East End.

There was another benefit of having Jenkins on board: she wasn't judgemental. On a few occasions she'd walked in on me while I was performing some of my more personal procedures. I'd look up and she'd be standing in the doorway, watching. When she realised I'd seen her, she'd smile, nod as if in approval of what I was doing, and back out of the room, softly closing the door behind her. She never discussed what she saw.

This may have been the first time she let down me, but something in my gut knew this was more than a slight oversight on her part. Like a parasite wriggling through my stomach, turning my good day into a bad one, I knew exactly what she'd done. After everything I'd given her, the cunt had upped and left without a word.

The message light on the phone at the reception desk blinked furiously. I listened to a few messages from women enquiring about procedures. It seemed the clinic had finally gained some notoriety.

In my office, I fired up my laptop and discovered why we'd become an overnight sensation. Our social media evangelists were doing what we'd hoped, posting pictures of their flatter stomachs, praising the service they'd received at the clinic and spreading the word. They even thanked me profusely for my assistance in achieving their more sculpted forms. I didn't read all the replies—we'd used this approach a dozen or more times before and the comments rarely changed. It was a simple way of getting the word out, an idea for which I had to thank Nurse Jenkins—

The fucking bitch!

I could hear the phone on the reception desk ringing. The message service would have to cope for the day. I was too angry to talk with anyone.

I flicked through some financials, trying to calculate how much I'd have to turn over to cover the initial costs of set-up in Belgrade, but I couldn't concentrate. My focus kept sliding into rage. It was one thing to dump me after a successful job but doing it when the social media wave was about to break was spiteful. What the fuck had I done to Jenkins to cause such hate? Unless I could get some payments in, this whole charade was going to end up costing me money.

My thoughts became consumed with revenge. I'd track her down, teach her not to fuck me around. She'd be sorry she'd ever met me. As I visualised the tortures I'd inflict on her, I realised someone was in the clinic again. Through the frosted glass, I saw a figure in a white nurse's uniform. Springing to my feet, I flew to the door and threw it open.

"Where the fuck have you been?" I snapped.

The woman looking back at me shrugged, a smile on her face.

"Who the fuck are you?"

"I didn't mean to startle you, Doctor. I was looking for Nurse Phillips."

"There's no Nurse Phillips here. There's a Nurse Jenkins, or at least there was, but she's disappeared and left me in the shit."

"I was sure she'd be here. I've been looking for her for some time." The mystery nurse's smile faded. "Did Nurse Jenkins perhaps ever use another name?"

I shrugged.

"She probably did, when she was picking up men at bars, but she's always been Nurse Jenkins as far as I know. Either way, it matters not, because she's gone."

The smile returned.

"I could help out if you like. On a temporary basis, naturally."

"I'm sorry," I said, trying to present a calm and rational front. "I doubt you have any idea how this clinic operates, so you won't be of much help. Good luck with looking for Nurse Phillips. I assume you know the way out."

"Doctor …?" She gave me a quizzical look.

"Fairweather," I replied.

"Doctor Fairweather, with respect, I have a lot of experience in cosmetic clinics," she said. "In the past, in clinics where I've been employed, I've implemented several methods to increase patient numbers without impacting on the … shall we say bottom line."

"Bottom line?" I asked.

"I have a high degree of local knowledge," she continued. "Serbia attracts many socialites from the Eastern bloc where the great and good have access to untraceable funds. There are certain clinical services these clients seek. Without being presumptuous, I think I could help increase your revenue."

"As I said—"

"My experience would allow you to focus on other things," she said. "You know, the things which fire your passion for surgery."

I froze, a momentary panic overwhelming me. I was being paranoid; there was no way she could know anything about Petra or my long-term plans.

"As I said, I don't think you'd be right for this clinic. I apologise for the inconvenience—"

"No, Doctor Fairweather, it is me who should be apologising," she said. "I may have been presumptuous and only wanted to help. I'll be on my way, but if I might be so bold as to leave my telephone number. You can always call me if you need some assistance in the future."

As she turned to leave, I realised I'd gained an erection. In my anger, I'd failed to notice how beautiful she was. A natural beauty. Her make-up was minimal, her hair simply styled, but everything about her screamed perfection.

As her heels clacked across the waiting room floor, I made sure my erection wasn't obvious and followed her.

"Nurse, hold on a minute," I called before she reached the door.

I'd been so hung up on the treachery of Nurse Jenkins, I hadn't considered the bigger picture. The mystery nurse was the ideal base for my *magnum opus*. I'd found my flawless woman, one who I could rebuild and adapt, corrupting her inherent beauty to create a monster, a hideous and perverse troll, my ultimate freak fuck.

She had one flaw: her voice wasn't the best. She had an American accent, but one of those whiny ones, like a rusted bandsaw cutting through a sheet of metal. If she kept her fucking mouth shut, I might be able to tolerate it. I'd rip out her vocal cords at the first opportunity.

"On second thought," I said, "I'm in a bit of a corner, what with my nurse disappearing, and it doesn't make sense to close the clinic for an indefinite period. If you were to work here for a few days, as a trial, we could discuss whether it's working out at the end of the week. What do you think?"

"Do you want me to start today?" she asked.

"No. I have a few things to sort out. Come back tomorrow morning and we can start from there."

"No problem," she replied with a grin. "I'll see you tomorrow morning, Doctor Fairweather."

"Yes, I'll see you then, Nurse … sorry, but I don't even know your name."

"Nurse Hooper," she replied, "but when we're not working, you can call me Hoop."

I sat in silence long after Nurse Hooper had left. Even if Belgrade ended up costing me money, at least I'd found that elusive someone to violate. Her only flaw was that fucking dreadful, screeching accent of hers, but there were ways to sort that out.

I wasn't about to forget Jenkins and her fucking treachery though. What goes around comes around, and if I ever saw the bitch again, I'd teach her the cost of a lack of loyalty. The irony was her disappearing act had actually done me a favour. The Belgrade money would have been nice, but having a perfect subject was worth so much more. There'd be other cities and other nurses in the future.

I wasn't sure if it was the arrival of Nurse Hooper, but I was struggling to remember what Jenkins looked like, or what her voice sounded like. It was as if I was emerging from a dream.

The dilemma I faced was what to do with the clinic. It needed to appear operational in order to ensure Nurse Hooper turned up every day, but once I had her on the treatment table, did I really want the hassle of running the place just to scam a few halfwits? Maybe I was better off cutting my losses.

As exciting as the potential for Hooper was, I still had Petra to deal with. She'd been the highlight of my trip so far, but with Nurse Hooper on the horizon, I was struggling to remain enthusiastic. Despite my waning passion for her, I still held a torch for her snout. I could sit and gaze at it for hours.

I stood and went to the treatment room door. Producing the key, I felt myself harden as I turned it in the lock. A shudder passed through me, a sexual tremor, as I fought back the urge to prematurely ejaculate. It wasn't just the thought of seeing Petra's snout which aroused me; it was also knowing that soon it would be Nurse Hooper on the gurney.

Petra was laid on the bed, head perpetually nodding as the drugs washed over her. Dressings obscured her face and her breathing was slow. I was disappointed she wasn't snorting. I clearly hadn't done enough to make breathing through her mouth uncomfortable.

I planned to concentrate on her eyes next. They were one of her better features, an icy blue that verged on grey. It was a shame they didn't get the exposure they deserved. I wanted to change that, to bring them to the fore, to make them the jewels which emphasised her snout.

Like a small child with a present on Christmas morning, my fingers trembled with excitement as I carefully removed the dressings. The snout was perfect, the delicate stitching around its edges giving it emphasis. The teeth were another matter; jagged shards of enamel, flecked with blood where her tongue was lacerated. They defiled her natural beauty, but they weren't a compliment to the snout. In the future, I either needed to brush up on my dental skills or leave teeth well alone.

I pulled back the white sheet covering her body. Her stomach was further distended, and her thighs were splattered with a mix of blood and shit, the tapeworm fragments bulging out of her arsehole. Her skin had taken on a mottled appearance, a greyish hue spreading as the lack of nutrition became more obvious.

I administered another dose of Propofol and prepared my instruments. Positioning the surgical light so her face was well illuminated, I made the first incision. The scalpel sliced easily through the thin eyelid as I ran the blade from her tear duct outward. I worked slowly to ensure I didn't damage the eyeball. I knew it wouldn't take long for her eyes to dry out, the cells of her cornea flaking off before the eyeball became infected and ulcerated. I wanted to get some practice before that happened. Any clumsiness once Nurse Hooper was under the knife would forever flaw my *magnus opus*.

With the upper eyelid removed, I set about the lower. Once one eye was finished, I swabbed the wounds and stood back to admire my work. The eye looked magnificent, an ivory-coloured orb with a flash of blue-grey standing out like a beacon above her snout. It appeared to float out of her blood-smeared face, as if separate from her skull. Its size was surprising. She looked both startled and seductive and I laughed to myself at that.

Taking a few moments to compose myself, I set about the other eye. Resisting the urge to rush, I sliced through the skin and carefully removed the lid, trimming up the glands beneath the epidermis to give it a more surreal floating appearance.

My cock was pulsating as I admired the work, the modicum of beauty she once possessed destroyed by my masterful hands. I was a fucking genius.

Releasing the restraints, I pulled her down the bed until her hips were on the edge. Then I removed my trousers.

The knots of tapeworm and compacted bloody shit made it difficult to push my cock fully inside her anus. Once I'd achieved entry, I started to thrust, gazing at her face, the wild unattached eyes, the snout, the ragged teeth. It didn't take long for me to reach my peak, and I howled like a demented animal as I spurted my seed into her broken body.

I hadn't intended to, but as I ejaculated, I thought about Nurse Hooper.

The first few days working with Nurse Hooper were an exercise in patience. At times, her shrill, trashy accent made me want to tell her to get the fuck out of my clinic. On other occasions, I wanted to drag her into the treatment room and fit the bitch with a snout. Instead, I smiled with good grace, listened to her nonsensical babble, and let her work her way through the phone messages arranging the initial consultations.

She also had an uncanny knack of turning every conversation into a string of questions. I'd ask her to ensure the plants in the waiting room were watered, and within minutes she'd be quizzing me about the stock of anaesthetics, the storage of patient records, and was I sure I didn't know a Nurse Phillips. While it had been the search for the unknown nurse that first brought her to me, I soon got fed up with the sound of the woman's name.

Nurse Hooper was, in a word, nosy. She wanted to know everything about everything. My concern was how long it would be until she got curious about the locked treatment room.

Petra was in decline. She didn't have long left for this mortal coil, so I wanted—in fact, I needed—to get her out of the clinic as soon as possible. I couldn't wait for nature to take its course. As tempting as it was to keep the hot fix in case Nurse Jenkins ever returned, Petra was a problem I didn't need. Her presence could screw up my plans for Hooper.

As the working day ended, I wished Nurse Hooper a pleasant evening and watched as she left. Then I headed into the treatment room. Petra was comatose on the bed, unaware of my presence as I removed the dressings. Although my interest in her had faded as my objectives changed, I was still proud of what I'd achieved.

The Phenobarbital was still holding her under, so I prepared her final injection, the hot fix of heroin laced with sodium cyanide, before undressing and climbing onto the treatment table next to her. Holding her clammy body close to mine, I manoeuvred her head so I could administer the shot into her carotid artery. As the drugs washed through her I felt her body temporarily relax. It wouldn't take long for that to change as the other additives took over from the heroin.

Waiting for her imminent death, I suppressed a giggle. If she'd been on time for her original appointment, she wouldn't be about to die. She'd be out there in the world, more sculpted and a few pounds lighter, do whatever she needed to do. Instead, she was here. Guts and anus bloated with tapeworms, her face mutilated, vital organs shutting down.

In that moment, I wished she was awake and aware, so I could show her where her tardiness had led. I wanted her to understand she'd been the architect of her own demise. She'd probably think I was the one in the wrong, the evil and twisted one, but the truth was she'd been late which showed a lack of gratitude. She'd deserved everything I'd done to her. Anyway, how could she accuse me of being cruel? I'd made love to her. Would a monster do that? I don't fucking think so.

I felt her start to convulse as the other chemicals in the cocktail went to work. It wouldn't be long now. I placed my ear against her chest and listened to the bubbling as her gullet filled with frothy sputum. As it flowed into her throat, she sucked the muck back into her lungs and began to asphyxiate.

My cock hardened, not with desire for Petra, but with excitement for what was to come. Petra was the starter, the appetiser, but Nurse Hooper would be the main course.

As the flood of white foam flecked with blood emerged between her lips through the broken and jagged teeth, I masturbated furiously. Petra was dying in my arms, and her demise would give birth to my ultimate freak fuck. It was the circle of life, and for a moment, I even heard the stirring musical nonsense from *The Lion King* in my head.

Petra's body twitched violently as she entered her death throes, and as she slid into the darkness from which there was no return, I pulled her head down and shot my load over her face. I watched the tension in her cheeks ebb away, her eyes fading, the muscles drooping as her visage—splattered with my spunk—contorted.

I'd gone through a number of options for disposing of the corpse, settling on dumping her in a small industrial town outside Belgrade. The place had a problem with transient trash in makeshift camps, so hopefully a vagrant would find her and fuck the corpse, or at least jerk off over it. That would give the local police the DNA they'd need to hunt the poor fucker down and pin the murder on him.

I spent some time cleaning Petra's body, making sure there was nothing which forensically tied me to her. To delay any chance at a positive identification, I cut off her fingers. Given the fucking mess I'd made of her teeth, dental records would be unlikely to help, and I had no need to pop out her eyes as they were already degrading and becoming ulcerous.

By the time I'd finished, it was dark and the streets were empty. Collecting my car from the parking lot, I left it outside, trunk open. Petra didn't have a scrap of meat on her bones, and even wrapped in a tarpaulin, she was easy to carry. If anything, the bulk of her weight came from the knot of worms clogging up her guts.

With her corpse loaded, I set off into the darkness, heading out of the city.

I drove through the suburbs and into the countryside. The roads were quiet as I headed south.

In the distance, the darkness was interrupted by a series of tiny lights. I was close. Turning off the main road, I headed toward the small town.

As I approached, I spotted a tangle of ramshackle buildings which housed the local flotsam and jetsam. These low-down cunts probably made their money thieving, whoring, and selling drugs to kids. Hopefully, the dirty fuckers would be unable to resist a dead woman and would rather screw the corpse than inform the authorities.

I pulled off the street, away from the shacks. As I dragged the corpse from the car, the night calm was broken by a dog barking. It wasn't a bark of alarm or warning; more a lazy attempt at asserting its authority. It summed up this settlement of vagrants and itinerants: slothful bastards. They didn't work, contributed nothing to society, and certainly didn't pick up their own shit; they just laid down in the middle of it. They were the type of scum who no doubt bred with their own sisters and daughters. The kindest thing would have been to douse the whole place with petrol and strike a match, but I wasn't here to solve Serbia's social problems.

I positioned Petra against a tree. It took all my strength to crack her hips as rigour had set in. Emulating the traditional porno pose, I sat her with her legs spread, cunt on display. I tried to make her look like a tramp's wet dream. Before I left, I pulled a sack over her head.

Making my way back to the car, I struggled to hold in my laughter. Some poor cunt would find her, start wanking, and when he was ready to spurt his muck over her nakedness, he'd whip off the sack. His cum would be dripping off her snout and septic eyeballs as he contemplated the murder charge he'd soon be facing.

As I drove back to Belgrade, back towards Nurse Hooper, I switched on the radio. Eric Clapton was limping his way through 'Wonderful Tonight'. It seemed apt, given how I'd left Petra, so I turned it up full volume. With the speakers vibrating, I joined in the first refrain, screaming the words out through the open window into the Serbian dawn.

"And then she asks me: do I look alright? And I say, yes, you look wonderful tonight."

They say you don't appreciate the worth of someone until they're gone, and with Jenkins gone, I realised she was worth fuck all. Maybe I'd been too kind to the old bitch, allowing her to drift along doing the minimum she could get away with. She had one positive characteristic: her face was like a bag of dogs' bollocks that had been given a severe kicking. I never wanted to fuck her, even when I was loaded up with the animal variant of Viagra, so it kept things simple between us and on a business-only level.

Nurse Hooper turned out to be something of a powerhouse when it came to managing the clinic. While she didn't appear to be putting much effort in, her results were twice what Jenkins had been delivering. Even though I'd written off any chance of making money out of this Belgrade clinic, every day since she started, we were hit with a tide of potential patients that didn't abate from the moment the doors were first opened in the morning until we closed them in the early evening.

I was tired from my late night farewell to Petra, but I didn't get a chance to rest. The lumpy, bumpy, and generally podgy wannabe socialites kept coming through the doors. I sat behind my desk, watching them undress and parade their mutton-ugly bodies while I listened to their pleas for me to apply a touch of magic and make them young again.

I promised them all the body of an angel, and they queued up for Nurse Hooper to take their payments. We were making money hand over fist, but I felt detached from the whole charade. For once, money wasn't getting me excited, and the process felt flat, dull, a chore I'd rather not suffer.

I realised the only time I felt any excitement were when Nurse Hooper was bringing in the next mark. She'd explain what they'd like done in the pursuit of extending their youth and hand me the notes. Each time she did it, I got hard. I imagined her legs amputated above the knee, her stumps bleeding while I jerked off onto the nubs. I pictured her with no fingers, struggling to wank me off with her ball-like hands. I dreamed about injecting her breasts with virulent bacteria, her tits swelling to such a degree her nipples permanently oozed blood and pus.

I would violate her beauty, destroy her, mutilate her body and create a freak to fuck until I'd purged myself of the disgust I felt for her and all the other vane, precocious, beautiful people. I needed to start work on Hooper as soon as possible. It would be perfect, especially if I could force her to keep her fucking mouth shut!

The flow of prospective patients wound down, and soon the clinic was empty. Nurse Hooper walked into my office and, with a grin of self-satisfaction, declared the day was done. She displayed a tinge of arrogance; nowhere near as pompous as Petra or the dozens of other good-looking cunts I'd meddled with in the past, but she exhibited that inevitable link between beauty and ignorance.

"I think you owe me a drink," she announced.

"I think we deserve one," I replied. If she was about to bite, I didn't want to miss the opportunity to hook her. "There's a bar down the street with a roof terrace. We might as well enjoy the pleasant evening."

As we sat watching the sun set, working our way through a jug of margaritas, Nurse Hooper gave me her feedback from the day.

"I hope you don't think I'm being presumptuous, but one thing which would improve your business is better communication."

I took a moment to try and understand where she was going with the conversation, before replying.

"I don't see how. There's only you and me. If we need to talk, we just close the office door and talk."

"Imagine how much more impact your consultations would have if I knew what you wanted before we even spoke."

"You're not going to tell me you believe in telepathy, are you?"

"Telepathy? No. I'm talking about technology. Let's say you're seeing a patient who wants a breast augmentation. While she's there, you realise you could also sell her a tummy tuck. Knowing what you're thinking would allow me to persuade her to go for the double procedure, thus increasing the potential revenue."

"I know how to sell cosmetic procedures," I said, pissed off by her dismissal of my ability to upsell. "Anyway, we'd still need to have the conversation about the patient, so I don't see any advantage."

She picked up her handbag and rooted around inside, producing a small, plain cardboard box.

"Not with this, you wouldn't."

Opening the box, she placed what looked like a miniature metal dome on the table. With a slight whirring sound, it moved, hundreds of tiny legs appearing, propelling it towards me.

"What's that?" I asked, watching as it approached.

"It's the latest smart device," she said, a noticeable level of excitement in her voice. "It allows those who are wearing it to communicate with each other using just their thoughts."

"Jesus, you'll buy anything; a fucking salesman's dream."

"Trust me. It works."

"You said anyone wearing it. How the fuck do you wear it?"

Nurse Hooper picked up the device and held it her head. The legs extended and gently clamped onto her ear. She grinned and shook her head, the device staying put. Then she looked at me, winked and laughed.

"What?" I asked.

"You'd know what I was thinking if you were wearing one of these."

Raising a finger, she gently touched the centre of the dome and the legs released, allowing her to remove the device. As she placed it on the table, I took the initiative.

"Okay, moving on, I have a question. I've been casting my eye over you, and I don't think you've had any work done."

"Correct," she replied. "Never have and never will."

"Never is a long time."

"I'm like you," she said. "I love the money but not the product. That's what attracts me to your *business model*. The clients pay for their vanity, but never go under the knife. It's a win-win."

I froze for a moment. She knew I was running a scam but didn't seem to care.

"You're not like me, Hoop," I replied. "I love the product, but I don't believe most people deserve it. Cosmetic surgery is wasted on fat, ugly people who do nothing to better themselves. Cosmetic procedures should be to enhance, not to make silk purses from sows' ears."

"Tell me more."

She leaned forward, gazing with an intensity which made me feel uncomfortable.

"I'd love to, but I've got somewhere to be. Wealthy clients are hard work; they need to be nurtured."

We got up to leave.

"Don't forget your thought machine," I said sarcastically, pointing to the device.

"Oh, that one's for you. I have my own."

"Really, I'm fine—"

"It's a gift," she said, "a thank you. It'd be rude of you to decline."

Picking up the thing, I pushed it into my jacket pocket and headed for the stairs.

After leaving Nurse Hooper, I drove toward the outskirts of the city. In a depressing neighbourhood, I found somewhere to park and headed into the side streets filled with bars and strip joints. I needed to buy something to deal with Nurse Hooper. I hadn't expected her to have an aversion to undergoing any procedure. I'd hoped by playing to her vanity, I could persuade her to agree to a modest nip or tuck. Once she was anaesthetised, I'd be free to do what I wanted. However, her reluctance forced me in a different direction. I'd have to slip something in her drink.

While I had the right drugs for intravenous anaesthesia, I needed something that would be reliable when administered orally. I couldn't risk delivering an intravenous administration without her knowledge, not unless she was already heavily sedated.

Strolling along the road, a young girl fell into step with me. She was slim, nice body, pretty, but with one flaw: her nose was fucking huge, like a hawk's beak. I could sort that out for her if I had the inclination, but I didn't.

"Howdee Pardner," she said with a grin, her fake American accent influenced by countless western films.

"Wrong country," I replied.

"English?"

I nodded.

"Do you want to see a bed show, mate?" she asked in a terrible Dick Van Dyke-style fake cockney trill. "Two girls, two drink minimum, no cover."

"No thanks."

"C'mon, mate, two drink minimum, one can be for me. What do you say?"

I slowed, and said, "Listen, what I want—"

"A boy?"

"No, not a boy. Are you going to fucking listen or should I take my business elsewhere?"

She stopped grinning, her eyes burning with contempt. For a mouthy little cunt, she didn't like it if you gave her some back.

"I want some Rohypnol."

Hawk Nose's face cracked into a mischievous leer.

"You got a date, have you? Don't she feel the same as you do? Can you only get her to fuck you if she's knocked out?"

"It's for a friend."

"I bet it fucking is." She cackled. "Must be a friend who doesn't know she's a friend yet."

This bitch was getting on my nerves.

"Spare the chit-chat. Can you get it, yes or no?"

"What's it worth?"

"It's worth what it's worth. Is it yes or is it no?"

She held up her finger, a momentary halt called in the conversation, before jogging back to the neon-illuminated doorway she'd appeared from. A few minutes later she returned.

"It'll be five thousand dinars."

"What's that in real money?"

"Around fifty dollars."

"You're still in the wrong country," I quipped. "Even so, isn't that a bit pricey?"

"Okay, see you later, mate," she replied, but made no effort to walk away.

I fished out my wallet, produced a five thousand note, and held it out. As she tried to take it, I whipped it away and tore it in half.

Handing her one piece of the bank note, I said, "The other half stays with me until you come back. I'll be in the bar on the corner. Okay?"

She wasn't happy but headed off up the street. I found a space at the bar and gave myself a four-drink deadline. I was finishing the second when she returned. With the pills in my pocket, I gave her the other half of the bank note.

"So, how about that bed show?" she asked. "It might not be on the same scale as your rape plans, but you might enjoy it."

There was something about her that really got under my skin, something distasteful, and it wasn't just the monstrosity she called a nose. She had that entitlement, just like Petra, like many of the others in the past, and to a degree, a bit like Nurse Hooper.

"I don't do voyeurism," I said, "but if you're in the mood for some one-on-one company, I might be interested."

Her place was a small, bleak room in what appeared to be a derelict block of apartments. I told her to undress. Once she was naked, I pushed her onto the bed and wrenched her legs apart. Despite my aggression, she giggled and stroked herself, a grotesque puppet of a good-time girl.

On the bedside table was a pack of cigarettes. I hadn't smoked in years, but I picked them up.

"Is it okay if I have one?"

She nodded.

I lit one and gently pulled her closer. As she closed in, I stubbed it out on her nipple.

The air was torn apart by her scream. I pushed the big-nosed bitch down on the bed and forced my mouth onto hers. Feeling her lip between my teeth, I bit. Warm coppery blood filled my mouth.

A driving punch to her ribs took the fight out of her. Gasping for breath like some old woman, she looked afraid. I knew behind the terror another scream was building, ready to blow the top off everything, to upset the apple cart, to burn my bridges.

I pushed my hand over her mouth, stopping her from screaming and holding her down at the same time. Her big nostrils flared as she sucked in air. That nose was a joke; the world didn't deserve to be affronted by the sight of that every time she went out.

Opening my mouth as wide as I could, I leaned forwards, fitting her monstrous, ugly cunt of a proboscis inside. Then I bit, locking my jaw like a mad dog. I felt my teeth go through her skin; a crunch as they hit the gristle. She was bucking and shaking, her howling muffled by my hand.

With my jaw locked, I shook my head violently, feeling her nose start to tear away from her face. Her blood was warm and thick, mingling with snot. It bubbled as she struggled to breathe. It took two or three hard shakes to tear the thing right off her face. Her thrashing had stopped. She'd passed out. I did the only thing I could: spat out her nose and pushed it into her cunt.

Driving back to the hotel, as I crossed the bridge over the Danube, I wound down the window, fished in my pocket for the device Nurse Hooper had given me, and hurled it into the water.

"How come you didn't try it?" Nurse Hooper asked. "You said you would."

I'd only just walked in the door, and for a second, I had no clue what she was talking about.

"What was I supposed to try?"

"The bug—the communication device I gave you. I thought you'd give it a go last night, but I didn't receive any messages."

As the realisation hit me, an alarm bell sounded in my head. What was her fascination with that crackpot techno junk? Did she have shares in the company, or was she trying to sell the idea of an investment to me? Either way, she wasn't going to get very far. Surely, she'd realise I of all people knew a fucking scam when I saw one.

"I didn't get back until late, and to be honest, I was beat. I went straight to bed."

It sounded like bullshit, but I just wanted to end the conversation.

"You should have tried it," she said in her screechy way, admonishing me for my tardiness.

The last thing I wanted was for her to have access to what I was thinking. If she knew even my most innocent thoughts, she'd run a fucking mile. However, this was my chance…

"Well, are you in a rush tonight?"

She smiled at me and said, "No. I've got nowhere to be."

"Perhaps, when we've seen today's patients, we could grab a drink and talk about the … thing, you know." I pointed to my ear. "I'll give you my full attention. I promise."

She nodded enthusiastically. Fuck me; the girl had personality issues if her idea of fun was messing around with a headset. All I needed was to get through the day, and then my *magnum opus* would begin.

The day's procession of patients was a blur. Their dreams and dramas washed over me as I listened without interest before pointing them and their credit card towards Nurse Hooper. As they complained about their misshapen tits and droopy piss-flaps and oozing sphincters, I doodled in my notebook, toying with the changes I'd be making once Hoop was in the treatment room. I sketched her without arms, without legs, even without a face. Absent-mindedly I drew her with nothing on her face except a vagina, the labia loose and cascading like flaps of rotten meat.

None of the patients noticed how little I cared. The silly fuckers took my dismissive approach as a mark of professionalism When the human flotsam and jetsam eventually cleared I could hear Nurse Hooper pacing in the waiting room, probably doing menial tasks to kill the time until we had our chat. It unnerved me how keen she was to persuade me to wear her fucking headset. Paranoia worked its way into my thoughts, casting its ominous shadow over any attempt to rationalise the situation.

After Nurse Jenkins's unexpected disappearance, Nurse Hooper had arrived without explanation. Allegedly on the trail of the mysterious Nurse Phillips, she'd turned up at my door. Why? There were several large hospitals in Belgrade, along with numerous health centres, dentists, therapists, and other general quacks. What made her think she'd find this Phillips character in a small, low profile, cosmetic surgery clinic? It was too convenient, too orchestrated to be down to chance.

She certainly wouldn't have known I needed a replacement nurse. In truth, I didn't know I needed one until I realised that selfish fuck had abandoned me. Hooper arrived ten or fifteen minutes later, at the most. She hadn't come specifically to look for work, but she was pretty fast to get herself involved.

I knew nothing about Nurse Hooper, yet I'd allowed her to worm her way in, and now she was up to something. Was the whole bug scenario an attempt to track me, and if so, why? Was she investigating the clinic?

Hooper knew about the scam; she'd told me as much in her coy comment last night. Given her work rate, she'd put in effort to make it even more profitable. Would she have done that if she was from Interpol? If she was law enforcement and had got herself involved in expanding the scam, it had to be a case of entrapment. Would they go that far to arrest a conman? I was probably too small fry to be worth the effort. Most of the women I'd conned would have been too ashamed to report the fraud. Imagine them standing up in court and declaring they'd paid me thousands to make their slack twats a bit tighter. But if Hooper wasn't looking to bust me for the clinic, what was her angle?

If she knew about Petra, if she was tracking me for the murder, it still didn't make sense. I hadn't killed Petra when she first arrived, and surely if she'd suspected what I was about to do, she'd have arrested me before I could act.

I went out into the waiting room. Nurse Hooper grinned and stopped rearranging the leaflets on the reception desk. I grinned back and went into the toilet. Splashing cold water on my face, I tried to calm my thoughts. The paranoia was rampant.

She was just a fucking crook, much like I was. She was a chancer who'd got lucky. The bug was bullshit, maybe a little side-hustle she was trying to get off the ground. There was no such thing as mental communication. Anyway, what did it matter? In less than hour, she'd be anaesthetised, and my work would begin.

Taking a deep breath, I headed back to my office, leaving the door open. By the time she decided to join me, I'd poured two glasses of scotch and pushed the one I'd prepared for her across the desk.

As she settled into the seat, I jumped in, preventing any talk about her fucking stupid device.

"Here's a funny thing, Hoop. I don't know anything about your background. I don't know where you're from, where you grew up, if you have any siblings, what your hopes and dreams are, what fears you have. Tell me all about yourself."

"It's a long story," she said. I knew she was going to try and put off telling it.

"Well, start at the beginning … unless you have somewhere else to be. We can always have this chat another day."

She tried to give me an abridged version, but I constantly interrupted, asking for more details. I feigned interest, ensuring she didn't feel like I was questioning her. In truth, I didn't give a shit. I was waiting for the Rohypnol to kick in.

It took until her high school years before she started to slur, and by the time we got to college, her eyes were heavy. Struggling to keep them open, she tried to tell me something about taking a gap year to travel the world, but I couldn't understand a word. Pouring another round of drinks, I excused myself and went to the toilet. When I came back, she was sprawled in the chair, unconscious, a ribbon of drool hanging from her lips.

She was mine. I had won.

Getting Nurse Hooper onto the treatment table wasn't as simple as I'd thought. She didn't have a lot of bulk to her but felt a lot heavier than she looked. I figured I was tired after lugging Petra around, and tearing up the lippy bitch with the hawk nose had taken a toll on my stamina. With Hooper strapped down, I administered a dose of Propofol.

I anticipated the procedures might last a few hours, maybe even longer, so I prepared a second syringe in case things ran over. With women I'd worked on in the past, I didn't care if they were regaining consciousness toward the end. Their spasms and reactions to pain just made the process more satisfying. However, I didn't want that with Hoop. Even the slightest reflex action could mess up my work, and I wanted her adjustments to be perfect.

With the anaesthetic administered, I laid out my tools: a selection of scalpels, scissors, forceps and clamps, along with swabs and sutures. After fitting a new blade to the bone saw, I was ready.

The first task was to cut off her clothing. Naked, she looked tempting, but I promised myself waiting would be better. A moment of gratification before I started her transformation would spoil the climax I'd hit once she was disfigured.

Patience, I reminded myself, was a virtue.

Nurse Hooper was my ultimate, and I wanted to let my creative juices flow. The best approach was to start with a blank canvas. If I stripped away her features, I could rebuild her as a stunningly grotesque freak. The only thing I knew for certain was that she needed a snout.

Remembering the debacle with Petra, I vowed not to attempt any dentistry. You have to know your limits.

Pulling her lips apart, I checked her teeth. White, straight and uniform, they didn't need any work. In fact, they were so beautiful it was a shame not to show them off. I slid the scalpel under her top lip, pierced the flesh, and ran the blade around from under her nose to her cheek. Repeating the incision on the other side, I carefully removed her top lip. The bloody gums and white teeth made me smile, and as I peeled away the lower lip, I felt myself getting hard.

I moved to her nose, slicing down the ridge before stripping the epidermis away. With the cartilage exposed, I sliced it away in fine slivers to free up the space for a snout. I didn't want to tear it out. I'd got away with ripping it free when I worked on Petra, but with Hoop it was critical to retain a good base for the rhinoplasty. The foundations needed to be solid. Petra's snout was magnificent, but Hoop's would be the snout to end all snouts.

With the main structure of her nose removed, I stemmed the bleeding and closed up the incision.

My cock was throbbing as I inserted the sutures. Without her lips, her teeth seemed long and thin, almost like enamel fingers reaching out from her gums. Because I'd removed the bone structure of her nose, the nostrils sat above the teeth like puncture wounds. She already bore the look of someone who'd been ravaged by a psychopath. Knowing I'd been the one who'd done the damage made me want to cum.

As I finished putting in the stitches, I noticed a minor spasm as the needle went through her skin. It was time to top up the Propofol.

The surgical tray still had my tools neatly laid out, but the syringe wasn't there. I checked around the treatment room but couldn't see any sign of it. As a sanity check, I opened the box of vials. Two were missing. I had definitely prepared another dose, but where was it?

Putting it out of my mind, I decided to call it a night. I didn't want to overdo things; it was critical her body had time to recover from the first procedure, and doing too much in one go would slow the healing process.

I stood above her, looking down at what I'd done. Although I still had a lot of work to do, I couldn't see any harm in rewarding myself. I deserved a fuck for all my hard work. She owed me that much.

Loosening the restraints, I dragged her toward me into a more accessible position. Pulling her legs apart, I hesitated. I figured it would be nice to save her cunt until all my work was done. It would be the pinnacle, a freak fuck to end all freak fucks. For now, I'd content myself with sodomising her.

Wrestling her into place, I spat on my fingers and worked them into her anus, making sure there was some lubrication. With my cock throbbing, I dropped my trousers and forced myself inside her. She was tight. I guessed her butt hadn't been screwed, certainly not on a regular basis. Once in, I started to fuck her while focusing on her face. Leaning forward, I let my tongue dance around the incisions, licking at her bloody gums and teeth.

As the frequency of my thrusts increased, I heard a noise which sent a spike of nervous itching across my skin. Nurse Hooper was laughing. Not a drug-induced giggle, but a full-on belly laugh, a hysterical outpouring of mockery. Her laughter wasn't feminine. It was base, guttural, male. Then the cunt opened her eyes. They seemed older, cold and bitter. I tried to pull out, but her sphincter gripped my cock like a hand, holding me in place while she howled out her demented shrieks of hilarity.

Something was rippling. I looked down and her stomach was distending, swelling and rolling as it filled out. Her tits lost their shape, the firm breasts became sagging flesh as the nipples spread, thick black hairs sprouting around them.

I still couldn't pull out. It wasn't just the tight grip of the sphincter; sharp barbs had pierced my prick, locking it in place. The agony was searing. I pushed the voluminous belly up to see what was happening, and that's when I realised her cunt was a flaccid cock, the helmet crusty, a long pubic hair stuck to the muck.

Her face had changed. Looking back at me was a grinning, obese man, sweaty and unkempt. Unable to look away, ensnared by his eyes, my head spun as the room grew darker. My legs buckled as the sound of his spiteful guffaws filled the room. I reached out and grabbed at the tray, snatching up a scalpel. He didn't flinch as I waved it in a threatening gesture, his laughter increasing in volume.

"Who the fuck are you?" I screamed.

"I'm Sonny Hooper." He giggled. "But you can call me Hoop."

In panic, I slashed at his throat, the bubbling blood and spray of fine crimson droplets doing nothing to silence his ever-increasing mockery.

Then he rose, sitting upright, his eyes still locked on mine. For a moment, he stopped laughing, before bellowing, "Fucking scumbag!"

I saw the syringe in his hand too late, and before I could react, it was embedded in my neck.

I felt like I was inside a kaleidoscope, the chaotic jumble of colour and light dancing all around me. Sounds echoed somewhere in the distance, a threatening, malevolent cacophony rumbling like impending doom. My body tingled with burning cold, from my extremities right to my inner core. Something was wrong, very wrong, but I couldn't understand what.

Waves of pain ebbed and flowed through my body, a battle between discomfort and relief. A spike of agony would erupt, and soon after a rush of endorphins would wash over it, masking it from my brain. I wanted to move, to wake up, to cry out for help, but I was smothered by an unavoidable fatigue. Nothing made sense.

Where was I, and what the fuck was I doing here? Something had happened, but my memory was fuzzy, distorted, like I was looking at a scene through a puddle of oil. Fear started to build. No, not fear but terror, smothering me, suffocating me with its awfulness. The only thing I knew for certain was I was alive, although in what state remained a mystery.

Alone, weak and distressed, I floated in a haze, unsure of my condition. All I felt was nothingness; absolute nothingness. I wanted to fade, to recede, to disappear back into the darkness, but instead I felt like I was surfacing, emerging, heading inevitably towards … it, whatever the fuck 'it' was.

Struggling to overcome the confusion, I tried to latch on to something, anything, which gave me a clue. My condition had a shred of familiarity, a spark of past awareness, and then it hit me: I was regaining consciousness, but from what?

Opening my eyes led to a shrieking agony, the blinding light piercing my head with shards of brilliant white pain. Closing them again, I tried to speak in order to hear my own voice. I tried, but my mouth and throat were too dry, burningly arid. It made breathing difficult, but I was somehow managing to get air in and out. Each time I inhaled, something clicked, a subtle sound off to one side of where I lay.

I tried to lick my lips, but my mouth was blocked, a hard unexpected object between my teeth. It took me a while to realise it was the mouthpiece of a respirator.

Why was I on a respirator? What was going on? I was close to the surface, almost ready to emerge into real-time, when the reality dawned on me. The sensations I felt, the chaos, the confusion, all made sense. I was emerging from being anaesthetised.

Everything I felt, everything I heard, told me I was in a surgical theatre, but my memory was fragmented. Why the fuck had I needed an operation?

I tried to open my eyes again. Struggling against the invasive brightness, I shook my head and something dark fell through my vision, an unknown entity whizzing past my eyes. Then it was gone.

The room was quiet but there was motion. I wasn't alone. A blurred figure moved closer. Blinking, trying to focus, the definition of my vision slowly improved, and it all came flooding back to me.

Sonny Hooper stood over me, his face bearing a grin which was more smugness than humour.

"You're back with us, are you?"

I tried to speak, to ask what was happening, but words wouldn't come. He reached out and clumsily removed the respirator.

"What have you done?" I croaked, struggling to speak.

"Relax, Doctor Fairweather, or whatever it is you're calling yourself today," he said with a humiliating edge to his tone. "They say imitation is the sincerest form of flattery, don't they? Well, all I've done is flatter you. I've performed the procedures you'd planned to carry out on me … well, you'd planned to carry them out on who you thought I was."

I couldn't understand what he was saying. Nothing made sense. I was in my treatment room, but he was the one in control and I was on the table. The other difference was the room bore a stomach-churning stench, an overwhelming odour of shit and decay.

"What's that smell?" I asked, barely able to finish my words.

"I can't smell anything," he replied with a smile. "What does it smell like?"

"Like shit," I croaked trying to lift my head.

Again, something dark moved across my line of vision, there for a second or two, then gone. What was it? I reached out my hand to feel my face, but I couldn't touch it. No matter how much I moved my arm, I couldn't connect.

"It's your nerves playing a little game with you," Hoop said with a chuckle, watching me intently.

"What do you mean?"

"Oh, come now, Doctor. You should understand, given your medical background. Your nerves are telling your brain that your arm is still there. I believe it's called phantom limb syndrome."

"But that happens after an…"

I tried to touch my face with my other arm, with no result. Had he really removed my arms? Despite the terror, the confusion and the overwhelming fatigue, I involuntarily screamed out loud.

"FUCK!"

Sonny Hooper laughed, as if giggling at the foolishness of a small child.

"That's right, Doctor. Let it all out."

"What have you done?"

"As I said, I've only done what you planned for me. Now you're the freak: an armless, legless, slug of a human. If you had any hands, you could check your undercarriage, and you'd find you're as smooth as a baby's bottom down there too. You're a freak, Doctor Fairweather, a freak that no one wants to fuck. Ironic, eh?"

I tried to slow my breathing, to take stock of what was happening. The stink of shit grew worse.

"What's that fucking stink?" I screamed.

"My bad," Hooper sniggered as if playing a game. "I forgot to mention I connected your olfactory canal to your colon. It's a little joke I was sure you'd appreciate. You'll smell your own shit, all day, every day."

I wanted to vomit, the noxious faecal stech filling my lungs with every breath I took. As I tried to sit, again the dark shape danced across my field of vision.

"What have you done to my eyes?" I asked, my voice pleading rather than demanding an answer.

"Nothing. What makes you think I have?"

I battled with my inability to make sense of things. She was a nurse or had been a nurse. In fact, he'd been a she, but now he was … I screamed again, a howl of confusion and pain.

He, she, or whatever Hooper was, had somehow carried out a series of complex procedures. The fact my extremities had been removed without me dying showed he had a good level of ability.

"How did you manage it?" I spluttered, trying to hold back the tide of rising bile in my throat.

"I had a little help. The Devil makes work for idle hands; that's what people say."

"You're the fucking Devil," I spat.

"Always one for flattery, eh, Doctor? I'm honoured you recognise my power and authority. It's best to accept the situation and embrace the retribution. It's so much more dignified than begging, don't you think?"

I couldn't comprehend what he was telling me. It all sounded nonsensical.

"Listen, Hooper—Hoop—can we make a deal?"

"Too late for deals, dear Doctor."

I pleaded, I whined, I begged, but he stood looking down at me, the same shit-eating smile on his face that I wore when ripping off my patients. I knew the look, and it told me he didn't give two fucks about my despair.

"Okay," I rasped, my mouth still feeling like it was filled with ashes. "If there's no deal, kill me. I'll give you all my money to kill me."

"I don't need your money."

I lifted my head to try and see him better. He was a grubby, overweight, excuse of a man. He needed my money.

"Hoop, think about it: more money than you've ever had. I swear, it's yours. Just kill me."

"You don't deserve death," he said, coldly.

"Why..."

I gave up trying to ask. I knew why. I let my head drop back onto the treatment table, and as I did that dark object once more flopped across my vision.

"Well, I'm done here," Hooper said matter-of-factly. "I've made arrangements for you. You'll be collected later today. I couldn't believe freak circuses still existed, but luckily for you, I found one. They're quite the thing in some circles. You'll be taken around the countryside, mocked and ridiculed, abused for the entertainment of others, and at night I daresay the showfolk will use you for their own pleasures. That's your eternity, a living hell; that's your penance. It's come full circle, hasn't it?"

"For fuck's sake, kill me," I howled as he turned to leave. "I've got no arms, no fucking legs, and all I can smell is my own shit. You've even hacked off my cock. What more do you want?"

Hooper turned back and smiled, for once a genuine and warm smile.

"You've still got your cock."

"You said—"

"You've still got your cock. I just ... moved it."

As he left, the dark shape once more swung across my vision, and as it started to urinate, my piss splashed over my face and trickled into my eyes, burning like acid as it mingled with my tears.

# THE TRAP HOUSE

Drew Stepek

"Shut the fuck up, motherfucker," I whispered into the junkie's ear as I stuffed my forearm into his mouth. Good thing I wore my thick denim jacket. This piece of shit's chipped-away fangs would have torn into my flesh. I probably would've gotten hepatitis or AIDS if I wasn't as careful as I was. Dirty junkies in K-Town were like a catcher's mitt for bad shit like that. A bum's teeth ripping into my arm plus blood from his gums when I smashed his head into the wall equaled contamination. At the very least, HIV. Yeah, sure they could cure that shit, but it would be a hassle to tell my dads that I needed money and shit to get rid of "the bug." Besides, he hadn't spoken to me in five months or so since he and his motherfucking gold-digging wife kicked me out.

The meaner, uglier junkies hung out in Koreatown. That was what I was left with though. Some motherfucking racist pig slaughtered a bunch of bums, two of his partners, and some retarded kid downtown on Skid Row. So the rest of the LAPD was working overtime to clean up their name. You couldn't walk two blocks anymore without seeing flashing lights or a perp spread eagle on the sidewalk.

This K-Town junkie was so deep into the nods, I didn't think he would have noticed me robbing him. I suppose I didn't have to smash his head against the wall at all. Stupid me. I woke him up. He looked awake when I spotted him. Then again, the alleys behind all-night karaoke bars and Korean BBQ restaurants were almost always pitch black. Nobody wanted to walk into them. Nobody wanted to look at the trash that lived in them…including me.

I *had* to go into their dens to make money. Pretty easy to understand, I stole from the poor and gave to the rich. Sometimes I had to kill the poor to keep the kids at Beverly Hills High School and their habits in check. I was a thugged-up Robin Hood. I got this street product, cooked it back down on a hot plate, mixed it up with ephedrine and other assorted scrips, and re-packaged it as The Snap: a mixture of heroin, tar, coke, meth, and cold meds I stole from drug stores. Whatever. There wasn't any recipe for it. It was just drugs. It was kind of like mixing all your dad's liquor into a cup when you were a kid. The bitches from Bev Hills High didn't complain. They didn't give a fuck what I was feeding them as long as it got them high.

I tugged the needle out of the junkie's arm and raised the syringe shaft close to my eye. I couldn't see shit. I couldn't tell if there was anything left in it. I needed a flashlight. I told myself that every single time I went out. Other things always seemed more important.

The druggie shook a little, but he still seemed too far out of it to do shit. I might have given him a concussion. Who knows? He certainly couldn't make a fucking sound because my entire mid-forearm was all up in his fucking mouth.

After I shoved his lighter and spoon into the front of my jean jacket, I started digging around in his pockets, trying to locate his uncooked bag. It was real fucking smart of me to pick up those steel-woven work gloves from Lowe's on my way downtown from Beverly Hills even though I forgot the flashlight I made the whole trip for. Gloves were more critical, and I was happy as a motherfucker with my decision to wear them. This piece of shit had a fucking dirty-ass needle in his front, right pocket. We called them "HIVES" or "HIV knives." The streets of downtown LA and K-Town were littered with them. It was a good thing I always wore Timbs because I didn't want to be *that* bitch. You know, the fucking dipshit in flip-flops who stepped on a HIVE, got fucking AIDS, and died like some pathetic nobody. From my experience, people with AIDS always wanted to give their shit to everyone else. They were worse than fucking zombies.

The bum's eyes opened, the whites lighting up right in front of me. That stinky ass started shaking and trying to bite into my arm with his toothless gums. He bounced back and forth on his butt as his arms shot up from his sides. He wrapped his filthy hands around my neck and dug his claws into my throat. The stench of his hands nearly knocked me unconscious. He must have wiped his ass with them after he shit dumpster Korean BBQ all over the streets.

I grabbed one of his wrists with my free hand. "Get off me, bitch!"

His entire body tensed up and twitched. He began pushing on my neck to try and get leverage over me. The thing was, I was about twice his size. I dropped my knees onto his legs to plant him back on the ground. I yanked one of his arms free from my throat and started pounding his head harder and harder against the brick wall. Junkie AIDS blood splatted sideways behind him. Luckily, I closed my eyes and pursed my lips so none of that shit got inside me.

After a loud crunch, I felt the back of his skull crumble. The hand still around my throat went limp, and his toothless mouth unlocked from my jacket. His eyes disappeared into the darkness of the alley.

I pulled a little baggie out of his back pocket and felt around for anything remaining. It didn't feel like much, but I could feel some lumps of heroin powder inside.

Not getting too close to what I figured were his final breaths, I slapped him across the face to see if there was any fight left in him. He didn't move. So I got up off of him. His back slumped sideways into the same position that I had found it.

I wasn't sure if I killed him. That motherfucker was probably gonna die from an overdose or AIDS eventually. I just sped things up.

Exiting the alley, unable to tell if that bitch-ass was breathing anymore, I thought, if I got AIDS and my pop didn't spring for me to be cured, at least I could say I *was* somebody.

Danny Snaps: "The Skinny Little White Kid Who Can Spit."

I didn't check the booty until I got back to the G Wagon that I had parked in a garage down by the Staples Center.

I popped open the tailgate before taking off my gloves and carefully pulled the syringe and baggy out of my pocket.

"Motherfucker AIDS bitch."

The syringe only had a few drops left and the bag was almost empty. Those bumps I felt back in the alley were just parts of the bag that got cut by the other dirty-ass needle that was in the cocksucker's pocket.

I rolled that useless trash into a grocery store bag and tossed it into a garbage can next to the stairs. Looking at the arm of my jacket that I smashed into that junkie's mouth, I muttered, "Fucking waste of my goddamn time, yo."

The jacket arm did have blood on it, but I was pretty sure it would wash out. There was no way I was gonna ditch that thing. It was my thirteenth birthday gift from Young Guns.

My dads threw me a huge bash and invited everyone in the industry. They all came to celebrate Danny Snaps becoming a man. I still had every single gift I got. Most of it was in the back of my G Wagon because my dads got all fucked up at me and told me to get out. He wouldn't have booted me if he wasn't with that evil, cunt, gold-digger wife of his.

My dad was *the* Russ Sapperstein. He and this DJ named Cutty Jax started a hip-hop label in the early '90s called Phresh Coat Records. They made bank as one of the first Westside record companies to bring the sound of LA street life into the ears of suburban white kids. After they made millions together, they had a falling out. Unable to work together anymore, they sold off PCR. Cutty started a heavy metal label called Black Coat, and my dads moved on up to a mansion in Bev Hills where he still guest produced and discovered new artists.

He didn't need the money, so new talent became more of a hobby. That was… until he discovered me.

I jumped into the driver's seat of my whip and pulled up the video on YouTube.

When I was eight, one of the top artists from the PCR era, Young Guns, brought my ass on stage with him at a concert to knock out a couple of my own bars. I was standing in front of around twenty thousand peeps. I just started this sick flow that I freestyled while hanging out all the time in my dad's home studio where Young Guns was working on an album.

I pulled my cock out and started reliving the night. My night. My stage. My motherfucking debut.

Before all that happened, my dads would cut out the vocals on the tracks of his artists and teach me the fundamentals of rhymes, verses, and hooks.

My lit performance was interrupted on my phone.

"*Every single day in the United States, an animal is abused...*" the ad began.

"Fucking YouTube."

This annoying fucking ad came on for some fucking send-your-money-to-save-dogs-and-cats shit. Fucking beggars. It seemed like every time I tried to watch a video online or a TV show, *that* pathetic beggar shit ad came on. They had some slut who used to be on some fucking lousy TV show talking over a video clip of some whimpering dog, all skinny and fucked up, shaking in a cage. The cage was all rusted and shit and the dog's back legs were covered in frozen piss.

For what seemed like an eternity, the dog looked directly into the camera, directly at me. I stared right back at that motherfucker and yelled, "Why don't you feed that motherfucker? You've got a fucking camera on him, bitch. Give that shitty mutt a treat."

After 15 seconds of that torture, the ad ended. My video, interrupted at the worst possible moment in the middle of my signature eight bar, came back on. I destroyed the mic and the crowd went crazy ballistic. No matter how many times I watched it, I was never bored.

That video from the Young Guns show blew up in the early days of YouTube. Eight-year-old Danny Sapperstein became the great white hope known as Danny Snaps: "The Skinny Little White Kid Who Can Spit."

The popularity of that video led a talent recruiter from the music competition show *The Stage* to contact my dads to see if I would try out for the show. She promised dads that I would glide by easily. And I did. I made it to the final four contestants. The judges re-dubbed me "Lil Snap," and Vegas odds had me as the clear winner of that season.

Then Cutty Jax was brought on as a guest judge. My dad was furious and threatened to sue the network and the talent booker who got me on the show. They eventually came to an understanding and my dads pulled back. So I performed in the semi-finals of the show.

Cutty heard about the beef between my dads and the network. When it came time for the judges to give their opinion of my song, he dissed my dads and me calling me "cultural appropriation incarnate." Or some shit like that.

So, on live TV, I called my dad's former best friend "a fucking bitch faggot with AIDS."

I was cut from the show about ten minutes later. And I was robbed of my shot at becoming the next huge rapper. You see, my dads and I recorded a whole album for Danny Snaps a.k.a. Lil Snap a.k.a. "The Skinny Little White Kid Who Can Spit" called *Snap. Snap. Snap.* We were gonna surprise drop that motherfucker the day after I took *The Stage* crown.

After that night, no one was interested because bitch-ass Cutty cried to everyone who'd listen. My dad's cred in the record industry disappeared, and I was over before I got started.

I did get the last laugh though. Cutty died in a mental institution from AIDS a few years later.

"Sir, you can't park there," some bitch collecting shopping carts at Lowe's hollered. She tapped the hood of the G Wagon. Backing up a little bit, I parked directly outside of the front doors. My right tire hopped the curb, making the bitch jump back.

I cut the engine and hopped out, tossing her the keys. "Park it then."

She caught the keys and looked at my platinum keychain. "I'm not a valet. We don't have a valet here. This is a hardware store, fool."

"Then it stays here," I said as I snatched my keys back. Waving my finger around the parking lot, I added, "You shouldn't be up in my shit, Cart Bitch. You got more carts to collect. Hop to it."

She looked around the garage, following my finger. "It's gonna get towed, sir," she said. She knocked into another cart, adding it to the train she was having difficulty pushing around.

I walked through the doors into Lowe's and called back, "No, it won't, you dumb ho. I'm just gonna get a flashlight."

She might have said something clever back to me, but I didn't hear it. The automatic doors closed and I put my hand up behind me to let her know that no one was listening to her nag. If I had the time, I would've complained to the manager about that bitch harassing customers instead of doing her fucking job.

The second I got inside, a giant inflatable Frankenstein and a creepy skull inside a globe making fucked up screaming sounds reminded me it was Halloween time. And that reminded me about TT Love's annual Halloween bash. It was the largest shindig at Beverly Hills High School. At least it was since I stopped doing my Halloween party. That was the true fattest joint ever. My dads got in trouble though for me serving booze and giving drugs to underage girls…and guys. So he made me shut it down. Last year, Danny Snaps fanboy Todd Love ripped my party off and started doing the same party…with his name on it.

I never formally gave that kid permission to copy *my* thing. Still, TTL kept me in the game by buying drugs from me, which became my principal cash flow source until I got back into the hip-hop game. On top of that, Love's career was also kinda blowing up, and he told me I could guest on one of his tracks. So, I had to deal with being robbed. It was just a matter of time before I was back on top, and when that day came, TT Love would be *my* bitch again. Even though he was a Danny Snap wannabe, I never hated him for it. If I hated everyone who tried to bite my blueprint, there would be other bodies piling up all around LA that weren't just junkies and bums.

After stopping to check out some of the Halloween decorations, I dragged my ass over to the gardening section. Knowing that HIV was all over the streets, I grabbed two more pairs of those steel gloves. I still had that pair that I used the night before in Koreatown, but you could never have too many pairs of gloves in my business.

I walked around for a bit, looking for someone in a Lowe's vest. After what seemed like forever, I found some asshole using a pen and a clipboard to count light fixtures.

"Yo. Where the fuck is the flashlights, fool?"

Homeboy didn't look at me. He just continued counting and said, "Aisle 15."

"I'm over here, bitch," I said as I tapped on my chest with two fingers.

He continued to disrespect me and mouthed *193, 194, 195.*

"229, 345, 899, 406, 758," I yelled into his ear.

His clipboard dropped to his side as he turned to me with a shitty look on his face. "Aisle 15. That's where the flashlights *are*, sir."

"Was that so fucking hard, bitch? Jesus, yo." I walked away. "How do they train you motherfuckers here? Laziest entitled fucking people I've ever met."

He didn't say shit.

When I reached aisle 15, I dumped a couple of flashlights in my cart with the gloves.

"You're next, sir," the chick overseeing the self-checkout said to me.

Stepping up to the checkout, I realized she was the Cart Bitch from the parking lot. "You get a promotion?"

"Excuse me?"

"Yeah. Ten minutes ago, you were hassling me in the lot."

"Please scan your items, sir." She pointed behind me. "People are behind you."

I slid my middle finger up my thigh, and when it reached my stomach, I turned it up in her face. "They'll wait, bitch." Taking my time, I dragged the gloves and flashlights across the scanner. When I was done and COMPLETE CHECKOUT appeared on the screen, I ignored it and paced back and forth in front of the candy and drinks.

Someone in the line sighed.

Tilting my head back toward them, I said, "You got something to say, partner?" to the pasty kid directly behind me. I pointed a fist full of Snickers bars at him like they were guns.

A black lady side-stepped behind the kid. "He didn't do it, fat boy. Hurry up."

"Yo, sista. I got no beef with you." I pointed a bottle of Mountain Dew at her.

"I'm not your sister, asshole." She looked at the Cart Bitch, then back at my ass, and tapped her watch. "Hurry up, Karen. I got places to be."

"Karen? What the fuck does that shit mean?"

"You know what it means, Heavy D."

"You better check your shit, *sista*."

Before she responded again, someone else on the line shouted. "Holy shit. That fat fuck is Danny Snaps!"

Everyone paused and stared. Then they all lifted their phones and started taking pictures.

I threw the candy bars and the Dew back on a ledge by the checkout counter and pressed checkout on the touchscreen. "Y'all better pay me for those pics, motherfuckers," I said as I fumbled through my wallet for my Amex Centurion Card.

As soon as I found it, I held up the card before I swiped it. "You gotta make a cool million a year to have one of these, folks."

The pasty-ass white kid held up his phone like he was recording me. "Maybe you should buy a million candy bars with it."

Everyone in the line busted out into laughter. The black bitch patted the pasty kid on the shoulder and then doubled over, dropping her phone.

A larger crowd gathered.

"That ain't Lil Snap," someone said.

"You better believe it is," the pasty kid retorted. "His fat ass is buying a million candy bars. Maybe you should go see an eye doctor and get new contacts. That's Lil Snap!"

"What happened to him? He was such a cute kid," some hood rat bitch said.

I ran my card to pay and pressed CREDIT on the touchscreen. A DECLINED message popped up. WAIT FOR CASHIER.

I turned back to the Cart Bitch. She was taking pictures with her phone, too.

"Fuck you, bitch."

I pulled the card through again.

DECLINED.

And again.

DECLINED.

"Yo, this machine is all fucked up." I handed the card to the Cart Bitch. "Fix it."

The crowd and the laughter grew.

Now recording me, she opened a drawer in her workstation. She pulled out a pair of scissors and smiled. "Sorry, Mr. Sapperstein. The bank is insisting." She cut the card in half and tossed it back into her drawer.

"I told you all that was Danny Snap. He's Russ Sapperstein's son," the pasty kid screamed.

"Looks like you're outta candy, Tubby. Hope you don't starve to death," the black bitch said as she turned her phone to the crowd. They all cheered.

"Fuck all y'all," I said, wiping sweat off of my forehead.

As I walked out the doors, the Cart Bitch said, "Come again. Thank you for shopping at Lowe's."

I jumped in my G and cranked up the new Young Guns track. Some of the crowd followed me out of the store and continued to record me. I rolled down my passenger-side window.

"You're all a bunch of fucking nobodies." I spit out the window, my loogie hit that Cart Bitch right in the neck.

Trying to peel out of the parking lot, I hit the curb again. That pushed my G up against a tool shed they were selling out in front of the store. The scratching of metal tearing into my white matte fender drowned out the laughter of those punk bitches who were trying to play paparazzi at a fucking hardware store.

"Fuck you. Fuck all you."

"Hello, son," my dads said, answering his phone for the first time in five months.

"Yo, nigga! Why the fuck did you cut my Centurion card off?"

I could hear shuffling around on his end.

"Answer me," I demanded.

He cleared his throat. "Daniel. Please don't use that term when addressing me. Don't use that term to address anyone."

"What term? Fuck. Fuck you, bitch."

"You know that's not the term I'm talking about, Daniel. Please. Don't act dumb. I didn't raise you to speak to people like that."

"You didn't? That's news to me, bitch." I looked at myself in my rearview and tugged my lid down over my eyes. "I got a 'hood pass' from Rok5, fool. I can use that term whenever I want. You just jealous."

"Daniel. Rok5 told you that over ten years ago, and he only told you that because I asked him to." He went silent for a couple of seconds again. "We wanted to make you feel better about yourself when people in the media were calling you a phony. Remember? When everyone found out that you were my son?"

"Sure, nice story, bruh. Me and Rok were gonna do a collab, and he told me that I had the skills to pay his motherfuckin' bills."

"What do you want, Daniel?"

"I already told you what I want. Why the fuck did you cut off my Centurion card?"

"You'd think after a few months you would have understood. You have to start fending for yourself. Taffy and I can't continue to support—"

"Taffy?" I shook my head. "Why the fuck you gotta bring that bitch up? Wake up, old man. That ho is diggin' right through your bank account like a motherfucking gopher. She fucking kicked me out of my house. That's fucked up you would choose some busted bitch over your only kid."

"Daniel. You drowned her dog."

"Fuck that little asshole. That motherfucker bit me."

"He bit you because you were tearing his hair out in clumps and poking out his eyes. For the love of God, the poor animal was protecting itself."

"That's bullshit. That dog bit me. Totally unprovoked."

"We watched the security video. We know exactly what happened. You know this isn't the first time this happened. Your mother and I spent years taking you to therapists because of all the squirrels, cats, dogs, birds, and bugs you tortured as a kid. Remember when we took your knife collection away? *That* was why. You killing Bobo was the last straw."

"Bobo? Was that the dog's name? Fuck that queer-ass dog. He got what was coming to him. You don't bite *the* dog."

"You need to grow up, son, and you need to get help. You're not well. Every time my phone rings, I fear it's going to be the police telling me you're dead or you killed someone."

"How do you know I haven't killed anyone? I'm a fucking straight G, motherfucker. You made me G."

I heard Taffy say something in the background.

Turning up my radio, I yelled into the phone. "Tell that gold digger to shut the fuck up or I'm gonna come over there and jam a fucking MAC-10 up her wrinkly-ass gash."

"Don't threaten my wife, son. I am tempted to call the police right now. You don't think I can track the Mercedes? You don't think I can track your phone? I paid for both of them."

I turned up the music a little more, so I didn't have to hear all that.

"Where are you anyway?" he said after a minute of listening to the track. "What are you doing?"

"I'm writing rhymes, bitch. Waiting until you kick that ho out and we can get back into the studio."

"That's never going to happen, Daniel. That's never, ever going to happen. You had more opportunities than anyone in the world and you threw everything away."

"How that? Because I made a joke about some faggot who had AIDS on some pop star reality show?"

"He was my friend. He was my dearest and oldest friend. He was like a second father to you."

"You gay, too?" I flipped a bitch and headed toward Beverly Hills. "Well, I'm gonna swing by and pick up all my recording gear. I can sell that shit."

"None of it is, or ever was, yours. All that equipment is mine. The studio is mine. The Mercedes you're driving around in right now—that's mine. I know this is difficult for you to swallow, but…you don't own anything."

"Oh, fuck you, you Jew bitch. You just made all your money by stealing from the street. I'm on the street now. I'm living in my whip. You made me G. That's what I am. I bet I'm more G than any of those fucking kids you're fucking with now. I'm gonna do a collab with TT Love, motherfucker. That's what's up. Old-ass punk bitch, you don't even know what's going on in the game anymore. I'm at ground zero. I'm the next thing."

"Sell the Mercedes. That will at least get you some money to get by until you find a job. Goodbye, Daniel."

I spun back around and headed back toward K-Town. "FUCK YOU!"

"Yo, motherfucker!" I hopped backward as a massive plate of nachos dripped down the front of the jean jacket YG gave me.

"I'm so sorry, buddy."

"This jacket is worth more than your car, Biggie."

He looked me up and down and cleared his throat.

"You got something to say?"

He reached out with his nearly empty plate, using it as a dustpan for the food he dumped all over me.

"I wasn't looking," he said in a disgusting Boston accent. "Please accept my apologies." He started scraping the plate full of slop off my coat with the long nails on his sausage fingers.

I pushed him away. "Get off me, you Masshole bitch."

"I'm actually from Rhode Island," he said as he cowered and tossed the plate into the garbage.

"Bruh. You totally fucked up my gear." I began flicking corn chips, jalapeños, and several kinds of meat at him. "This is one-of-a-kind."

He pointed at my sleeve, "Looks like it was already pretty stained with…" he said, adjusting his thick glasses. "What is that? Ketchup?"

I lifted my coat to show him I was packing. "Yeah, that's *ketchup*."

"I don't want any trouble, mister," he said, raising his hands. "I tell you what. Why don't you come into my store? I'll try to make this right."

He pointed to the store directly behind me. The neon sign read "HOOP'S WORLD OF ELECTRONICS."

"What the fuck happened to Julio's? I was just here last week." I covered up my gun. I already sent the message. He knew I wasn't playin'.

"Julio couldn't pay his lease." He walked toward the front of the shop and waved me in.

"Julio was my homie. So, what? You just jumped in and took it over?"

"Something like that," he said as he unlocked the security gate and pulled it back.

I stepped into the shop. It looked nothing like Julio's. All the walls had been painted white and were covered top-to-bottom with TVs. Not crackhead pawnshop TVs like Julio had. Nice shit.

"You saw what was under my coat, right? Why would you invite me in?"

He shrugged and said, "Nest. On." All the TVs and other top-shelf electronics turned on. He pointed out six security cameras throughout the store and walked behind the counter.

"Go stand over there," he said, pointing to a red box in the corner.

"Why?"

"Because it isn't in view of any of the security cameras. It's a safe zone. You can take off that coat, so I can give it to the dry cleaner at the end of the block, and you can hide your gun under your shirt."

"Is this some kind of trick, Nacho Man?"

"I have several tricks, I assure you." He set up several weird robot bugs on the counter. "But this is about treats."

Running the tip of my Timbs on top of the box, I asked, "You're not like some child fucker, are you? Is this a trapdoor?"

The robot bugs walked themselves up in a line across the counter. "No, sir. I'm not a pervert. And that is not a trapdoor."

I stepped into the box and started taking off my jacket.

He slapped a smartwatch onto his wrist. "Why would that concern you? You're not a child anymore. Are you, Danny?"

"How do you know my name, motherfucker?" I rested my palm on the handle of my gun.

"Danny Snaps, right? Lil Snap. Russ Sapperstein's kid. Hip-hop royalty." He put his watch up to his mouth. "Nest. Play 'Tag Out' by Lil Snap."

My music blared out dozens of speakers in the shop.

"H-h-how do you have this?" The song was going to be my first drop. My dads was gonna release it the day after I was set to win *The Stage.* After being kicked off the show, Dads buried the track and everything else we planned to release. "This never came out."

The kick on the song shook the store. The robot bugs danced to the beat. Disco balls and tripped-out visuals appeared on every screen.

The track cut for a hook. The Nacho Man put up his finger and shushed me. He mouthed my favorite bar of the track.

*I punched that bitch,*
*Cause she made me itch,*
*My dick was hurtin',*
*So, I strangled her ass with a curtain.*

I hadn't heard the track in years. I bobbed my head and wrapped my gun into my stinky jacket. "Didn't get your name, friend."

"Name's Sonny Hooper." He extended his hand and waved me out of the red box. "You can call me Hoop."

"Whatever happened between your father and Cutty Jax?" Hoop asked as he leaned in toward me, expecting the scoop.

"Creative differences. Jax wanted to make old people's music. My dad wanted to make hip-hop. Phresh Coat was a rap label. Not some heavy metal shit."

"There's really nothing more to it than that? Cutty Clyde Phillips was one of the best DJs in the history of West Coast rap."

One of the robot bugs crept to my fingers. "Who the fuck is Clyde Phillips?"

He tilted his head. "Cutty Jax's real name wasn't Clyde Phillips?"

"Fuck no. Who told you that? I've never heard of Clyde Phillips. Cutty's name was Cameron Jackson." I flicked the bug away. It stood on its butt, hissing and showing its hundreds of tiny wire legs. "Bruh. Get these fucking scary-ass bugs away from me. What the fuck are these anyway?"

He pressed his watch. The bug somersaulted backward and crept up Hoop's arm. When it reached his ear, it latched itself on. "I was gonna give you one of these to apologize for getting nachos on your coat. It's a communication device. Unlike anything you've ever seen or used."

"Oh, hells no," I said, dabbing him. "I fucking hate bugs. That goes for robot bugs, too. If a bug crosses my path, I step on that bitch. If a centipede or a worm is crawling on me, I cut that motherfucker in half. When it's finished squirming around, I smash it."

Nacho pushed his glasses back up his nose. "Ahhhh. Well, I want to make this good." He pointed around the store. "Pick anything you want."

I scratched my chin and immediately looked at the 120-inch TV in the center of the wall. "I want that shit, but—"

The robot bug climbed back down his neck and into the front pocket of his shirt. "But?" he said.

"But..." I hesitated. Apparently he was a big fan, and I didn't want to tell him I was homeless. "I'm between cribs right now. Can't even fit that thing in my G. I could really use a flashlight. No bug-ass flashlight, though. No bug-ass nothin'."

"Hmmm." Nacho put the arm of his thick-ass glasses in his mouth. He still had nacho cheese stuck in his goatee. He snapped his fingers and pointed at me. "I've got just the thing." He bent down behind the counter and unlocked a cabinet. I didn't really want to know what that weirdo locked up in the store, but if he had a flashlight for me, we'd be good. After fucking around and moving shit back and forth for a minute, he finally stood. He placed an orange construction helmet on the counter. He spun the helmet around so the headlamp attached to the front faced me.

"The fuck is this shit?" I knocked on the top of it with my ring. "I need like a Maglite. Something I can put in my mouth while I use my hands to do my business."

He chuckled as he tilted his head and pulled his greasy-ass hair out of a ponytail. "You need a flashlight to jerk off?" He put the rubber band in his mouth, ran his fingers through his hair, and tied it back tighter.

"Fuck no. What is this? You a narc?"

Rolling his eyes, he said. "If I was a narc, wouldn't I have busted you for carrying an un-permitted firearm?" He patted the top of the helmet. "This is more than a flashlight."

"What are you talking about?"

"This little baby…" He lifted the helmet and pressed a button on the side. Black glasses popped out of the brim. "…is quite special. It will allow you to see things in the dark you don't think are there."

I ran the bottom of the glasses across my palm. "You mean like infrared?"

He handed it to me. "Kind of like infrared. More like X-ray vision."

"What the fuck are you talking about, bruh?" I batted the helmet away and snorted a couple times to let him know I wasn't some sucker he could unload his bullshit on.

"See for yourself, Danny." He pushed it back.

"Fuck that stupid X-Men shit. Does the flashlight work?" I looked back at the other shit in the store and noticed the dog beggar commercial was on all the TVs. "Yo, dude. Turn that shit off."

He pressed his watch and changed the channel. "You don't like abused animals either?"

"Does the flashlight work or not?"

"Sure it does." He clicked it on and off a few times. "But there is so much more—"

"Don't care about any of that other bullshit. I just need a flashlight, Nacho."

"Call me Hoop."

"I just need a flashlight. Mother. Fucker."

"Alright then." He pulled out a bag, shook it open, and put the helmet inside. As he started to hand it to me, he asked, "Is there anything else I can give you to say I'm sorry?"

"Yeah, actually." I looked at the security cameras and leaned into him, whispering. "Do you sell the other stuff that Julio did? You know what I'm sayin'?" I nudged my head toward the backroom and winked.

"Look in the bag, Snap."

I opened the bag up, turned the helmet sideways, and saw two new clips for my gun. "Wait. How the fuck did you do that?"

He winked at me. "Trade secrets," he whispered back.

"You the man, Nach..."

He tilted his head.

"Hoop," I said, correcting myself.

He straightened up and pulled the tails of his shirt over his gut. "I'm not the man, Snap. You the man."

"What about the…," I dragged my finger under my nose. "You know."

"The drugs?" He shook his head. "I'm a new business. The guns are bad enough. People who have guns and need ammo have money. Drug addicts hanging around would raise suspicion. You feel?"

I laughed at his attempt to talk street. "Yeah, I hear you, bruh. It's not for me anyway. I don't touch that shit. I mean, I smoke blunts and shit, but that's all legal."

"There is this…" He paused. "Nah." He waved me away. "I shouldn't be opening my big mouth."

"Spill it, Hoop." I tapped on my gun under my shirt.

He nodded, knowing I wasn't there to fuck around. Whispering again, he said, "Have you heard about that trap house in Bel-Air?"

"No. What's up with that?"

"Word on the street is there's an old, condemned house tucked away in Bel-Air that some kids are running and living in to get high."

I licked my lips. "No shit?"

"No shit. Here's the thing. These are just a bunch of rich kids who know nothing about dealing drugs. Some guy I know was invited over there to buy some drugs. When he got there, all those dumb punks were passed out with needles on their arms."

"So what did he do?"

"He didn't do anything. He got cold feet and left because he said it was too dark inside to look for the motherlode. But he did say he heard the kids talking about a closet upstairs. Probably the closet in the master bedroom. He got freaked because he thought one of the kids was dead. He high-tailed it out of there through the kitchen in the back because he's on parole and was afraid that the cops could be there at any second. He did say there was no security in the house anywhere. Just a bunch of dumb, wasted kids."

"What?"

"Yeah. I told that pussy he was an idiot for not trying to take advantage of the gold mine he walked into." He looked at my bag. "Of course, a street-smart individual with the right equipment probably wouldn't pass up an opportunity like that. Worse comes to worst, and that enterprising young man can't find the product, he could, hypothetically, just rob these rich kids. Even steal the needles right out of their arms."

I stroked my chin. "If an enterprising young man was interested in such an opportunity, would his new friend be able to get an address of said location?"

"He could. The friend could text it to the enterprising young man later today after he spoke with his chicken-shit associate." Hoop put his watch to his mouth. "Nest. Add contact. Danny Snaps "

"*Ready*," a female voice boomed through every speaker in the store.

Shrugging my shoulders, I read out my digits.

"*Thank you, Danny Snaps,*" it said.

"Yes. Thank you, Danny Snaps. I should have your jacket all cleaned up for you sometime tomorrow. Not sure if my dry cleaner is backed up by Halloween costumes."

I shot Hoop some deuces and headed out of his shop.

"Oh, Lil Snap," he called back to me.

"Yeah, bruh?"

"Have a happy Devil's Night."

Love studied the side of my G as he threw his backpack onto both shoulders. "Yo, Snap! What the fuck did you do to your ride?"

Not wanting to tell him what went down at Lowe's, I said, "Some ho."

"Damn." He dragged his finger up the side of the fender. "What? Did she attack you with a chainsaw?"

"That bitch was crazy, yo."

"You must have done something really fucked up."

I pointed between my legs. "You know what's up?"

"Shit." He reached into my G through the passenger side window and put out his fist.

"Bitches wanna be with me because they think I'm gonna make them a star and shit. Know what I'm sayin'?" I fist-bumped him. "They know who my dad is."

He tilted his lid. "I heard that, Snap."

Todd Love, or TT Love as he called himself, was still at Beverly Hills High. Homeboy pretty much bit everything from me to start his hip-hop career. The only difference was that his shit wasn't fire like mine. I should've been mad that he was a wannabe, ripping off my flow and my swag, but he was a longtime friend. On top of that, he promised me that he would do a collab track with me and bring me back into the game when he got signed—even though his bubblegum crossover shit wasn't my thing.

"You know tomorrow night is my Halloween Joint, right?"

"Yo, bruh. Of course. I wanted to track you down today and make sure that we were on the same page with the product."

"Yeah, man." He looked back over his shoulder. "There's gonna be around two large at this joint. I need as much H, Chuck, and Molly as you can get your hands on."

"Low inventory right now on Molly, kid. What about that Snap shit I been giving you?"

"Man, that sent three chicks to the hospital last time." He scratched his temple. "What about moonrocks?"

"There ain't nobody doin' that shit anymore." I laughed. "You wanna buy me a plane ticket to Florida? That's where I can get you some moonies."

"Yeah, yeah. I know," Love said as he rubbed his shoulder. "I just need something for the bitches."

"That's what coke is for, bruh."

"You know high school bitches." He tugged at his gold chain. "They think coke and heroin are gonna fuck them up."

"I'll see what I can drum up." I looked up at the oil well on the high school property, thinking about how I could get my hands on some cheddar if I didn't score at Hoop's magical trap house. "I can get you some real rock. Throw that at these prude bitches. Looks like candy."

"High school girls don't like crack, Snap. They think it's for poor people."

I lit up the cigarillo blunt I had tucked behind my ear. "Yo. Speaking of money. When are we gonna cut that collab? We've been talking about it for years. Let's get into my dad's studio before Thanksgiving and drop some shit."

He hesitated and then said, "I thought your dads kicked you out a few months ago."

"Nah, dude. We squashed that beef. He's kicking that gold digger out and your boy is moving back in. Maybe I can twist him to produce our track."

"Y-yeah, sure, Snap. Tell me when you're back in and I'll get my manager to call Russ."

Blowing smoke from my blunt in his face, I said, "We don't gotta do nothin' like that. Let's just get in the studio and spit. I've been working on beats."

"Sure," he said, waving the smoke away and coughing a little bit.

I pointed at two girls walking by. They also went to BHH. Changing the subject back to the drugs, I said, "Those bitches wouldn't know the difference between crack and moonrocks."

One of them noticed Love was looking at her. She also must have seen the plates on my G and known TT was talking to LILSNAP.

"Hi, Todd." She tried to play it cool, but when she waved, she dropped her phone. Her friend started giggling as she bent over to pick it up for her.

I waved TT out of the way. He stepped sideways as I reached over the passenger seat and opened the door. "You pretty ladies wanna go for a ride?"

They looked at each other and started laughing. "Gross," one of the sluts said.

"There isn't nothin' gross about Lil Snap, bitch," I said, patting the seat.

The ho who dropped her phone threw me a gas face and asked, "Who's Little Snap?"

I scratched my nails on the passenger seat like I was playing with a kitten. "I'm Lil Snap. Danny Snaps. You'll be screaming my name in seconds and never forget it. I'll take care of you ladies."

The friend whispered in her ear and swiped on her phone.

"Come on, little girlies." I turned my hand over and twirled my fingers, inviting them into my G again.

Love stepped in front of the door between the hos and my whip. "Lighten up, Snap."

"What? Are you a little bitch now, too, T?"

He tried to block out the door as he opened up his jacket. A big wad of dollars stuck out of the inside pocket. "You want the money or not?"

I tapped him out of the way.

The girls were holding up their phones. They looked at each other and became hysterical. "It's him!"

I bent my lid sideways like TT had earlier and took the blunt out of my mouth, offering it to them. "That's right. Danny Motherfuckin' Snaps."

"Fat pig. Why don't you go have some fried chicken?" the friend said between fits of laughter.

"Or some Snickers bars," the bitch holding the phone added.

Love closed his jacket and closed the door. "Bruh. You need to focus on getting me what I need for the party."

"What the fuck was that all about?" I asked. "You turnin' my peeps against me?"

"What? No. Those girls are freshmen. They're like 14. Campus security has a stricter policy about talking to strangers now."

Faking confusion, I pretended to look around the inside of my G. "There's no stranger in here." I pointed to the oil well. "I used to run this motherfucking school. Those bitches know who I am. Besides, if there's grass on the infield, I always play ball."

"You better get that beat-up ride off school property before we call the cops," one of the girls yelled.

"It's all good, Bree," Love shouted back. "I'll get rid of this guy."

As her laughter turned into heavy breathing, the bitch named Bree said, "He knows who I am!"

I rolled down the back window and reclined my seat. "I know your name now, too, bitch. You're gonna take this fucking big-ass dick!"

"Dude," Love said, using his hand to try and cover the back window. "We're talking business here. If you can't get me what I need, I'll go somewhere else."

"Oh, so that's how it is? I'm just your mule now. That's how it is, Mr. Bigtime?" I got my seat back up and opened up the center console. "My nine is right there, bitch. We playing gangsta shit now?" I took a massive pull off my blunt and held it in my lungs

"I didn't mean it like that. If you can't get me the product, I'll just find someone who can."

I exhaled. "You better give me that wad in your jacket, T."

He continued to wave my smoke. "I'm not giving you shit until I see that you're giving me something in return."

"We never did it like that before." I ashed my blunt into a Mountain Dew can.

"Well, Danny. You don't seem real certain you can get me what I want. You aren't the only person I go to for drugs. I'm doing you a favor because I know you're in a bad spot. All you want to do is talk to little girls and shit. My Halloween Joint is the biggest party of the year. People need to know they can get what they need."

"Bitch. Imma get you what you need." I flicked what was left of my cigarillo and spit the strawberry aftertaste into the can. "You stole that party from me anyway. That was my thing when I went to BHH."

"What? You own Halloween parties now?"

"I guess that *is* how it is." I started to put my G in drive. "I'll get your drugs for you and all your gay-ass teenybopper friends."

"Good. Meet me out back of Pinks tomorrow morning at 10." He put out his fist to bump again. "We'll sort this out and I'll buy you some Halloween breakfast."

"I don't need your charity, bitch. Lil Snap has a few cards up his sleeve. You know what, bruh? I don't want to waste my fucking brand or my dad's time doing any fake-ass crossover drop with your pussy ass. You're gonna regret biting me and fucking this…" I flipped my thumb back and forth between us. "…up."

I ignored his bump. Just as I was about to slam the pedal and leave his punk ass hanging, he said, "Yeah. You might wanna check out *The Roach* today, homie."

"Why the fuck would I do that? You drop a song with the bitch from *Stranger Things*?"

"Your Young Guns video is trending on social."

*DANNY SNACKS!*

That's what the headline on fucking Hollywood gossip site *The Roach* said.

Below the giant headline were hundreds of pictures and videos of me holding up fistfuls of Snickers bars at Lowe's.

*Son of record mogul Russ Sapperstein and blink-and-you-missed-him rapper Danny Snaps was spotted at Lowe's in Mid-City LA looking unsatisfied with their SNACKS. After his credit card was declined, he went on a tirade. Good thing annoyed customers, and loyal* Roach *readers, sent us plenty of pictures and videos of the chocolate-covered meltdown.*

"Those motherfuckers," I said as I pounded my steering wheel. It was super obvious they Photoshopped me to look fat and like I was drooling over the candy bars. "I'm gonna sue the fuck out of you."

I continued to scroll.

*If you don't, like most people, remember Danny Snaps (or Lil Snap, as nobody called him beside himself), he made it to the semi-finals of the third season of* The Stage. *He was the Vegas odds-on favorite to win the whole competition. That was until he broke out into a homophobic rant live on the show. And, it was directed at his father's former business partner/co-owner of Phresh Coat Records, Cutty Jax.*

"Homophobic? That bitch died of AIDS. I was speaking the truth. Y'all should have listened to me. All I spoke was the truth."

There was a link to some gay-ass video called "Cutty Jax: Hip-Hop Trailblazer."

I ignored that bullshit and kept reading. There was an ad in the middle of the article with Roach owner Tanner Devereux. He was smiling with a sippy cup in his hand. It said, *Got Gossip? Contact The Roach.*

"Faggot bitch," I said. "You better watch your ass. Nobody reading this shit cares about you." As I put my thumb over his smug face, I saw an article about that ho Chastity O'Neill on the side of the screen. I almost fucked her before she went berserk and killed a bunch of people.

"Oh, shit," I said, snapping my fingers. "That fucking prude offed herself in jail." I covered my mouth and laughed. "Man, am I lucky I didn't fuck with that." The truth was that I was making out with her and her big ass nose got in the way. I told her to go see a plastic surgeon. She split. "Fuck her. No talent."

I went back to the article about me.

*The would-be star, whose real name is Danny Sapperstein, rose to D-list fame after appearing on stage with one of his father's artists Young Guns. Ironic now, the video of that performance was titled "The Skinny Little White Kid Who Can Spit." The video went viral and everyone felt Snap was the next child artist to break into hip-hop. Of course, that pretty much ended when everyone found out he was Russ Sapperstein's son. The attempt at a culture vulture cash grab was said to have led to Russ and Cutty parting ways and selling off Phresh Coat Records.*

"Yeah, boyyeeee! Grab that cash." I snapped my fingers like I used to do on stage after I belted out a sick freestyle. "That's what the fuck I'm talkin' about."

*After the accusations of nepotism faded, Danny auditioned for* The Stage *as his new alias, Lil Snap. He wanted to prove to the world he could spit with the best and he wasn't another label-manufactured child star.*

My epic video with Young Guns was linked below.

"Danny Snaps is back! People are gonna remember this now."

The world needed a reminder of how great I was. Everyone needed to hear my tracks. No doubt me and dads were going to sue *The Roach* and its insect motherfucking owner Tanner Devereux.

I scooted my seat back, unbuttoned my pants. I slid my hand under my gut and started tickling the head of my big-ass dick. While waiting a second for the song to pop up, I held my phone sideways and prepped my thumb to push play. I was pleased to see that the "The Skinny Little White Kid Who Can Spit" video had gotten around a million new views since I checked it out the day before. I made sure that the sound on my phone was paired with the G's sound system. A little chime told me it was.

"Danny Snaps is back," I repeated as the shaft of my cock filled up my hand.

I pushed play and started punching my dick back and forth.

"*Every single day in the United States, an animal is abused—*"

There I was, face-to-face with that beggar dog again.

"Fuck you, mutt!" I continued slugging away.

Its pathetic eyes looked directly at the camera as sleet pounded its fucked-up, starving-ass body. It shook as it tried to lick piss off itself. If I could have reached into my phone and ripped that motherfucker's eyes out, I would have. It all reminded me how great it felt to rip the hair out of my dad's whore's precious little fucking Bobo. When it took its last breath after I drowned it, it became limp in my hands, just like my dick after I blew my wad.

As I always pointed out when I saw that ad, I said, "Somebody's gotta be there to give that bitch-ass dog a treat. That dog should move where the food is."

I felt a little bit of cum gathering around my head, so I slowed my stroke. Thankfully, the "skip" button came up on my screen.

"Finally!"

The appetizer was over, and I was ready for the main course.

Right as Young Guns said, "Get out here, Snap," I closed my eyes. I hardly ever watch the video. I was there. How could I forget any second of the best moment of my life?

I was backstage when Guns called me on stage. My dads straightened out the blue bandana around my neck that Guns gave me a few weeks earlier. It was from his set, the Shoreline Crips. Dads put a Band-Aid under my left eye. He grabbed me by the shoulders and winked at me.

"I'm proud of you, son," he said.

Before I got the chance to thank him, he spun me toward the stage and tapped me on the head.

I Crip Walked out to Young Guns, gazing at the packed forum. I gave them all the finger. They erupted like they just witnessed the birth of God.

When I crossed Guns on the stage, I threw my hand and he tossed me the mic. We had that alley-oop shit timed perfectly. We rehearsed it for hours before the show because we wanted to be sure that the second after that mic hit my palm, I would start spitting. My dads wanted my introduction to the hip-hop world to be so large that it would instantly become legendary.

I mouthed my own science as I slowed my hand to a more sensual and passionate stroke.

*You ain't never seen no kid,*
*Dealing lids to the other kids on the skids,*
*Smack, crack,*
*What's that?*
*Up your nose, in your arm,*
*I mean no harm,*
*I'm a street dealer bigger than a pharm-*
*-aceutical corporation,*
*Taking over the nation,*
*I pay off the pigs and send them on vacation,*
*To swim with the other fishes,*
*Bitches and snitches,*
*I'll create all your darkest wishes,*
*Then leave you in stitches.*
*My name is Snap,*

*Snap,*
*Snap,*
*Unloading rounds from my Gat,*
*Gat,*
*Gat.*

I acted like I was holding an Uzi.

*Rata-tat-tat,*
*Rata-tat-tat,*
*Rata-tat-tat.*

The beat stopped.

*It's too late when you hear MYYYYYYY...*

And then kicked back in with an earth-shaking explosion.

*PAP,*
*PAP,*
*PAP.*

Everyone in the Forum threw their hands in the air. A pit started in front of the stage. Young Guns stood behind me, bobbing his head to the beat and scratching his chin.

*Name is Snap,*
*Snap,*
*Snap.*

The crowd started singing along with the bridge.

*I'm here to tap,*
*Tap,*
*Tap,*

*That bitch under your arm,*
*She doesn't think I mean no harm,*
*Stay calm,*
*Hit the deck,*
*Stand still while I flex my,*
*Skills,*
*I ain't paying that bitch's bills,*
*I'll use her up,*

*Fuck her dry while she cries,*
*And get her hooked on rocks,*
*Then send her corpse back to you in a box,*
*You can dump your load in her. It's better than you using a sock.*

I put up my fingers.

*"Peace,"* I said, putting an exclamation point on my debut.

I walked back to Guns, fist-bumped him. He nodded his head in approval.

Before I handed him back the mic, I yelled:

*Fuck the bitches in red. We repping that Shoreline Blue, nigga!*

And then, as I C-Walked my eight-year-old ass off the stage and the crowd roared for more, Young Guns said, "That's my boy Danny Snaps. That motherfucker is a cold G."

I tugged away at my cock. I had managed to time it so that I shot my blat almost when Guns called me "a cold G."

I grabbed a shirt tucked away from behind the seat and used it as a nut rag.

I sat back in my seat and felt the memory of that moment. My goo shot out several times, getting the palm of my hand a little wet when it seeped through the fibers of the shirt.

Nobody came out that hard ever again in the rap game. It was long overdue for me to take back what was mine. I was meant to be the motherfucking king. And no matter how many faggots or bitches lined up in front of me, I only got stronger.

Just as I was about to fall into an afternoon nap, my phone buzzed.

Looking through one eye, I saw a text from a number I didn't recognize.

*"It's Hoop."*

I typed with my free hand that I wasn't using to still mop up my jizz.

*"Yo. What you got for me?"*

He sent through an address in Bel-Air and a Maps link to the location.

*"This is that house I was telling you about. You should send it to your broker. It could be a good investment."*

He sent a wink emoji next.

*"Shit, yeah, Hoop. I think I can make that happen,"* I typed back.

I put my phone down on the G's center console. It buzzed again.

*"I thought you might want this."*

After a couple of seconds, an attachment came through.

It was an MP3 for my buried track "Tag Out."

*"You gotta release this track, Snap. It's been in my rotation since I found it last month."*

I typed back. "*You don't think I want to drop this shit? I don't have the masters, motherfucker! We recorded a whole album that I've never even heard all the way through. My dads musta leaked that shit to pay for a new summer house.*"

*"You should go get them!"* Hoop finally wrote.

The phone rang for the twenty-third time on the security call box outside the gates of my dads' driveway gate.

"Yes, Daniel," he answered.

"Yo, dads. I—"

He quieted his voice. He must have been in the same room with Taffy. "What do you want, Daniel?"

"I. I need help. I really need help."

I heard a click on the other end. A beat in the background went silent. He was in the studio. "I already told you I can't give you any more money, son. You need to pick yourself up. You need to be a man now."

"I don't want money," I said, almost whimpering. "I need help. I need to apologize to you and Taff. I want to start over. I love you. I can't take back all the awful things I've done and said, but I can try to make things right. I want to be my own man. I *need* to be worthy of calling myself your son."

"It's not that I'm not concerned about you, Daniel. I just don't trust you to do the right thing anymore. I'm at a loss. On the one hand, I love you more than anything in the world. You know I have done everything in my power to help you through your issues. On the other hand, you scare my wife." He paused. It sounded like he was getting choked up. "You scare me. No father wants to be afraid of his blood. No father doesn't want to do everything he can to help his son succeed."

"You know most of that is just me frontin'," I said, acting like I was touched by his speech. "I need to let all that go now. I need to be your son. If you'll only *please* help me. The first step is me getting on my knees and begging you, and Taffy, for forgiveness. If you don't want to help me out, that's okay. I just need to walk into my new life by starting to clean up my messes. I don't want to be out of your lives. And, even if it means you aren't supporting me, I can't move forward without stepping back and righting all the wrongs."

I heard some whispering. Clearly, Taffy was in the studio with him. Fucking gold-digger bitch was probably singing over my beats

Finally, he said, "You can come in. But I have to be clear. You can apologize to both of us and we will try to figure out a way to move forward. If we can't, we can't. And sadly, I will have to count on you to do this on your own."

I heard a buzzer and the gold gate blocking my entrance into my home started to open.

"Thank you, father," I said, holding back laughter and disguising my amusement with tears and sniffling. "I understand, and I will try my damndest to not let you down."

"Taffy and I are out back in the studio. We *both* look forward to hearing what you have to say."

Before I went through the gate, I tapped the call box, reminding myself of all the security cameras my dads had throughout the estate.

I drove up the long, palm tree-lined driveway, counting security cameras. I had some great times in this giant yard growing up. It was one of the few huge yards in Beverly Hills. And since I didn't have a whole lot of friends growing up, I spent a lot of time playing on the grounds, at the tennis courts, in the pools…by myself. That was only when I wasn't in the pool house my dads converted into a massive studio out back. That was where my *real* friends were. Every West Coast hip-hop legend came in and out of that studio, and all of them treated me like I was their best friend. They talked to me about the hip-hop world. Showed me how to program a drum track and flip a sample. Taught me how to build verses, hooks, and rhymes.

With toys like that, I never needed coloring books, video games, and action figures. I was raised by the game. My toys were real people, and they actually responded to me when I spoke to them and told them what to do.

"The palace that Phresh Coat built," I said as I passed the main roundabout in front of the mansion. It was the truth. Even after Phresh Coat was sold off, every player in the game still wanted to get Russ Sapperstein's signature sound on their track. The estate and the studio became known in the industry as "The Westside Graceland." It was the center of Los Angeles rap. Everyone tried to duplicate the sound and the boom, but no one came close.

My dads's white Rolls and Taffy's cherry red Bentley were parked out front. No other cars were there; they were alone. I opened the center console of the G and tickled the trigger of my gun.

As I pulled up to the entrance of the studio house, I counted the final camera that was tucked away on the far side of the basketball court. 24. Only 24 cameras caught me driving onto the estate grounds.

I threw my gun into my backpack before I climbed out of my G. I had illegally tinted windows on my whip, so no camera would have caught the weapon anyway. I grabbed my phone and cued up the MP3 of "Tag Out" that Hoop sent me.

"Let's do this," I said to myself as I slapped my fingers together with a loud *snap*! I pulled my shirt down over my belly and made a desperate face into my side mirror. "Still got it."

Straightening myself up so I looked like I was sincere, I walked past the *big* pool in front of the studio. The ladder by the entrance to the water caught my eye. Fucking Bobo. That little fucking shit did bite me. I didn't really want to drown him. I never wanted to kill any of those animals. If anything—man, dog, squirrel, ant — fucked with me, I took them out. Those were the rules of the game that brought me up. My dads forgot that when he moved to Beverly Hills.

It was good to be home after five months. The air smelled fresher than it did in the bum-fucking alleys of Koreatown. That motherfucking part of the city smelled like dead fish and garbage. Beverly Hills, especially my yard, smelled like perfection. I tapped the lion statues on each side of the walkway up to the studio. It was something I always did as a kid for good luck before I went in to cut a track.

Shaking my head, I tried to drum up water in my eyes. I would have just rubbed them red, but I knew dads was watching me. I didn't want him to think that I was trying to get my tracks before letting me in. If he knew that, he would turn me away and most likely call the 5-0 to get me off the property.

I had to be slick and use every bit of the street to take back what was mine.

My hard work.

My ticket to fame.

The life that was taken away from me by all those motherfuckers who were jealous of my skills.

"Yo," I said into the two-way camera tablet on the side of the studio entrance door.

My dads's face came up on the screen. "Daniel, I have to be clear before I let you in. I am not going to give you money and I'm not going to invite you back to live in *our* home."

"I'm not here for a handout, dads." I wiped my nose on my sleeve and made sure I was looking directly into the tablet camera. "I need to give you what little I have left in me. I'm not in a good place. You're right. It's far past time for me to man up. Please." I lowered my voice to a whisper. "Please just give me the chance to make things right between the three of us."

He looked back at me, searching my face for bullshit. "One step at a time, son," he said as the door unlocked. "So you're aware, Taffy is going to stay inside the studio. You can apologize to her through the com in the control room."

"Understood," I said as I readied the play button on my phone and slid my backpack down to my elbow.

Shuffling through the lobby and foyer of the studio, I passed all the silver, gold, and platinum records my dads produced over the years. Every name that meant something to West Coast hip-hop was framed for everyone to see. Except one was missing.

Danny Motherfucking Snaps.

I stood outside the door to the control room as I lightly tapped the door. The RECORDING light above the entrance turned off, and that door unlocked, too. I laughed. It probably would have been easier for me to break into Fort Knox. The thing was, a lot of rappers and producers were getting gunned down in their studios when my dads built our home and studio. It was always better to be safe than sorry in the Westside hustle.

I put my head down and counted to three. And then entered.

Dads spun around in his producer's chair after pulling down some sliders on the main mixing board. The heat from all the equipment immediately caused sweat to build on my forehead. The analogs, rack effects, and sequencers blinked and ticked.

I was home.

"Have a seat, son," my dads said as he pointed to the couch against the back wall. He had a new puppy that looked like Bobo's twin brother in his lap.

"Who's that little rascal?" I said, pointing to the new mutt.

He pulled the dog in closer to his waist. "This is Gizmo." The mutt licked at my dad's fingers as he gave it a treat.

"Damn, dads. That's a cute, little dude. That might be the cutest dog I've ever seen."

I looked beyond the studio glass and saw Taffy sitting on a piano bench. As if that ho even knew how to play the piano.

I waved. She looked at my dads and then, reluctantly, waved back.

"Is here good?" I asked before sitting down on the couch.

He nodded.

As I took my seat, I sat my backpack against my shin. My gun rested on the tip of my Timbs.

"Okay, Daniel. Before I turn on the com so you can apologize to Taffy and beg her to forgive you for killing Bobo, I need to know what this is all about?"

"I wanted you to hear something before we got into all that."

I pushed the play button on my phone. "Tag Out" came on. I rolled my shoulders and started mouthing my lyrics. "You remember this?"

"Where did you get this?" He nodded his head to the beat.

"Some guy I met found it online." I turned up the volume. "I didn't even know it ever made it out of this room."

"It shouldn't have." he laughed. He started getting more into the song, bouncing his head around and using his fingers to mimic the drum fills.

I threw the phone on the floor. His eyes followed it as I reached into my bag and grabbed my gun. "You're right, motherfucker." I pointed the gun at his head. "It never should have made it out of this room."

"Daniel?" he said, putting up his hands. The new dog jumped out of his lap and ran to the door that led to the studio. Inside, his mommy shot up from the piano bench.

"Sit the fuck back down, you fucking gold-digging skank," I yelled through the glass as I signaled "down" with my gun.

She did as she was told. Gizmo started scratching at the door.

"Where the fuck…" I said as I Crip Walked over to him, continuing to target the center of his head. "…are my masters, bitch?"

"Why are you doing this?" he wheezed while hiding his face behind his hands.

I didn't answer. I pressed the nose of my gun against his head.

He pointed to the wall. "The original masters are in that red box. There is a hard drive in there that's labeled *Snap. Snap. Snap.*

"Get up and get it for me, you old motherfucker."

I looked back into the studio. Taffy was starting to make a move for her phone. It was sitting on top of the grand piano in front of her.

I shook my head "no" and continued to press the gun against my dads's head as he slowly got up and headed toward the shelf with all the masters.

Crying, he said, "Daniel, please. I will help you. I'll give you anything you want. Just don't hurt us."

"That doesn't sound sincere, bitch. Beg me."

He stood on his toes and grabbed the red box. As he came back down, his crying grew louder. "This isn't you, son. We love you. You know that."

"Then why did you ruin my fucking life, motherfucker? Why did you release my tracks and try to cut me out?" I snatched the box out of his hands.

He took cover under his arms.

"I love you, Daniel."

In sync with the beat of "Tag Out" coming from my phone, I knocked off five rounds, right in that bitch's head. Blood flew all around the control room. Gizmo started to bark. Taffy screamed.

Dads had one last second to look into the eyes of the legend he created before he tumbled into the shelf, bringing his life's work to the floor with a huge thud.

"Fuck you. Fuck your bitch-ass charity."

Out of the corner of my eye, I noticed Taffy inching closer to her phone. She reached it, but her hand was shaking so hard that she knocked it off the piano and onto the floor.

I charged over to the studio door. It was locked from the inside. Using my gun, I smashed the glass and unlocked it. Before I entered, I grabbed that motherfucker Gizmo by the ear and cupped his little head into my hand. He squealed just like his old brother had when I pulled that little bitch's ear completely off.

Desperately, Taffy fell to her knees and tried to grab her phone. Before she had the chance to unlock it or make an emergency call, I was standing over her.

"Please, Danny," she begged as she threw her phone across the room. "Please."

"You ruined my life, you fucking gold-digging bitch." I held Gizmo up to my face. He licked some of his daddy's blood off my cheek. "See, he likes me." I aimed my gun down at her.

"You'll never get away with this. The neighbors are going to hear all the shots."

I looked around the studio and laughed, pointing to the walls. "There ain't nobody gonna hear nothin' in here. This place is soundproof. You couldn't hear a parade two inches outside that door."

Her tears caused her makeup to run all over her face. When it got in her mouth, she tried to spit it out, but her hair got in the way.

"But since you're so concerned with bothering the neighbors with our *business,*" I said, digging my gun into Gizmo's stomach. "I'll use a silencer."

I pressed the dog and the gun into the front of her face and capped both of them. I flicked at the trigger until my clip was empty. I drop-kicked her in the chest and let her kiss the ass of her dead-ass fucking dog.

"Now who's the fucking big dog, ho?"

I sat down in my dads' producer's chair. I tickled the faders on the mixing board, remembering what life was like before Taffy came into the picture. After a few moments of remembering the good old days, I went through every security camera on the network from his workstation. I deleted all the video that was recorded that day. After I was in the clear, I turned off all the cameras and erased the backup on the network.

"Smack, crack, what's that?" I said as I dropped my gun and the *Snap. Snap. Snap.* hard drive into my backpack. "Danny Snaps is back."

Hoop advised me to hit the trap house after dark but before 10 p.m. According to his friend who chickened out trying to rob it before, that was the prime time to roll in undetected. That was when most dumb kids would all be faded from their first couple of helpings for the night. It made sense. As I knew from my robberies in K-Town, when these motherfuckers were about half a bag into the night, they were as useless as ragdolls. It was as easy as taking candy from a baby.

I pulled into a parking garage at the north end of Westwood near UCLA and checked how far the house was from me on Google Maps.

*Five miles? Fuck. My ass isn't walking five miles uphill*, I thought.

Just as I threw my G back in reverse, three college bitches rode by the garage on electric scooters.

I snapped my fingers. "Word up! Forgot about those punk-ass things."

I put the G back in park and put everything I needed into my backpack. Gun. Gloves. Flashlight?

"Motherfucker. I still didn't get a flashlight."

And then I remembered Hoop giving me that dumbass construction helmet. I opened the back of the G and dug through my belongings, looking for the Hoop's World bag. When I grabbed my clips out of the bag, I almost threw that shit away. I was glad I didn't.

"Bingo," I said as my knuckles knocked into the hard plastic. Before I tossed it into my bag with the rest of my shit, I clicked the light on and off a few times. As Hoop promised, it worked. It looked stupid as all fuck, but since the house would be pitch black, it would have to do.

I connected my phone with no problem to the Bird scooter that I immediately found outside the parking garage. I would never have been caught dead riding around on one of those things. Still, I wasn't going to take the chance of having the G and my LILSNAP license plate being caught on any of the thousands of cameras around Bel-Air.

As if rich-kid drug addicts reported stolen drugs anyway? Even though I didn't plan to kill anyone else, it was best to cruise in on a scooter to avoid suspect behavior.

I threw my backpack on, put in my buds, pulled a bandana over my face, and covered the rest of my head with a hoodie. I hit repeat on the "Tag Out" MP3 Hoop sent me. I would have preferred listening to the entire *Snap. Snap. Snap.* album, but the hard drive only had unfinished mix tracks on it. No big deal. Once I got T Love his drugs, I'd be swimming in fucking money. The plan was to roll up at Young Guns' house and drop those masters in his platinum-touched hands. I always thought he had more cred as a producer than my dads. And since he stopped working with my dads, his career skyrocketed. Besides, my dads' face was splattered all over his studio. That motherfucker wasn't turning knobs for anyone ever again.

Two frat boys trying to carry some drunk ho back to her dorm room waved at me, laughing. She had barf all over the front of her shirt. Those punks, who were probably named like Tailor or Bryce or some gay shit like that, were most likely gonna get their dicks wet. Good for them. Everyone deserved to get lucky on Devil's Night.

No cop or campus security dudes fucked with me as I drove through campus. Why would they? I looked just like every other rich-ass kid who went to UCLA. It was a cool school, and it was a hop skip and a jump away from *my* mansion. Too bad my dads and I agreed early on that college wasn't for me. Sure, I also split from Beverly Hills High before I graduated, but I'm sure he could have just bought my ass in. He had connections all over town, and it would have been one or two phone calls to make it happen.

He never said it, but I think it had a lot to do with him seeing me as his meal ticket after Phresh Coat was done.

I crossed Sunset and pulled over before getting too close to the security gate that led into Bel-Air. I knew my way around the streets up there because most of my dads's friends lived there. It was the home of every rich-ass record executive in the world. As I cut through the woods, I dragged the scooter behind me. Once I knew I wasn't anywhere near the gate and the Bel-Air cops, I got back on the scooter. I looked at my phone. The trap house was buried way back on the other side of the neighborhood, so I still needed the scooter to help me get there.

Much to my surprise, no one was on the streets and not one security car passed me. I guessed that the little shits in Bel-Air didn't go out and egg houses on Devil's Night.

As I approached the long, winding driveway leading up to the house, I ditched the scooter in the overgrown bushes next to what used to be the mailbox. I looked into the night to try and see anything at the end of the driveway. Nada. It just looked like a big, black hole. Those junkie-ass rich kids sure were serious about not letting on to what they were doing. No lights at all, and since I couldn't see the outline of the house in the moonlight, I figured it was also buried in the overgrowth of trees that blocked it out.

"I know you're there," I said as I looked at my phone again. The Maps app told me it was there, about 300 yards directly in front of me. I looked back toward the center of Bel-Air again, almost second-guessing going forward.

"You need this, Snap," I told myself. "There ain't nobody gonna make you a star again besides you."

Rather than running away like that other bitch, I walked into the darkness.

Much to my surprise, there was a house at the end of the driveway. I took a deep breath. I couldn't see a motherfucking thing. Nothing. I waved my hands in front of my face. Couldn't see shit. It was so dark I couldn't even see movement. I was close enough that if I put on the Hoop helmet, no one would be able to see me coming up the path. If anyone was there at all.

I slowly took off my backpack, not making any sound. It was so quiet in that house that it might as well have been out in the West Virginia boondocks. There wasn't even any sound coming from the estate yard because there wasn't any wind. No birds. No rodents. Nothing.

I unzipped my backpack and felt around until my hand touched the brim of the helmet. My shirt was heavy and soaking from the walk and my armpits were squishing my wet tits. Sweat rolled from my neck and into my belly button. The rolls in the back of my neck filled with more water and opened up as I bent forward. One by one, they emptied sweat onto the back collar of my shirt, some of it seeping down my shoulders.

I leaned against the house and hung the hanger strap of the bag on my wrist. I pulled the helmet out of the bag and slipped it onto my head. Feeling around, I flicked the button on the side of the headlamp.

Nothing.

The light didn't come on.

I pushed the button again.

Still nothing.

*Goddammit, Hoop, you Nacho motherfucker,* I thought.

After pressing the button one last time to the exact same nothingness, I remembered what Hoop told me back at his store:

"This little baby is quite special. It will allow you to see things in the dark that you don't think are there."

I quickly started feeling around the side of the helmet for the other button he showed me that dropped the glasses in front and turned on the infrared. With no light, there was no way I was going to find the drugs inside the house. I doubted I would even be able to find my way back down the driveway to the scooter.

And then…my finger hit the button. The inside of the helmet locked onto the top of my head just like the robot bug had locked onto Hoop's ear. As I tried to pull it off, it suctioned to my skull. The glasses descended, and suddenly I could see everything around me. I mean, *everything*. Pink and turquoise light rays bounced everywhere between the gaps in the trees. I looked up at the sky. It looked like a cosmic orgy of every color I could imagine. The world became a rave.

I turned to see all the way down the driveway to the scooter I hid in the bushes. I could actually see the scooter. I spun around and looked up and down the front of the house. I could see inside the house. Every room. I could see old plates in the cupboards. And I could see the Bel-Air rich kids slumped against walls and in corners of all the rooms inside.

I put my hand in front of my face again. I could see every vein, every bone, and all the blood flowing in every direction. Hoop was right. It wasn't infrared. It was an insane acid trip of colors. I felt like I was looking into another dimension. I wiped my hand down my wet shirt and looked up toward the second-story bedrooms. As if I were playing a see his heat, I could use the helmet to walk down the halls, in and out of doors, and up and down the stairs.

With my eyes.

At the end of the hall, I spotted the last and largest bedroom. I walked through the door and started phasing in and out of the different closets. I was almost ready to leave and check out the other bedrooms when I noticed some kid passed out under a towel cabinet with a needle between his toes. I widened my eyes and took a peek inside. My chest filled with excitement and thumped to the beat of "Tag Out," which was still looping in my head.

The cabinet was filled with the motherlode. Every drug on TT's list was either wrapped in brown paper or already cut up and stuffed into little baggies. The kid underneath didn't move, but I could see his heart—I could actually see his heart! — thumping and pushing blood through his still body. If this dude was the gatekeeper, this heist *would* be easier than taking candy from a fucking baby.

After walking to the front door only to find it was locked, I remembered that Hoop's chickenshit friend said he left the house from the rear kitchen door. I went back into the place with the helmet. Through the foyer. Around the family room and the dining room. Down another long hall. Finally, into the kitchen. Two more kids were passed out at what was left of the kitchen table. I walked around them and looked at the back door, my entrance and my escape. Not only was it unlocked, it was cracked open. Maybe the kids were chasing the dragon and didn't want to get hotboxed. Regardless, shit, could I have had any better luck?

I walked around the dark house. I studied the dead trees and weeds ingrown everywhere. Like the faded-to-shit kids in the place, I could see inside them. All the plants pulsated in unison as if they were breathing. I knew plants were alive, but I didn't think they were *that* alive. Even stranger, they seemed to open a walkway for me, leading to my entrance. Even *they* wanted me to have those drugs.

When I reached the back door, I laid my backpack on the step and pulled out my gun. I made sure that the safety wasn't on and pushed the door open with my Timbs. No squeak. Still not a sound. The only thing I could hear was me. Me performing at the Forum with Young Guns. Me destroying the other three finalists on *The Stage*. The beats and rhymes I unleashed on *Snap. Snap. Snap.* And the explosion of applause whenever I jumped on a stage.

I slipped through the kitchen undetected. Dozens of unconscious kids laid in the halls. I stepped over them. Finally, I made my way to the decaying staircase in the center of the foyer. I wanted to run up the stairs, but with so many fucked-up rich kids around the house, I played it cool. My booty would wait, and nothing was going to stop me from taking what was mine.

Once I reached the top, I looked down the long hall leading to the master bedroom and let the helmet carry me to my future. Every few feet, I stepped over another kid. None of them moved. But I could see through their invisible skin that they were alive, each one of them breathing in unison like the plants outside.

"This is my day," I whispered as I opened the master bedroom door. "This is the day Danny Snaps becomes king."

Creeping through the bedroom, I looked through the walls. I could see in between every piece of wood and every crack inside the cement. I could see disgusting ants and termites bustling all around. It was as if the house had come to life and the insects were its blood. It was unlike anything anyone had ever seen.

I stepped into the bathroom and saw the gatekeeper, still in the same exact position he had been in when I entered the house using the helmet. I inched closer, noticing the towel cabinet had a steel lock on it.

"Fuck," I said under my breath. I raised my nine and took aim at it. Before I fired off a round and woke up the entire house from their nods, something caught my eye. The gatekeeper had a key around his neck. He actually had a key around his neck and he was passed out right below the treasure his dumb-fuck ass was supposed to be guarding! If Hoop's friend had any idea how easy this was all going to be, whether he was on parole or not, he never would've split.

"His loss." I bent forward to grab the key. I could have been firing my gun in the air and that little motherfucker wouldn't have moved an inch. He was so fucked up that the world was spinning around him and all he could do was sleep. As I latched onto the key and grabbed onto the chain that held it around his neck, I saw something move inside of him. It wasn't blood. He gurgled and his eyes burst open. I put my hand over his mouth to silence him. The thing inside him slithered up his insides and burst through his face. As if he vomited, it crawled down his torso. As it grew wider through the opening in his head, it forced blood and slime to spray and cover the walls.

I pushed myself away from it, looking behind me for the quickest way out of the bathroom. The thing crawled over my Timbs and inside my track pants. Thousands of tiny legs tip-toed up my calf and then my thigh. Within seconds it was crawling over my dick and up the front of my body. The faceless gatekeeper convulsed as the never-ending, giant millipede exited his body. It was as if his intestines came to life. I batted at it with the handle of my gun, but nothing was slowing it down. I was shaking so hard that I dropped the gun, and it slid across the filthy bathroom tile.

When the thing reached my neck, it coiled its way around my face. I tried to bite into it, but its body was rough and slimy like an eel. It started to constrict around my head with no other mission than to suffocate me. I couldn't see anything because the helmet glasses went black as if the batteries were dead. Dropping forward, I tried to crush the insect with all my weight. I felt around the floor for my gun as thousands of grubs and spiders detached from the thing and filled the corners of my eyes, nose, and mouth. I jammed my eyes shut and started spitting the babies from the back of my teeth. The ones that hadn't yet made their way into my nose and throat began biting into my gums.

Just when I was about to stop breathing, my fingers felt the cold metal of my gun. Without thinking, I started firing at the gatekeeper. That thing came from him. It had to be part of him. After I knocked out several rounds, my gun jammed. But the damage was done. The millipede unlocked itself from my head like a ball of unraveling yarn, became goo, and dropped onto my shoulders. It mixed in with my drenched shirt and became heavy as it hardened on my shoulders.

The biting of the grubs and spiders filling my skull also ceased. I could feel them melting, filling my facial orifices with slime. Did I get dosed? I tried to shake the millipede master off, and even though I could still feel its thousands of legs creeping all over my body, it wasn't there anymore.

I felt around the pitch-black bathroom and tried to grab onto something to lift myself away from the gatekeeper. Somehow, I managed to find the corner of the tub. I pulled myself up with one hand and put the other down on the tiled floor to support my weight. But my hand didn't touch the cold tiled floor. It touched a foot. Nothing moved. Nothing made a sound. I pulled myself toward the tub, planning to get into it.

The glasses on the helmet flickered back on.

*"AAAAHHHHHHH!"*

Thousands of screams filled the room.

Standing over me were the rest of the druggie rich kids. All naked, they lifted their fingers and pointed at me. I tried to rip off the fucking helmet. If I didn't see it, it wasn't there, right? That's what Hoop had said: "You can see things that aren't there."

I slipped sideways toward the tub and reached inside. The bathtub wasn't filled with water. It was alive.

Cockroaches, worms, and more centipedes dug themselves into my skin. All at once the rich kids' bodies began bubbling everywhere. One by one, they started falling. Their living, ravenous blisters popped open like their skin was giving birth. Dogs, squirrels, raccoons, rats, and opossums dug through their organs and chewed them to pieces from the inside out. Each of the husks held dozens of animals. I hammered away at the helmet with my gun. It wasn't budging. It had somehow meshed with my head and it ripped at my skin whenever I attempted to push it off.

As the bugs in the tub covered my arm, chaining me in place, one of the rich kids crawled toward me. When he felt my body, he grabbed onto my shirt and showed me his face.

It was the eyeless, hairless, bloody face of Bobo. He started snapping at my face as the rest of the fucking disgusting mutant animals attacked and bit at me from every direction. Two bigger millipedes crawled into each of the openings at the bottom of my pants. Once again, my skin froze as their legs crept continuously up my body.

I looked beyond the bathroom into the master bedroom and saw something through the helmet that I hadn't noticed before. Under the window, on the far side of the bed, there was a flashing red box just like the one in Hoop's store.

With every bit of strength I had left, I started flapping my arms and kicking my feet. I shot at the buzzing rich kids that were piled up on the floor. I managed to kick Bobo away and unhook my arm from the creatures in the tub. The more I shot, the more things turned to mush.

"Fuck you, Bobo!" I said, managing to plug a hole in the center of its eyeless face.

I torpedoed myself over the pile of bodies and stumbled out of the bathroom.

"Fuck all of you! Fuck all of you motherfuckers. I'm Danny Motherfucking Snaps. I'm the big dog."

Trying to make it to the red, flashing square, I tripped over one of the rich kids. The monstrosities from the bathroom piled up on each other, chasing me like I was their dinner. One of the millipedes trapped between my gut and my leg began pushing itself into my asshole. I felt the rugged, rubbery hide making its way into my stomach. I got back up and threw myself, butt first, onto the red square, the safe zone. As I landed, the creature melted inside me and dripped out of me like warm diarrhea.

"I'm Danny Fucking Snaps," I yelled. "I'm Danny Fucking Snaps."

Just as the horde reached the corner of the red square, the walls closed in, and a bright light flashed, tearing through the beasts like a thousand machine guns. The screams all went silent and in a split second, the walls were painted with everything living in the room. All the monsters became lifeless mush and what was left of them dripped from the ceiling and walls like a rainstorm of tar.

The floor rumbled under my ass and as the entire mansion cracked and broke to pieces, the pink and turquoise lights from outside bounced in. Tree limbs and vines came to life and smashed through concrete. The world tipped sideways, making me vomit. I tried to curl up into a ball to avoid being crushed as the entire mansion imploded around me.

Everything went white.

And as the world re-opened, the red square became a rusted cage. Sleet pounded into my shivering and achy body. For some reason, I was standing on four legs. The matted fur covering my body was clumped together with blood. It was almost impossible to stand on my right front leg because the bones were shattered from top to bottom and wrapped with a greasy oil rag.

I tried to speak. I wanted to cry out to anyone, but I didn't have any voice. I could almost whimper, but the shaking made it difficult to make any noise other than the chattering of my few teeth. The overpowering fumes from my urine became thick and I couldn't keep my eyes open. I tried to bend my head back to catch some of the rain to cleanse them, but that only hurt more. The sleet felt like darts piercing my eyes.

The blur of two bodies moved toward me. I tried to stand straight and look directly at them.

*"I'm in here! It's me, Danny Snaps!"*

Nothing was coming out.

I limped closer to the fence. The figures became two men wearing raincoats.

*Help me, please.*

"Wow. This dog is really fucked up," one of them said. "Glad we followed this tip. There is definitely abuse going on here."

*Dog? It's Danny Snaps. You know, Lil Snap? The Skinny Little White Kid Who Can Spit!*

"Zoom in on his eyes. Make sure you get it looking directly into the camera. This is the worst example of animal abuse I've seen in a long time."

*Animal abuse? It's Danny Sapperstein. The son of Russ Sapperstein.*

The second figure, a fat guy with a camera over his shoulder, bent toward the front of the cage. He winked at me behind his wet and foggy glasses. "Copy that. You're the director," he said.

I could barely make out his face, but when I saw the thick glasses and heard the accent, I knew it was that motherfucker Hoop. He must have somehow dosed me back at the Trap House. Motherfucker!

"Man," the first guy said as he shook the chain cage. "We're gonna get paid from this footage."

Hoop blew into my nostrils, making me sneeze. It felt like I had rocks lodged in my throat. "Hundreds of millions of people are going to see this mutt every day. Over and over again. It will be almost as if they are living his despair on constant repeat. This will be the most famous dog in the world."

"I hear you," the director said. "This is even better than the footage we got of those cats that were starving to death. Should we get him out of there?"

"You know the rules." He took his camera off his shoulder and wiped the lens with a cloth. "We can't get involved." Staring directly at me, he added, "Besides…" He tapped on a lock on the front of my cage. "…he's locked in."

"We can break that lock." The director pointed back into the heavy sleet, which was becoming snow. "I have a crowbar in the van."

*Let me outta here! Please. Let me out.*

Hoop stuck his finger in the cage and flicked me on the snout. I growled and bit at it.

He pulled his hand out. "We could be dealing with rabies here, Sam. Who knows what kind of diseases this little snapper is carrying. Like I said, it's best we leave it to Animal Control and get back to the hotel."

"Little snapper. You Rhode Islanders sure have a way with words. Lil Snap," the director, Sam, giggled. "Whatever happened to that loser?"

Hoop stood up, continuing to stare at me. "He was a bad kid. Bad kids eventually get punished."

"Should we at least give this poor fucker a treat?"

"All I got are these." Hoop reached into the pocket of his poncho. He pulled out two Snickers bars.

I licked my chops, and my back leg gave out. I fell into a pile of my own shit.

The director started walking away. "Give them to him and hurry up. I wanna get into some dry clothes and hit the bar."

"What are you? Stupid?" Hoop said as he unwrapped one of the candy bars. "Dogs can't eat chocolate. That'll kill them."

"If I were that fucking dog, I'd want to be dead."

*Please kill me.*

"You're going to finally get the fame you deserve," Hoop whispered into the cage.

"What was that?" the director called back as he flung open the side door of his van.

"Doesn't matter. Let's call it a day. I got the first round," Hoop said as he took a giant bite out of his Snickers bar. "Trick or treat, Lil Snap."

# THE
# SCRATCHING POST

DANI BROWN

Goddamn cats kept staring at me like I owed them something. The tap in the bathroom dripped. My parents were on a cruise ship holiday drinking cocktails and avoiding explosive diarrhoea-inducing infections. They forgot to deposit extra into my bank account for emergency repairs and expenses and expected me to live with the dripping tap.

Furry faces glared. I suppose it was better than looking at their shit-crusted rear-ends. They liked rubbing those in my face no matter how many times I sprayed them with the water bottle. If they didn't look so good on my social media profiles, I'd consider dumping them.

One of the beasts decided the food I provided wasn't good enough and took it out on my foot. I stamped on its tail. I saved these cats from a lifetime of cat shows and children dripping ice lollies into their glossy fur.

Beloved family pets my arse. I walked past my latest acquisition's missing poster each time I went for an ice mocha with extra cream and chocolate drizzle. Some bitch is claiming how much her children love the cat. No, I think she loves the money that comes with being a cat influencer.

I resumed my scrolling. My phone was set up with my actual social media accounts under my actual name. I had four different tablets set up with four different identities; three female and one male. It is much easier that way. No more signing out and signing back in. All I do is grab a device off the coffee table and agree with myself in a comment posted by my alter egos.

It wasn't long after I started scrolling again that I heard the tell-tale sound of a cat pissing on my hardwood floors. I launched a throw pillow in the general direction. They should be grateful I gave them a home and provided them with friends. They must get lonely when I leave to get an iced mocha with extra cream and chocolate drizzle. It isn't like the barista gets my order right the first time, so

I always have to wait for a second one to be made.

The cat hissed before running off. The other cats looked but didn't follow. All that inbreeding for the finest pedigrees didn't allow for intelligence.

I locked in on my newest target—Sophie. She's Charlie's new girlfriend, and I can't wait to *help* them. Charlie thinks he's my best friend. Let's hope Sophie is mentally stronger than his last GF. A picture of her in her underwear stared back from my phone screen on Charlie's profile. I added a heart react and went to commenting.

*I would be so embarrassed to show off my stretch marks like that. It is nice to see someone who doesn't care.* I picked up a tablet and added *I know she's so beautiful.* With my second tablet I added *She's setting such a good example. Companies airbrush models. It is so nice to see someone not afraid to show their tiger stripes.* And with the male tablet *Such an inspiration.* Someone else was typing. *I know, right?*

My phone chimed. I picked it up. Charlie sent me full-frontal nudes of her. He knew what I liked without being told. His last girlfriend was furious when she found that out. He told her she had nothing to be ashamed of and everyone loves her, but she was still mad, which is why she's an ex. I saved them to my album. You never know when something like that will come in handy. By the time I saved the pictures of Sophie and responded to them, ten more comments had been added, all agreeing with me.

Charlie surrounded himself with my accounts, which in turn altered how he saw the world and then attracted more people who agreed with my point of view. Everyone else was wrong. They had a bad worldview. But Charlie didn't need to know much about everyone else, he just had to believe me when I told him who was toxic.

I left to get my iced mocha with extra cream and chocolate drizzle. He messaged me while I was out, but I couldn't very well respond with the coffee in my hand.

The cats' former collars jangled when I entered my flat. I saved them all, but I couldn't remember which one belonged to which cat. I loved that sound. I liberated them from their bells. They no longer had to hunt birds either. I provided all the cat food and treats.

I sat on my sofa and read through the messages. Turns out his new girlfriend did not appreciate being put on display, much like the last one. I talked him through how to handle it and was glad to hear he'd already promised her a new job working for his parents. It was much better than collecting on the dole. I responded about how helpful he was. There's no way that girl would be able to get a job on her own. She'd just have to put up with his snap-happy fingers if she wanted to eat and not be homeless.

He sent me more blocks of text, but I was already reading his passive-aggressive status update about having to remove the pictures. I laughed and had a sip of my ice mocha.

These cats were relentless. The friendlier cats started head butting me for attention. The wretched felines couldn't see I was busy. I doubt their previous owners gave them any affection. Little Jenny decided now was a perfectly good time to drag her rear-end across my hardwood floor leaving a trail of shit. That wouldn't look good on social media. I liked giving my cats new names. I based them off the ungrateful little snobs I took under my wing. They always abandoned me in the end.

*Are you still there?*

I texted him, *Yeah, sorry, one of my cats has made a mess, I'll be right back.*

I grabbed her by the scruff and rubbed her squashed nose across the mess. She tried to resist but knew better than to claw me. Last time one of the feline fuckers decided to try to take a chunk of my flesh I covered all of their feet in baby socks. Her white fur came away in my hands.

I covered the trail with paper towels. It wasn't my job to wipe up shit. That's why I had a cleaning lady two times each week. My parents wouldn't let her come a third. It was so unfair. They didn't know how bad living with ten fucking cats smelt. I sprayed some air freshener. It wasn't the same as the scent of Kadine's cleaning products.

I sat back down on my sofa to read Charlie's texts. The foam moulded to fit my body perfectly. I didn't want him to screw up things with this girl until the timing was right, unlike the last girl. That was a complete disaster. I didn't even get a new cat out of the ordeal. She had a massive fucking stick up her arse. And he pushed her too far too soon.

I told him things like *free sex takes a bit of warming up to first*, but he didn't listen to me preferring instead the advice of his cock. I guess he wanted to impress some people he hardly knew with the size of her breasts and her willingness to climb abroad and ride, but she wasn't willing. She wasn't bi-curious, bi-sexual or bi-anything either despite all the sex with women and mood swings.

We both could have found ourselves in a lot of trouble if she decided to go to the police. Luckily, so far, she hasn't. At the start of the relationship, he had her grooming some girl whose boyfriend left. Only she didn't realise she was grooming. She thought she was lending a shoulder to cry on. The police won't see it like that and she'll go down too. The girl wasn't in a frame of mind to consent to anything, and Charlie still had sex with her after his last girlfriend worked some chat magic.

According to the texts, this one wasn't willing to engage in promiscuous group sex either, but he hadn't given it time to work on her. She claimed she didn't have the time to *help* another woman going through a rough patch. *I'm reading your texts now. Give me a few minutes. Remember, these things take patience.*

He texted back right away. *She's texting me now. She's just going off on me.* I responded with my form reply. *Okay, calm down. We can fix this. You need to think positive.* Charlie could have been any other of the guys I speak to. They were all the same. I needed more women in this little online social circle. The men always scared them away so they never wanted to meet up in person.

I spread myself out and took a sip of my extra iced mocha with cream and chocolate drizzle. I bought two so I wouldn't have to go out again today. People were being weird out there and I didn't want to get caught in rush hour and the school runs. I hated children. They were always in the way. Rush hour could prove interesting, but only when the schools weren't in session. Throw children into the mix and everything gets screwed up. Parents never approved when my foot connected with a child's fat, usually wet arse and lifted them a few feet into the air. More than one have threatened me with the police over a little kick. It isn't like the police ever actually do anything. But I wasn't in the mood for any drama today.

Timmy decided now was a good time to sharpen his claws on my sofa. I whacked him over the head with a cushion. I wished I lived in a country where declawing was a thing. I couldn't even find someone on the black market willing to carry out the procedure. At least he doesn't have a squashed face, but his fur was looking awful and matted. I'd have to brush him later to look good in my social media uploads. Unfortunately, it took too long to *Photoshop* the matts away.

"Fuck off you little shit."

These text messages were important. We couldn't afford another screw up. Charlie might start thinking for himself, which would be dreadful. It is a lot easier to pass Charlie's exes as crazy than it would be to convince Charlie he's crazy.

*Can you screenshot her messages?*

I scrolled while I waited. Chanel had a new range of handbags. I checked my bank account. I couldn't get extra from Mummy and Daddy while they were on their fucking cruise. They didn't understand the importance of the latest designer handbag either. I couldn't show up anywhere with last season's. Claimed they were grieving over DiDi and needed to get away from the world. It has been two fucking years. They needed to get over it. They've been on and off cruise ships since the funeral. They spent more time on and refused to pay for the roaming charges.

My sister was a stupid bitch anyways. She lacked any comprehension about how the world worked. She tried to convince my parents that they should start cutting the apron strings and I should get a job. She made her choices and wasted years of her life at university. She paid into a pension and she'd never get to spend it. A total waste.

I found an article about consent and posted it on my social media page. Articles like those kept the heat off me. People in my circle knew better than to question my behaviour because I was so anti-rape. Whoever the douchebag on the other side of the three-typing dots was lapped up all my words. They'd be sure to repost it with their own word-salad opinion. If it's a man behind those three dots he'll leave out the part about how he wears down a woman until she gives in. I'll have Charlie repost it in a few minutes.

The screenshots arrived. They were angry, typed out in caps. She just said "no" repeatedly and clearly explained her reasons for not wanting her bedroom snaps online. *Tell her she needs a doctor. She isn't making any sense. Say you're worried about her. Your parents won't hire her if she acts all cray-cray.* She'll relent by the end of the day. Tomorrow, Charlie will have her grooming some unsuspecting woman for a threesome. *But most of all, be patient. The ones that resist the most are the ones most worth it. Sophie could be your future wife.*

I picked up a tablet to interact with the article I just posted. *It isn't hard to ask for consent. It is like asking if someone wants sugar in their tea and respecting the answer.* I picked up the next tablet to like that comment. I had to be careful about how the accounts interacted with each other. I didn't want anyone in real life to be onto me.

Max, who is like the love of my life but doesn't realise it yet, will block all my accounts if he knew about them. He's just frightened of his feelings. Men need time to get used to them. I checked on his profile before I went to the next tablet.

A quick search of his name brought up more pictures from a secret *Twitter* account I didn't know he had. The same girl appeared in lots of them. I clicked. I needed to know her name. I accidentally liked the picture as I clicked. *Undo! Undo! Undo!* I threw the tablet across the room. It seemed to be glitching and kept liking and unliking the picture.

I just wanted to know who the girl was. I took a sip of my second iced mocha to calm myself. I couldn't risk shaking hands while finding out who this girl was. It'll let Max onto me. The girl looked like a total prostitute with her fake eyelashes and frosted lips.

I decided to set up a new identity specific for learning about this girl. I didn't want to compromise any of my other profiles if my thumb slipped again. Luckily, I had ten extra email addresses already, so all I had to do was assign one to a sleeper social media presence, ready to be utilised beyond online stalking if the need should arise.

The cats gathered around me.

"What do you want? I've fed you. You have fresh water. It is nearly time for a photo-shoot to earn those likes. I'm busy right now. Go play on your cat-tree, I paid enough for it."

I didn't add a photo to the new profile, only a generic name. I could be anyone clicking on those photos and finding out who stole Max's attention. She had a stupid smile plastered across her face in every image, all except the one that was taken from above with her mouth open. She looked like a largemouth bass waiting for a spray of cum to land on her tongue while someone pulls on her girlish pigtails.

Max needed to get it all out of his system before he settles down with me. Satisfied this girl was nothing more than a cheap whore, I set up the camera for the cats. Taking selfies with them was a sure way to instant social media superstardom. I even recorded a short video with plenty of duck lips from me and added an old song. It is easy to get cats to do what I want.

I woke up to a terrible banging from next door. The bells on the cats' old collars jinged from the front door. This place was meant to be soundproof. I was sold on a lie. I couldn't even phone my parents to complain. They fucking lived on cruise ships these days.

The cats sat watching the wall move from all the banging. *What the actual fuck was going on in there?* I threw a pillow but that wasn't hard enough to get them to stop. It was too early for this shit.

I stumbled out of bed and put my foot in a warm puddle of sick. Goddamn fucking cats! I don't get why Kadine wouldn't come an extra day without pay. She should be grateful to be in this country and have a fucking job.

The banging next door opened the kitchen cupboards. Food boxes toppled and spilled all over the floor. I couldn't hold in my scream any longer. Someone needs to get here and fix this shit. It looks like an earthquake happened inside my flat.

I grabbed my phone and ignored the notifications. I don't care if Kadine wasn't scheduled to be here until tomorrow she needed to get here now. She didn't reply to my text, so I started phoning. I hate talking on the phone. It went straight to voicemail. That stupid bitch should be accessible one hundred percent of the time. She needed to learn her place in this world.

I couldn't think straight with that incessant noise next door and the kitchen cupboard contents strewn across the floor. I had to get out.

My phone chimed. It wasn't fucking Kadine but Charlie. I didn't bother to read it. It could wait. I had to get out now.

I grabbed my keys from the counter. Somehow they escaped a dusting of flour. I couldn't find my handbag and shoes, so I ran back to my bedroom. The banging was louder in there. I hit my fist against the wall but all that accomplished was pain.

I found a handbag though. It smelt of fresh cat piss, and when I picked it up, urine poured out and down my arm. I ran into the en suite and wiped myself with wet toilet paper wipes. If they can clean my arse after curry night, then they're good enough for cat piss. There was no way I was going to take a shower with all that racket.

It was becoming increasingly hard to think with the banging next door. My phone chimed again. Charlie. Again. *I'm having a crisis. Someone is banging next door and the cats peed all over my handbag.* I didn't bother reading what he wrote. It wasn't as important as what I was going through. I didn't bother to read his response either.

I dug through my wardrobe trying to find another handbag. I had loads, but I needed to be seen with the right bag and matching shoes. I found a pouch full of the dustcovers but couldn't find my handbags. I bet Kadine stole them. She's the only other person with access.

The banging from next door grew louder and more incessant, shaking the centre of my brain. I pulled stuff out of my wardrobe. Kadine can sort it out. She needs to iron the clothes, too. The cats watched.

"Which one of you motherfuckers pissed on my bag?"

At the very back of the closet, I found my bags. Kadine can put them in the dustcovers when she puts everything back. I'll have to sleep in the guestroom tonight unless she answers her fucking phone. I made my distress clear in the messages I sent her.

Something smelt awful as I made my way to the lift. A weird combination of cheap fast food and human faecal matter with undertones of cat piss. I can never escape the scent of cat piss. It follows me everywhere. My stomach bubbled.

I kept pressing the button. The damn thing needed to move quicker. If I didn't get out of here, I would have a total panic attack. Finally it arrived. That's when I noticed the grime on my pressing finger. I reached into my bag, but this one had just come out of my wardrobe. Any wipes in it would long be dried.

I stamped my feet. The lift couldn't move fast enough. We stopped at another floor on the way down. Some woman that I've never seen before stepped in with a pram. Her child's sticky hands reached for my clean dress.

"This is silk."

The woman looked at me.

"There's plenty of room for both us."

"I was here first. What are you doing in here anyways?"

I looked her up and down making note of her grubby canvas trainers and stained three quarter length trousers.

"You clearly don't belong here. Who are you working for?"

"I live here."

"I doubt that."

The lift spat us out at the bottom. I ran to the concierge without even stopping in the toilets to wash my finger.

"That woman doesn't belong in here."

I was careful not to cross my arms with the filth on my pressing finger.

"Look at what the child did to my dress. Tell me who she works for so I can lodge a formal complaint."

He ignored me and instead turned to the woman. I smirked from the desk.

"Good day, Mrs Duckworth. How's the little one?"

"Excuse me, her brat ruined my dress."

The concierge turned to me.

"Shall we replay the CCTV? There was plenty of space for you to move away from her pram."

The concierge made faces at the snot-nosed brat.

"Any mail?" Mrs Duckworth asked.

"Let me just see."

"Aren't you going to do something?"

"He's a baby. He did what baby's do. It is your responsibility to stay out of the way of his fingers."

"I'm going to report you to management."

"You do that."

"You just wait until my parents hear about this."

"They still off on their cruise? Did they leave their thirty-year-old daughter all alone in the big city?"

"Don't talk down to me. My service charges pay your wages."

Two men tried to get into the building with a sofa.

"Isn't there meant to be a side entrance for that?"

"It is out of order today."

"Well then fix it."

"I've alerted the correct people but with the weekend looming, there's nothing they can do. I can't let them leave the new tenant's stuff out on the street now, can I?"

"Is that what all the banging was? A new tenant? He fucking woke me up."

"Watch your language, Amy."

"Don't tell me what to do."

"You're the one standing here trying to start an argument."

"You aren't doing your job. I pay your wages."

The sofa stuck in the doorway.

"That door isn't wide enough for a fucking sofa."

The concierge looked up.

"What the fuck is wrong with you people?"

All eyes were on the sofa stuck in the entrance. I needed to get out of this building.

"That's a fire hazard! I'm going to report you."

"Just a minute, gentlemen, and I can have that door opened right up for you."

The concierge stepped out from behind his desk. I stood in front of him and put my hands on my hips before remembering the grime on my finger.

"You need to call the fire brigade immediately."

"Will you get out of my way, Amy, I have a job to do. But you wouldn't understand about that."

"It isn't my fault my parents love me and you have to slave away."

He stepped around me and went to a cupboard. He found a pole inside.

"What is that going to do? Hook the sofa in?"

My phone chimed from my bag. If that was Kadine she wouldn't be able to get in the building. I took it out. It was Charlie again. He really didn't understand about a crisis.

"Will you get out of the way, Missy?"

I looked up. The two men had the sofa inside the building.

"That's not how you ask someone to move."

The concierge held the pole in a hook in the glass front of the building and was pulling it shut. I didn't realise the front could open up like that.

"Will you please move out of the way, Miss, this is heavy."

The man put on a fake posh accent. I moved.

"What's your problem?"

"This is heavy and you're standing around having a strop."

While the movers were busy distracting me, the woman with the baby left without saying how she was going to pay for my dress to be dry-cleaned. At least it wasn't my job to clean the muddy footprints the movers left on the way to the lift. That better be cleaned by the time I get back.

"Concierge." I put on my sweetest voice and waved him down like I would a waiter.

"Yes, Miss Amy?"

"Will the lift be cleaned by the time I get back? My dress has already been damaged by the awful offspring of that dreadful woman and there was dirt on the button when I was pressing it to get down. That dirt ended up on my finger without my notice and now it is on my dress. Who is going to take it to the dry-cleaners and pay?"

"Amy, your dress is not my problem. Dresses get dirty. You need to get over it. The cleaners won't be in until Monday."

"Monday! They should be here every day."

"It is the weekend. They only come in for mornings, and people who work, they like a day off once in a while."

"The nerve."

"I know. The nerve of people needing rest and wanting some time with their families, maybe they're working on getting a degree."

He started to ramble. I left. I wasn't going to stand there and listen about other people's pathetic lives. It isn't my fault their parents didn't love them.

I left the flat without any breakfast. Each restaurant I walked past had too many people. With a dirty dress and a season's old handbag, I wouldn't get preferred treatment and would have to wait. I wasn't about to eat fast food though. Yuck! Fridays unleashed the worst of humanity from office blocks earlier than usual. Even the unemployed came out in droves to window shop for items they'd never be able to afford.

Christmas specials and reduced Halloween sweets sat side-by-side as if we needed an imported American celebration of poor dental hygiene and obesity. The wind kicked up with a chill to travel right through my dress before it was gone and the unseasonable heat returned. Winter delayed further every year. All those stupid Americans and their huge 4x4s and denial of manmade global warming. Anything less than is deemed unpatriotic. I wouldn't complain except I hated carrying around enough clothes to cover me for four seasons in one day.

The wind came back to push up my skirt from behind. I ducked into the nearest restaurant. The greeter was busy with a family of four and then after them another family. Children should be banned.

To kill time, I pulled out my phone and replied to Charlie.

If it's still windy after breakfast, I'm going to have to stop and pick up some new clothes. My parents didn't leave enough money for me to go boutique shopping. I'll have to get a mass-produced autumn jacket. Autumn jackets and silk dresses don't match, so I'll need a new dress which will further cut into my budget. My allowance won't clear into my bank account until next week. Budgeting is so stressful.

I didn't know the passwords for my other social media accounts, so I had to cope with my own account without anyone to backup what I was saying. I couldn't even stalk Max or find out more about that girl he was seeing.

The children in the restaurant kept screaming. It made it difficult to think. The shrill cries went right through the centre of my head. I waved over the waitress and asked for whisky to go with my breakfast. It was past lunchtime on a Friday, no one would raise an eyebrow.

Once I purchased the new dress and jacket, I went to the makeup counter. I had no intention of buying anything, but the free makeover would sort out my face. By the time I left the shop, I looked put together, but people still made a funny face at me. One looked like disgust after smelling something rotten.

I stopped at a supermarket for cat food and deodorant. It still wasn't good enough. I overheard the child behind me saying *Mummy, why does that lady smell bad?* I turned around and bared my teeth. I would get them filed into points but that puts off everyone, not just the people beneath me.

Boxes were being moved in when I arrived home. The concierge didn't seem to care. I had to wait longer for the lift than I should have.

"Why isn't the service lift working?"

"I already told you, Amy, it is the weekend. No one can come out until Monday at the earliest."

"I need to get this stuff home. I don't have the time to be waiting around here."

The lift opened.

"There's your lift. Goodbye, Amy."

I stepped in and it was blissfully empty, but it smelt terrible, like rotten fast food. I just bought these clothes and with the lift being so slow they're going to pick up the scent. Finally, it stopped at my floor without anyone getting in on the way. The movers were waiting when I stepped out.

"Hey, do you know why the entire corridor smells like cat piss?"

I didn't bother to give them a response. I just wanted to get in and bathe and check up on Max.

I dropped my shopping. The cats waited by the door.

"What do you want from me?"

They stared.

"Stop looking at me. Go on now. Go to your cat tree, I paid good money for that."

I grabbed my tablet with my secret identity connected to it on my way to the bath. I ran the bath with an added bath bomb. I went to log on to the social media accounts and the connection was gone.

I ran to the sofa for my other tablets. The WiFi was gone on all of them. I couldn't waste time logging in and out of various accounts on my phone. I didn't even have the passwords. The tablets saved those automatically.

At least the banging next door had stopped, but without my WiFi, my night was as good as ruined. I sat on the side of the bath while it ran and used the 5G on my phone to check if the network was down. Apparently it wasn't.

Not all my tablets could be broken at once. I ran to the modem. It had the red light. I knew the bill was paid. It went out of my parents account by direct debit every month. I don't even think they noticed and they were on a cruise. Cancelling my WiFi was not their top priority.

I turned it off and back on again after waiting thirty seconds. I ran to check on my bath. A cat caught under my feet and I went down. This was not shaping up to be a good day. I screamed and banged my fists on the hardwood floor. By the time I pushed myself up, I heard the water splashing over the side of the tub.

My phone chimed. That would be Charlie again. I doubted it was Kadine. As soon as my parents get back, I intend to bring up the issue of the cleaning woman with them. She absolutely sucked.

I switched off the taps and lapped up the water with a towel. I didn't know where the mop was stored. I tried phoning Kadine but she once again wouldn't answer. Surely she could tell it was an emergency?

The banging next door started again. I really don't give a shit if they have furniture to assemble. They've already clogged the lift and made the corridor reek of fast food.

My phone started ringing. It should have been fucking Kadine. It wasn't. It was Charlie. He should know better than to phone me. It wasn't like I was going to answer.

I invited him over via text when it finally stopped ringing. It'll be better to sort this out in person and he could clean my floor. I grabbed my tablets from the sofa and shoved them into my wardrobe. Someone might notice the other personas not being active. I grabbed my pink satin dressing gown while I was in there. I took off everything else. I could use the family bathroom to shower. Even though I really wanted a bath, I didn't want to miss Charlie's ring.

Fifteen minutes later, I buzzed him in.

"It smells out there."

He was a cat person so the scent of *eau de* cat piss didn't register.

"Quick before the cats get out."

He was visibly upset but there were more pressing issues beyond his new girlfriend. The cat collar bells jangled.

"Did you get more cats since I've last been over?"

"Probably."

He followed me in.

"The WiFi is down and I don't know why and the en suite flooded. Can you help me with the water? I don't know where Kadine keeps the mop. If it starts seeping through the floor the concierge is going to come up here and start shouting. Why won't this day just fucking end?"

"Where's your modem?"

I pointed. He switched it on and off.

"I've already done that."

He unplugged it at the wall.

"Wait a few minutes. That might do it. Did you check to see if there's any service issues?"

"Yes. There weren't any. At all. Anywhere."

"Have you phoned the company?"

"No. I don't know the account number and it is set up in my mother's name. They're on a cruise right now."

"Well, let's hope we can get it working."

The cats came over to see what we were doing. Charlie fussed over them.

"How much does a cat like this set you back?"

I wouldn't know. I shrugged.

He plugged the modem back in. The lights started to flash, but it was nothing more than false hope. I couldn't tether everything to my phone. That would slow down all the devices.

I sent a text to my mother in hopes she'd be able to respond soon. They didn't like having their phones on while out at sea. They'd get the same roaming charges wherever they ported next. I think my parents kept their phones off because they didn't want to deal with my needs. They should have equipped me better for the real world.

Charlie cleaned up the bathroom for me. His phone kept ringing while he was doing it.

"Don't answer," I told him. "She has to learn."

"I upset her before."

I shrugged.

"How she reacts is her problem. Not yours."

My fingers traced his neck as I said this.

"Yeah, fuck her," he mumbled.

With a twitch of my shoulder my dressing gown opened revealing how I wasn't wearing anything underneath. I had seduction down to an exact art and I knew exactly what Charlie liked. His phone rang again.

"Switch it off."

I pressed my body against his. His erection pressed into my thigh. I went for his belt buckle.

"Tell her you're in an open relationship when she asks where you were. You have to lay down the rules with her early on, otherwise she'll walk all over you."

I went to my knees in front of him. His dick tasted sour, like he hadn't washed. Normally, he tastes of soap. If Max can have fun with some hussy, I can too. It will help us settle down when we're finally together.

My salvia washed away the taste. Charlie moaned a little. Not a loud sound. It is how I imagine Max would sound. With my eyes closed it was like sucking off Max. Charlie's hands held my jaw and laced around the back of my head. I knew what was coming next and braced myself for it.

I have loads of practice giving head. I know to stop before he cums if I want something in return. I usually know just when that moment will be, especially with Charlie. We've been here so many times before.

Charlie slipped my dressing gown from my shoulders. The lights in my flat are designed to be flattering. I know I'm not perfect, but my company doesn't need to know that.

He sat back on the sofa and lowered me onto him. He reached between my legs to put a condom on.

After a few minutes of soft and sensual, I screamed and started riding him hard. I didn't care if the condom tore. I knew I was clean. Besides, there's treatments for just about everything these days.

We went through an entire box of condoms. It was obvious his new girlfriend wasn't putting out. No man can last that long.

"I should go," he eventually said.

I was naked in his arms pretending he was Max. He started to sit up. I followed the movements of his body with my own until I too was sitting. He stood and stretched with a yawn.

"Don't switch your phone on until you get home," I advised.

He nodded.

"It looks cold out there," he said.

The cats meowed at him as if in agreement.

"They're so sweet."

He bent down to scratch one behind the ears.

"Did you have a coat?"

He shook his head.

"I'll see what I can find."

I went into the guest room. I keep a selection of men's clothing in here just in case. I found a coat that looked like it would fit him. I tore the tags off and put them in the pocket. I didn't want him to know that I kept new clothes for visitors, but I did want him to know how much I paid for it.

"Maybe we'll see winter this year," I said as I handed him the coat. "Thanks for coming over."

"No problem. Thanks for the girlfriend tips. And the coat."

I winked.

"She needs our help, Charlie."

I yawned even though I didn't need to. I wanted him gone. He leaned in to kiss me on the cheek. I stood there and let him.

"At least your building isn't like a maze."

The tap was still dripping when Kadine woke me up with loud proclamations of "gross" in her Caribbean accent. I assumed she found the used condoms. She's pretty used to cat shit by now. If she's going to live and work in this country, she needs to get used to the British way.

She works on a Saturday. I don't get why no one else does. The world doesn't stop just because it is the weekend.

"Can you keep it down in there? I'm trying to sleep."

I rolled over. She didn't even try to apologise. The cats ran out of the bedroom upon realising they weren't getting any food from me yet.

Last night, my vagina had a bit of a dull ache from the heavy riding. When I woke up, it was an active throb and itch. Charlie gave me something! The nerve of him. I went to shower in the family bathroom. Kadine left it sparkling. I didn't even hear her come in to mop up the rest of the mess in the en suite. These things need a professional touch. Although I must say, Charlie did an excellent job.

I felt hot and a bit shaky. The water cooled me off. I took the showerhead down to run over my vagina. It seemed swollen. The cold water felt good in a nonsexual way.

The new neighbour stumbled out of his flat as I locked my door.

"Why does it smell like cat piss out here?"

I don't know if he was talking to me or asking the air. I didn't respond. His loud American accent travelled right through me. I already felt feverish. He followed me to the lift.

"I know what you were doing last night."

He smiled with unclean teeth.

"I thought America had the best dentists in the world."

"Call me Hoop."

He held out his hand, but I didn't take it. I wasn't about to touch him.

"My associate Phillips mentioned London has the best hookers in the world."

He smiled.

"Do Americans ever know when to shut up?"

"He never mentioned about the lack of water in the toilets. How do you lot stop them from streaking?"

The lift opened. He followed me in. Right after the door shut, he lifted his leg to fart.

"Going down."

I rolled my eyes. He made rude sex gestures with his hands and his tongue pressed against his cheek.

"If London's hookers are anything like how you sounded last night, I'm going to be in for a world of a good time. I certainly hope they are better than the surfing. Newquay was like riding my board through sewage. I never rode waves at Misquamicut, but kids shit in that water all the time and it is cleaner. If it weren't ocean, I'd swear you could drink it."

I assumed he was talking about where he was from.

"Then why don't you go back there?"

I had the last word. The lift opened and spewed us out.

The concierge looked busy, and I was in too much pain to stop and wait. I'd phone management later, once the painkillers take effect. I went to the chemist before picking up my iced mocha with chocolate drizzle and whipped cream. This seemed like a day for a normal mocha. That would also come with cream and chocolate drizzle.

There was a long queue to speak with the chemist. I needed treatment right now. I didn't want to have to take the tube to the hospital so some student nurse could put my feet up in stirrups and poke and prod and make the swelling worse. I whispered my problem to the male pharmacist. He was kinda cute but this would ruin my chances with him.

"Howdy neighbour."

I breathed deep—or rather tried. The smell of fast food emanating from his grotesque form made me gag.

"What are you doing here? Did you follow me?"

Hoop didn't answer my question. Fine by me. I already hated his nasally American voice. The pharmacist returned with ointment and painkillers. He took the tube out of the box.

"Now, and I can imagine this is difficult, only use it twice per day. You can use an ice pack between your legs, but you really need to see a doctor. I can sell you three days' worth of codeine. Don't take with any other products that contain paracetamol."

I think the entire shop heard him. He rang up my purchases as I went bright red. He can go suck cocks in Hell if he thinks I'm only using the cream twice per day.

I was in such a rush to leave home I forgot to bring all my tablets. The coffee shop had free WiFi. This was not shaping into a very good weekend. At least my new neighbour didn't follow me in.

On the way out, some American tourists bumped into me and asked for directions to Buckingham Palace. I told them to go fuck themselves. I think I reached my limits for dealing with Americans for one day. I deserved a medal for not having a meltdown.

My weekend would have been uneventful if it weren't for Hoop, my vagina, and my lack of WiFi. My parents still haven't returned my text messages. They must port somewhere at the weekends. I know they answer my brother's texts. He told me. He told me they check their phones nightly with the ship's roaming. It was an emergency. I had to go out and buy a Blu-Ray player so I'd have some form of entertainment.

Hoop stepped into the lift with live lobsters.

"I think those are illegal."

"Oh, I'm not going to eat these. They're for my fish tank."

He winked and smirked. He held them up to my eyes. Their claws were tied with elastic bands.

"You know, in Rhode Island we can go into a restaurant and choose whatever lobster we want to eat right out of the tank and the chef comes and boils them alive."

"You know lobsters are like the vacuums of the sea, right? They literally live off fish shit and you eat them."

He farted in response. I held my breath. But I couldn't make it all the way up to our floor without breathing.

"You're going a bit red in the face there." He poked my stomach. "Getting a bit pudgy, too, I see. Is it all those mochas? I like cream myself. I remember the cream from my last trip to Cornwall, so much better than the surfing in sewage."

The lift opened and I ran out, tripping over my feet.

"Opps." He laughed. Then he sniffed the air. "Is the smell of cat piss stronger? Those are your cats, aren't they? You need to change their litter box."

He waved around his bag of live lobsters while talking. I don't know how many he had in there.

"Don't tell me how to look after my cats. I know what I'm doing. You on the other hand are not allowed to have live fucking lobsters in this country. It's cruel."

The bag broke. Live lobsters and water with lobster shit landed on me. I screamed.

"Opps. Sorry neighbour. It's this bag. So flimsy and cheap."

"Get them off me! Gross. Real fucking gross."

"I already told you, they're for my fish tank."

"And then you're going to fucking eat them."

"I thought you said they are gross, why do you care what I do with them if they're so gross."

"Get them off me." The water soaked through my wool-cashmere blend coat. "This was expensive."

"You didn't pay for it, so why do you care?"

"My parents bought it for me, it has sentimental value."

"Like everything else in your flat?"

"I smell of fucking lobster."

"I'm sure your vagina looks like you were fucking a lobster. Still walking a bit funny, aren't you?"

Neighbours started poking their heads out of their flats.

"Help me."

They slammed the doors. All except one, some bratty super-rich Asian kid of Instagram or whatever the fuck they call themselves. He started to film with the latest goddamn iPhone.

"What are you looking at?"

Hoop still made no move to get the lobsters off me. They were crawling all over me. One went into my hair. I started to cry. The super-rich Asian snickered with his phone pointed.

I could hear my cats meowing at the door. They wanted their mummy. I reached for a lobster and ripped it off and threw it.

"Now, now, that's a bit cruel," Hoop said. "And to think, you accused me of cruelty. You're just regurgitating what you're told."

I made a decision there and then, Hoop was going to pay for this. I didn't care what it took, but he was going to pay.

"Hey, Amy," the super-rich Asian brat said.

"What?"

I looked over.

"You're internet famous. My live stream has over five million viewers with more coming in every second."

This wouldn't have happened if it weren't for Hoop.

"You should be filming him." I pointed at Hoop, but the phone stayed trained on me. "He's the one who dumped lobsters on me. I fucking hate lobsters. They're gross. They eat sea-shit and then people think they're a fucking delicacy. It isn't even legal to have live lobsters in this country. He's meant to buy them frozen. It is cruel to boil them alive."

"Shame you can't capture the smell on that phone of yours," Hoop said to the Asian kid.

"This entire hallway smells of cat piss and it all comes from her flat and yet she calls me gross for wanting to add some lobsters to my fish tank."

He winked when he said fish tank. I knew he was going to boil them alive. The Asian kid knew he was going to boil them alive. The viewing audience knew he was going to boil them alive.

"No one keeps lobsters in a fish tank."

"I do." He picked up the lobster I threw and waved it in front of my face. "What have you done to little Clawie?"

"How long can those things survive out of water?"

"Oh, a good forty-eight hours." He smirked.

He held the lobster right up to my nose. The stupid rich Asian brat stepped out of his flat and held the phone right over me.

"Stop fucking filming me."

"Why, Amy? We had to listen to your meltdowns and weird sex noises for the past year now. Me and my sister, we can't take anymore."

I grabbed another lobster and threw it at him. He dodged out of the way.

"Stop throwing my lobsters."

"Then get them off me. And buy me a new coat."

Hoop collected his lobsters. When it was clear the incident was over, the stupid Asian brat slammed the door to his flat. He lived a life of luxury on the bank of Mom and Dad. I didn't get why he had WiFi and 5G and I didn't. I had some 5G signal on my phone but no 4G signal.

"Hey," Hoop said, "Sorry about your WiFi. My guys will be in to fix it within the next few days."

"What the actual fuck? You did that?"

"Yeah, I said sorry."

I had no more lobsters to throw at him. I threw my mocha. It was ruined anyways with lobster water. There was no way I was going to drink it.

The lift opened. The concierge stepped out. Hoop was already back in his flat with his stinking live lobsters. I pointed.

"He has live lobsters and the bag split on me."

"I know, Amy, the entire incident was caught not just on CCTV but on your neighbour's live stream. I'll send the cleaning bill to your parents."

"What? He had my WiFi cut off and probably knows why I'm not getting any 4G signal and only patchy 5G."

"Internet problems are external. I saw you throw a cup of coffee and a lobster."

"Phone the police. He isn't meant to have live lobsters."

"Actually, Amy, there isn't a law to prevent it or prevent him from boiling them and eating them. There's only calls for one." He sniffed the air. "And why does it smell like cat piss up here? You're the only resident with a cat."

"She's been sick. I've taken her to the vet."

"Really? CCTV hasn't shown you leaving with a cat. Bringing in cats, in the plural sense, yes, leaving with a cat, no."

"CCTV is wrong."

"Is it now? What would happen if I called an inspection on your flat? How many cats do you have in there? You know, you lecture your neighbours about animal cruelty, yet you keep god knows how many cats in a two-room flat. Sounds a bit hypocritical to me."

With that, he left back down the lift. He didn't even help me up or assess the damage done to my clothing.

Hoop waited until the concierge was gone before he played what some people might classify as music on speakers pressed right against my wall. It sounded like angry men shouting and grunting while sat on a toilet with a bottle of laxative and occasionally masturbating a guitar.

I like to look on the bright side of life. When the music stops, I'll know it's safe to plant a little present in his flat for the cops to find.

I went for a shower. My lace knickers were soaked through with green vaginal sludge. The smell was awful. The cats followed me into the bathroom and had a sniff. They seemed to like it.

"Get out of here."

I threw a bottle of soap at them.

"Fucking gross cats."

I wanted to post about the green sludge on one of my sock accounts to increase sexual health awareness, but my WiFi wasn't working and I couldn't get any 4 or 5G signal on any device. I sent my father a text message this time. It'll go through when the signal comes back. Maybe he'd respond.

The music played continuously. Even at night, but Hoop had the common sense to turn it down. I only knew because five minutes after I stopped hearing it, I pressed my ear against the wall. Once heard, it couldn't be unheard as I lied there in bed. The dripping tap provided a clashing beat.

I had a little surprise for that American bastard. I had lots of little surprises underneath my floorboards. I kept them for when I needed to get rid of someone fast.

Kiddie porn. Cocaine. Heroin. Bestiality. Kiddie and animal mash ups. I decided to start light with a bit of coke and teenage girl nudes. They had little rosebub breasts and pubes. If that didn't get rid of Hoop, I could go more extreme all the way down to a baby being fucked by a dog.

The shouty-grunt-grunts and guitar masturbation woke me up too early on Monday morning. I sat on the toilet straining. When the pee finally came it burnt past my swollen flesh.

The shit the chemist sold me didn't do any good and I only had one day worth of painkillers left. I'd have to see a doctor for this. I made an appointment. At least I could still make outgoing phone calls.

The nurse didn't think there was anything wrong other than some bruising. She was brutish with the examination, and she wouldn't ask the doctor to okay a codeine prescription. Apparently, I should avoid leggings and synthetic fabric until the swelling goes down.

When I left the doctor's, my phone started chiming. It wasn't my parents saying they sorted out the WiFi and they'd do something about the new neighbour. I couldn't even scoop out the cat litter box. Not like the little darlings used it. They preferred shitting in my shoes and dragging their arses across the floor. Kadine is going to have a right mess to sort out when she comes tomorrow.

I read Charlie's message. The girlfriend went to the police. *With what?* I responded. She had no evidence. *I tried messaging you yesterday but the messages sat on unread.* Fucking Hoop. We'd have this sorted and she'd be on her knees sucking Charlie off while fingering my arsehole right now if Hoop hadn't interfered with the signal. *Okay, sorry, there aren't any signals hitting my flat. Want to meet up? Has she already gone to the police?*

I stood in the middle of the sidewalk—oh shit, I'm fucking thinking in American. It isn't a sidewalk. What the fuck is that word? That goddamn lobster-eating pig is fucking with my brain now, too. People pushed past me aggravating my swollen vagina.

*Yes,* he responded.

*Yes to what?* I waited.

A toddler walked right into me. I kicked it while screaming "ouch."

"He's just a baby," some foaming-at-the-mouth foreigner shouted.

"Stop draining our NHS bitch," I shouted back.

I flipped her off, too. Her toddler cried in a delayed reaction.

"He isn't even hurt. He just wants attention."

She scooped the brat up and ran off.

*To both. She's gone to the police already about posting her bedroom photos online. I was only trying to give her some self-esteem, like you said. Where do you want to meet up? We need to sort this out. This is bad. This is very bad. She's accused me of all sorts. Apparently I coerced her into sex as well. I was only trying to help her. I made sure she said "yes". Then she accused me of trying to get her to sleep with women while I watched. It was only a suggestion.* He was rambling. I couldn't read that and take it all in, not with this pain.

I thought my vagina was going to burst open by the time the lift arrived at the ground floor. At least my mental stream wasn't referring to it as an elevator. Yet. If someone didn't sort out Hoop soon, that might happen.

On top of Hoop, I had Charlie's nasty-ass skank to deal with. I don't know who she thought she was. Going to the police like that.

Charlie and I could destroy her. She's the one with the bad background. Our parents love us. Her's chucked her out to fend for herself. She doesn't even have a degree. She probably doesn't have any qualifications.

When I stepped out of the lift, Kadine was laughing at something Hoop said.

"What the fuck, Kadine? Don't talk to him, he's dirty."

"No, Amy, you're dirty. I'm not cleaning up after you anymore. Hoop has offered me double pay. I start immediately. I guess you'll have to change your own cat litter boxes and pick up your own disgusting used condoms." She looked me up and down. "But I guess you won't be having sex for awhile."

"Just wait until my parents here about this, you'll be chucked out of the country."

"Really?"

She raised her eyebrows.

"Yes."

"And what exactly are they going to do? I was born here. My parents were born here. I'm a UK citizen. I can work here legally because I'm British. There's nothing they can do, and from the sounds of things, they aren't returning your desperate texts. They texted me to see what you wanted. I told them I didn't know. That you're usually in bed when I arrive and don't wake up until sometime after I leave. I mentioned you acquired more cats and that there's even more missing pet posters about town. They didn't seem too happy about the used condoms left everywhere as well."

"What the actual fuck? You're bluffing. And I'll report you to the Home Office myself."

"Come on, Kadine, you don't have to take that."

Hoop put his hand on her shoulder and looked back at me with a wink and a smirk.

"Laters."

I flipped them off. She was bluffing about my parents. She had to be. Why would they text her and not me? She was the help.

Hoop! This was all about Hoop! Everything started going wrong when he moved in and now I might be taken in for questioning because I didn't get Charlie's messages.

"Why did you have to come here? Why? What did I do?"

He didn't respond but instead walked off with my cleaning lady.

"He farts in the lift," I called after them.

I waited by the door all day with the cats coming in to sit with me. That was one of the nice things about them. They knew how to comfort. I could take pictures, but I couldn't upload them anywhere for instant likes. Hopefully my timed posts were going out without signal. I should have checked but Charlie's texts had me worried.

I heard Kadine leave. She sounded positively joyful. It was sickening. She was a cleaning woman. There was nothing for her to be happy about. That vile American probably shagged her pressed against the window and gave her a host of diseases, especially considering the way he talked about hookers.

Shortly after she left, Hoop left. Through the peephole, I watched him lumbering down the corridor with his heavy breathing and commentary on everything even though he had no one else to talk to. He left that god-awful music on though. It sounded like pigs being raped with a cactus.

There were too many people about during the daytime. That rich Asian kid and his stupid girlfriend were always in and out of the building. I knew Hoop's little trick now. All I'd have to do would be to wait for him to leave tonight and ignore the music. He wasn't fooling me with the foul sounds.

I stood up and went to the loose floorboards. I concealed the spot underneath a rug so it only sounded a bit squeaky and no one knew it was loose. If I was caught with this stuff, I'd be the one arrested. The police wouldn't listen to my pleas of how I saved people from it by collecting it. They didn't understand noble intentions. They were too busy accusing Charlie of rape and revenge pornography. But if I reported the neighbour for having this stuff, it'll take the attention off me and therefore my name would never come up in conjunction with his case. The police wouldn't listen to how Charlie and I promote sex positivity.

It is such a shame Kadine threw out those used condoms. I could also point my finger at Charlie if he tried to bring my name into it.

Without internet access I had nothing to do. Life was so boring. I couldn't even try phoning my parents without a signal. I needed something to occupy my mind, so I went shopping.

Harrod's was fucking packed with planeloads of American tourists only buying something small so they could take home a little green bag. There was no way I could reach the makeup counter around the throbbing mass. Americans perfected mouth breathing. Each one must account for two people given their girth.

This was completely hopeless. I would have to get my makeup from Boots instead. I should probably pick up some maxi pads while I'm in there to collect my vaginal sludge before it runs down my leg. There's a pretty intense smell to match the texture. The security guard at the door looked ready to heave when I shuffled past.

Boots wasn't as busy. Their carrier bags weren't world-famous and therefore didn't have the status symbol pull of Harrod's.

With my makeup and extra thick maxi pads I stopped in a coffee shop for my mocha. The air finally found a pre-winter chill to strip the leaves from the trees. I found a table in the back away from other customers. Unfortunately, it was right next to the toilets. I put my shopping on the other chair so no one would dare sit next to me and took out my phone.

Still no response from my parents. The nerve of Kadine abandoning me like that and then making up shit up about my parents. They were just busy coming to terms with DiDi's death. She was a worthless waste of space. I don't get why they mourned her. Her suicide looked bad on the family's reputation anyways. It was the things found in her office that led to it. But my parents never believed she was a dirty paedophile. They thought she'd been framed.

Some snot-nosed brat stared at me while waiting for the toilet.

"I hope you piss yourself," I said only loud enough for the child to hear.

I bared my teeth. When the child stepped back the mother turned to look at me, blushing. I smiled.

"What's gotten into you," she asked, shaking his arm a bit.

I turned back to my phone. Without my other accounts to really get communication going, I didn't have many notifications. People only agreed with my status updates if someone else had already. That explains the basic mentality of humanity. Followers the lot of them. I was a leader. I set the trends. My friends list just followed.

I scrolled looking for gossip about Charlie. The news didn't look good. Lots of posts about him befriending girls when they were depressed and then me and him tag-teaming them into thinking the only way to rebuild themselves was with sex. Words like "rape" and "coercion" came up more times than was comfortable. A few people focused on the pictures Charlie posted. Some even brought up his various exes and said this same thing happened with all of them.

I would have to distance myself from him. I hit unfriend, thought better of it and blocked him for good measure. I didn't block his phone number though. I needed to know if I'd be implicated in whatever bullshit his new ex was spouting off to the police.

I stayed in the coffee shop long after my mocha was gone. I would have stayed for longer, but I could feel the vaginal sludge seeping out of my trousers. People gave me funny looks when I walked past. I knew this infection was somehow Hoop's fault. I have the immune system of a goddess and then he moved in. Everything went wrong when he moved him, even before I heard his awful American accent.

The music was still blaring into my bedroom. I checked the corridor for the stupid rich Asian brat and his girlfriend. They must be out taking social media-worthy photos of their stupidly expensive dinner covered in authentic edible gold flakes. That always takes a long time. And he needs to show off his latest car. Really, he was only announcing to the city that he had a very small penis.

The disc didn't fit in my pocket, but I had a memory stick next to a little bit of blow. I didn't know what sort of devices Hoop had, but I was prepared for every situation. I even had printouts of underage girls posing without any clothes on. In case he wasn't straight, I had nudes of boys as well. Thousands of thumbnails on the memory stick plus a few video clips to upload to his computer. Plus the DVD in my hand.

These locks were surprisingly easy to pick. The doors were heavy, offering nothing more than an illusion of security. I checked over my shoulder to make sure CCTV wasn't trained on his door. I took out my lock-picking kit. A few turns and I heard the spring in the door come undone despite Hoop's abysmal tastes in music.

I opened the door with caution just in case he was home. He left dishes piled up high on the work surfaces in the kitchen. A massive pot sat on the hob. It looked large enough to boil lobsters. His flat had a distinct smell in it of fast food and farts. Typical American. They were all the same and they wondered why they were the fattest nation on Earth.

Takeaway containers sat piled by the door. I knocked down a tower of them and held my breath. Nothing happened. Hoop didn't randomly jump out from behind a shut door.

He really needed to open a window. Not even that would get rid of the smell.

I walked into the living room. The smell was stronger. The sofa that blocked the door had centre stage. I didn't want to touch it. It looked like there were cum stains over every inch.

There was an open laptop on the sofa. I didn't even need to utilise my hacking skills. There wasn't any need for a password. I popped my memory stick in.

While the memory stick was loading, I shoved printouts underneath the cushions while trying not to think about what he did on that sofa. I went to one of the bedrooms and planted more underneath the mattress. I didn't know which room he slept in. It didn't really matter. Kiddie porn was kiddie porn.

I could place the tip anonymously, posing as an escort he hired not just for a good time but for what turned out to be some real kinky and questionable shit.

The door to the other bedroom creaked open. My stomach dropped and my bowels turned to liquid. I clenched my arse cheeks shut despite the immense shooting pains that exploded in my vagina. Hoop stepped out of the room.

"Come in, Amy." He waved towards his bedroom. "I've been expecting you."

I backed up against the wall, shaking my head.

"No? I thought you wanted to plant something in there. Let's see what you have."

He took a step towards me and ripped the printouts from my hands.

"Kiddie porn. Very nice. Little boys and little girls. I bet that disc in your hand has some film footage of an underage orgy. There's a TV in the bedroom with a DVD player, let's find out together, shall we?"

I couldn't back against the wall any further.

"No? Okay, well, I suppose the TV in the living room is good enough. You'll have to sit on my sofa though. I've been having a real good time on that lately trying out London's hookers. Phillips was right. London really does have the best hookers in the world. I should know."

He winked. My stomach clenched. My mocha was going to come out one way or the other.

"What's the matter, Amy? You look a little sick?"

He stepped towards me and took my upper arm, pulling me to the living room. I had no resistance.

"If you need to shit yourself or vomit, just say so, none of that bothers me."

We arrived in the living room. It seemed to take forever with him breathing on me. His breath was absolutely rank. I didn't want to vomit though. I had the impression he got off on such things. It really didn't come as any sort of surprise.

"Ah, I see you've already been in here. What is that you're uploading to my laptop? More kiddie porn. Oh wow. You really like me, don't you, Amy?"

He showed no signs of disgust even when he pulled printed images out of the sofa cushions.

"Where did you get all this kiddie porn? You must have quite the connections."

He paused to examine each image before throwing it on the floor. He sat down and patted the cushion next to him.

"Take a seat, Amy, me and you, we're going to have a little talk. Don't worry, we'll have the chance to watch that film in your hand. I'm sure it is really good. Probably something not even I have seen before."

"Do you ever shut up?"

"I will, once we're watching that film."

He snatched it off my finger.

"Always careful not to scratch it, aren't you? Shame you aren't careful with those cats you hold prisoner in your flat."

"They're my babies."

"They're someone's babies, but not yours."

I tried to run for the door, but my feet wouldn't move.

"Now that I think of it, I have a better film we could watch together. Hard to believe there's anything better than kiddie porn, but I feel confident you'll like this more."

I had no choice but to sit. My mocha seeped out of my arse.

"A bit squelchy, aren't you? You haven't been feeling so well lately, have you? I can feel the fever coming off you. Perhaps this film will help you feel better?"

He pressed some buttons on the remote. He didn't even bother taking the kiddie porn out of the DVD player. It was like he just didn't give a shit.

My dead sister smiled from the screen.

"Look at those cheekbones. Strong family resemblance."

DiDi twirled in her small studio apartment, tears streaming down her face. She didn't have on any makeup to smudge. She couldn't afford it after my parents cut her off.

"Her last dance. She just received her eviction notice. She had nowhere to go. No friends. No family. You saw to that."

The disc skipped. It took years to bring DiDi down from her pedestal. My parents were so proud when she graduated with a double first in internal medicine. Then she went onto paediatrics.

"How did you break into your sister's office though? Hospitals have so much security."

I swallowed hard.

He turned back to the TV.

"Ah, that's right, you befriended the security guards with promises of sex. One of them took home a chlamydia infection for his pregnant girlfriend. You didn't even bother to wash between them. You naughty girl."

Images of my legs over my head flashed on the screen. It cut to me on my knees.

"Why are you doing this?" I asked once I found the words.

"Look at you go. You can suck a dick dry. Bet your friend enjoyed that the other night. It'll be last time his dick is going to be sucked in a long time."

He slapped my knee.

"Don't touch me."

He put his arms around me and pulled me in a hug.

"I said, don't touch me."

"I heard you, but you're hardly in a position to make demands. I know there's more kiddie porn where that came from."

His breath engulfed us as the TV screen changed. It wasn't my sister's bright office anymore but a dark alley alive with flies.

"What do we have here? Is this one of your friends beneath all the flies?"

The camera zoomed on the vomit-strewn alley.

"This doesn't look like a nice place to die. But, wait... is that mass beneath all the flies still breathing? I think she might be. The rats look hungry."

A pale hand with a broken manicure reached from beneath the blanket of flies. Hoop turned the volume up and held a hand to his ear for dramatic effect.

"I learned that trick from you, but we'll get to that, for now listen."

I had no choice. I could hear whoever was underneath that blanket of flies groaning.

"Sounds like she's in pain and still conscious. I wonder what happened here.

Only one way to find out."

The images moved backwards until the screen showed the inside of a packed nightclub and a woman on the floor, crying. She was surrounded by people on their phones

"You know that woman, don't you? She was one of your inner-circle."

Hoop reached over and placed his hand over my ear. Something slimy crawled inside.

"What the fuck?"

I jumped off the sofa. Vaginal sludge leaked down my leg mixed with what liquid seeped out of my arse. The TV paused. Hoop sat there laughing.

"Should I make some popcorn? Would you like some?"

He didn't show any signs of moving. I dug my finger into my ear to find what he put inside me.

"You won't be able to remove it, but please, keep trying."

"Wait until my parents hear about this. They'll…"

"They'll what? Review the footage of you framing your sister? They'll recall every word you said to them during her trial. How you came between them and their successful daughter. You already suspect they know something. You're on borrowed time with them, Amy, and you know it, so why don't you sit back down and watch the highlights of your life with me. You'll actually be able to feel with that device in your ear."

"What are you talking about, I can feel?"

"You think you can. You're feeling pretty sorry for yourself right now. That infection from your friend's unwashed dick must be pretty sore and itchy. I know it smells bad. I'm going to have to air out this flat and still need to use industrial strength air freshener once you leave."

"I get to leave?"

"I don't want you in here forever. The sooner we finish the movie, the sooner you get to go home. I'm not sure how much longer the flat next door will be your home though."

I pulled at the thing in my ear. Little tiny legs dug themselves in. Hoop patted the sofa cushion next to him. He saw the look of disgust on my face.

"It is only a bit of dried cum. Oh, right, the infection. Cum probably isn't your favourite thing right now."

He flipped the cushion over. I hope that's dried chocolate. Hoop leaned over and licked it. I gagged. I never felt such revulsion before.

"See, told you that you couldn't really feel anything before. Now you can."

I swallowed down my vomit.

"Seat is good as new."

Droplets of Hoop's spit sparkled in the overhead lights. The stain was still there. I took a step back.

"Stop making things hard on yourself, Amy. The sooner you get this over and done with, the sooner I let you go."

He pulled a handkerchief out of his pocket and laid it on the cushion.

"Fresh this morning. Only used it once."

He scraped at a big green smudge with his dirty fingernail. There was no getting out of this. It was like one of my father's lectures about helping your fellow man and how we have a responsibility to help the needy because we were born into wealth.

Sarah sat on the floor of a nightclub on the TV screen. The faces around her were frozen in laughter. I could feel the humiliation as if they were laughing at me. Their hands held phones that no doubt they were sharing footage of Sarah's home movies caught on hidden camera with a guy she didn't even like. The stubble left behind by her pubes gave him a rash. He and I had been sure to let the world know.

"I'm surprised you remember her name. She wasn't your only victim, was she?"

Tears threatened to stream down my face.

"That's better," Hoop said, "and you can feel now, can't you?"

He pulled me into an embrace.

"Little Amy is growing up." He smiled. "Shall we hit play?"

Hoop didn't wait for my response. The nightclub came to life. People towered over me. I was in two places at once; sat on the sofa and in the nightclub. Lights flashed on their phones.

"She didn't consent to being filmed having sex, did she? You had to set up a hidden camera. She didn't even like the guy. You told her how she couldn't do any better and threatened to ruin her reputation if she didn't sleep with him. You told everyone she was judgemental of promiscuous sex, even though she had better things to think about. She lost her job because of the footage. You tried to convince her to star in her own homemade porn to earn an income."

Hoop slapped my knee.

"Can you feel that humiliation? All those eyes looking at you? There's no use adjusting your skirt, they've already seen. Those images will stay with the audience for a very long time. Long after her body is found in the alley."

Someone tried to help Sarah up but instead of taking her hand, he squeezed her breast and pulled down her top. My own breast sent tendrils of pain through my body.

"Hurts, doesn't it?"

I grabbed my breast. I couldn't help myself. Tears ran down Sarah's face. Tears ran down mine. Once the man grabbed her breast she fell back down on the floor. I felt the pain travel up my tailbone and jar the swollen flesh between my thighs.

I don't know how Sarah afforded to get in. She was jobless and the JobCentre was giving her a hard time. A man came into view with two drinks. He stood over Sarah.

"I thought you were a nice girl. I would have never swiped right if I knew about your home movies."

He threw the drinks on her and stormed off. That explains how she paid the club's entry fee. I don't know how anyone could miss her homemade porn. That footage was everywhere.

"Come on, babe, let me help."

Some creep made a grab for her. The bouncer came over. He looked directly at Sarah.

"It is time for you to leave."

"I don't have any way to get home."

"That isn't my problem. You have upset the people in here tonight. You aren't welcome here."

The bouncer grabbed her upper arm and yanked her to her feet.

"People come in here for a good time and to forget their problems for a few hours. We can't have the likes of you with your travelling drama-circus upsetting that."

My breast still hurt from the squeeze and now my upper arm felt like it was coming up in bruises. My ankles twisted as Sarah was dragged across the floor. I looked down and watched them. The bouncer threw her onto the cobbled street. A few men followed her out.

"Let me walk you home. I'll make sure you get there safely."

They crowed around her.

"Leave me alone."

Hoop turned to me.

"Can you feel that? That is fear. Actual fear. Not this petty little scared girl act you have going on."

I was shaking. The infection in my vagina didn't like that, but I couldn't help it.

"You better not be leaking green sludge onto my handkerchief."

Sarah eventually found her feet after the men left. She had a long walk ahead of her to get home. She didn't see the group of men hiding in the shadows.

My heart thumped in my chest. I couldn't catch my breath. At the same time an invisible belt tightened around me. Black shadows appeared in my vision.

"Oh, little Amy is starting to grow up. She's having her first actual panic attack."

Hoop took a camera out from somewhere and started snapping pictures. Each click came from far away but at the same time the sound penetrated deep down to my soul.

"Sarah didn't see those men. Those black patches on your vision, she couldn't see them, plus they were in the shadows, waiting. They figured as she was so willing to put out on film, they should get a piece."

The TV paused again.

"I have all day, Amy, I'll just wait for you to compose yourself. It is a bit harder to get a Xanax prescription here, isn't it? No worries, this is your first real panic attack anyways so you wouldn't have any on hand."

I clutched at my throat. Hoop sat there taking photos and laughing.

The TV started to play again. Sarah walked fast with her shoulders up. That tension was going to hurt in the morning. The men crept out of the shadows and pulled her into an alley. She screamed but no one noticed.

"What's the matter, baby? We've seen your film. We know what you're all about."

"Yeah, we know just how you like it."

Sarah tried to fight them off.

"Please leave me alone, I just want to go home."

"See what I don't get, is why you put out on film, but won't give us any?"

"Yeah, we not good enough for you?"

"Go away. I didn't consent to that. I didn't even like the guy."

"Then why'd you fuck him?"

One of the men in the alley was missing a front tooth. Sarah stepped in a puddle of vomit.

"Let me go."

She screamed, but if people heard, no one did anything. The man with a missing tooth pulled down her top.

"That's right, show us those breasts."

He pinched her nipples. Another man came out of the shadows with a knife.

"Leave me alone."

Sarah tried to pull away. The knife-man poked her flesh.

"Why is your skirt so short if you don't want any?"

Another man ripped her skirt off.

"Look at that sexy thong."

He flicked the string across her hips. The knife man held it and cut it away.

"That's better."

"Who's going first?"

Sarah kicked. Her shoe came off and landed in the puddle of steaming vomit. Rats scurried away from the shuffle with indignant squeaks. Sarah stumbled. One of the men caught her.

"That's better, baby, right into my arms."

Sarah spat into his mouth.

"Now, now, don't be like that. We know you want it."

"You wouldn't be out here walking alone otherwise."

People walked past the alley. Sarah had their attention, but they ran off like the rats.

A man grabbed her from behind lifting her up. Another man grabbed one of her legs. Yet another grabbed her from the other leg. She squirmed.

"I like it when you move around like that."

A man walked towards her with his dick out.

"Don't try to deny it. I know you want it."

He forced himself in. Sarah screamed.

I felt him enter past my infection and swollen vagina. It stung. He thrust himself in and out. Each thrust brought me fresh pain. Hoop clapped me on the back.

"Don't care for that, do ya?"

Bile rose in my throat as another man had his turn.

"Such a pretty little mouth. Would be such a shame if something happened to it."

The man flashed his knife.

"I suggest you stop screaming."

Sarah spat in his face and squirmed. The man holding her arms and upper body dropped her. Her head banged against the concrete. My vision went white.

"Hit your head? Don't worry, it'll pass."

Somehow, I heard Hoop in the centre of my brain without any other sound. Pain spread like a flower blooming across my skull. Sarah came to with the man thrusting himself into her.

"Please stop. Why are you doing this?"

Her speech came out slurred.

"Ah, little baby doesn't know what she's saying."

The man looked up.

"Do you know what she's saying?"

Each thrust brought me fresh pain that throbbed in sync with my head. The man stabbed her side when she tried to crawl away. I felt the warm blood seep down my ribs. I lifted my shirt to look. But there was no blood.

"Oh, this won't leave any marks on you," Hoop sneered. "Not physical ones, anyway."

Once all the men had their turn, one pissed on me/Sarah before running out of the alley. I felt the warm liquid splash against my bare flesh.

The rats came back. The early morning brought flies. Sarah tried to swat them away, but she didn't have the strength. The street cleaners never bothered to look down the alley. She was still alive when revellers came out the next night, covered in more flies. The rats started to gnaw on her once the sun went down.

"Please help me."

No one heard her. The screen went black.

My mind recovered from Sarah's injuries.

"We're just warming up, Amy. I won't show you another like Sarah. She experienced the full range of consequences. No one was really able to pick up their lives and move on once you showed the world their nudes, but Sarah experienced the worse. They didn't discover her body until that alley started to smell worse than usual, but you already knew that. Saw it in the news."

"Why are you doing this?"

"Why not? Who is that boy you stalk? Oh yes, Max. He's quite the playboy, isn't he? Let's see what he's up to."

Images came onto the TV screen.

"That looks like the sexual health clinic. I wonder what he's picked up."

Hoop turned to me and smiled. His teeth were filthy.

"Let's find out."

Max went into the exam room and dropped his trousers. His dick looked red and swollen. Discharge dripped out of his pisshole.

"Unfortunately, I don't have smell-o-vision, but just spread your legs and you'll get an idea of the odour."

The nurse was visibly shocked and disgusted.

"I'm going to need to take a sample of that discharge. Is it sore? It looks sore?"

Max just shook his head. The nurse came at him with a cotton bud.

"I need you to hold your penis steady. I'm going to have to insert this into the tip."

Max screamed and then started chewing on his lip while tears fell from his eyes. The nurse swallowed her vomit. Once he left the room, she puked into the bin.

"People have been doing that after you walk past, Amy. Your infection isn't a sexually transmitted disease like what Max has, although it was sexually transmitted, wasn't it? Charlie doesn't wash, does he? He also passed it onto that ex-girlfriend of his who is being questioned by the police as we speak. I think they'll want to talk to you, too, what do you think? Although before we see what she is up to, let's find out what Max has?"

On the screen, the nurse returned with grim news.

"What do you mean there's no treatment?" Max asked.

"That particular gonorrhoea infection you picked up is resistant to antibiotics."

"Wait, there's more." Hoop laughed. He looked positively gleeful.

"The syphilis you have…" the nurse continued. "The lab has never seen anything like it before and they've seen a lot of syphilis. That can't be treated either. That's what is causing all those sores, not the gonorrhoea. It mutated somehow."

"What's going to happen to me?"

"We aren't too sure. This is a new type of syphilis. In terms of the gonorrhoea, you'll just have to learn to live with it. And always use a condom."

Max shuddered. It was obvious his penis was still inflamed even if I couldn't strictly feel that.

"We think the syphilis will follow the course of a normal syphilis infection, only it'll be more extreme. I see you already have the sores spreading across your feet and palms. Next, you'll go blind and insane. Finally, it'll kill you."

"Sucks to be him." Hoop laughed.

I planned on having his babies. I couldn't do that now. My skin started to itch. I scratched, but it hurt at the same time. Hoop waited to change the scene while I scratched myself raw.

A cat meowed on the screen. The cat was familiar; the house wasn't. A small hand stroked it.

"Don't worry, Cuddles, Mummy is getting your food now," a child's voice said.

"You must be very hungry."

A woman's feet appeared in the frame. She bent down with a bowl of cat food.

"There you are, Cuddles."

"That looks like one of your cats, doesn't it?"

The scene changed.

"Where's, Cuddles, Mummy? Why did she leave? Does she not love us anymore?"

The scene changed to another cat curled up in bed with a strange woman. The cat was purring.

"Another one of yours? How much was the reward for these cats?"

"Not high enough." I gritted my teeth.

"You've been stealing cats for years, long before it became fashionable. Do your parents know where your cats come from or why you don't take them to the vet?"

"They're fancy cats. People don't actually love them. They only get them for the prize money at the cat show and Instagram likes."

"Really?"

Hoop raised an eyebrow and turned back to the TV. A cat chased a feather attached to a stick.

"Looks like a family pet to me."

The scene changed on the TV again. The police banged on a non-descript door. The sun was only starting to come out.

"I wonder who lives there, is it Charlie? Do you think it is Charlie? I think it is Charlie."

Charlie answered the door in his underwear, his phone clutched in his hand.

"I bet I know who he has been frantically messaging all night. He hasn't had any more of your guidance though, has he? Even if your internet and signal were working, if it didn't look like the rape and humiliation of his ex could be traced back to you, you would have blocked him. For being negative, am I right?"

"Charlie Ryan?"

"Yes."

"We're placing you under arrest. You need to come with us and answer some questions."

The screen cut to Charlie at the police station.

"Looks like he is cooperating."

He unlocked his phone for the officer. They let him get dressed before they brought him in. That was nice. The messages flashed on the screen.

"All those messages look like desperate pleas to you. Before you stopped responding, you were giving him instruction in how to handle this and convince the girl that she was crazy and didn't know what she was talking about. Times have changed, Amy. This will be a test case."

"Why are you doing this?"

I started to cry. I couldn't help it.

"Those crocodile tears won't work on me. They've taken you far, but this is the end of the line."

Some dream I had. The new neighbour is really fucking with my head.

A furry paw print pressed on my windpipe. I tried to brush it off and turn over, but I couldn't move. The cats started to meow. It sounded like all of them were clustered around my bed.

Suddenly they decided at the same time to hack up fur balls. The sound was worse than their meowing. The one on my windpipe wouldn't even move to do it. I tried to push it aside so I could breathe and not get cat sick on me, but I couldn't move.

One took a swipe at my foot. I didn't know where the duvet was. Cold winter air danced across my naked skin. The Indian Summer was officially over.

I gasped for air. Another cat swiped at my face.

I wanted to scream, but my throat didn't work. I tried to roll over. My muscles twitched, but they wouldn't contract. Now I knew what a person in a coma felt when people clustered around their bed discussing switching off the life support.

The cats pounced on me all at once with their claws out. The Siamese had sharp teeth. I knew that one started biting first. Which other cat would it be? I tried to focus all my energy on opening an eyelid so I could at least see but they were crusted over.

Growling and screaming vocals came from through the wall. Someone banged on the door. I knew it was the police. They'd save me from the cats. My little babies turned on me after I saved them from their wretched existences.

Another cat started to bite. Warm drops of blood pooled from my body. A cat swiped at my eyes. The delicate skin of the eyelids didn't do much to protect it. They stayed well clear of my vagina but had no objections to chewing on my outer thighs. A claw found my nostrils. Unfortunately that didn't remove my sense of smell. They were all covered in shit like they had been rolling in it from the smell of things.

The banging grew more distant as did the guitar masturbation section of whatever the fuck Hoop classified as music.

The cats took turns using my ribs as a scratching post until the skin was gone. They started on the muscle. White overtook the blood on my vision. I think that was more in my head though.

A cat claw swiped my eye, digging all the way in. I both heard and felt a pop. I knew sight was lost in that eye, but the white was still there.

A cat bit my nose. I felt the teeth sink all the way through. It took a few tries for the cat to chew it off.

I knew I should have stolen dogs. They would have made this quick. I couldn't even post about my dying agony.

# THE PROFILE

RYAN HARDING

Kessler queued up the video for his Quantico group, the latest profiler hopefuls preparing to stare into the abyss.

White letters appeared on a black background on the auditorium screen:

ARCHIVAL FIELD FOOTAGE

INTERVIEWER: AGENT JOHN KESSLER

SUBJECT: FILO PRESTON

MANGUM MAXIMUM SECURITY PRISON

JUNE 6, 2018

The title screen cut to a small room with pink walls and the pressure of an ambient hum in the speakers. Two men sat across from each other at a table, Kessler to the right and Filo Preston to the left, half a decade into one of his life sentences and already aging in dog years behind bars.

"I appreciate you seeing me today, Filo," Kessler said.

Filo snorted. "Beats busting my ass in the laundry. You coulda been a Jehovah's Witness and I'd still be sitting in this chair right now." He looked around the room, shaking his head. "Thought I might get a break from these walls. Feels like I'm stuck in fuckin' Barbie's Dream House. Ain't no Barbie to dunk off in, though."

"So you don't think the pink curbs some of your more violent impulses, then."

"Shit no, man. It just makes me think of pussy all the time. "

Kessler chuckled. "Well, I don't need pink walls for that."

The image froze as Kessler paused the video. "You can see right there, I surprised him. It feels less formal—just two men in a room talking. Now he's thinking about lowering his guard. Sometimes it takes that push to build a rapport because otherwise they'll sit there and try to play innocent. You know, their lawyer is *always* appealing, their case is *always* about to be overturned, there's *always* some compelling new evidence."

A few people in the audience laughed quietly.

"Now, some of what I do here may seem shameful or immoral, particularly in this more delicate social climate we find ourselves. A serial killer's mind is no safe space, however, and never will be. You won't be proud of it, but unfortunately there's no politically correct way to buddy up to a man who has raped and killed a couple dozen women. You'll have to soil your thoughts and fear your mind."

He presumed this common knowledge to everyone here, but a couple of them jotted it down anyway. Maybe they liked the quote.

"As a word of warning, that's probably the most polite way you'll hear me try to meet Filo Preston on his own terms, I'm afraid."

He started the video again.

Filo unfroze and laughed uncertainly. "Yeah, I hear that. Maybe if I could have just shut that off once in a while, I wouldn't be stuck here with all these bastards trying to play musical chairs with my asshole. " He gestured toward the video camera. "Man, what's all this for, anyway?"

"Come on, Filo. You know the score. I want to pick your brain a little and revisit your greatest hits."

"This shit ain't admissible as evidence, right?"

"I'm just here to listen. This won't add anything to your sentence. That goes both ways, though. It won't take anything off either, either. "

"Shit, that figures. You're coming to me for escort service, but only offering crack whore rates."

"Hey, I'd love to throw you a bone. Give up some new bodies so we could confirm to these boohooing old ladies, 'Yeah, your missing daughter is a pile of bones somewhere because she was dumb enough to hitchhike,' but…the Bureau." Kessler shrugged. "You know how it is. So, you're good to record?"

Filo grinned. "Now, you know I ain't camera shy."

"That's right. I've seen your oeuvre probably about as many times as you have."

"My ooh *what*?"

"Your body of work."

"You seen all my movies, huh? They told me they was gonna burn them. Shoulda known that was a crock. Pissed me off, man. That's one-of-a-kind shit. No sequel for none of those twats, neither."

"Solid gold like that, Filo, no way I'd let them feed that to the incinerator."

"Yeah?" He squinted suspiciously. "What was your favorite?"

Kessler didn't miss a beat. "Priscilla Wyrick."

"Shit yeah. I put her through some freakin' paces, Jack!"

"Inspired use of a curling iron, I'll grant you that."

"She screamed so loud, my ears rang for two days." He smiled serenely, closing his eyes, leaning back in his chair. "Just my good fortune she'd packed it in her bag. Sometimes the universe smiles on you."

"I'm sure you'd like to see those clips again."

Filo frowned at this. "I dunno."

"You don't know? I thought for sure you'd have been thinking about those movies for the past five years. When you weren't thinking about pussy, that is."

"Eh, same difference. But naw, it's just..." He crossed his arms, looking toward the ceiling as if he'd find the right words to explain up there. "I was in a school play back in second or third grade. I only had a couple lines, but it was a big deal. My parents came to see it, and they acted like it was *The Godfather* of school plays after the show. All the parents did, you know, so we all thought we were the shit. My mom and dad got a copy from somebody who brought their video camera. And I watched myself on that tape a few days later, wondering why the show seemed so different from how I knew it was in the moment. Because there was no getting around it...me, the lead girl, the whole class, we fuckin' sucked, dude."

"So what, you're saying you sucked in your own snuff movies?"

"No, but a video camera can't capture the magic of actually doing it. I didn't start off taping 'em, but I thought it might be a good way to hold on to it, make it last. So I started recording it. I didn't want to go right back out. Yeah, it'd be killer to pack up the ol' rape kit night after night, keep drilling new bitches, but I knew I was playing with fire. It don't matter, though. One day it's not enough to think about it and watching it just reminds you what you're missin'. Like porn. Even the way something really happened can become a bad copy, a lie. So you go out again. And again. Then they get you."

"A promising career cut short."

Filo laughed, shaking his head. "You ain't who you say you are, Jack."

Kessler shrugged again. "Everybody has a secret face."

Kessler watched the Priscilla Wyrick clip in his office after the lecture, on his laptop. A far cry from the hi-def quality, but at least it came from a digital camera. Most of Filo's videos were dull static shots, but he'd gone handheld for Priscilla, a twenty-six-year-old restaurant hostess. Kessler would have deemed it an ass that wouldn't quit, but that's exactly what happened when Filo plunged the curling iron into her anus. It almost looked like a vibrator. She clenched around the iron, spasms jolting her as steam curled from the scorched orifice. The shrill scream could have been a whistling tea kettle, even with the volume nearly dragged down to zero.

Kessler moved his cursor over the time bar to start the sequence over.

Pendleton rapped on his door. "You following this mess in Chapman?"

"No, sir. What mess?"

"Bodies. You can probably lip synch it with me, but police had ostrich syndrome on serial activity. Started with three over a couple months, but there's been two more in just the past ten days. The mayor's calling in favors. She wants our best and brightest. I said I'd send you instead."

Kessler laughed.

Pendleton entered the office deep enough to get an angle on the laptop. He winced. "I don't see how the hell you can keep watching that stuff without going crazy."

"I owe it to the men and women who went through it. My job's the easy part. I just have to learn from it."

"I wouldn't want to keep that in my head all the time. How are you going to cope if you ever get married again?"

"Marriage is the kind of torture I don't have to see, sir. Who do I ask for in Chapman?"

They never liked to see Kessler coming—not the suspects and especially not the police forces the Bureau sent him to help. Bill Forsythe, South Chapman chief of police, expressed gratitude with his mouth while the rest of his body language offered wishes for Kessler's swift departure and/or lingering death.

"Rothman, Perez, Cartwright, and Billings caught the calls," Forsythe said. "They're all working it. You want Nick Rothman. He's the lead dick."

Heads turned as Kessler re-entered the maelstrom outside Forsythe's office, an acid trip of voices upon voices. The male cops looked at him as if they'd all received the same memo—*This guy put the bricks to your mama and never called her back.* The female officers seemed slightly less hostile, perhaps intrigued by the aura of celebrity, but still as skeptical as their counterparts. They all believed in the home team, and no outsider could tell them their business. Especially not a glorified psychic in an expensive suit which would have netted an IA investigation for any one of them.

Eyes dropped as Kessler navigated the maze of desks. Detectives growled into phones. Uniformed cops keyed in details provided by citizens sitting across from them with bovine looks on their faces, or haughtily demanding action be taken *right by Christ this second.*

"Well, well," said a detective who'd stopped at a busy intersection on his way back from the break room. Coffee steamed from a Styrofoam cup in his hand. His rumpled shirt needed a couple of minutes on an ironing board, and razor burn flared on his neck. "It's the Mind Stalker right here in our *po-lice* station."

Kessler halted. "I'm looking for a Detective Rothman. Do you know where might I find him?"

The detective smirked.

"You *might* find him back that way," the man said, gesturing to a couple of offices in the back corner with smoky glass.

"Much obliged, detective."

"Don't mention it…I know you usually don't." He projected his voice for the benefit of anyone listening in. "Guess it's true what they say, eh? The Mind Stalker always gets his man…he just needs a shitload of help from the cops."

This earned him some laughs and light applause.

On the other side of the station, a suspect in handcuffs struggled to pull away from the detaining officers dragging him off to the holding cells. *"I didn't kill them! I only wanted to free their souls!"*

An elderly woman waiting in front of an unmanned desk nudged her husband as Kessler passed. "We saw him on the Netflix! Look!"

It was about the only semi-flattering thing he overheard as he wove his way toward the corner offices. He spotted the name ROTHMAN stenciled on an open door, but no Nick Rothman inside. He recognized the name BILLINGS on the office beside his, though, and poked his head in just in time to see a redheaded woman hang up her phone and reach for a brown leather jacket. She stood up to stick an arm into one of the sleeves. She had to be just an inch or two shy of six feet.

"Detective Billings?" he said. "Agent Kessler from the FBI."

"Not much of a good luck charm, are you?" She picked through objects on her desk until she jingled a set of keys.

"How's that?"

"Or maybe this really is lucky, if you're as good as they say. We think we have another murder."

"I'm supposed to meet up with Nick Rothman."

"Uh, you already did." She gave him an apologetic look.

"The lead dick, indeed," Kessler murmured.

"Come on, you ride with me. Don't even think about asking to drive."

Billings expertly swerved them in and out of traffic like the other cars were standing still.

"Look, if you can help us, I'm glad you came," she said. "The others are a bit less thrilled."

"So I gathered."

"It's nothing personal, they just hate your guts."

"Gathered that, too. But I didn't have to be a profiler to figure that one out. They weren't shy. Especially Rothman."

"Oh, yes. I was his least favorite person around here too."

"Congratulations. How'd you change his mind?"

"I didn't." She gave him a thin smile. "You showed up."

Someone sat on their horn as she sliced into the other lane with inches to spare. "I just want the case solved. Rothman's the type who'd rather sit on pivotal info than share with another department. He wants the case solved too…as long as he's the one doing the solving. And taking the credit."

"That's me too, according to him."

"You've built up something of a mystique. I saw the thing about the Crossville Mutilator on Netflix."

Kessler shrugged. "Not one of the more challenging cases, but he had a memorable name."

"They haven't pinned one on our guy yet. That's about the only thing going for us." She rode up on an empty sidewalk, blue light flashing on the dash, rolling past a line of cars stuck at an intersection. "Have you kept with it at all? Any preliminary thoughts?"

"I'd like to wait until I've seen this newest crime scene," he said.

"Okay," Billings said, turning into the lot of a run-down warehouse. Several police cars, a coroner van, and a forensics unit sat parked out front. "How about now?"

They waited a bit while forensics had the run of the place, collecting their samples and taking pictures before Chapman's finest could troop in and contaminate everything.

Rothman waved to them, grinning at Kessler. "Fancy meeting you here."

Two other detectives arrived minutes later, initially pairing off with Rothman.

"We get a make-up trailer set up for him yet?" Rothman asked his pals, just loud enough for Kessler to overhear.

Laughter ensued, including a donkey-like bray from one of them with a face to match.

"Yeah, we want him to look good for TV," said his partner.

The donkey brayed again.

"The one with the charming laugh is Jeff Cartwright," Billings said. "I get to hear that every day. Lucky me, he thinks everything out of Rothman's mouth is a riot. His partner is Carlos Perez. Carlos is okay on his own, but a knucklehead with those two."

Perez and Cartwright came over for a formal introduction a moment later. They shared their gratitude for Kessler's help with sincerity equal to their chief's.

Billings quizzed one of the cops setting up a perimeter to keep the media vans out. The neighborhood didn't seem like a rare occurrence for a crime scene.

"Who called it in?"

"We think some homeless guy looking for a place to squat. Called in on a cell."

Billings turned to Kessler. "May be our guy himself, anonymously."

"No roof over his head, but owns a smartphone," Cartwright said. "What a time to be alive."

"No one should miss out on meme wars or The Fappening just because they're homeless, you classist fuck," Perez said.

One of the forensic techs signaled them from the doorway.

"Showtime."

She and Kessler went through the entrance. "We have an ID yet?" Billings asked.

The tech shook his head. "No ID. No face, either."

The warehouse stood mostly empty apart from dust-ridden boxes and machinery that had yet to be removed by the prior owner, but the techs obscured the main attraction as they packed up their equipment. The scene held a faux celestial aura, with rays of light beaming through panes in the high columns of windows overhead. It appeared that someone had broken them out strategically so the dead body would be bathed in intersections of light.

"God," Billings said. Her mouth curled in disgust.

The body had been posed nude in a sitting position with both arms held out in a Zen-like pose, palms up. In one hand, the man's eyeballs stared sightlessly to the east and west. In the other hand lay a hunk of withered flesh that Kessler might not have recognized if he couldn't see the gap carved into the man's throat. This was probably his larynx. His open mouth implied a continuing scream they would hear if he still had that tissue back where it belonged. Something drooped from both of the empty eye sockets, like tracks of black tears.

"Are those…rosary beads?" Billings said.

"I think so."

"If there's a crucifix, it's gotta be…inside him." Billings shook her head. "God."

As promised, there was no face. It had been flensed right off, leaving behind a *Gray's Anatomy* nightmare of exposed muscle and teeth. The skin tone elsewhere and black hair suggested Asian descent. The victim's penis had been replaced with a black candle, which had melted into a pile of wax around his scrotum.

Rothman and his cronies caught up with them. Kessler knelt down like a golf pro surveying the green to plan his putt, now at eye level with the body—or where his eyes used to be.

"You got it all figured out, superstar?" Rothman asked.

"Give it a rest, Nick," Billings said.

Rothman smiled at her with his lip curled. "Fucking figures you'd be on board with this guy."

"I don't even wanna know what's going through this freak's head," Cartwright said.

Kessler wasn't sure if "freak" referred to himself or the killer. He ignored it.

The mutilation of the face arguably didn't even qualify as the most gruesome aspect of the scene. Kessler circled behind the body in a crouch to get an unimpeded view of the angel wings the killer had fashioned for his prey. He'd sliced open drapes of back skin to unveil the dual staircases of the rib cages, then somehow sheared through the flank of each rib with something sharp—perhaps something like bolt cutters. The bony half columns were wrenched up and out, the makeshift wings sticking past the arms. Along with the skinned rictus of the face and the ironic radiance, it seemed like a mockery of both anatomy and theology.

The killer performed the handiwork in the building, rather than transporting it after the fact. The body sat in a pool of blood, some of which had been used to ink symbols like numbers on a clock in a circle. Perhaps he had posed the body as it gradually stiffened, allowing it to be fixed in this upright position.

Rothman whistled and waved over a couple of the uniforms. They approached hesitantly, obviously unsettled by the mutilations.

"I want you two to start rousting all the bums and junkies out there, ask if they saw anything. Long as our boy didn't look like two cents waiting for change, they hit him up for a buck coming or going with their usual bullshit sob stories."

"The hookers too?" one of the uniforms asked.

"Yeah, long as they're not wearing dark glasses and poking around with a white cane. You come get me if there's anything promising."

Kessler stood up. To Billings, he said, "Before I talk about a profile, maybe you can show me some of those other cases you think are connected."

"Think are connected?" Rothman echoed. "The guy who's supposed to bail us out of this shit hasn't even done his homework."

Cartwright brayed again.

They'd commandeered an office for the case, hanging up crime-scene photos, maps, and writing down leads and theories on a dry erase board. Any persons of interest had been cleared or deemed not so interesting after all. The photos displayed more grisly tableaux, obviously the work of the same devotee who conducted the mutilation orchestra in the warehouse.

"They're piling up fast," Billings said. "Five murders, two in the past week and a half."

Nathaniel Drucker. Discovered just off path of a hiking trail. Beheaded and eviscerated, the head tucked into the chest cavity. Flesh skinned from the shins down, kneeling in a pile of his own entrails.

Brenda Aguilar, nineteen years old. Found in a barely used junkyard, wedded with twisted metal like some strange combination of a ghastly sculpture and an altar. Organs neatly stacked on various intersecting, corroded limbs, one impaling her vaginally.

Rick van Zandt, twenty-four years old. Left in an abandoned house, several tendons and muscles peeled and stripped and used to hold him upright like puppet strings. An acolyte in the process of prostration but his arms outstretched in cruciform, scrotum pushed through a groove sliced into his pelvic region.

Catherine Nichols, fifty-three years old. Posed in front of a hole in the wall of a closed factory. Back skin removed and sewn over her face like a mask. Both arms severed and posed as if someone were climbing out of the wall behind her. Scalp partially incised with the flap positioned between the fingers of one of those extremities, to suggest dragging her into the darkness, the mouth of Hell.

"There's not much of a cooling off period, if you can even call it that," Billings continued. "It's too methodical and ritualistic to just be some frenzy. This isn't someone carrying out a private fantasy. He obviously believes in all this occult stuff."

Kessler examined the pictures. Occult symbols appeared at every scene, always inked in blood. While the full complement varied, one sigil showed up every time—a circle within a larger circle and the letters A M D U S I A S spread out clockwise between them. A maze of smaller symbols interlocked within, including a circle with the Roman numeral III and a larger circle featuring an uneven cross where the vertical bar became an oval on the bottom, part of a line of three.

"It would appear that way," Kessler said.

The mutilations impressed him. Flesh incised, excised, punctured, undraped. Organs transposed, removed, sculpted. Human beings remade as abominations, repurposed as vessels to damnation.

"What do you mean, appears that way?" Rothman led his entourage into the office. Detective Jeff Cartwright smiled with a set of teeth that would have earned the Gary Busey seal of approval. Carlos Perez wore a close approximation of this amused look. Rothman undoubtedly held court in Kessler's absence, skewering him for his captive audience.

"Just what I said. These crimes all appear to be the work of one man."

"You know, it's telling that you ducked out with actual police work underway."

"Why? I'm not a cop."

"We could have had our big break on the case, though. Anyone on that street could have seen the killer."

"And did they?" Billings asked.

"Well…no."

"What do you know about this...Amdusias?" Kessler said.

"He's a demon," Rothman said. "A fallen angel and a great duke of Hell."

"Have you ever heard of the Woodsman?" Billings asked. "Kind of a modern myth. Some people believe him to be Amdusias."

"And they think that little girl who disappeared in Clayton was taken by this Woodsman," Kessler said. "A demon of the woods."

"Her name was Gwendolyn something," Rothman said. "But we all know that girl wasn't taken by any monster except the human kind. It'll be someone with kiddie porn on their rap sheet, some playground wienie-wagger who crossed the line to murder. I'll bet you the guy we're looking for now has something like that, too."

"Why?" Kessler asked. "None of these cases involved children."

"Remember all those stories about ritual satanic abuse back in the 80s?" Rothman said.

"Totally *discredited* stories," Billings said.

"Just because the McMartin thing was a crock, doesn't mean all of it is. This is where all these satanic trips lead to—orgies and child rape."

"I'm partially in agreement with you," Kessler said.

"You are?" Billings said.

"You are?" Rothman echoed.

"Looking at the body today, I see inexperience," Kessler said.

"Is he joking?" Rothman asked Billings.

"*Are* you joking?" Billings asked him.

Kessler shook his head. "I can understand the temptation to group this latest killing with all the rest of these. I see anomalies, though."

"Wait, you're really saying you don't think this was all done by the same person?"

"Definitely not today's."

"Man, you're crazy," Rothman said.

Billings looked plenty skeptical herself, but she didn't say anything.

"The murder today has a noticeable lack of precision," Kessler said. "It's like someone tracing a drawing under a sheet of onion skin paper. It may seem like the same thing, but if you look closely enough, you'll see the flaws in the pen strokes."

"Hey, speaking of strokes," Rothman said, "are you sure you're not having one right now? Because there is no fucking way this is some copycat. There were so many details we never released to the media from the other murders, not least of which was the symbols. These were a perfect match for the other crime scenes. It'd be one thing if they were generic pentagrams, but seals of Amdusias are way beyond any beginner's level shit."

"Now wait," Billings said. "Let's just hear him out on this."

"This is a waste of time."

"Do you have any idea how many killers Kessler has put away in the past couple years?"

"I actually do," Rothman said. "Because the answer is zero—not a single one. Go check the arrest reports and tell me if you see his name on there."

"Don't worry about what I think," Kessler said. "Why don't you tell me about the person you believe you're looking for, detective. All of you."

"Just one of those nuts hiding in plain sight. He must be at least semi-functional because he needs a car to pick these people up and transport them. The crime scenes are several miles apart and none of the victims lived in easy walking distance."

"I put him in his early thirties," Billings said. "Young enough to have a conviction in his beliefs and a compulsion to act, but seasoned enough to be organized about it. Maybe someone who grew up in a home with a strict religious upbringing that pushed him into occult studies?"

Cartwright chipped in. "Somebody with medical training. Maybe just veterinary studies, but you can't cut somebody up like that if you don't know what you're doing."

"He may have an artistic background," Perez said. "It's always real showy. The way the light hit the body through the windows, he went to the trouble to do that. He believes in presentation."

"Probably paints naked kids," Rothman said. "Fuckin' freak."

Kessler nodded, scanning the room. "That all sounds quite logical." He paused on Rothman. "Mostly. However, I think for the one today, we're looking less for someone downloading child porn than someone closer to that age demographic. No job, no training, barely out of high school. Still living with a parent."

Billings, Rothman, Cartwright, and Perez shared dumbfounded looks.

"How'd you pull that out of your ass?" Rothman said. To Billings, he said, "You really thought this guy could help? I don't think he could find his own ass with GPS."

Her cell vibrated and moved along the tabletop as she received a text. She unlocked the screen. "We have an ID on the victim," she said. "Kwan Choi, twenty-eight years of age. Looks like they've already pulled up Instagram and Twitter accounts. His roommate reported him missing yesterday."

"Let's look into him," Kessler said. "Because I'm willing to bet our unsub had some kind of connection to the victim."

His profile was bullshit, of course. It was all malleable and ephemeral, same as his identity.

After tagging along with the detectives all afternoon—Billings in particular, who suffered him gladly—the man (or mind) calling himself Kessler settled into his hotel room. He queued up video footage on his laptop, running it through multiple windows. Filo Preston's snuff footage through Windows Media, Leonard Lake and Charles Ng "home movies" through VLC, and rape and torture videos from the Schoolgirl Murderers Paul Bernardo and Karla Homolka through RealPlayer—the latter allegedly destroyed by the Canadian government, but the FBI had it in the archives anyway. He'd spent the last three years devouring material like this, always claiming it for "research purposes." As far as the Bureau could tell, it paid off, and it was about to once again.

He worked his inches as Preston and company humiliated and mutilated their victims with satanic delight. While it barely moved the needle of his own lust, he thrived on the loathing and horror of his host body. He could hear the agent's scream in what the usurper considered the "under-mind." What must it be like to dedicate yourself to the pursuit of depraved killers, then be relegated to some recess of your mind as someone else took the wheel and essentially raped your body and will in the process? Three years of this torment, seeing his career flourish with commendations while elsewhere corruption proliferated.

The usurper had arranged for the dormant Kessler to feel a vestige of the release as he expelled his load to pixilated teary eyes, begging mouths, and spurting arteries. The agent would have all these memories to keep him warm when he regained control of the body some distant day when the usurper had cause to move on, and what would he do then? No one would believe Kessler if he tried to explain it.

Sated for the moment, the usurper logged into Kwan Choi's Facebook page. Back at the station, they were waiting for the authorization to access it and seek any clues and connections to other victims. For him, it was like sliding a credit card through a flimsy lock. He was in, seeing the proliferation of sad emojis and testimonials on the page as close friends voiced their despair at Choi's loss. He moved on to movie and band pages Kwan followed.

Next he logged into an interface he had used many times before to bypass the numerous security protocols and anonymously access the FBI watch list. Even with all his prestige, he couldn't freely browse the list. It was one thing to have someone in mind and discover their internet search history raised a red flag on some related matter. It was quite another to have no lead and go looking for a sacrificial lamb. That wouldn't look good if anyone ever did some digging.

He found a connection to Choi with potential. Not a direct friend, but somebody local who'd firmly established his presence on the list a couple of years ago. Not yet old enough to legally drink, either.

It would take a little more than that, though. He cross-referenced the name with another resource—InterphaZ's Interdex. He smiled after a moment.

Kessler had just found his next killer in a storied career.

"Tyson Bryant?"

The young man at the door blinked, obviously figuring the group on his porch hadn't dropped by to deliver a massive check from Publisher's Clearing House. He may have just rolled out of bed, judging by his tousled hair. He wore a shirt with a barely readable band logo—CORPSE FROTHER—and a crude drawing of a naked dismembered woman whose genitals seemed to be missing in the human jigsaw. In letters stretching across the bottom of the shirt, it said WHERE'S ALL THE PUSS?

"Tyson? Who's at the door?" a reedy voice asked from deep in the house.

"It's for me!" he shouted back. To Kessler and Rothman, he said, "What's this about?"

Kessler smiled disarmingly. "I'm John Kessler with the FBI. These are Detectives Billings and Rothman."

Tyson's eyes bugged at "FBI," the gears clearly turning in his mind—what had he illegally downloaded lately, and how could he pawn it off on someone else?

"Mind if we come in and talk to you for a moment?" Billings said.

He obviously wanted to say no, but he replied, "Uh, yeah, sure. Follow me."

He paused as he led them toward the basement when the reedy voice said, "Is that Vance? Who's at the door?"

Tyson sighed and vanished down the hallway, saying, "It's for me. You need to get back in bed, Mom."

Satisfied she'd obeyed, he returned to lead Kessler, Billings, and Rothman to the basement down a dim flight of stairs. Kessler caught the look Rothman shared with Billings—pure skepticism.

As they studied the décor of the basement, though, Billings gave Rothman a look of her own, like *See?* A poster tacked to the wall featured a pornographic scene of a man with an intense look of effort as he thrust into a woman well on her way to being thrice his size. Blue lower case letters read "libido airbag" in the upper left corner, and red text near the bottom said KNEE DEEP IN HER PUSSY in caps. Kessler supposed the profile angle of the sex act seemed to fulfill the promise of the title.

On the opposite wall, Tyson had taped up a collage of vaginas from various pornographic magazines. Some of them were pierced, others stretched with fish hooks.

"Interesting artwork," Kessler said, nodding at the collage. "Not too big on faces, are you?"

"A pretty one helps, but you can't see 'em while they're blowing you, so…"

Billings curled her mouth.

There wasn't really anywhere to sit but an unmade bed and a beanbag chair, so they all remained standing. It seemed too warm down here, magnified by the stale air. A guitar and amp stood against the wall, the red guitar covered in several unreadable band logo stickers modeled mostly on blood and semen. Beside that, a CD cabinet with the shelves crammed full of jewel cases.

"Not sure why you want to talk to me," Tyson said after several awkward seconds. "I haven't done nothing."

"No?" Kessler said.

"I guess I was a little late signing up for the draft, but I registered."

"Why don't you tell us about your band."

"You want to know about Corpse Frother? You don't exactly look like porno grind maniacs. No offense. "

"Porno grind?" Billings echoed.

"Yeah. Like Gut, CBT, the Meat Shits, Creamface, Libido Airbag, bands like that. Real heavy shit with a lot of porno samples. I have a bunch of them on my racks." He pointed to the CD cabinet.

Billings' eyes were locked on the Libido Airbag poster. "This is…music?"

"Ha…sort of. My CDs are on the dresser, feel free to grab one on your way out."

"Who else is in Corpse Frother?" Rothman asked.

"It's just me."

"What does that even mean?"

"It's what it sounds like. One who froths on corpses."

"And you're Corpse Frother?" Billings said.

"That's the band name, but I go by Giallo Killer."

"Giallo?"

"Giallo movies are sort of mystery thrillers with real brutal deaths in them. Usually psychos in black gloves laying waste with razors, knives, drills, all sorts of shit. Giallo just means yellow."

"So you're Yellow Killer," Kessler translated.

"Like Asian," Rothman said.

Tyson shook his head, confused. "No, they're Italian."

"Someone's killed a few women around here lately," Kessler said. "You hear much about that?"

Tyson paused before answering as the familiar ground of music and movies abruptly became shaky. "A little, I guess. A few news clips."

"And did you hear about Kwan Choi?"

"Who's that?"

"You don't know? He tagged Corpse Frother on a Facebook post. He went to one of your shows."

"Okay, so? I don't know someone just because they watched me play or tagged my page."

"He posted a picture of the two of you, too."

"Wait, how do you even hold a concert?" Rothman asked. "I thought you were a one-man band."

"Yeah, I use a drum machine. I play guitar and do the vocals on stage during the samples and drum beats." To Kessler he said, "I don't doubt the picture, but do you know how many people came up to me after a gig to get a picture and say they liked the show?"

"Two or three?" Billings said.

Tyson smirked. "Are you guys butthurt about Corpse Frother, is that it?"

"We haven't even heard it," Kessler said.

"I can tell she has some opinions." Tyson hooked a thumb toward Billings. "But I mean, when that porno grind dude in Ohio shot those people, Bandcamp, Spotify, and those other pussy sites started kicking off all the porno grind bands. I lost my account because of that."

"An incalculable loss to the music world, I'm sure," Kessler said. "What will they do without your oeuvre?"

"Ooh-*what?* They only just let me back on Bandcamp. For all I know, you guys are making me a suspect because I play that kind of music. Because suddenly everyone who plays porno grind is some kind of maniac."

"Not so sure about suddenly," Billings said.

"Listen, I don't know anything about these dead women or this Chew dude or whatever."

"Choi."

"I still don't know him."

"Still living at home, are you?" Kessler said.

"For now. My mom needs my help. She's all fucked up in here." He pointed to his head.

"Apple doesn't fall far from the tree," Billings muttered.

"Let me guess," Rothman said. "She needs you for interior decorating?" He nodded in the direction of the vagina collage.

"That's going to be the next album cover," Tyson said. "*Get Up in Those Guts.*"

Looks all around.

"Okay, you say you don't remember Choi," Kessler said. "What about the women?"

"What about them? It hasn't been all women, has it?"

"I thought you didn't 'know that much about the crimes."

"I hear people talk, is all. I just think it's messed up how they make a bigger deal about the women. The guys probably didn't have any more of a fighting chance, especially if this maniac jumped them with a knife, but people think it's somehow fairer. Same as me having to sign up for the draft. Bet you didn't have to do that." He said this last to Billings.

"They care more about the women?" Kessler said. "These anonymous people who can't stop talking about these murders you're not following at all?"

"You know what I mean. When that dude in California shot those people five or six years ago, the news stories were always about his manifesto and how much he hated women. A bunch of guys got capped, but all they could talk about was 'misogyny.' I just get tired of the woe-is-me victim bullshit when they're always on a pedestal."

"You're coming off like an incel," Billings said.

Tyson laughed. "I've probably crushed more gash than these two combined." He nodded toward Kessler and Rothman, and after a pause added, "Maybe all three of you."

Billings' face turned an angry red, almost a match of the guitar. "What do you have against women?"

Tyson deadpanned, "Hopefully my dick."

Rothman cracked his knuckles. "Kid, you know anything about patching up a wall after someone's head goes through it?"

"Okay, chill out," Tyson said. "I'm sorry. I don't have any problem with them, okay?"

Billings scanned the back cover of one of the Corpse Frother CDs on the dresser. "Here are some choice cuts from *Bad Jams and Corpse Butt-Slams.*"

Tyson smiled faintly.

"'Strangled With Your Own Stockings.' 'Poondoggle.' 'Blowtorched Twat.'"

"There aren't even any lyrics," Tyson said. "I'm just making sounds...gurgles and screams, no words."

Billings continued. "'Manifesto for Exterminating Cunts.' 'Satanic Pussy Barbecue.' 'Find a Fold and Fuck It.' 'Runny Cream-Pied Cunny.'"

"No lyrics. I repeat, no lyrics."

"'Felch My Beef Broth from Your Sister's Prolapsed Rect—.'"

Tyson interrupted. "Okay, yeah, it sounds bad when you read it like that, but it takes longer to say the title than listen to that song. That's the joke."

"You're sure you don't know anything about Kwan Choi, Mr. Yellow Killer?" Kessler said.

"No! Stop acting like I'm some kind of racist. Dude, I've got like half a terabyte of Asian porn on my hard drive, okay? And it's *Giallo* Killer."

"My mistake. I'd hate to take anything away from a gurgle icon like you. I don't suppose anyone can corroborate all your whereabouts yesterday, can they?"

"I was here. It wouldn't mean anything if my mom backed that up or not. She might tell you I'm not here right this second and I just saw her."

"Do you think anything about Amdusias?" Rothman asked.

"Amdusias? No, I'm not into black metal."

"Okay," Kessler said, "I think that's plenty for now. Thanks for chatting with us, Tyson."

"I didn't do nothing," he repeated.

"We'll let you get back to your misogyny," Billings said.

"Appreciate it."

He led them up to the ground floor, and shut the door behind them.

"I don't like him," Billings said.

"Personally speaking, or you don't like him for any murders?" Kessler asked.

"Take your pick."

"I told you this was a waste of time," Rothman said. "Sure, I'd like to wring his skinny little neck, but I wouldn't trust that shit-ass to microwave a Lean Cuisine. He hasn't killed anything but music. Maybe you can bring him in for that."

Kessler smiled. "We'll see."

Kessler went back to Tyson's house after nightfall. He parked his rental car a block away and waited. A little neighborhood activity, but not much. In the first hour, a woman walked an Australian cattle dog and a Siberian husky. A few cars returned home. In the second hour, a man in a fluorescent orange helmet and reflector pads rode past in a bicycle. A ponytailed lady in Spandex jogged by on the opposite sidewalk. In the third hour, teenagers returned from a date and the boy walked the girl to the front door, kissed her good night, and left. Her bedroom light flipped on a minute later on the second floor.

Nothing happened in the historical home of the songsmith of "Molest the Corpse Butt" fame. Soft light glowed in the basement windows the whole time. Half past hour three, Kessler stepped out of the car and made his way over. He knelt by a window on the side of the house with some shrubbery cover. No one could see him from the street. The curtains were sheer enough to reveal Tyson in his bean bag chair, engrossed by something on his laptop. Kessler took a wild guess at what the purveyor of porno grind might be watching. Music played over speakers, extremely down-turned guitars with throttling drums and vocals so low they sounded like bass rumblings. He doubted it would sound any more coherent from inside the house, but he'd be finding out anyway.

He sat in front of the window, which acted as a veiled television screen. He concentrated on drawing aside the veil, projecting his mind, his essence. Allowing Tyson to unwittingly absorb it, an assimilation beneath the boy's perception, as though Tyson breathed him in, but instead of oxygen, the usurper manifested as consciousness. And like someone sliding their fingers down a panel of circuit breakers, he switched off Tyson in an instant.

The agent's body remained where he'd left it, Kessler essentially on pause. Like hanging up a coat that he could slip back into when he was ready to walk out with it. Kessler would know nobody was home, but he couldn't do a thing to regain control. He remained trapped and comatose, thoughts with no responding vessel.

Tyson thrashed in the under-mind, panicked by the loss of control, but it amounted to little more than a whisper down a long tunnel. Even someone who'd mastered mind over matter well enough to sit still while they burned alive couldn't do more than scratch at the psychic door if they'd assimilated InterphaZ nanotechnology at some point through unwitting transmission. Everyone on the Interdex could be manipulated. With the nano seeding, he could keep someone suspended while he overtook another mind, and inhabit a person with all of their experiences and mannerisms at his disposal, rather than overwriting them for the duration.

InterphaZ had found several creative ways to disperse their influence. He'd been there for that nascent stage of nano research in the mind of a scientist named Yves, which the institution developed to clandestinely mutate a subject's anatomy and alter his or her will. The recent assassination of Dr. Braedon Obrist by a quintessential patsy suggested they'd come a long way with it, but remained quite primitive compared to his own private manipulation of the nano potential. InterphaZ might as well have wielded a stone and sling while he launched atomic bombs of psychic warfare.

The porno grind artist formerly known as Tyson tried to make sense of the menagerie of images on the laptop. The way storefronts used to display a wall of televisions, Tyson had carefully resized several porn site windows to play clips simultaneously, a tic-tac-toe board of perversity. A double penetration here, a POV blowjob there, a line of veiny men in the top left corner screen anointing a chair-bound woman with load after load (true to Tyson's word, she was Asian), aggressive bondage and strange rubber apparatuses in the opposite corner. A blindfolded woman tied up and stationed on some kind of saddle sex toy, the vibration settings of which were controlled by a naked man in a Mexican wrestling mask. The woman moaned and shuddered in ecstasy, but she'd begun to bleed between her legs. She had no idea as she twitched in another orgasm.

He minimized several of the browser windows, wondering just how much he might have embellished Tyson's profile after all. His dick was out, or at least Tyson's was. He kept it that way for the time being, partially erect. A pump bottle of lotion stood within arm's reach, but he wasn't lathered up and hadn't been holding the organ when he overtook Tyson's consciousness. This was just part of Tyson's prolonged masturbatory process. It would seem he had an affinity for ritual after all.

The usurper guessed correctly about the music—if possible, it sounded even more incomprehensible to him without the filter of insulated walls. The mercifully short burst ended, followed by audio from a vintage phone sex ad of the VHSage.

"I'm so looooooonely and horny, lover. Why don't you call me up and tell me how you like your *massive* dick sucked. You know I'll do it for you, and I won't let a drop of your *precious* ball sauce go to waste. I'll swallow it *allllllll* down. I'll be frigging my clit waiting for your call. Only five dollars per minute."

Riffling through Tyson's thoughts, he figured out how to shut the music off. The ensuing silence sat in his ears with the sort of pressure that could warp a submarine. Almost immediately he heard the reedy voice from this afternoon: "Tyson? Who's at the door?"

He took the laptop and walked up the stairs, his cock engorging. Her voice became clearer as he ascended. A detour to the kitchen rewarded him with a fillet knife to take to mommy dearest's bedroom. He followed the voice down the hallway toward the back corner of the house, his penis pulsing as if drawn to the sound.

By now he knew from his access to Tyson's mind that she'd exhibited early signs of senility and he tried to keep her confined to bed, mostly so he didn't have to deal with her. The bedroom glowed with the cool blue light of flickering images from her TV, an older model mounted on her dresser. A candle on the nightstand provided a warmer glow near the bed.

He set the laptop down where its built-in webcam presented a wide angle of the room. He initiated its record function. The picture looked dark, so he flipped on the overhead light. Tyson's mother blinked against the brightness, sixty-two years old with all gray hair dyed black, an unbecoming amount of eye shadow and a short nightgown that covered little of her thick white legs. She looked Tyson up and down, this young figure poised above her with a knife clutched in his hand and a hard-on jutting from his open jeans, bouncing with his frenzied heartbeat.

"Vance, is that you?" she asked, squinting. "Good Lord, look at that! Why don't you guide that stud missile right here?" Her legs parted slightly, where Tyson could see hair and the absence of underwear. She slapped her mons pubis as if trying to coax a cat onto a seat cushion.

He stood rooted to the spot in a rare moment of indecision, but as the screams of his host mind hit a shrillness undreamed of, he smiled and crawled onto the bed, guiding that stud missile right where she'd indicated. He stuck the fillet knife into the corner of the mattress, away from the action.

*NOOOOOOOOO!* Tyson hollered, now much louder down that long corridor.

A few strategic flips of that circuit panel and Tyson could feel the way his body responded to his mother's moist inner walls as their mouths joined. Her netherlips sucked Tyson's girth like a second mouth, suggesting some serious Kegel maneuvers in her day. The usurper experienced a mental rapture as euphoric as that shuddering warm embrace. Many times had he used a host's body with a willing (and oftentimes unwilling) partner, but this was the first time for an incestuous encounter where the recipient *wanted* it to happen, even if she wasn't in her right mind at the moment. That wasn't a loophole that would be of any comfort to Tyson, especially as he withdrew the stud missile and broke off a kiss to lick his way down her navel and belly before sinking his face between her thighs.

*STOP IT, OH PLEASE GOD, STOOOOP IIIIIIIIIIIT!*

"Oh God Vance what are you doing don't stop don't stop don't stop," Mom said.

Tyson's tongue and fingers obliged her, denying the prisoner's request. The mother's thighs quivered uncontrollably.

*OH GOD WHAT'S HAPPENING I'M IN HELL I'M IN HELL*

"Oh God my pussy's exploding, Vance, eat me eat me eat me—"

He ate. Her words choked off and her body went stiff before a wave detonated inside her and Tyson discovered firsthand-and-face that his beloved old ma was one righteous squirter.

After her passionate tsunami and bafflement that it had never been so good with this Vance person before, he climbed back up to sink Tyson's erection home again...where it all started for her number one sonny-buns. The torment had already hit its pinnacle, and there were only meek sobs from his host as he unloaded his precious ball sauce into his mother's sucking vagina. He wondered if she would have swallowed it *allllll* down if he'd finished in her mouth.

Her shuddering began again as he planted a pillow over her face and drove the knife into it five, six times. Blood bloomed through the tears. Her struggling arms flopped to her sides. He tossed the pillow aside, satisfied she'd spent the worst of her screams. He wanted all of this to be discovered, but not until he'd finished the prerequisites.

The meek sobs boosted in volume again, horror and despair. It made the usurper half-hard again, even after a profound orgasm where he still felt fluid dribbling from the tip of the stud missile.

He incised her face over several seconds, patiently sawing through the layers of skin. He fashioned a flower shape in her flesh, like a full circle of daisy petals, which he peeled away from her skull one at a time as though she bloomed in a death repose. It lacked the precision of the Kwan Choi job, uneven as it was and interrupted by multiple stab wounds, but no denying the startling effect of someone's face opened in such an unnatural shape.

Tyson's moaning became background static throughout the process.

He began to inscribe the symbol of Amdusias across her stomach with the blade, etching everything from memory, including other arcane symbols, the acts of a faithful disciple. Like drawing mazes in her flesh, labyrinths for which the center led to damnation.

In his ministrations, his eyes fell upon a vacuum cleaner in the corner of the room. When he had completed all of the sigils, he slid off the bed and dislodged the vacuum wand from its attachment, rolled it all over to the bed, and plugged it in. Not sure if it would work, he affixed the opening of the wand over the mother's anus and turned it on. The nightgown had climbed up to her breasts while he stabbed her, and he observed strange movement within the skin as the suction pulled at her insides. The machine whirred and the opening to the wand sputtered as it engulfed something in its orifice.

He pulled the wand back and something came with it—a bulb of coiled flesh prolapsed from the rectum. More withdrew from peristalsis as the vacuum tugged. He teased out the rope of her insides, dragging it across the bedspread like a mutant tail.

Tyson's static screams soared back into consciousness over this humiliation of the corpse. The usurper shut off the vacuum, which relinquished the intestine. He guided the length up the front of her body to her mouth, feeding it down the passage of her throat. The blooming mutilation of the face and the passage of waste rerouted to its source suggested fecundity and infinity.

He walked over to the laptop, the fillet knife once more in hand. He set the laptop to broadcast live to Facebook. "I am the slayer of Kwan Choi earlier this week and now my mother, as a final sacrifice. The seventh gate will open at last. May all whores and untrue sons of Satan perish in flames!"

So saying, he grimly set the fillet knife to the base of his penis and began slicing through the skin. It gave with frightful ease. The usurper shut down his pain receptors, but kindly rerouted them to the under-mind.

The inner Tyson shrieked.

A few reaction hearts fluttered across the screen, then emoticons with shocked faces.

As crimson pumped from the severed arteries, he took the castrated member back to the bed and inserted it in the mother's runny cream-pied cunny. Hot blood spritzed upon the carpet, the bed, the walls, the mother's legs. He gripped the pillar of the nightstand candle and set the flame to the stump, faux shrieking as the veins and arteries sizzled and popped like a campfire frank. Here he flooded from the gurgle icon's mind back to Kessler's body and unhurriedly strolled back to his car. Whether or not Tyson survived the blood loss was immaterial.

Kessler caught the call from Billings on his way back to the hotel, seconds after a line of squad cars blew past in the other lane, sirens wailing.

"New theory, Billings? I was just about to call it a night."

"You're never going to believe this," she said. "Tyson Bryant just dropped a new Corpse Frother promo on Facebook and we've got a fucking bloodbath. I'm en route. Do you know remember how to get back to the house?"

Kessler smiled. "I think I can find it. Be seeing you."

Rothman beat him to the crime scene again. Red and blue lights washed over the detective's face from the ambulance and squad cars. The red in particular suited his sour expression. "Lucky fucking guess."

A media van stopped in front of the house and a crew burst from its doors, almost synchronized. They had the death beat down to a fine art. A uniform ordered them to stay on the street. Neighbors watched unabashedly from their lawns.

Billings emerged from the house.

"What happened here, detective?" Kessler said mildly.

Billings blew out air. "One dead. Tyson did his mother, cut off his own dick, and…uh, did his mother."

"Look, just because he said he snuffed Choi doesn't mean he really did it," Rothman said. "I could find ten stewbums right now who'd take credit for that."

"So, ten more than those cops found in the interviews yesterday?" Kessler asked. To Billings, he said, "Tyson confessed to Choi?"

"On Facebook. He's recanting now, to put it mildly."

Paramedics guided a stretcher through the front door—the man of the hour, restrained, sobbing, raving: *"It wasn't me! I didn't kill her! I was possessed!"*

"He carved the Amdusias symbol in his mother's flesh," Billings continued. "Looked accurate to me. He recorded the whole thing before the Facebook broadcast. Don't watch it until you have a trash can or toilet to puke in."

"Bully for you," Rothman said to Kessler. "You're a modern day Nostradamus. You plucked some kid off Facebook who sings about raping and killing women all the time, and he raped and killed a woman. How did you ever know?"

*"I told you there weren't any lyrics, motherfucker!"* Tyson screamed from the stretcher.

"There's the pot calling the kettle black. I saw what was dripping out of your mom in there, Corpse Frother, and it wasn't maple syrup. "

*"There weren't any lyrics! There weren't any lyrics!"*

"Get this dick-less piece of shit outta my sight!"

Kessler heard one of the news crewmen say, "Holy shit, is that the Mind Stalker?"

Rothman rolled his eyes. "Here we go. Bow for your adoring public. A woman's dead and full of her son's load, but oh well, who was that masked man? Just know, your nutcase didn't cop to the other killings and we won't find any evidence connecting him. This isn't over."

Kessler watched them shut the ambulance doors, cutting off Tyson's latest declaration of innocence. The siren chirped as it rolled out of the driveway.

He turned back to Rothman. "I never said it was."

Kessler's agent called as he stepped off the elevator back in Virginia.

"John boy, the phones are blowing up again!" Wyatt said. "The crime shows want in while this Cunt Killer thing is all the rage."

"Corpse Frother," Kessler corrected.

"Hey, a rose by any other name, am I right? Bandcamp just deleted his page, by the way. Apparently 'Felch My Beef Broth from Your Sister's Prolapsed Rectum' cracked the top ten single downloads. Wait, did I just say rectum and cracked? Poetry."

Kessler frowned. There seemed like a lot more bustle as IT staff flitted in and out of the offices. Pendleton waited at the end of the corridor, surveying. He made eye contact with Kessler and nodded.

Wyatt rattled on. "Listen, A&E wants to reboot *American Justice* with you on a slew of episodes. Tubi's also launching a new unsolved crimes series, where you could be like the in-house expert. You know, get you to profile the sort of scumbag who'd have done it and hope someone says, 'Whoa, that sounds like Dad!' Their loved one fries in the electric chair, the victims get justice, everybody wins."

"Not really feeling cold cases," Kessler said.

"No? If you stepped in and cracked it—shit, I said it again—it'd be big, Johnny. I bet you could. You mean to tell me you couldn't hash out whoever snatched that Geisha Hammond woman in Bartok?"

"Who?"

"News anchor who disappeared, real looker. Her lips *really* belonged on a microphone, that's all I'm saying."

"Pass."

"Okay, what about that little girl who vanished in Clayton? Gwendolyn something. She was obsessed with that Woodsman thing, some demonic entity like Slenderman. Christ, were kids always this crazy?"

He knew of that one, of course. Billings mentioned it the other day. Amdusias again, though no relation to the Chapman murders. Although, could he *make* them related? Food for thought.

A beefy guy with glasses appeared beside Pendleton. Kessler had never seen him before.

"What about the cases no one expects you to bust?" Wyatt said. "Zodiac."

"Someone *not* named Arthur Leigh Allen. Next."

"Jack the Ripper. The classics never die, at least not for long, right?"

"If Patricia Cornwall already thinks she solved it, what could I possibly have to add? I'll give you a firm maybe on *American Justice*, but only if Bill Kurtis is involved. Talk soon, Wyatt."

"Wait—"

Kessler ended the call as he reached Pendleton and the sweaty stranger. "Something going on, sir?"

"We've had ourselves a breach, John. No *bueno*."

"Oh?"

"You're just in time to meet our new IT Security Director, Sonny Hooper." Pendleton clapped the heavyset man on the shoulder.

"Agent Kessler," the man said. He shook Kessler's hand with a moist palm. "It's an honor. I've never met someone the day after they were trending on Twitter."

"Before you get too smug, you should know 'beef broth' trended too," Pendleton said. "And for longer."

"I have nothing to be smug about," Kessler said. "A woman is dead." He had plenty to feel smug about anyway.

"We had a double hit last night," Pendleton said. "The watch list and the Interdex, apparently within minutes of each other."

"I have my team fortifying security measures on all the PCs in the building," Hooper said. "We're making sure there's nothing that shouldn't be there. We could just remote in and take control, but I don't know. I prefer the direct approach. We already checked over yours, but we understand there's a laptop too?"

"Correct." Still in the trunk of his car in the parking garage, where he planned to keep it. "I'll make sure to bring it in."

"We'd appreciate that."

"You suspect some kind of Trojan virus thing from InterphaZ? Kessler asked Pendleton. "Could they have shared their directory with us just so they could take a peek at our files? A little unsanctioned quid pro quo?"

"We suspect *everyone*. But nice to see you don't need a cadaver to start divining entrails."

The new security director said, "It might even be an inside job."

Kessler wondered if he could shut down Sonny Hooper's mind, hoping it wouldn't come to that. It didn't require InterphaZ implants but that offered the smoothest and most capable medium. He'd previously rooted through those directories with none the wiser. He wondered what had changed. Hooper also gave him a strange vibe. A familiar one.

Kessler's phone vibrated. He checked the text, expecting something from Wyatt about Bill Kurtis, but it was Billings.

*Can you come back? They just found another body*

"I'm afraid I need to get back on a plane," he said. "Nice meeting you, Mr. Hooper."

The man's eyes seemed to float like goldfish in his lenses. "Oh, please. Call me Hoop."

"Can't believe the reign of terror didn't miraculously stop with the Jello Killer in the hospital," Rothman said. "Almost like the whole thing was bullshit."

"Giallo Killer," Billings corrected.

"Bryant's still going with the demonic possession excuse?" Kessler asked.

"You know it."

"Speaking of things that are also bullshit," Rothman added.

They were back at the North Chapman HQ office, five around the table—Kessler, Billings, Rothman, Perez, and Cartwright. They'd added another dry erase board to the room with some of the latest highlights. Beneath a print-out of a picture of Kwan Choi still in possession of his face—probably a driver's license photo—Billings had written *Killed by Tyson Bryant?* Rothman had crossed the line out and written *Hell no, ALL CONNECTED.* Under pictures of Tyson and his mother Elaine, Rothman had also written *Related to each other, but not to our case.*

"Anything stand out to you about the latest?" Kessler asked.

Jesse Milton, a thirty-two-year-old white male found in an abandoned theater. With Kessler unable to observe the fresh crime scene, Billings made a video of it on her smartphone, which lent it a grimier aesthetic than the crime scene pictures.

"His car was nearby, so he probably wasn't taken there," Billings said. "No prints on the steering wheel but his. Didn't seem like any were smudged by gloves or intentionally wiped away."

"Why would he be there?"

"YouTube," Perez said. "He's one of those 'urban explorers.'"

"I've heard a little about that. They go into hospitals, schools, amusement parks, spots that were closed down years ago, right?"

"Pretty much. Milton had a channel called *Extreme Jauntings*. He'd hit places like that, but he was just as likely to climb to the top of a bridge or take an elevator to the roof of a tall building and hang off the edge with one hand. "

"Christ," Rothman said. "Should have called it *Extreme-ly Fucking Stupid.*"

"Lucky to make it as long as he did," Perez said. "I mean, until what happened."

Milton would have been better off splattering on the pavement in front of the Hyatt Regency. He'd also been molded into a religious pose like Choi, but on his knees with his arms raised heavenward. His hands were nailed to a wall to keep them aloft, with curtains of flesh sliced from his torso to expose both columns of his ribs—what was left of them. Every other rib had been broken off, potentially by the claw of the hammer that did the crucifying. The shards from the shattered ribs wound up on top of Milton's head like a crown, wedged into gaps where the hammerhead pounded open his skull. The Amdusias sigils once more appeared etched at the scene, this time on a ragged movie screen. The lack of windows prevented a final celestial touch, but Milton's lantern sat on the floor in front of him, retaining enough juice to throw his warped shadow across the screen like a projector.

Cartwright shook his head. "I can't even watch some of those daredevil videos. They make me dizzy."

"He did this channel by himself?" Kessler asked.

Perez nodded. "Must have thought it'd be an easy one last night, as long as there wasn't some meth'd-out hobo living in there."

"No video, I take it."

Rothman laid on the sarcasm. "Gosh, now why didn't we think of that?"

"He recorded all those videos with a pair of glasses," Perez said. "We searched hours for them and didn't find shit."

"Actually, shit was all we *did* find," Cartwright corrected. "Mostly rodent, but some of it was probably human."

"We're hoping a vagrant picked up the glasses and not the killer," Billings said. "Maybe whoever called in the body. Anonymous again."

Rothman shook his head. "Unless we start a 'trade in crucial evidence for Thunderbird' program, we'll never see those specs."

"If we *do*, though…" Billings knocked on the wooden tabletop. "Milton used night vision on some of those videos. I bet we'd have our guy's mug. Facial recognition might take us right to him."

"Let's assume we aren't getting a convenient video of him doing his thing," Kessler said. "Tell me about your killer."

Rothman scoffed. "Do you ever actually put together a profile, or do you just cherry pick from everyone else's ideas?"

"Your ideas didn't lead me to Tyson Bryant."

"For good reason—he doesn't have anything to do with this case. Now, whoever did this one killed Choi too, and all those others."

"What about you, Billings? Do you think it's the same killer?"

"I do." She seemed almost embarrassed to admit it. "But there's no easy explanation for how Tyson knew about the symbols."

"Maybe we're looking at some kind of cult here," Kessler said.

"For Christ's sake," Rothman said. "It's some lone nutcase who listened to too much Slayer back in high school."

"So, to summarize," Kessler said, "you're looking for a man in his early thirties with some kind of medical training, possibly a religious upbringing, and an artistic background."

Rothman held up a finger. "You left something out—this sicko is probably sitting on literal *mountains* of child porn."

"If he's sitting on literal mountains of illegal pornography, he should be pretty easy to find."

Cartwright brayed.

Rothman looked rather displeased. "You'll see when we get him."

Cartwright's phone rattled on the tabletop. "Sorry, I gotta take this," he said, trying to hurry out of the room, though not before they all identified his ringtone—Corpse Frother's "Beef Broth" song.

"Seriously, Jeff?" Billings said.

Cartwright gave her a "what can you do?" shrug and disappeared through the doorway.

"I don't think it's any accident that we keep finding bodies in these abandoned places," Kessler said.

"Well, he's not going to carry it out in a Starbucks, now, is he?"

"I think if we look through Milton's YouTube channel, we're going to find out that he explored some of our crime scenes in his past videos before they were crime scenes…and that someone used his channel to scout for some private real estate to make all those alterations to the victims without being interrupted or seen. It's fair to say Milton's mutilations demonstrate a philosophy similar to Choi's, but I don't see the same kind of brute strength it would have taken to twist Choi's ribs into angel wings. Whoever did the wings could have broken those ribs off with his bare hands, but that isn't what happened."

"Maybe it's a subscriber to Milton's channel," Billings said.

"All you have to do is run the names and look for a sex bust in their criminal records," Rothman said. "Especially if it had anything to do with child porn."

"Any ideas why your pedophile is preying exclusively on adult men and women?" Kessler asked neutrally.

"Because he's out of his mind! Why else?"

"*His* mind," Kessler repeated.

Billings seized on it. "What do you mean? Why did you repeat that?"

Kessler shrugged. "It's my belief that Jesse Milton was killed by a woman."

A woman named Priscilla York, to be precise. Another bad specimen the usurper pulled from the watch list and cross-referenced with the Interdex when he'd rooted out Tyson Bryant. Priscilla's illustrious criminal record began with possession of narcotics, then possession with intent to distribute, then back to mere possession as she apparently couldn't stop hitting up her own supply long enough to actually sell it. She landed on the watch list when she shared a seedy element of contacts after a prison stretch—people who bought and sold women into slavery overseas. An old cellmate may have hooked her up. It was suspected that Priscilla played mother hen to fresh street meat, setting up these newcomers to the skin trade with "talent scouts" from the operation. Several messages in probable coded language were intercepted and flagged—*I have a new friend you should meet shewud luv to travel*—and then there'd be more room on the street corner for the next group of desperate women to sell their bodies. Perhaps she informed any curious veterans on the blocks that she'd talked these naïve women into going back to their parents, safe from the jaws of a hungry and indiscriminate city.

Tonight, though, Priscilla would be involved with a whole other skin trade.

The convenient thing about a faithful druggie like Priscilla was that the usurper could take a body ride with her oblivious, which he'd actually done the other night for the first time after departing the Beef Broth Massacre crime scene (as the jaded social media audience had dubbed Tyson's matricidal frolic). She'd been a subscriber to *Extreme Jauntings* and had also viewed some Corpse Frother videos previously, probably to make a decision on whether she should make an appearance at one of Tyson's gigs at a club she frequented (she had not done so). These were tenuous connections among perpetrators and victims, but that didn't matter when footage of the murders existed.

The usurper saw the potential with Milton's glasses, and the explorer had serendipitously posted about shooting a new video that night (*late night creeping, y'all!*). It was nothing to take control of a wasted Priscilla in her studio hovel, then follow Milton to his destination in the late-night hours. The glasses had filmed Priscilla's attack in the theater, and now she wore them for a first-person view of tonight's "occult" killing.

He sat in the back pew of the church as Priscilla, waiting for late night penitents to finish their prayers and fuck off back to the streets. It forced him to pretend to pray and meditate for far longer than he would have believed necessary. Some old lady with a kerchief wrapped around her head held out so long, he started to think—hope—she'd died , but the old bag of bones eventually stood and walked out in a rickety fashion, as if she were in the middle of a private earthquake. That left Priscilla alone at last in the pews.

Someone from the clergy appeared at the front of the church, a mostly bald man in white robes. He might have even been a priest. He was here, so that was good enough.

Kessler stood, adjusting the glasses as he walked up front. He turned Priscilla's head briefly to check the entrance. So far, no one else.

"I was wondering..." Priscilla's voice said. He unzipped her purse, which he'd emptied back at the apartment this evening to have room for the dagger, a cleaver, a serrated knife, and hammer.

The man looked at her expectantly, late forties, early fifties. His eyes barely had time to register shock when the steel of the blade sank into his throat. The dagger twisted and a severed artery burst in a mist of hot blood. The white robe became a sodden crimson sail. The dagger withdrew and fell in quick succession, gradually taking the clergyman to the ground like a nail hammered crookedly.

Priscilla cut the robe open, revealing a wiry form beneath. The chest rose and fell rapidly, the man gasping and moaning, blood still misting from his punctured throat. He chopped through the clergyman's forearms, then hacked at the ankles with the cleaver. The gasping stopped before he stuck the serrated knife into the man's flank and sawed at the skin, creating a massive flap. The usurper carved another and another, as if fashioning scrolls of human skin from the back, the chest, the belly. He wasn't sure he could carry this out before another sinner wandered off the street for a sight they wouldn't be able to pray away, but his luck held. He crafted signs and symbols with the spreading pool of blood, including the ubiquitous Amdusias sigil.

He chopped the clergyman's penis off. Multiple crosses hung around the sanctuary, so he dug a couple of nails out of the purse, turned one of the crosses upside down, and hammered the base of the organ vertically. He tried to stretch it to cover more vertically, but the nail ripped through the skin and he had to pluck out another and try again. He nailed a bit higher from the base and didn't stretch as aggressively. He hammered the glans right where the horizontal piece intersected with the vertical.

Still no one came in off the street or from the recesses of the church.

He tacked the flesh scrolls to a massive carving of Christ, covering the face by pushing the skin through the crown of thorns. He let one of the clergyman's severed arms bleed into the holy water, turning it all red until he could see Priscilla's reflection in it.

He looked around at the remains—dismembered parts here, three-quarters skinned torso there. He removed Priscilla's yoga pants and spread her legs wide. The man who came to burn a candle for his mother's soul found Priscilla a bloody mess, jamming the clergyman's forearm into her vagina over and over again. He bolted screaming from the church. Beat police came back with him.

"The seventh gate is opened by the lamb's blood! I descend to the void!"

The usurper left her to face the music alone and reverted back to Kessler's body across the schism of the plane.

"Stop me if you've heard this one," Billings said as Kessler arrived at the church. "We have ritualistic mutilation by a Priscilla York, who claims she wasn't in control of herself, probably demonically possessed."

"Stop," Kessler said, following her into the sanctuary. "She recorded it?"

"Recorded and caught red-handed."

"And red-cunted," Rothman said, approaching from near the white shroud laid over the clergyman. "She was fucking herself with the guy's arm. Now, if your profile said that's what would go down, I'd respect it. You didn't say she'd fuck no arms, though, or nail a dick to a cross."

Paramedics fastened her to a stretcher, though for all her loud protestations of innocence, she barely struggled. Shock, perhaps. Maybe also sedation.

"She denies any killing," Billings said, frowning at Rothman's language in a sacred place. "But it's going to be on the glasses, at least this one and Milton's."

"She didn't do the others," Rothman said, as if daring Kessler to say otherwise. "Not this junkie and not that porno twerp either."

"We'll see what Perez and Cartwright find in her apartment," Billings said evenly.

They stood quiet for a moment, watching orderlies maneuver the stretcher around blood trails. One of the wheels spun in a circle, unbalanced.

"She probably *wasn't* in control of herself," Billings continued. "Her pupils were about as big as dimes."

As the stretcher drew near, Rothman held up a hand.

"We need to get her to the ER stat," one of the paramedics said. "She could have internal bleeding."

"It'll just take a second. And if she bleeds out, well, it's not the worst place it could happen to her. Presto change-o, deathbed redemption, right? Hey, Priss Priss."

She twisted her head to look at him, shaking.

"Who's in on this with you? I know you didn't kill the others, so tell me who we need to bring in."

She looked to Kessler and Billings, not able to focus on one for more than a couple seconds.

"Hey, sweetheart, you killed someone in a church. If you don't help me out, they're going to stick you with the kind of needle that won't get you high…it'll get you dead."

"Something controlled me!" With her head upon the stretcher, the tears trickled left and right. "I never killed no one!"

"*Who* made you kill?"

"The lord knows I'm innocent! Innocent as a newborn babe!" She fixed her gaze toward the ceiling. "Jesus, see your humble servant!"

"He can't…you covered His eyes with somebody else's skin, remember?" Rothman slapped the side of the stretcher in disgust. "Get this dick-nailing piece of shit outta my sight!"

They wheeled off with Priscilla still trying to set up a direct line to heaven without tin cans and a string.

"You're pretty good at setting us up for these one-off lunatics," Rothman said to Kessler. "I don't know what the deal is with them. Maybe they're really involved in some cult like you said, but my hunch is that it's a bullshit smokescreen."

"Let's hope so, then. The harder someone tries to mislead us, the more they open their mind to me."

"What a relief. But I'm not so sure it's our killer trying to set up the smokescreen. So what about the other murders, superstar? You keep giving us the lowdown on this stuff that's maybe related, maybe not, but what about the four before Choi?"

"I'm not ready to say, detective. I have a theory, but I need more time with the case files. I don't want to risk leading you in the wrong direction."

"God forbid." He walked away, looking back to say, "I'm going to go check out that whackjob's apartment with my own eyes."

Billings watched him leave. "So what do you make of Tyson and Priscilla both claiming they were possessed?"

"I think you're going to be hearing that story a lot over the next few weeks," Kessler said. "It's really getting around."

"I have a feeling they'll be missing the signs and sigils."

"Are you trying to say this woman and gurgle boy were really possessed by demons? The devil?"

"Of course not. Just that whether anything happened or not, they both believed it did. I don't think it was an act."

"It was orchestrated," Kessler said. "An excuse they all worked out in advance."

"How many do you think are part of this…cult?"

"Maybe five or six, but not all of them are involved in the murders. It's mainly one killer. Probably the cult leader."

"And he's the one who fits our profile? At least a little?" Billings practically had her hands clasped in prayer.

"I'd say he's roughly ten years older than you projected. He may have had some medical training somewhere down the line." Kessler watched a tech remove the flap of flesh off Christ's crown, wincing and then making the sign of the cross. "But these days…I think our killer is a cop."

Kessler took the call the following morning thinking it was Pendleton, but Facetime granted him the unwelcome sight of Sonny Hooper's face with the swimming eyeballs. He looked sweaty again, like no matter which room he wound up in, someone always set the thermostat to about eighty-seven degrees.

"Agent Kessler," Hooper greeted. "I'm sorry to bother you. I just wanted to touch base on the matter of your laptop."

"No bother at all, Mr. Hooper."

"Just Hoop is fine." He smiled crookedly.

"I don't suppose you've heard, but I'm still not back from Chapman. We've had some more murders."

"Is that right? Do you think it's climate change?"

"Climate change?" Kessler repeated.

"Yeah…is that why these killers don't have a cooling off period anymore? The temperature keeps going up?" He chuckled at his own joke.

Kessler forced a smile. The strange vibes Hoop gave him deepened.

"Honestly, I didn't think serial killers were even a thing anymore," Hooper continued. "If they talk about one now, it's only because they missed them in the 70s and 80s, like Green River or BTK. These days, they go for that whole mass murder deal. It's such an instant gratification culture now." He tut-tutted at the unfairness of this pendulum swing away from the rigors of old school serial murder.

"They're still out there," Kessler said. "I've just pulled several of them off the street before they slaughtered their way to notoriety."

"That's why you're the Mind Stalker. Quite the track record. It's kind of funny, but I looked up a few of the arrests you influenced and I noticed something."

"What's that?"

"They were all on the watch list." Hooper smiled all the while.

"No surprise. It doesn't take much for someone to end up on it, and these psychopaths are curious in all the wrong ways."

"I'm sure you're right. Well, I hope you'll be coming back soon so we can finish out our business together."

"Of course. I haven't forgotten."

"Happy hunting."

He called Rothman immediately after.

"Rothman."

"It's Kessler."

"Have you narrowed down our suspects? Maybe a certain professor or colonel in the study with a lead pipe?"

"I'm running behind this morning. Some unexpected Bureau business."

"I hope things are *better* now," Rothman said. He laughed. "Get it? Like the Better Business Bureau?"

"I'll see you in an hour or so. You can fill me in on what they found in Priscilla's apartment."

"Okay. Hey, do me a favor and see if you can come up with some leads on a sense of humor to go with that murder profile."

Kessler ended the call without acknowledging this parting shot. Then he drove to Rothman's house.

Billings didn't know the half of it, Kessler discovered. Rothman would apparently withhold information from someone else's department and his own to boot.

The detective lived in a lower middle-class neighborhood where people seemed to mind their business. A better business bureau that paid Kessler no mind as he drove down the street to the dark cedar house he previewed with Google Maps and Zillow last night. It looked like it should be somewhere in the woods.

Kessler negotiated the lock on the back entrance in under a minute. The detective had set up a bulletin board in a spare bedroom doubling as an office, featuring diagrams of the murders, the symbols, the victims, the most tenuous of connections. He'd also boned up on the subject of the occult—black arts in particular, from books like *The Magick of Inversion Precepts, The Grimoire of Othoth, Summoning the Lords Infernal,* and *Transposition of the Nether Planes*. He'd dog-eared several pages obviously pertaining to the ritual murders in Chapman.

The whole thing went beyond a pet psychosis, though Rothman would assume the murderer acted only out of some misplaced devotion to the occult. How shocked Saint Nick would be to discover that completion of this ritual opened a gate to Hell, one that superimposed itself over a limited zone of the physical world. The magus could then directly petition the summoned entity—Amdusias, in this case. Anyone caught within the nether plane would be sacrificed.

Able to relate to a ritual manifesting in multiple murders of his own, the usurper had wanted this intrepid butcher to succeed in his rites. He'd tried to drive him away from the abandoned sectors here with the smokescreen, to places where he might find less scrutiny and fewer walls closing in. Based on a report out of a place called Naughton, it seemed the magus took the hint and quite possibly completed his grand sacrament. Kessler still had to do an offering of his own—someone to sacrifice for all the sacrifices.

Well, no one better than the guy with all the how-to books. And if he had an alibi for one or two of the deaths, he had a secret cult carrying out his commands.

Kessler woke up Rothman's computer. Password protected, but he used the same one from his work computer—Kessler had watched him. He brought something to crack it anyway, but saved himself a few minutes. Kessler went ahead and sent the text to Billings he'd told her to await.

Next he popped in a flash drive to unzip the files and programs he needed to sign into the FBI watch list and Interdex, as well as an archive of MPEGs for Rothman's department to discover on the computer—stuff that would almost make the murders a secondary consideration. He covered his tracks a little with the Bureau watch list sign-in to make it look good, but Hoop would track it down on his end. It left a convenient excuse for Kessler, too—Rothman hacked the watch list on Kessler's laptop as a frame-up. It wouldn't be ironclad, but the Bureau wouldn't want any controversy. Kessler's success in the past three years spoke for itself, and few would miss the watch list fodder.

He opened a desk drawer while he waited for the MPEGs to unzip. Detective Rothman was the owner of an InterphaZ self-gratification device known as the oSheath. These things were a nesting ground for nano-tech seeking urethral ingress.

As he wrapped things up and repocketed his flash drives, he saw silhouettes streak past the curtains in the room. Not Billings yet, he didn't think.

Kessler withdrew his Glock from its holster as he exited the office. He hadn't needed it at any point in the past three years. He paused in the living room, halfway between the front and rear exits. Maybe an exit in the garage?

The back door sprang open. Cartwright drew on him, not looking like such a dope now. The front door sprang next. Rothman, Desert Eagle aimed, and Perez close behind.

"Working on your profile, Agent Kessler?" Rothman said. "Why don't you drop that piece before we drop your ass."

Kessler bent down and slid the gun away. "You should be familiar with it, detective. We're looking for a white male, early forties, motivated by an occult fixation, myriad job stressors, and professional jealousy. Someone forsaking protocol for personal gain, capable of using his detective status to influence desperate citizens to further his sickness."

"Fuck's he talking about, Roth?" Cartwright said.

"He's bullshitting you!"

"Check his office," Kessler said. "Everything you want to know about the murders is in the books."

"For Christ's sake. It's called detective work. "

"Detective work you weren't sharing with your partners?"

A look passed between Perez and Cartwright.

Rothman closed the gap between them and belted Kessler across the temple with the butt of his gun. Kessler went with it, grateful for the chance. He stayed motionless on the carpet.

"He's the one you need to be suspicious of," Rothman said. "He gets here and our killers multiply, broadcasting this shit or doing it in public, which is the opposite of what we'd been seeing. Cartwright, I asked you to tail this weirdo today and he took you right to my house. That doesn't seem the least bit strange to you?"

"Come on," Perez said, "You really think he mind-controlled Bryant and York?""

"Hell if I know. But they swear up and down they didn't do it. Hell, CIA did MK-Ultra, you don't think the Feds can pull off some shady shit like that? Set him up with some zip ties."

Rothman's mind opened to Kessler as easily if he'd used the same password as the detective's computers. The astonishment would be only too short-lived, but he enjoyed the dawning revelation happening in the under-mind as Rothman understood he'd been locked out of control of his own body.

Billings' tall silhouette appeared in the front doorway. "What the hell is going on here?" she asked. "What did you do to Kessler?"

"The tenth aire is open," Rothman said. The usurper shot Perez first, point-blank, painting a blood face on the mirror as wet leaves of bone and brain exploded from the back of Perez's head.

Cartwright shouted, raising his gun. Rothman squeezed the trigger three times on his .357. The throat which brayed so doltishly in the past few days blew apart like creek water impacted by a stone.

Billings' gun flashed before Rothman could turn toward her. She hit him dead center mass. He sprawled against a table, and his weight brought it all to the ground. Blood filled his mouth; she'd punctured a lung.

The usurper jettisoned himself back to Kessler's body. The detective's mouth opened uselessly, back in control of himself but unable to do anything about it.

"Billings?" Kessler said. He groaned, lightly touching the bloody wound on his forehead for dramatic effect. Spent gunpowder and bowels overtook the Potpourri scent of the room. "What happened?"

"Rothman killed Perez and Cartwright in front of me," she said, crouching as if to avoid smoke inhalation. She talked between deep breaths. "You were right about him. I shot him. It's over."

"I was right about you too," he said.
"Thanks. But I think I'm going to be sick now."

Kessler watched the news clip on his flight back.

"Detective Olive Billings credits FBI agent John 'the Mind Stalker' Kessler with creating a profile indicating the involvement of a law enforcement officer. A disturbing picture is developing about Detective Nicholas Rothman, the suspected killer of as many as five men and women in Chapman. Authorities are additionally reporting their investigation of Rothman's personal computer uncovered what one anonymous source is reporting as 'literal mountains of child pornography.' The question remains…was Rothman the dark messiah of a murderous cult, and are there still unknown members who must be brought to justice? We'll have more later in the hour as details emerge on this breaking story. Right now, our weatherman Jimmy Lee Tone will let everyone know if they can break out the short sleeves for tomorrow's boating extravaganza. Let's go live aboard the newly christened schooner the *Beef Broth.* Ahoy there, Jimmy!"

Kessler wasn't ready to go home from the airport. Since he hadn't risked eating on the plane, he stopped at a diner on Hanbury Street, almost walking distance from his house. He ordered a grilled chicken sandwich and a plate of fries with coffee. He scored one of the last booths. The dinner rush was still in full swing, but the waitress brought his order back before he could read the latest raves about his intervention in the Chapman murders. She barely made eye contact, hopping to the next person wanting to order, wanting a refill, wanting the check.

Kessler hoped to enjoy his meal without anyone pointing out that he was the Mind Stalker, sitting here eating just like any other regular person who wasn't always knee-deep in dead bodies as an occupation.

It wasn't to be.

"Mind if I join you?" Sonny Hooper slid into the opposite booth. His paunch rubbed against the table. His lips glistened, like he'd made sure to keep licking them every other minute.

"Looks like you already did." Kessler struck the bottom of a ketchup bottle with the flat of his hand. A red dollop became a thick spreading pool against the stark white of his plate.

Hooper surveyed Kessler's repast. "Not quite a hero's welcome for the amazing Mind Stalker."

Kessler's eyes narrowed. He stared at Hooper and pushed ever so slightly at his mind to test its boundaries. Nothing doing for incursion. It would be like trying to go through a mountain with a pick.

"I'm not quite a hero," he finally said.

Hooper laughed. "There's some truth in advertising." He grabbed some fries off Kessler's plate. "So, you finally have that laptop for me to look at…Phillips?"

"Oh, so you managed to follow my little breadcrumb trail?" He smiled. "Great job with that racist cop in LA, by the way."

"So you heard about that?" Hooper reached for more fries. Kessler slapped the top of his hand.

"FBI all-star, remember?" Kessler withdrew his badge from his inner jacket pocket. "I suspected it was you when we met the other day, Hoop. I just couldn't figure out why you took the body of this fat fuck."

"What about you? You've really been wearing this do-gooder's husk for three years?"

"Why not? Pulling the strings of degenerates and reaping all the pleasure with none of the consequence…even heaven can't make an offer that good."

"You're going to like my offer even less," Hooper said. "It's time for you to come back where you belong, Phillips."

"Yeah, I don't think so." Phillips took a bite of the grilled chicken. "I haven't even finished my sandwich."

A man dressed in white—shirt, pants, chef beret—stepped through the swinging kitchen door with a meat cleaver at his side.

"Hey, you shouldn't have that out here, Arliss," one of the waitresses said.

Arliss swung the cleaver at the head of a customer eating at the counter. The blade chopped through the side of the diner's head, lopping off a huge divot of his scalp. The man dropped his spoon and screamed. The stretching of his jaw snapped a flimsy thread of skin and his ear dropped into his bowl of clam chowder. A woman sitting beside him plucked the steak knife from her napkin and thrust it into his open mouth. He spat a mouthful of blood on the counter with the tip of the knife jutting through the back of his head.

Phillips' prior waitress raised a meat fork, headed for Hoop. A burly man two booths down slid out to intercept her. He wrested the fork from her and jammed it into her face once, twice, three times for six bleeding holes. The last jab burst one of her eyes with the stark thunk of prongs embedding in flesh. She went limp, still glued to the fork until her dead weight yanked her free. The eye and a clump of trailing brain matter clung to the tines. Two other diners snatched hold of the burly man, wrestling him to the ground and pushing the top of his head until the fork penetrated the underside of his jaw, pounding it through the roof of his mouth.

A baby began crying with a siren wail.

Another cook rushed out of the kitchen with a griddle held before him like a shield. Steam hissed, curling from his hands as they cooked on the titanium. He screamed, darting around the counter in Kessler's direction. A man slid off his stool to block the way. The griddle struck his face and the cook tackled him, trapping the man beneath his burning shield. The cook bore down on him. Flesh hissed and crackled. He wrenched the griddle up and slammed it down again, mashing the customer's face. His own fingers continued to cook in the process, skin dribbling and oozing like fat.

All around the diner, customers threw themselves into the sudden chaos, taking up knives and any other makeshift weapons available. A seven-year-old girl stabbed her mother in the back; her mother jammed a fork in her ear. A man grabbed the jug from a water dispenser, spilling gallons of water between the kitchen and serving floor. He barely swung it one time before Arliss's cleaver punched through the crown of his head.

Others used their hands, gouging out eyes or pushing them deep into skulls with their thumbs. A woman reached her slender hand into her boyfriend's mouth and grabbed a handful of throat organs. She tore them out in a bloody fistful. A stocky man lifted her up and dunked her head first into the fryer. She came out scalded into something barely recognizable as human, the eyes melted like runny eggs. An electric carving knife whirred to life, wielded by a grandmotherly lady wearing cat-eye glasses. She stuck the knife into the stocky man's stomach and sliced across the half-moon of flesh in a cascade of flying crimson giblets. He staggered back, blood-soaked palms attempting to staunch the wound and instead catching handfuls of sloughing entrails. A younger woman took the electric knife away from the grandmother and pushed the grinding blade up one of the old lady's nostrils. She rattled as if the blade's vibrations could be felt through the entirety of her body, expelling blood and tissue from her nose. The violent motion caused the knife to grind through her face and sever part of her cheek bone, which struck the floor like a shard from a broken plate.

Something thumped loudly against the front window. It did not shatter, but the loud squalling from the crying infant ceased.

A pile of fingers rolled across the black and white checkered floor as Arliss chopped through a woman's defensive hand. He swung at her neck, hacking deeper and deeper into the groove until her head rolled away, spurting across the floor. The neck stump continued to vomit its own contribution of arterial blood as errant feet trampled the woman's torso in the melee. The serving floor became slippery from the spilled jug and severed bodies. Someone picked up the head by the hair and swung it as a bludgeon. Arliss continued hacking his way through the flailing mass between him and the booth where Phillips and Hoop sat unfazed in the eye of the storm.

Within, however, on a metaphysical, higher level of consciousness, their minds were knotted together. Hoop's had become a black hole, absorbing Phillips' like a snake swallowing prey too big for its body with gradual peristalsis.

A struggle between two women for the electric carving knife resulted in it cutting its own cord. The tail of exposed wires dropped to the wet floor. Blue currents of light ignited and sizzled across the pool of water and blood. Sparks blew from the outlet. A woman's eye burst apart like overheated sauce in a microwave. Several of the people kneeling in the wetness shuddered and flailed, dropping their weapons as they fried. This included Arliss, who had nearly crawled to Phillips with the cleaver.

Phillips flashed a quick smile in the sudden pregnant silence. “I won’t see you in Hell…Hoop.” He soared out of John Kessler’s mind the instant the lights blew out in the diner.

# THE DINER

Drew Stepek

"Really appreciate you hiring me to fix this for you." I squinted to make out the name tag on her waitress's uniform. "Stephanie?"

She smiled and pointed to a massive pool of muck on the floor behind the counter. "Beverage line burst or something. Normally, we don't give work to people who come in off the street, but this needs to be fixed now. If someone slips on this shit and sues, we'll all be out on the street with you."

I put my tool kit down on the counter next to the apple pie. "I'm not homeless, ma'am. Just need some work."

"I didn't ask for your life story," she said, picking a piece of meat out of her teeth. She studied the morsel through the tops of her glasses that rested on the bulb of her nose.

Rather than continue talking about my desperate situation, I nudged my head at one of the guests across the diner. "Is that…"

"Yep. That's *the* Mind Stalker." She wiped the meat that she unearthed from her back teeth on her pink sleeve. "Comes in here all the time. Never talks to anyone. Never dines with anyone." She winked at me. "Leaves terrible tips. I asked him for an autograph one time."

"Oh yeah? How'd that go?"

"Fucking asshole just tapped his finger on his coffee cup and said, 'You got the wrong fella, lady.' Of course, he had his FBI badge on full display on the table for everyone to see. Fucking whore."

"Ouch. So, you're telling me not to ask him for his autograph?"

She scratched at the back of her hair with a pencil. "Not unless you want to be kicked out of here. Mr. Big Shot threatened to sue us if we told the press he comes here."

"Speaking of that. Did you hear? He just broke that huge case. The Satanic ritual thing." I keep up my phone. "Saw it on *The Roach* this morning."

"Like I said. Whore." She looked back over to Agent Kessler's booth. "Well. What do you know."

"What?"

"Take a look for yourself." She pointed to Agent Kessler. "Looks like he has a friend after all."

A fat guy with thick glasses and a ponytail joined the Mind Stalker at his booth. I could practically smell the sweat rings soaking his armpits as he struggled to fit into the booth.

She tucked a pencil behind her ear. "Probably another fan or paparazzi. I should probably get rid of him." She chuckled. "Don't want to get sued."

"Why bother?" I pressed against the counter to unlatch the magnet that held it closed. "Sounds like he deserves to be harassed a little."

"You know what?" She took a sip of coffee. "You're right. Let him deal with it. He's the one who wanted to be a big TV star."

I pulled back the door under the counter. Soda sludge filled with food spilled out all over the floor. "Jesus fuck!"

"Oops." She spat up a little bit of her coffee. "I probably should have warned you about that."

"You *really* shouldn't be serving right now," I said, kicking the deepening puddle of shit away from us and the server traffic coming in and out of the kitchen. "This is dangerous."

"What are you? The fucking health inspector? Just fix it, pal."

I bent down to get a better look at the leak that seemed to be coming from the soda fountain. I couldn't be sure, though, because multiple beverage lines were all twisted around each other. I put my knees into the sludge and began running my bare hands up and down the hoses, looking for a leak. I didn't find anything. That meant the leak was more than likely coming from the pipes.

Stephanie put her hand on my shoulder and bent over me. She wreaked of cigarettes and dozens of cups of coffee. "You find anything?"

"Looking." I bent further into the cabinet. The soda sludge smelled better than her awful dragon breath.

"I don't think it's any of the hoses. Let me get back in there and cut the $CO_2$. Then, I'll search the pipes."

"Of course, it's the hoses, dummy." She pressed all her weight onto my back as she leaned in further. "This shit all over the floor is soda. There ain't no soda in the pipes."

"Can you hand me my tools?" I said, in an attempt to get the stench of her mouth as far away from me as possible. "I have a flashlight in there."

She turned around to unlock the toolbox. "You want the flashlight, right?"

I waved my hand. "No. No. No. Don't go in there. I need the whole box."

"What's your problem? I'm trying to help you, you bum."

I continued to wave my wand. She would have found my gun if she had opened the box and lifted the top section. I was planning on robbing the diner, but I had a change of heart when I saw the Mind Stalker. "Just give me the whole thing, please."

As soon as she picked up the kit, one of the chefs walked through the swinging kitchen door. He had a dead look in his eyes and a meat cleaver at his side.

"Hey, you shouldn't have that out here, Arliss," Stephanie yelled at him. The chef walked by her, knocking her out of the way. The toolbox fell onto my head.

Everything went black.

When I woke up, Stephanie's smashed face was floating in the soda sludge between my legs.

I screamed and struggled to my feet as her fingernails dug into my thighs. She lifted her mangled head out of the blood that mixed with the mess from the soda fountain.

"Help me," she managed to say while pulling herself on top of me. As she gagged on the filth from the floor and coughed, her teeth dropped into the front pocket of her waitress uniform.

"Jesus fuck!" I screamed. "Get the fuck away from me."

She clawed the front of my shirt. "Please. Help me." The gash in her head cracked down the side of her face. Her right eyeball swung back and forth a few times until it came loose and hit my crotch. She looked down and screamed. Her tongue flapped out of the side of her exposed jaw like she was a panting dog.

Putting up my knee to barricade her from me, I yelled, "Don't fucking touch me, lady!"

In the dining room, a baby cried uncontrollably, followed by the screams of customers.

I plunged my hands into the sludge to find my tools as I tried to push myself away from Stephanie.

Stephanie pawed at my face. "Please. God. Help me."

Before she was lip to lip with me, I felt my pipe wrench behind me. Without wasting a second, I swung it out of the soda puddle, cracking Stephanie across the face. She fell to the side. Her body convulsed, and her last breaths bubbled in the soda and blood that had risen shoe-deep.

"I'm sorry," I said, lifting the wrench and pounding her head into the tile floor. Soda splashed in every direction as I crushed her skull and ripped into her brain. After one last strike, she let out a final few wet dog shakes and stopped moving. After one last bubble surfaced from the sludge, her misery ended.

I pushed myself back up against the counter and looked into the mirror that reflected the entirety of the diner. Bodies filled the booths.

The screaming baby sat in a highchair and picked at his mother's head. It was broken like an egg on the table in front of him. Other than the baby, the only survivors were the Mind Stalker and the fat man who sat down to join him minutes before. They were in some sort of weird trance.

"I *won't* see you in Hell…Hoop," the Mind Stalker said as the lights went out.

I tried to hide myself among the hoses under the counter, but there wasn't enough room.

"Motherfucker," the fat man said in a thick Boston accent as he picked at the fries on Kessler's plate. "Fucking motherfucking Phillips."

He took a bite from a half-eaten burger. "FUCK!"

Shocked and seemingly out of his trance, the Mind Stalker jumped to his feet. His eye widened as he looked around at the massacre. "Who? Who are you? Where? Where am I?"

"NEST," the fat man said. "Head."

Immediately after that fat man spoke, the Mind Stalker started swatting at the air as if he were being attacked by hornets. He started ripping out his hair in clumps and covered his ears. "What is this? What the fuck is this?" he screamed. He danced around for a second until he shot straight up, extending his back and neck like he was trying to jump out of his own skin. He dug his fingers into his face and began tearing the skin from his cheekbones.

The fat man counted backward from three with his fingers. "Three… two…"

When he reached one, the Mind Stalker's head erupted like it was a tomato filled with dynamite. What was left of his hands fell to his sides. His body dropped to the floor like a heavy bag of laundry.

My teeth began chattering. The air conditioning from the diner and my drenched clothing combined with the fear and horror that spun uncontrollably through my body. I put my pipe wrench in my mouth and bit into it, trying to stay quiet.

"Fuck me. Is there someone still here?" The fat man looked into the mirror, making eye contact with my reflection. I hid my face behind the web of hoses.

And then, as suddenly as they went off, the lights returned. The baby stopped crying, and the jukebox back by the bathrooms started playing music. A bell rang from the front door.

Another man entered the diner.

The fat man closed his eyes. "Jesus fucking Christ."

While he was preoccupied, I began feeling around in the soda sludge. Then I remembered that I had my gun in my toolbox.

"Ahhh. They're playing my song." The new guy sashayed his way across the diner, making his way toward the fat man's booth. "'I'm a little bit country," he sang, jumping into the booth and taking Kessler's seat. "And I'm a little bit rock and roll!'"

Keeping his eyes closed, the fat guy said, "Hey, man. I guess I should have known you were tracking me."

"Oh. Hey, Lou." He looked around the restaurant. "Wow. Great job. Really. Just outstanding work."

The fat man became silent.

"You know what's funny?" The new guy put his hands behind his head and relaxed in the booth. "I could have sworn that we told you over 100 years ago not to let this guy go. As a matter of fact, I distinctly remember us telling you not to develop your own technology, as well. You weren't supposed to come here. At all. And, yeah. You were easy as fuck to track because you left a pile of bodies in your wake."

"Why don't you just catch him, Chris?"

"Ummm. Let's see, shitbag." He adjusted his glasses. "First of all, *he* shouldn't be here. *You* shouldn't be here. And, well. At the end of the day, I'm your boss."

"Your father is my boss," the fat man sighed as he took his hair out of its ponytail.

After letting out a snort, the new guy tapped his fingers on the table. "You were told never to develop any tech that would jeopardize everything we've been doing down here. You were banished for eternity, dummy. You know what that means, right?"

The fat man picked up some ketchup on the table. "Why are you still wearing those dumb glasses?" After unscrewing the cap, he started pounding on the bottom of the bottle until he covered the plate. "Do you want me to call you Koresh? I think you need to stop living in the past. Waco didn't really go as planned."

Leaning forward in his seat, the new guy said, "Look at you, brother? As if you weren't already the vilest creature in existence, you took this human turd as your host? Hoop? Come on, Lou. At least the humans that we influence spread our message and make us money."

"Oh, come down off the cross." The fat man used a fork to dig into the newly sauced fries. "Those evangelists and preachers are just as greedy and fucking evil as any host I've ever taken. You should be sending those assholes my way, not using them to fleece the human race."

"You dumbfuck. We've been doing this all since before I was born. We spread our influence. We make the company money. There's no side hustle here. There's no dastardly sister company. There is only *the* corporation."

Chomping on his fries, the fat man said, "I could easily kill you right now, you know. Right here. You're in the flesh here and now." He pointed at the new guy with his fork. "I bet your old man would give me a promotion. Lord knows you haven't exactly crushed it in the past two millennia."

"Promotion? Lou. Come on, man. Promotion to what? We already gave you hell, asshole. What the fuck else do you want?"

"Does He?" the fat man pointed at the sky. "Does He know I'm here? Does He know that Phillips escaped?"

"As far as I know, you're good." The new guy stood up. "He doesn't really talk to me a whole lot, Lou. Look. You gotta get this guy. His influence is spreading *quickly*. He is a menace and a danger to the operation. I should just take your shitty tech. But I'm not gonna get my hands dirty with this guy. I've been told that I'm not exactly on Dad's favorite list anymore. If I die here trying to clean up your mess of malevolence, I'm likely going to be trapped in a desk job for a *long* time."

The fat man lowered his head. "I'm sorry, Chris."

"No, you're not." While making his way toward the diner exit, the new guy added, "And, Hoop… Lou… Satan… whatever your name is now."

"Yes, my Lord."

"This." He kicked the Mind Stalker's headless corpse. "This shit is all on you. What the fuck?"

The bell rang again as he left. The lights and the jukebox shut down again. The baby let out a gigantic shriek.

I looked back toward the swinging door to the kitchen and debated whether or not I could make a break for it. Then again, there was no escape unless this fat guy wasn't some delusional weirdo.

Before I got the chance to crawl to the doors, he said, "You can come out now."

As I quietly tried to slide back underneath the counter, my foot kicked the gun. I kept my eyes on the mirror and reached forward to grab the only thing that could possibly save my life.

He chomped on the meat in his ketchup soup and gazed at me again through the reflection. It was as if he were standing directly in front of me. His evil hovered all around my body. The teeth-chattering started again, but it had less to do with me being cold and more to do with me feeling my life coming to a close.

"Look, homie. I know you heard all that." He took a huge breath and somehow managed to work his gut out from under the table.

I latched onto the pipe wrench again, and I released the safety from my gun. "Don't come back here. I'm armed." I took the mag out and re-inserted it to make sure he heard the gun.

"Put the gun away. For the love of Christ, put the wrench away, too. Like I said, I know you heard all of that. And if you understood what we were talking about—" He laughed, popping a loose button on the bottom of his blood-drenched shirt. "—Then you know your weapons are no match for the fucking devil. Ha. That sounds so fucking stupid to say aloud."

I continued to watch him in the mirror.

"The name's Sonny Hooper." He waddled to the counter and took a seat. He then folded his arms and rested them on his stomach. "You can call me Hoop."

Pressing the cold handle of my gun against my face, I asked, "Was that other guy Jesus?"

He put his hair back in its ponytail. "Yeah. That snake oil salesman."

"You really expect me to believe all of this?" Tears began streaming down my cheeks. "That I just witnessed Lucifer and Jesus Christ having a conversation. In *this* diner?"

"I'm sorry to say that you're probably going to be blamed for everything that happened here, plumber. You are a plumber, right? Well. I mean, you told the nice owners of this establishment that you were. Surely, you weren't going to rob them, were you?"

"They were throwing me some work because I'm about to lose my home." I swallowed and pushed the gun across the checkered tile floor so he could see it.

He lifted the cover off the apple pie and then pressed his fingers into it, testing its freshness. "Is the pie any good here?"

"It looks terrible."

"So tell me. Were you going to rob these nice folks?"

I took a deep breath. "Yes. I was going to rob them. I need the money."

"You fucking scumbag." He re-covered the pie. "You deserve to die."

"I was going to pay them back. I promise."

"Sure, guy. Anyway, you're going to get blamed for this bloodbath. Be smart. Tell everyone what you heard here. Let them know that both Jesus and Satan are here on earth. Convince people that they are in the middle of a Holy War."

He stood up and headed toward the door. Then, he started singing.

"I'm a little bit country," he said and stopped to pat the crying baby on the head.

The bell rang again, and he headed out.

"I'm a little bit rock 'n roll."

Ryan Harding

# FUCK YOU

Dani Brown

Lewis Kelly

Peter Caffrey

S.C.

www.ingramcontent.com/pod-product-compliance
Lightning Source LLC
Chambersburg PA
CBHW031944260626
47157CB00017B/2305
* 9 7 8 1 9 4 0 2 5 0 5 2 6 *